MIDNIGHT'S KISS

5 Stars! TOP PICK! "[Grant] blends ancient gods, love, desire, and evil-doers into a world you will want to revisit over and over again." —*Night Owl Reviews*

5 Blue Ribbons! "This story is one you will remember long after the last page is read. A definite keeper!"
—*Romance Junkies*

4 Stars! "The world of the Immortal Warriors is a thoroughly engaging one, blending powerful ancient gods, fiery desire, and touchingly human love, which readers will surely want to revisit." —*RT Book Reviews*

4 Feathers "*Midnight's Kiss* is a game changer—one that will set the rest of the series in motion."
—*Under the Covers*

MIDNIGHT'S CAPTIVE

5 Blue Ribbons! "Packed with originality, imagination, humor, Scotland, Highlanders, magic, surprising plot twists, intrigue, sizzling sensuality, suspense, tender romance, and true love, this story has something for everyone." —*Romance Junkies*

4 1/2 Stars! "Grant has crafted a chemistry between her wounded alpha and surprisingly capable heroine that will, no doubt, enthrall series fans and newcomers alike."
—*RT Book Reviews*

MIDNIGHT'S WARRIOR

4 Stars! "Super storyteller Grant returns with . . . A rich variety of previous protagonists [which] adds a wonderful familiarity to the books." —*RT Books Reviews*

5 Stars! "Ms. Grant brings together two people who are afraid to fall in love and then ignites sparks between them." —*Single Title Reviews*

MIDNIGHT'S SEDUCTION

"Sizzling love scenes and engaging characters fill the pages of this fast-paced and immersive novel." —*Publishers Weekly*

4 Stars! "Grant again proves that she is a stellar writer and a force to be reckoned with." —*RT Book Reviews*

5 Blue Ribbons! "A deliciously sexy, adventuresome paranormal romance that will keep you glued to the pages." —*Romance Junkies*

5 Stars! "Ms. Grant mixes adventure, magic and sweet love to create the perfect romance story." —*Single Title Reviews*

MIDNIGHT'S LOVER

"Paranormal elements and scorching romance are cleverly intertwined in this tale of a damaged hero and resilient heroine." —*Publishers Weekly*

5 Blue Ribbons! "An exciting, adventure-packed tale, *Midnight's Lover* is a story that captivates you from the very first page." —*Romance Junkies*

The DARK WARRIOR series by
DONNA GRANT

MIDNIGHT'S PROMISE

DONNA GRANT

St. Martin's Paperbacks

MIDNIGHT'S PROMISE

Copyright © 2013 by Donna Grant.

For information address St. Martin's Press, 175 Fifth Avenue, New York, NY 10010.

ISBN: 978-1-250-01729-1

Printed in the United States of America

St. Martin's Paperbacks edition / November 2013

St. Martin's Paperbacks are published by St. Martin's Press, 175 Fifth Avenue, New York, NY 10010.

10 9 8 7 6 5 4 3 2 1

To Dad—
For telling me I could do anything or
be anything I wanted

ACKNOWLEDGMENTS

So much work goes into getting a book ready, and I couldn't do it without my fabulous editor, Monique Patterson, and everyone at SMP who was involved. Y'all rock!

To my amazing agent, Louise Fury, who keeps me on my toes.

Melissa Bradley, my assistant and my rock. Thanks for everything you do. You make my life easier, and for that, I owe you so very much, and a chocolate cake.

A special thanks to my family for the never-ending support.

And to my husband, Steve. For the laughs, the adventures, the date nights, and your continual support. I love you, Sexy!

CHAPTER ONE

Rothiemurchus, Scotland
October

The weather didn't matter. The temperatures didn't matter.

No feelings, no emotions.

No entanglements.

That was the kind of life Malcolm Munro led. The kind of life he'd come to accept.

He had already been walking down such a road when the primeval god inside him was unbound. Evil had infused him and, had he been worried about his soul, the god might have had a chance to take over.

But Malcolm hadn't been worried, nor had he cared what happened. He was dead inside. The only thing that kept him attached was the thread of family that was all but severed now.

Malcolm hunkered next to one of the two-hundred-year-old pines. It was private property he was on, but with Rothiemurchus being the largest surviving area of ancient woodland in Europe, there was nowhere else he wanted to be.

The forest was a living being. In every tree, every flower there was a timeline of history waiting to be discovered. Malcolm had no need. He knew what was there.

The past.

He put his hand on the bark of the pine and inhaled deeply. Just a few steps away was a tree well over three centuries old. It stood strong and unyielding, a protector for the forest.

Malcolm once thought himself such a guardian for his clan. How easily things changed, and always so unexpectedly.

He picked up a scent of deer, splintering his thoughts out of the darkness. His eyes snapped open and they hastily scanned the dense forest of rowan, birch, holly, willow, and juniper to name a few.

A herd of red deer was nearing. The thrill of the hunt was the only thing that caused any sort of excitement to rush through him.

Malcolm's enhanced hearing picked up the sound of the deer running toward him, their hooves pounding upon the ground. He remained squatting near the tree, waiting.

His heart began the rhythmic thumping of expectation, of eagerness. A slow tilt pulled at his lips when he felt the rumble of thunder through his body. A mortal wouldn't have heard or felt it, but Malcolm was different—in so many ways. Lightning sizzled in his veins, yearning to break free.

It was always the case when a storm rolled in, and the one coming was going to be vicious.

With the hunt and the storm, for just a moment, Malcolm felt a smidgen of contentment. Just as soon as the emotion was named, it vanished. He refused to think more about it as the deer came into view.

His claws, long and maroon-colored, extended from

his fingers. He could go days without food, but hunting helped to curb more of his . . . ferocious . . . parts.

Malcolm shifted silently, his gaze locked on one of the does. Just as he was about to give chase, a wave of magic—untainted and exquisite—brushed him.

He paused, giving the deer time to pass him. It wasn't the first time he'd felt the magic over the past week. Each time was the same. It was strong magic, pure magic. And it glided over him like the softest down, the smoothest seduction.

It cajoled, persuaded. It enticed.

This time, however, it was closer. Though Malcolm knew he shouldn't, he found himself rising to his feet and turning toward Aviemore where the magic originated.

His claws and fangs disappeared and his maroon skin faded as he walked to the small, charming village. There was no hesitation, no thought. He had to see who the magic came from and why it affected him so deeply.

When he arrived, Malcolm kept to the shadows between buildings as he reached the center of town. He watched the traffic around Tesco's with lazy abandon. People rushed in and out, sometimes with one bag, sometimes laden with groceries.

Aviemore was one of the busiest towns in the Cairngorm area. In the summer, tourists came to golf, hike, bike, and see the beautiful scenery like Rothiemurchus. In the winter, it was a skier's paradise. Slopes in every direction. It didn't matter what time of year it was with the many distilleries near and around the River Spey to visit.

From his spot situated between the buildings, Malcolm observed a young family walk out of Tesco's. The parents were holding hands while their two young boys raced each other to the car.

Malcolm wondered if they knew how precious their smiles and laughter were. He couldn't recall the last time he had done either. There hadn't been a reason. At least not for him.

There wasn't much left of his soul, but what remained reminded him often of what his life could have been had he not traveled that road from Edinburgh to MacLeod Castle five centuries earlier to check on Larena and Fallon.

Deirdre would never have sent her Warriors to kill him. Broc wouldn't have found him near death, nor would Broc have brought him to the castle to be healed.

Sonya wouldn't have used every bit of healing magic she possessed, and he wouldn't have woken to find himself scarred—and maimed.

Malcolm wouldn't have faced a bleak future of not ruling his clan and having nowhere to go. He wouldn't have looked at each day as if it were a curse instead of a blessing.

He wouldn't have left MacLeod Castle. He wouldn't have been trapped by Deirdre and had his god—a primeval god he hadn't known traveled through his bloodline—unbound. He wouldn't have been blackmailed by Deirdre to do her bidding in order to keep Larena safe. He wouldn't have been pulled forward through time by four centuries.

And he wouldn't have lost his soul.

All because he'd wanted to see how his cousin fared.

Malcolm pushed away from the corner of a building and crossed the street to amble into Tesco's to see exactly what was inside. Even though he had been in this time for a couple of years, he still found it odd to witness how far his beloved Scotland had come in four hundred years.

Being pulled forward through time with Deirdre hadn't been something Malcolm was prepared for. He had acclimated quickly thanks to the primeval god inside him. Yet, he missed the way things were.

The quiet that settled over the land, the simplicity of life. It hadn't been an easy life. He'd had to hunt for his food, and if he missed a kill, he went hungry. It had been a learning experience every Scot endured—man or woman, child or adult.

The beauty of his land hadn't faded, but the people weren't the same. Not worse, not better, just . . . different. There was peace within the clans, which some would say was a vast improvement.

It wasn't as if Malcolm had enjoyed the clan battles. They had been a necessity of life as a Highlander, especially one who was son to the laird. A clan, after all, was only as strong as its laird.

Malcolm walked through the produce aisle before he turned left and went down another aisle. He heard a gasp from a woman beside him. There wasn't a need to look to know she'd seen his face.

Odd how he sometimes forgot the one thing that should never be forgotten.

"Did you see his face?" she whispered to her companion.

Malcolm couldn't blame her. He didn't enjoy looking in the mirror. It was one of the reasons he let his beard grow. Not only did it hide some of his scars, but he didn't need to shave and see the horror that was his face.

When Deirdre unbound his god, she also used her magic to hide his scars. His god, Daal, had been the one who healed the injury to his right arm and shoulder.

For a short period of time, Malcolm looked as he once had. On the outside.

Inside, he was still a broken, damaged man. There was no anger, no joy, no peace. There was . . . nothing. Because of that, Daal had naught to use to take over. Malcolm's icy demeanor, his bleak outlook, left him with an iron fist of control over his god.

As soon as the last bit of his soul was gone, however, things would change. Daal would take over, and Larena would be hunting him.

She wouldn't be alone either. The rest of the Warriors and Druids at MacLeod Castle would use every ounce of magic and power they had to track him and kill him.

If it came to that. Malcolm could make it easy on everyone and take his own head. It wouldn't be simple, but he hadn't been a superb hunter for nothing. The right trap would take the head off anything, even a Warrior.

He walked out of Tesco's on his way back to the forest when the feel of magic stopped him dead in his tracks. It wasn't just any magic either. It was particularly sweet, infinitely wild, and exceedingly sensual.

It left him reeling, listing.

Lurching.

He swiveled his head to find the source of the magic jogging across the street toward him while she held onto her purse.

Her hair was the color of chocolate and hung in large curls past her shoulders. Those curls bounced while she ran. When she reached the sidewalk on his side of the street, she smiled easily at a woman who passed her.

Malcolm couldn't tear his gaze from her oval face. From her high cheekbones and small nose to her full lips and gracefully arched eyebrows. Her eyes, a magnificent color of clear blue, were her most dazzling feature.

He swiftly stepped into the shadows behind a group of people and discreetly watched the Druid. Her khaki jacket hung open, revealing a deep purple shirt that hugged her breasts. As she passed, his gaze went to her perfectly shaped ass the jacket didn't cover.

Malcolm took a deep breath and slowly released it. She

was a *mie*, a Druid who used the natural magic they were born with.

There hadn't been a drop of the cloying, sickening feel of black magic used by the *droughs*, Druids who gave their souls to Satan in order to use the more powerful magic.

Once the Druid was inside Tesco's, Malcolm was going to walk away. Except he couldn't. He remained where he was for the next fifteen minutes waiting for another glimpse of her beauty, for another wash of her magic until she strolled out of the store.

She kept her gaze on the ground. As she neared him, she tucked her hair behind her ear and glanced in his direction. For the briefest of seconds their gazes met, clashed. Held.

Malcolm became lost in the clear blue of her eyes. There was no guile, deceit, no duplicity. Just wonderfully pure, beautiful magic—and a stunning woman.

He waited until she was back in her royal-blue Renault and drove away before he moved. Malcolm wasn't sure what happened with the Druid, or why he couldn't seem to walk away from her.

It wasn't just her loveliness or her magic that entrapped him. It was . . . her. The complete package. He wanted to pursue her, to learn more of her.

But his feet didn't follow. It would've been easy too. Her magic was different than any other Druid's he'd ever encountered.

He glanced into the window of Tesco's and saw his reflection. The mangled man he spied with long, wild hair wasn't fit company for anyone. Malcolm turned his mind away from the Druid to the forest where he should have stayed.

It wasn't until the sounds of Aviemore faded, replaced by noises of the forest as he let the trees surround him that he relaxed. It was always his curiosity of mortals that pulled him away.

And it was the mortals who sent him back.

His god, Daal, thundered for another feel of the Druid's magic. It would be easy to find her. Her magic was unique and too easy to follow. That in itself gave him pause.

His mobile gave a quick vibration to alert him of a text. Malcolm pulled it out of his back pocket and saw it was from Phelan.

Malcolm had assumed Phelan was like him—a loner. Everyone knew Phelan's only friend was Charon. Yet, to Malcolm's surprise, Phelan had called him weeks ago. At first Malcolm thought it was regarding the business of the *drough* they hunted—Jason Wallace—but it turned out to be much more than that.

He almost didn't answer the text, but Malcolm knew Phelan would keep on until he responded. It'd been this way since Phelan and Aisley's wedding. Phelan was still pissed that he hadn't lingered for the ceremony.

Malcolm quickly typed, "I'm fine," and hit send.

He snorted when Phelan sent another message asking him to meet with him, Aisley, Charon, and Laura in Ferness.

They were getting as bad as Larena, checking in on him. Though he didn't try to hide what he was becoming, he'd believed everyone was too busy to notice. Obviously he'd been wrong.

"Another time," he replied and returned his phone to his pocket.

Malcolm stayed off the well-worn trails through the forest. He preferred the untamed landscape and whatever animal he might encounter.

It was while he meandered through the trees that he allowed the memories of his old life to surface. He had been raised to be laird of his clan. It had been his destiny.

How was he to know his bloodline carried a primeval god dragged up from his prison in Hell by *droughs*? As much as that angered him, he couldn't blame the Celts for asking the *droughs* for help so many centuries ago when Rome had tried to take them.

The Celts held Rome off as long as they could, but the Romans hadn't given up easily. So many families sacrificed loved ones in their bid to remain free of Rome's rule.

The Celtic tribal leaders knew they were on the verge of losing. When the *mies* had no answer, they turned to the *droughs*.

The *droughs* used their black magic to unleash ancient gods into the best warriors of each family who volunteered. Those men, fearless and already seasoned in battle, became something otherworldly. They suddenly possessed unimaginable speed, strength, and power.

But they also changed appearance. Each god favored a certain power and color. When the god was in control, the men's skin changed hue. Long, dangerous claws extended from their fingers and fangs from their teeth.

They were no longer men—but Warriors.

When Rome was defeated, the *droughs* tried to pull the gods out, but the gods refused to relinquish their hold on the men. It was only the combined magic of the *droughs* and *mies* that bound the gods inside the men.

It was then ordered that all spells used in the binding be destroyed, as well as the spell used to unbind the gods. The *mies* complied, but as usual, the treacherous *droughs* didn't.

While the Warriors returned to men, remembering nothing of their defeat of Rome, the gods were moving through the bloodline to the strongest warrior of each family.

Until the time of a fierce *drough* named Deirdre. She

found the scroll detailing how to unbind the gods. She also found a name—MacLeod. That's where she began to build her army to take over the world.

The MacLeods, however, didn't go quietly. The three brothers, equal in everything, shared a god, and they fought Deirdre. When they got free they returned to what was left of their castle.

Malcolm sat and leaned against a tree. The MacLeods. He remembered when he was just a lad and first witnessed Larena shift into her Warrior form. He'd been amazed and captivated.

Larena was his cousin from a century earlier who had her goddess unbound to protect a scroll that held all the names of the first Warriors.

They were two lonely people who became friends. When Malcolm was old enough, he vowed to help Larena keep hidden from Deirdre. He never expected that promise would lead them to the MacLeods and Larena's mate—Fallon.

Malcolm liked Fallon MacLeod instantly. Fallon was a good man who was a perfect match for Larena in every way. MacLeod Castle became a haven for Warriors and Druids who stood against Deirdre.

Malcolm dropped his head back against the tree and grimaced. How he'd eagerly gone to the castle, excited to see a place so full of magic. Only he'd nearly been killed. That's when the castle became a reminder of what Malcolm's life could have been. The sadness of what it was, was a daily reminder.

Without the use of his right arm, Malcolm was inadequate in battle. The fact he wasn't a Warrior relegated him to remain behind. With the women. Where they, as Druids, would protect him.

It'd been too much for a man who was reared to protect others. Malcolm began to despise everyone in the castle. It wasn't fair or rational, but those had been his feelings.

Then he became a Warrior. He went from fighting against evil to fighting for it.

He wanted to say that was when his soul died, but Malcolm knew that happened when he, as a man with only one good arm, couldn't find his place in the world.

"A shitty world it is too," he murmured. "And still no place for me."

CHAPTER TWO

Evangeline Walker parked her Renault and sat in the car outside the rented house. She had just forty-eight hours before her two-week lease was up.

She moved every few weeks. Maybe she was being paranoid in thinking there were people searching for her, but she knew what she'd seen when she discovered some-one had hacked into her Web site. A site that spoke of the Warriors and Druids.

Most of the pages had been left alone, but whoever had hacked the site made sure to dig up her information from the page talking about the necklace.

She touched the piece of jewelry hidden beneath her shirt. It wasn't just any necklace, but a magical one. It had been kept in a secret vault in Edinburgh Castle by the king for years until he had it—along with dozens of other magical items—moved to London.

Those items were separated into three shipments. Two traveled by land, and one by sea. One of the shipments journeying by land never made it to London. Instead, the contents were buried beneath the ground in a temple meant to keep them hidden for eternity.

"All but one item," Evie said.

She licked her lips and grabbed her things before exiting the car. The groceries and her purse were dumped on the counter when she entered the house.

Evie looked around and felt her soul sigh in resignation. It was plain and neutral in every sense of the word. Perfect for a rental, but it had no style, no flair.

This constant moving was taking a toll on her. She hated it. Then there was Brian. There was only so much moving around she could do because there was no way she was leaving her brother behind.

She pulled the frozen dinner out of the bag and set it on the counter. It looked as horrible as it had in the store, but the money was running low and beggars couldn't be choosy.

"Bugger it."

She missed her nice dinners in the city where the food was as enjoyable as the atmosphere. Though she wasn't the worst cook in the world, it was more difficult to prepare a meal for one than to buy the frozen dinners that had as much taste as her rental.

Evie walked into the bathroom and splashed water on her face. She braced her hands on either side of the sink and looked at herself in the mirror.

She almost didn't recognize the person staring back at her. Is this what paranoia did? The dark circles beneath her eyes, lines bracketing her mouth, the furrows deepening on her forehead. How would she look in a year, if she made it that long?

"Am I being paranoid? So what if someone wants to know about the necklace. I put the information up there to see if Druids would recognize it." She rolled her eyes. "Why did I put it up? How stupid could I've been?"

She'd known in her gut it was a bad idea, but the need to see if there were other Druids in the world had been too much. Surely she couldn't be the last.

It had been that need, that curiosity that made her toss aside reasoning and choose to post the details of the necklace. Well, *some* of the details. She left out the fact that it held a spell her family had guarded for generations.

The necklace could be dangerous if it fell into the wrong hands. She pulled it out from beneath her shirt and held it in her palm.

It no longer resembled the pendant it had been when it was lost. Now it looked like any Celtic cross, but it had enough spells on it to keep it hidden from anyone searching for magical items.

With a sigh, she dropped the cross so that it bounced against her before she dried her face. The sound of Brian's special *Doctor Who* ring tone filled the stillness of the house.

Evie rushed into the kitchen and grabbed her purse. She reached for her mobile phone and smiled when she read her little brother's message of "Checking in."

It made her feel better if she heard from him every day. There would be no talking between them since Brian had been born without that ability. Sign language and texting were what kept them connected.

"Thank God for texting," Evie said as she drafted a response.

Each day when his classes ended he would text. As a teenager, he no longer told her all that happened during his day, but occasionally his excitement over a girl would show through his words.

She was looking forward to his winter break so they could spend some time together, but then she worried about where they would go if she still felt the need to stay on the move.

Unfortunately, Brian wasn't in the mood to talk and returned a curt message. Evie tossed aside her phone and plopped down on the hard cushion of the couch with a sigh that seemed too loud in the quiet house.

She'd had a good job as a software designer. It paid well and gave her flexibility when it came to Brian. Evie thought back to when she learned her mother, who she hadn't seen since she was five, died and left her custody of a three-year-old half-brother.

At eighteen, the last thing Evie wanted was to be responsible for herself, much less anyone else. But one look at Brian, and she hadn't been able to turn him away.

Their road had been a rocky one, but somehow they'd managed to muddle through it all. Evie couldn't imagine her life without him now.

She looked out her window to the views of the Cairngorm Mountains and the mist that settled over the peaks, which was the only saving grace to the rental. The mountains, called *Am Monadh Ruadh*, meaning "the russet-colored mountain range" for the way the pink granite turned russet in the setting sun, were magnificent.

"Come to ussssss."

The rocks were calling to her. For as long as she could remember the rocks and stones spoke to her—and she to them. But these were louder, more insistent. They were unrelenting and adamant.

How much longer could she ignore them?

As it was, she'd awakened the previous night to find herself standing outside facing the Cairngorms. Never had she sleepwalked before, but it seemed these stones did something to her.

"What do you want?" she asked them.

"You. Come to usssss, Evangeline."

"Not now."

"Yessssss. We need you. You'll be safe here. Hidden."

It didn't matter how far she was, the stones were louder

than any others before. She'd always heard them, but before they'd just whispered her name.

Now they clamored for her to come to them.

"Am I in danger?"

"Come to usssss," they insisted.

The same conversation had taken place between them for the last week. Part of her wanted to go. She wished to see these stones and find out what they sought from her. The fact they promised she'd be safe was an added benefit.

Evie scooted down on the sofa until her head lay on the armrest while the stones continued to call for her. She watched the sun sink in the sky and light it a magnificent golden tangerine before she rose and fixed her tasteless frozen dinner.

With the little cottage having no telly, Evie pulled out her laptop. She went through the back door of her server and checked e-mails. As usual there were several from coworkers and the handful of friends wondering where she was.

As much as she wanted to talk to them, she couldn't chance it. She'd probably done too much by telling them she was traveling when she first left.

No one believed her.

Was she that awful of a liar? Or just a person who was too predictable?

Evie exited her e-mail and checked her Web site. The hits to her site had been growing for the past three years, but there had been a spike over the last few months.

It was that spike that had her checking to see just who was visiting. The fact she had been hacked and had difficulty discovering who had done it was what kept her on the run.

The necklace was supposed to remain hidden, never to

be seen in case someone sought to use it. Despite her knowing that, she needed to know if there were other Druids. What was a picture of a necklace anyway?

She made the choice to put it onto the Web site because she instinctively knew that if there were other Druids out there they would recognize it as a magical item.

It hadn't taken long for e-mails to show up asking about the necklace. She easily put them off, but then came the hacking.

That's when the fear settled in her gut and grew with every hour. There were no e-mails demanding to know more about the necklace, but when the hacker managed to somehow go through dozens of firewalls and traps to discover her name, Evie knew real terror.

The hacker seemed to be a professional one minute with the ease and simplicity of how they got into her site, but then in the next instant, some of their keystrokes looked amateurish. As if they wanted her to catch them.

It had been enough to scare her into removing the page talking about her necklace weeks ago. Yet they continued to come back and get past every trick she knew to keep them out.

"Who are you, and what do you want with me?" she asked the computer.

She drummed her fingers lightly on the keys and tried to think of another way to find out who her hacker was.

"If only I knew magic that would help."

As if on cue, an instant message window popped up. Evie's heart began a slow, hard pound as she read the message aloud.

"Would like to talk to you."

She swallowed hard and squirmed on the sofa. "Just what do you want to talk about?"

Evie quickly typed in the words and hit enter. In a

matter of seconds the reply read: "You mentioned a neck-lace on your site before you removed the page. Would like to discover what you know of it."

She snorted. "As if I'd tell you everything." She took a second to think of a reply and then started typing as she said, "I only know what I had on the site after finding the picture of the necklace."

The cursor blinked, waiting for a response. Minutes ticked by with nothing. Could she have gotten them off her trail? She wanted to know why they looked for infor-mation on the necklace, but it would be a huge chance if she began asking.

Evie waited, and as she did, she realized the connec-tion was still in place. She quickly switched screens and began to trace it to the source. If the person wouldn't tell her who they were, she'd find out on her own.

Every time she figuratively hit a wall, she tried a dif-ferent route. And yet, blocks repeatedly came up to stop her. It took another five minutes before she was able to pull up the location of the server.

When she saw it was routed through about a dozen countries, Evie knew she was in big trouble. She immedi-ately disconnected the instant messenger and put in sev-eral more rounds of firewalls on her site.

Whoever this was wasn't playing. They knew she had information. And they wanted it.

Just how badly they wanted it and to what means they were willing to go to get it was what had her on edge. No longer could she afford to wait for the remainder of her two days at the rental. She had to leave that night.

Hours later Evie rubbed her tired eyes as she sat on the bed. It felt as if the entire Sahara desert had taken up residence in her eyes. Lack of sleep and ages on the com-puter had only made things worse.

The rain began in the middle of the night. She watched

it roll down the window in the hopes it would slack off enough for her to get on the road.

She was a horrible driver. In all actuality, she should never have gotten a license to drive. She'd bought her Renault because she loved the older cars, but the dings and scrapes on her beloved car were all her doing.

Evie glanced through the bedroom door at the clock hanging on the kitchen wall. It read 3:52. She jumped up, grabbed her purse, locked up, and ran to her car.

Earlier, she'd loaded her two suitcases into the trunk so she could leave at a moment's notice. Every vehicle light that came into view was sure to be the unknown hacker she feared would locate her.

Evie sat behind the wheel and thought of her life as it stood. She had done exactly what her grandmother had cautioned her not to do—show the world the necklace.

It had been a stupid decision, all because she wanted to find other Druids. Now she couldn't shake the feeling she was being tracked. Because the necklace had to stay hidden, Evie was on the run.

It wouldn't do any good to hide the necklace, not if the hacker found her. Evie imagined she could withstand torture, but it wasn't as if she knew for certain. She could design amazing computer software, but surviving torture hadn't been part of her courses at university.

Running wasn't her only choice. She could return to her flat and her job and wait for the hackers to find her. It was a choice she contemplated every damn day.

But the promise to her grandmother kept her from taking the easy road and handing the necklace over.

Evie started the car and put it in reverse. She pressed the accelerator, but in her haste, she turned the wheel too soon and backed into the picket fence surrounding the yard.

"Damn, damn, damn," she muttered as she put the car in drive and pulled forward.

Normally, she would have gotten out and seen to the damage, but there was an urgency she couldn't shake to get as far from the small cottage and Aviemore as she could.

On her second try, she backed out of the drive and only heard the screech as the wood of the fence scraped against the car.

Then she was on the road. At this hour, few people were about, which made driving a little easier. The rain, however, added a different, unpredictable complication.

She had great eyesight. Except at night. At night in the rain it was almost like she was blind. What Evie could see was so blurry and distorted she couldn't pick out a tree from a sheep if her life depended on it.

Evie gripped the steering wheel with both hands, sitting forward so that she looked like one of those little old ladies peering through the steering wheel as they drove ten miles per hour.

She choked on a laugh when she looked down to find she was driving ten miles an hour.

"I'm a ninety-year-old woman in a twenty-eight-year-old body. It's no wonder I'm perpetually single."

She sent up a hasty prayer that she was able to keep the car on the road and not hit anyone. With no idea of where she was going, Evie found herself following the road that led her deeper into the Cairngorms.

The thick tree limbs that hung over the road blocked some of the rain, but not enough. She took the sharp left and drove over a bridge.

At the next right, she was going slowly enough to miss a fox that ran across the road by mere inches.

Evie felt the adrenaline pump through her at the near miss. With her entire body shaking, she started driving again. She'd gone less than three miles when the trees thinned out in a section and the rain came down harder.

She squinted through the deluge and windshield wipers that were going as fast as they could and still didn't clear the window enough for her to see.

So she never glimpsed the deer walking across the road.

CHAPTER
THREE

Malcolm once more squatted near a tree downwind as he watched the herd of red deer. The rain cloaked his position as the deer looked around for what hunted them. He might not need to eat as a Warrior, but his form was still human and did weaken if he skipped too many meals.

But it wasn't hunger that had him tracking the animals through the night. It was the chase, the hunt.

The kill.

He called to his god. In the next heartbeat fangs filled his mouth and long, maroon claws extended from his fingers. Lightning singed along his fingers as he welcomed Daal. His enhanced senses picked up an approaching car. And a wisp of magic he wished he didn't recognize.

The deer's ears twitched in the direction of the vehicle. Malcolm shifted so he could see the advancing headlights through the rain and trees.

He looked at the deer to find them hurrying across the road. Malcolm summoned his power, making lightning fork from the sky and land behind the last of the deer. It startled them enough to get them running.

Everything would have worked had the car not sped

up. Malcolm pulled back his lips in a grimace when the vehicle turned the curve and headed straight for three deer that were still crossing the road.

He stood at the feel of the same stunning magic from earlier, startling the deer and sending them scattering through the forest. Malcolm sent another bolt of lightning behind the remaining deer, but their gazes were trapped in the car's headlights.

With a curse he rushed onto the road, but too late the woman spotted the animals and jerked the wheel of the car.

Tires screeched on the wet pavement and slid on a patch of water. Malcolm could only watch as the car careened off the road and flipped repeatedly, the crunch of metal loud and ominous in the rain as it rolled down the hill.

For a moment, he simply stared at the car, which had landed upside down. He was unsure of the need pounding through him to check on the Druid. It wasn't her beauty that called to him, though she was the most beautiful thing he'd ever seen.

It wasn't her magic either. It was something else entirely and he wasn't sure he liked it. It put him on edge, uncertain and hesitant to get near her.

Her pain exploded through her magic for the barest of an instant before it diminished. If the Druid died, it would be his fault. He had enough death to shoulder. He didn't want an innocent added to his load.

He used his supernatural speed to get to the car. Malcolm didn't pause as he rushed to the driver's side and peered through the shattered window inside.

The windshield was smashed with a spiderweb of breaks across the breadth and width of the window. Shards of glass from all four windows were everywhere.

The woman wasn't moving as she hung suspended by

her seat belt. Malcolm moved aside her long curls to see her face. Blood dripped from a busted lip and she was unconscious, but other than that seemed to be all right.

He unbuckled her seat belt and caught her in his arms before she could fall. He remained still for just a heart-beat and took in the feel of the Druid against him, her soft body cradled in his arms.

Then he carried her into a small grove of trees out of the rain and gently laid her down. Next, he felt along her limbs for any breaks and found nothing.

"Lucky," he said with a shake of his head.

To his horror, he ran the pads of his fingers down her cheek. Her skin was warm and soft as silk. That small touch wasn't enough though. He was about to repeat the movement when she moaned and moved her head.

Malcolm smoothed a hand down his thick growth of beard as he stood to study her. He wanted to walk away and not look back, but he couldn't take his eyes from her. The drop of humanity left in him told him he had to make sure she was all right.

He glanced at his fingers that had touched her to feel them tingling with magic. How could one stroke of her affect him so? His gaze slid back to the Druid and how she was lying so helpless upon the ground.

Her lips were slightly parted as if in sleep, but the blood trailing from the corner reminded him of what had happened. For several seconds, he did nothing but watch her, hoping she might wake.

And praying she wouldn't.

He stepped into the shadows to watch and wait. Her scent of jasmine clung to him. He might like the feel of the Druid's magic, but that didn't mean he wanted any part of her.

Or was he lying to himself? His arms could still feel

the weight of her, his fingers still feel the smoothness of her skin.

Want? He didn't want her, he craved her, hungered for her. Ached for her.

He flattened a hand on the tree as he struggled to get a hold of the rapid, swirling emotions within him. He was on fire. And all because of a stunning temptress who couldn't drive.

He watched as her eyes fluttered open. She winced and grabbed her head of wet hair as she slowly sat up.

"Oh, no," she cried when she spotted her car.

The soft lilt of her voice was pleasant. More than pleasant if he were honest.

"I knew I shouldn't have driven in this blasted rain."

A Scot. Malcolm leaned a shoulder against a tree. Her voice was sweet and flowing, with just the right amount of a brogue that told him she'd spent significant time in the Highlands.

He could help her. All he had to do was walk out of the shadows. Except he didn't, he couldn't. He wasn't sure he could hold himself back from touching her if he let himself be known. It was better for him—and especially her—if she didn't realize he was there.

The fact he remained left him ill at ease. The only people he helped were from MacLeod Castle, and then only because he owed them a debt that could never be repaid. If they had any inkling that he contemplated killing all Druids so there would be no need of Warriors they would probably take his head in an instant.

The Druid got to her feet by using the tree beside her. She swayed and wiped the blood off her lip with the back of her sleeve.

"Stop it, damn you. I'm tired of you calling to me!"

Malcolm looked around but saw no one. Just who was

the woman talking to? It couldn't be the wind since not a leaf stirred. The rain, perhaps?

It had been so very long since anyone had intrigued him that it took his brain several minutes to realize what the emotion was.

Once he did, Malcolm took a step back. The emptiness, the deadness inside him he'd gotten used to. Any emotion other than guilt, he couldn't process.

The Druid stumbled to her car as she stared at it in horror. She shoved aside her wet hair and looked from the broken window and then over her shoulder to where she'd woken.

She then looked around the trees. "Hello? Is someone there?"

Malcolm gripped the tree. She appeared so lost and vulnerable that he found himself considering stepping out of the shadows and offering his help. That was the old Malcolm, the one who still had a soul. He released a breath and glanced down to see it wasn't his fingers gripping the bark, but his claws sunk into the tree.

How had Daal been released and he hadn't even known it?

"I know you're out there!" she shouted over the rain. "Thank you for helping me."

The hair on the back of Evie's neck stood on end. Someone was watching her. Was it the same someone who had helped her? Or someone else? Perhaps the ones looking for her?

She dropped to her knees, wrinkling her nose in distaste as mud and water soaked into her jeans. Evie found her purse, laptop, and keys before she walked around to the trunk. When she unlocked the trunk, it fell open and both suitcases tumbled to the ground.

A look around showed her she had a heck of a climb

back up to the road, and a several mile walk to return to Aviemore. In the rain.

Evie dragged all her stuff into the trees where their thick limbs kept most of the rain away. She sat huddled on one of her suitcases, her arms wrapped around her to fight off the chill.

She knew someone had pulled her out of the car. Somehow she recalled strong, kind hands that had held her. She pressed her fingers to her cheek, wondering if she had dreamed the man's touch there as well.

Evie leaned her head on the tree next to her and closed her eyes. She was so tired, and her head hurt almost as much as her lip. At least she hadn't broken anything, which by the look of her car was a small miracle.

The call of the stones had grown louder since the accident. She couldn't hear her own thoughts over the voices.

Her bank account had suffered greatly over the last few months after she left her job. She thought she would've tracked down whoever searched for her by now, but they were good. Better than she expected, actually.

If she used the last of her money to fix the car, then Brian wouldn't have tuition for the next semester. Evie would have no choice but to return to work. *If* they allowed her to return.

Her gut churned painfully at the thought of going back to Edinburgh. She was exposed and easily tracked there. Yet, it wasn't just herself she had to worry over. There was Brian, and he counted on her.

With his disability, he needed to stay at his school. He'd finally found a place he felt he belonged, and Evie knew how important that was.

"I can't go back to Edinburgh," she whispered. "I just can't."

She knew in her heart it was the wrong thing to do. Something bad would happen to her. Then where would Brian be? No, she had to keep moving.

The how of that was the question with a wrecked car. If she wasn't going to use her savings to fix it or buy another, what option did she have?

She wasn't the woodsy type. Hiking, of any kind, certainly wasn't her cup of tea. And camping? There were bugs out there.

"Bugs out here," she corrected herself as she looked around for anything that might be crawling on her or toward her.

It was too bad she couldn't deal with the camping because it would be the perfect place for her to hide. She even mulled the option for a minute or two before she thought of having to go to the bathroom, meals, and washing.

"Come to usssssssss!" the stones called.

Evie lifted her gaze to the dark sky and the mountains surrounding her. What did she have to lose?

"Fine," she said. "I'll come."

With nowhere else to go, Evie slid her laptop, surrounded in its sleeve, in her oversized purse. Then she grabbed a suitcase handle in each hand after she slung her purse over her head to settle across her body.

She took a deep breath and said, "Tell me where to go."

The silent humming of the stones kept her on as straight a path as she could manage through the dense forest and uneven terrain.

All around her stones were whispering. She didn't understand why the ones she was walking toward were louder, or why they wanted her to come to them so desperately.

"I'll sort it out when I get there," she said with a grunt when she had to yank her luggage over a sharp rise of earth. "I just want to be dry. And warm. Bloody hell, it's cold as death."

The chuckle she gave quickly turned into a groan when she sunk into a patch of mud. It took all her effort to keep her foot in her boot and get it extracted.

She wiped her wet sleeve across her forehead and began trudging forward again. That's when she saw the range of mountains through a break in the trees. "Is that why you're so loud? Are you one of the mountains?"

"*Yesssss.*"

Evie had never lived on a mountain before, but there was a first time for everything. But man did she miss her mani and pedi times, hot bubble baths, and her shows on the telly.

It seemed she walked for three lifetimes before she found herself wincing at the loudness of the stones. She'd finally reached them.

She blinked through the rain with a smile. "I'm here," she said and bent to place a hand on a small rock protruding from the ground. "I'm here."

To her surprise, she felt the ground rumble beneath her feet. About fifty feet up a slab of granite that looked suspiciously like a door opened.

Evie knew this was her one chance to turn around. The idea of warmth and dry clothes, not to mention being hidden and keeping Brian safe was too good to pass up though.

What was inside? Why were the stones so adamant about her being here?

Evie had already made a terrible choice by putting the necklace on her site. She didn't want to make another bad decision.

"Cold, wet, and homeless," she mused. "Or dry, warm, and protected from the elements. Please don't let this be a bad choice."

She hurried to the door and stepped inside before she changed her mind.

Malcolm let out a long breath as he watched the Druid walk into Cairn Toul Mountain. "Well, well, well. What do we have here? Just who are you, Druid, to take over Deirdre's home?"

CHAPTER
FOUR

Wallace Mansion
Ullapool, Scotland

Jason Wallace smiled as he leaned back in his chair, the burgundy leather soft and cool. He drummed his fingers on the top of his desk while he stared at the computer screen.

"So, Evangeline Walker, you doona trust easily. No' to worry, lass. You'll soon come to see my side of things. I've got you on the run, trusting no one. Just as I knew you would. You'll be desperate soon, and that's when you'll find me."

Jason chuckled and reached for the crystal tumbler where a splash of whisky waited. He drained the glass, letting the smooth amber liquid slide down his throat to settle warmly in his stomach.

He left the instant messenger page up and blank, the cursor blinking as it waited for him to type. There was nothing else he needed to say. Not yet, anyway. He'd done just enough to set her on edge.

Jason smiled slyly when Evangeline disconnected

from their chat. She would be on the run again. Not that he was worried. With just a simple spell he could pinpoint her location.

It wasn't time to see her yet. That would come soon, but there was more work to do first. Right now she thought someone was out to hurt her. He would come in as a savior, giving her no choice but to trust him.

Once he did, she would be his. Jason wanted the necklace and whatever properties it held, but it was Evangeline herself that would be his prize. And what a prize she would be. She had no idea how she fit onto the chessboard he had laid out, but she was much more than a mere pawn as he was using her now.

It was later, when she became exactly what he needed her to be, that the true Evangeline Walker would show herself.

Through the keys of the computer he could sense her magic, her *mie* magic. He'd known before he contacted her, however. No *drough* in their right mind would put anything out onto the Internet about magic, Druids, or Warriors. Only a naïve, inexperienced *mie* would make such a crucial mistake.

Jason clicked a key on the computer and the screen popped up from Evangeline's site, including the page she had taken down regarding the necklace. He read over the passage about the necklace for what must have been the twentieth time.

She put it out there to lure potential visitors, and she made sure to add just enough to entice. But there was more to the pendant than she let on. Discovering what it was would be a bonus for all his plans coming together so easily.

It was difficult to keep his excitement in when all of his pawns were falling into place without them even knowing he was leading, nudging, and pushing them. By the time they found out, it would be too late.

How he relished the idea of seeing the faces of all those at MacLeod Castle when they ascertained the truth. Or, he should say when he *allowed* them to learn the truth.

Jason rolled back his chair and rose from behind his desk to walk to the roaring fire. He stood before the hearth staring into the flames.

He had used magic to learn Evangeline's name, but that wasn't all he'd learned. She wasn't alone in the world. She had a brother.

Perhaps it was time he took a drive to Brian's school and had a look around. If things worked out properly, Jason would have no need to use Brian. But Jason hadn't gained his position without always having a backup plan in place.

Jason shoved his hands into the pocket of his pants and spoke two quick words in Gaelic. Instantly an image of Evangeline Walker's face appeared in the flames.

Long curls in a glorious shade of the deepest brown hung well past her shoulders. A pretty enough face with clear blue eyes stared back at him.

She wasn't the beauty Mindy had been, but then again, Evangeline didn't need to be to accomplish what he wanted. There would never be another like Mindy again.

Jason turned away from the flames, anger simmering in his gut as he thought of Phelan Stewart, the Warrior who had killed his precious Mindy.

And Aisley, his cousin who had betrayed him and married Phelan.

Their time would come. Every Warrior and Druid at MacLeod Castle would pay for his suffering, but none more than Aisley and Phelan.

And Evangeline would help him.

Evie dropped her bags and closed her eyes as she was surrounded by the stones that seemed to . . . purr. Her magic swelled around her, twisting and turning faster and larger with each second that passed.

The sensation was heady, the power . . . intoxicating. She could feel her magic grow stronger just by entering the mountain. Could the reason be having the stones all around her?

"Finally!" the stones seemed to shout over each other again and again.

There hadn't been a time in her life when Evie had ever felt so wanted. It brought a smile to her face as she opened her eyes.

The granite slab of a door closed behind her with a soft thud. Then she was enclosed in darkness so deep and thick she couldn't see her hand before her face.

"Torchesssss. Light the torchessssssss."

"Light the . . ." Evie trailed off as she swallowed.

She concentrated on her magic and the torches. A few minutes later and suddenly the torch on her left blazed to life. One by one down the long corridor the torches flared, shining light into the darkness.

"Where do I go?" she asked.

"Here," came a distant reply.

Evie reached for the handles of her luggage and started down the hallway where the voice had sounded. If she'd thought it would be an easy walk, she was wrong. The ground was slippery and damp, and the floor itself was wide but rolling with many valleys and peaks.

The fact that some sections of the floor were worn smooth by footsteps made her apprehensive, yet she knew the rocks wouldn't call to her unless she was safe with them.

For someone who hadn't communicated with the stones, they wouldn't understand her conviction or confidence in what they could do for her. She never had to explain it, and she wasn't sure if she could.

It was deep in her soul, this faith she possessed in the rocks. It was part of her DNA, and went hand in hand with her magic.

As she walked the corridor, she passed many doors. "Am I the only one here?"

"Aye. Only you."

"All the rooms are for who, then?"

"From the past."

The past? Maybe now she could gain some answers to her numerous questions. "Who was here before?"

"Druids. Warriors. Wyrran. Mortals. Many," the stones answered in unison.

Evie halted. "There were Druids here?"

"Aye. Powerful Druids."

"Where are they now?"

"Gone from us. She left ussss!"

The anger in the voices of the stones caused her to wince. "How long have you been alone?"

"Hundreds of years. We've been so lonely waiting for you."

Evie released one of the luggage handles and put her palm on the wall. "I'm here now. You're not alone anymore."

"Not alone. Not alone. We're not alone."

She smoothed her hand over the stones, feeling their pain and loneliness. They were emotions she understood all too well. Though this wasn't a place Brian would enjoy, the mountain would be her haven.

For now, it would be a refuge. The stones needed her, and she needed them.

Evie took a deep breath and reached for her luggage once more. The stones led her down an ever ascending slope of a hallway that curved time and again as she went higher and higher into the mountain.

Her breathing was ragged and a stitch began in her

side when she came to an open door. "I really need to get my arse to a gym or take up jogging. This is pathetic."

The warm glow coming from inside the room caught her attention. She quickly forgot all about being out of shape as she stepped inside.

"Wow," she murmured.

The room was a sitting area with torches on each wall. The sofa and two chairs were in need of recovering, but the coffee table and two end tables were in decent shape, if not antique in their look.

Evie walked farther into the room and glanced through another open door. She caught sight of a bed and hurried forward.

"Unbelievable," she said and touched the four-poster bed. A vanity table sat on the opposite wall with a small stool before it. There was a large chest, a couple of chairs, and a massive tapestry of a black dragon hanging on a wall.

"Is there a kitchen?"

"Use magic."

"I'd rather not. Is there not a kitchen?"

"Not a place for youuuuuuu."

Evie sighed as exhaustion began to weigh upon her. Not only did her new quarters need a good cleaning, but it looked as though she would have to find a way to get food.

"Um . . . is there a bathroom?"

"Show us what you want."

Evie touched a wall and let her mind fill with the image of a bathroom with a large tub, roomy shower, sink, and toilet. She was just wondering how the plumbing would work when the mountain began to shake.

Almost instantly, the back section of the room started to tremble as the rocks shifted and moved. Evie stared in awe as another doorway was created.

When the vibrations halted, she walked to the new doorway and gasped as the image she'd seen in her head appeared before her. The tub wasn't porcelain or a clawfoot. Instead it was made out of the stone surrounding her. Same with the shower, toilet, and sink.

Even the faucets were made from stone. She'd never been so amazed. Evie ran her fingers along the smooth stone, thoroughly impressed.

"This is just what I saw in my head. Well, except for the running water."

"Use your magic."

That seemed to be the stones' answer for everything. She might have magic and know how to use it, but Evie had lived her life without it. Unless it had been important.

Did she dare to use it on something as simple as running water and food?

Suddenly a thought occurred to her. "The runoff from the rain. Can you collect it for me?"

There was more trembling throughout the mountain for a few minutes.

"Aye. It'll be routed to this room when you want it."

Evie laughed and twirled around the room. This all had to be a dream. How could anything be so fabulous and magical all at the same time? And be for her?

"Thank you!" she shouted. "Thank you so much!"

Again the stones seemed to purr in contentment. She knew just how they felt.

She was going to drop onto the bed when she saw all the dust and cobwebs. Evie hesitated for a moment before she used her magic to make the bedroom and sitting room clean with merely a thought.

"I'll do the others by hand tomorrow. I'm just too exhausted now," she told herself as she fell back on her now clean bed.

She laughed at how soft the mattresses were. And they

were mattresses, not the straw-filled bedding she had expected. The stones had said hundreds of years, but she was beginning to think it had been sooner than that.

Evie kicked off her wet boots and sat up long enough to peel out of her soaked clothes before she snuggled under the thick covers.

If the stones were right and she could use magic for anything, then she could make this as nice and cozy as she wanted.

There were some modern conveniences she missed, such as hot water for tea or baths, a hearth for a fire, and a stove. But she would make do.

The main thing was that she was safe. There was no way the stones would allow anyone in without alerting her.

CHAPTER
FIVE

Malcolm stared at Cairn Toul for hours. Memories of Deirdre and the horror she'd wrought filled him until he couldn't distinguish what were memories, and what was real.

The fury, the fear of when he'd become a Warrior seized him. The recollection of it taking him back to that fateful day when he was ripped apart only to come back together with a persistent voice in his head.

With those memories, Deirdre returned in all her glory. Her beauty, marred by the evil inside her, and her long white hair she used as a weapon.

Her insistence to rule the world, her disregard for life, it all slammed into him, breaking past the wall he'd erected in his mind to shut out such recollections.

Malcolm grabbed his head as he recalled the screams in the mountain, of death and destruction. He squeezed his eyes shut when he remembered how easily he'd killed for Deirdre.

What kind of man was he?

But he wasn't a man. He was a monster, a fiend not fit for anyone's company.

He dropped his head and opened his eyes. There was no use in looking to the past. He'd made his choices. He knew what the consequences would be, and he would gladly pay them when the time came.

Malcolm began to reach for his phone to alert those at the castle about the new Druid in Deirdre's mountain. But he paused at the last minute when he thought of Larena.

His cousin was still dealing with everything the X90 bullet filled with *drough* blood had done to her. One drop of *drough* blood could kill a Warrior. Jason Wallace had done something to make the *drough* blood in the X90s stronger.

Larena had died before the Druids could help her. Somehow, she had found her way back to Fallon. Malcolm still didn't understand how, but there were many things about magic he didn't comprehend.

Malcolm raked his wet hair out of his face and contemplated the situation. If he called the other Warriors, it would be Fallon who would want to bring the Druid to the castle. Fallon had taken it upon himself to save as many Druids as he could from the evil bent on destroying everything.

No one seemed to understand that without the Druids they wouldn't be in this mess. There was only one answer: kill the Druid.

A flash of clear blue eyes the color of a summer's sky flickered in Malcolm's mind. He shoved it aside. Beautiful or not, the Druid had to die.

There was only one reason for a Druid to be back in Cairn Toul. She was evil.

Or going to become evil.

Malcolm frowned. He'd felt her magic. It had been pure and magnetic, radiant and sensual. It had been . . . incandescent. There was no way she would have been able to mask her magic from him.

Yet, he couldn't fathom why a *mie* would be in such an evil place. The things that had taken place in Cairn Toul Mountain were unspeakable. The sheer number of Druids who had died by Deirdre's hand as she took their magic was unthinkable.

And the men captured and imprisoned in the hopes they held a god within them was unimaginable.

For over a thousand years, evil had ruled the mountain. That kind of wickedness left a mark, a mark that would remain forever. If the Druid didn't know where she was, then she could be in danger.

Malcolm found himself pulled in two directions again. He could get inside the mountain and confront the Druid. Or he could allow her to remain where she would most likely die or turn evil—then he would kill her.

He turned and looked over his shoulder to the forest. The deer were still there, waiting for him to resume his hunt. No matter how much he wanted to return to them, he couldn't.

For whatever reason, he had come across the Druid. Whether she lived or died was now in his hands. Whereas other Warriors might feel kindness or patience for her, Malcolm had no such difficulties.

He would evaluate her as the cold, calculating beast he was. If she left Cairn Toul, he might steer her toward MacLeod Castle.

If she remained . . . it would be his duty to end her life. There were enough problems caused by one powerful *drough*. One less *drough* wouldn't be missed.

His enhanced hearing picked up a slight whoosh from above. Malcolm jerked his gaze upward, searching the clouds. It would be just like the Dragon Kings to watch him.

The Kings were immortal like him, but unlike Warriors, they had been around since the beginning of time.

They could shift from dragon to human form and back again at will. It was their duty to keep the peace between the dragons and humans, which is why when a war broke out millions of years ago, they sent their dragons to another realm.

The Kings remained, powerful and influential. They hid behind Dreagan Industries, which also produced the most sought-after scotch in the world—Dreagan whisky.

Malcolm searched the skies for several minutes, yet he found no sign of a dragon nor heard anything that sounded remotely like a beating wing.

Which was good. He didn't want to explain himself to anyone. The farther he was from the others the better. They might not see it that way now, but they would eventually when it came time to hunt him. It was always easier to hunt something you didn't know than to kill a friend.

Malcolm faced Cairn Toul again. He'd never wanted to return, but it looked as if he would step once more into Hell itself thanks to this new Druid.

He had no doubt the stones knew he was there. Whether they had told the Druid or not, he wasn't sure. Deirdre had made certain there were ways for her Warriors to get in and out of the mountain besides using the main entry.

Malcolm jogged around the backside of the mountain regretting his decision with every step he took. When he finally reached his destination, the stones shifted and blocked the entrance.

He didn't bother trying to move the large boulder. Cairn Toul had another Druid in its bowels, and it would do whatever it needed to in order to keep her protected.

Malcolm leaned close and said in Gaelic, "*Fosgail*, open."

The stones had no choice but to allow him entry. He waited as the boulder rolled away and the entrance was once more revealed.

With a slight hesitation, Malcolm stepped into the mountain. For several seconds, he simply stood in the silence. The stones could have imprisoned him right then, but they allowed him through the small room and deeper into the mountain.

He knew there was only one place the rocks would have taken the Druid. Malcolm's boots didn't make a sound upon the stones as he made his way to Deirdre's old room.

The torches were lit to cast aside the shadows, but to Malcolm, it only made the shadows deeper, more sinister. Evil leeched from the stones until it enveloped him.

He wasn't sure what he would find when he reached Deirdre's chamber, but it wasn't the Druid fast asleep and buried under a mountain of blankets.

Her deep brown curls streamed across the pillow behind her as she lay on her side, one hand beneath her cheek. Lips, full and tempting, were slightly parted and her breathing was deep and even.

He wanted to spy on her for a few days to see what she was about, but the stones would no doubt tell her he was there.

There were few choices left to him. He could leave. He could make himself comfortable in one of the chairs and remain until she woke. Or he could go to another part of the mountain and wait.

Malcolm contemplated all three options and the consequences. Each held its own appeal, but in the end there was really only one choice.

Evie wasn't sure what yanked her so unceremoniously from her much needed sleep. One moment she was dreaming, and the next she opened her eyes—to find a man leaning over her.

She gasped and found herself gazing into the most

spectacular azure eyes the color of the brightest sapphires. They glittered like gems as he stared dispassionately at her.

"What are you doing here?"

His voice, dark, rich, and sultry, sent a tremor down her spine to settle in a warm flood between her legs. His blond hair, a golden color that made it seem as if he were born of the sun, hung wet and tangled about his shoulders.

"Did you no' hear me? What are you doing here?" he demanded again, his tone even, but brooking no argument.

She wanted to answer him, but she was arrested by what her eyes saw. Even with the thick growth of a beard she spied his angular jaw, strong chin, and cheekbones so high they could cut her.

Then she saw the scars. He didn't hide behind them, but displayed them as if waiting for some poor soul to try and pity him.

It took just a glance to see that there were five gashes that slashed across his face from his left temple to his right jaw. One even went over his eye, making her wonder how he hadn't lost it.

"Answer me," he growled dangerously.

Evie jerked her gaze back to his and licked her lips nervously even while she tried to stay calm. "I needed a place to stay."

"And you knew of this place how?"

There was something in his tone that told her he knew exactly how she knew. After all the running, all the hiding, she'd finally found a place she felt safe. She was tired of being scared. A wave of anger filled her. "Don't patronize me."

"Ah," he murmured. "You've a spine then."

It was only when she managed to pull her attention from the gorgeous—and frightening—specimen before her that she finally heard the stones. They were deafening as they shouted her name over and over. With one word she could have the stones hold the man, and it might come to that, but she wasn't ready to take that action. Yet.

Just knowing she had that option gave her the courage to stand up to him.

"Do you live here?" she asked.

"I asked you a question first."

She pulled her hands out of the covers and shoved at his chest. He was like a wall of granite, hard and unmovable. Her hands tingled from the contact, the warmth and power she felt urging her to touch him again, to learn the thick sinew she saw beneath his tight shirt.

When he didn't move, she did. Evie climbed out of the covers and stood on the opposite side of the bed. Only to realize she was in nothing but her bra and panties, having been too exhausted to riffle through her luggage for her jammies. She hastily grabbed one of the blankets and held it against her.

His gaze slid down her, but no desire flared in his eyes. She should be thankful. Yet all she could do was marvel at the man before her. He stood tall and commanding, large and impressive. His arms hung by his sides, belying the alertness she sensed within him.

He wore the charcoal-gray tee as if it were a second skin. It molded to every hard muscle and valley of his body, making her yearn to tear the shirt off and see him in all his glory.

The dark jeans were still damp from the rain and hung low on his hips. She had the insane urge to ask him to turn around so she could see his bum.

Evie let her gaze rake back up his trim hips to the deep V of his chest, to his impossibly wide shoulders. That's when she saw more scars half hidden on his neck by his hair and shirt.

He was danger and torment hulking in the doorway with a mouthwatering body and enthralling azure eyes. He was sex in its most primal and untamed form.

And she couldn't believe he was within reach.

His deep, sultry voice was a weapon on its own, but combined with his eyes and rock-hard body, Evie had to force her mind to remember what they were talking about.

"You asked a question, and I answered. Seems only fair you answer mine," she said in a voice calmer than she felt as she met his eyes.

The man set her on edge, her body seeming to come alive with him near. It was as if it recognized the very masculine, very dominant man would ease the deep ache within her.

She didn't know who he was though. For all she knew he could be the one who hacked her site.

And she didn't care.

He was frightening in the way he stared at her as if she could be the enemy, but he was also exciting and . . . stirring.

"Nay."

She swallowed and ignored how tempting his full lips were. "Look. I'm not being unfai—"

"Nay, I doona live here," he said as he crossed his arms over his chest.

Evie fiddled with the edge of the blanket. "Oh."

"Now. How did you know of this place?"

She had never told another soul she was a Druid, and now that the time was upon her, she wasn't so sure she wanted to talk about it.

"Shall I tell you?" the stranger asked. "You're a Druid, and you heard the stones."

It took a moment for Evie to realize her mouth was hanging open she was so shocked. Belatedly, she closed her mouth and dragged in a deep breath. "Are you . . . are you a Druid?"

"No' even close."

"But you know of Druids?"

He gave a single nod.

Evie stopped herself short of rolling her eyes. "Can you tell me what you know of them?"

"You know you're a Druid and you doona know of them?"

"It's complicated," she said with a shrug. "Will you tell me who you are?"

"I'm the worst thing that could've crossed your path, Druid."

CHAPTER
SIX

"I doona like this," Phelan said as he paced the length of floor-to-ceiling windows in Charon's living room above the tavern. "Malcolm is keeping to himself more and more. This doesna bode well."

Charon set down his glass on the coffee table and put his hand on Laura's knee. "We could always have Broc find him."

Phelan came to a halt when Aisley stepped in front of him. Her fawn-colored eyes held a wealth of concern. He tugged on a long lock of her black hair. "No' yet."

Broc was a viable choice since his power as a Warrior was to find anyone, anywhere. But Phelan wasn't ready for those at the castle to know how concerned he was over Malcolm.

"Any word on Larena?" Aisley asked.

It was Charon who said, "No' since Fallon told us Britt was close to finalizing the antidote that could help."

Phelan turned to look out the windows. The darkness couldn't hide the thick clouds that filled the sky. With the intermittent rain and cool temps, it had been a dreary day, which didn't appear to be letting up anytime soon.

"Text him again," Laura suggested.

Phelan closed his eyes when Aisley came up behind him and wrapped her arms around him. She laid her cheek on his back as he covered her hands with his. "It wouldna do any good. Malcolm will respond when he wants to."

"He's been distancing himself from all of us," Charon said. "I didna expect him to do the same to Larena."

"That's what tells me things are bad."

Aisley squeezed him. "You said yourself you didn't imagine he'd agree to meet us."

"Nay." Phelan turned and drew her against him. "I didna, but I also have a feeling something is going on with him. Before . . . well, before he talked. Now he willna even do that."

Charon got to his feet and poured a glass of wine that he handed to Laura. "How close to the edge do you think he is?"

"Verra," Phelan answered with a grimace. He wished it wasn't true, but he'd glimpsed it in Malcolm's eyes the last time they were in battle.

"You didna see the things I did in Cairn Toul," Charon said. "There are some men who couldna be saved, Phelan, no matter how much someone might want to. It's up to the Warrior to make that decision."

Phelan had been spared witnessing what Charon and the others had suffered at Deirdre's hand, but he experienced something else entirely, something no one could begin to comprehend.

Perhaps that's what led him to want to help Malcolm. Phelan had been where he was before. Somehow Phelan had found his way back. He wanted to give Malcolm that chance as well.

"All you say is true, but Malcolm is different. You know this," Phelan argued. "He didna suffer in the bowels of that hellish mountain. Deirdre tried to kill him first."

Laura uncrossed her long, jean-clad legs as she rose from the couch, wine in hand. "Neither of you were at the castle during the time Malcolm was recovering from those wounds. It might help if we could get someone else's opinion of how he was."

Phelan was shaking his head before she finished. "It's a good idea, but I'm no' ready to include the others. Fallon will worry, and so will Larena. Both need to concentrate on Larena getting better."

"Not to mention Jason's next attack," Aisley said.

Phelan tightened his hold on Aisley. Wallace had nearly taken her from him just a few weeks earlier. It was Aisley's Druid ancestor who had informed her she was a Phoenix, able to be reborn again and again. If it hadn't been for that, Aisley would be dead and Phelan would be right where Malcolm was.

"Jason needs to be killed for good," Laura said with a shiver.

Phelan watched Charon pull his wife into his arms and whisper something that made Laura smile. If anyone had asked Phelan a year before if he and Charon would ever find their mates, he'd have laughed.

Now it seemed that Aisley and Laura had always been a part of them, just waiting until they could join their lives together. All Phelan knew was that he couldn't survive without Aisley.

"I know my cousin well enough to know that he'll keep striking when we least expect it," Aisley said into the silence.

Phelan met Charon's gaze as smiles pulled at their lips. "Are you thinking what I'm thinking?"

Charon chuckled. "Oh, aye."

"Care to fill us in?" Laura asked as she pushed her long, dark hair behind her ear.

"We attack him just as we did Declan," Phelan answered.

Aisley pulled out of his arms and looked at him with fear and anxiety. "You can't."

"We can, and we will."

"No. You don't understand, Phelan. Jason is more powerful now. If he can come back from death, regenerate a new body, and triple his powers, how do you think attacking him will destroy him for good? If you do this, Jason will kill you."

"He's tried. And failed."

Laura set down her wineglass. "Aisley's right. I went up against Jason before his powers grew. I was also part of the battle after he seemed to more than double his powers. He's different."

"We know," Charon said. "It's Warriors who feel a Druid's magic. Neither of you are telling us anything we doona already know."

"Then why be so damned foolish?" Aisley asked Phelan. "Don't you understand? I can't live without you."

Phelan dragged her into his arms. He rested his chin atop her head and simply held her. She was shaking, not because she didn't think he could kill Wallace, but because she knew all too well what Jason could do.

"Wallace wants revenge against you still," Phelan told her. "I'm sure he knows you've regenerated. He'll be coming for you."

Charon sighed loudly. "We can no' wait for him to attack again, and Aisley says we shouldna strike first. What do we do then?"

"Set a trap?" Laura offered.

Aisley said, "That didn't work so well last time. He knew what was being planned."

"Then what?" Phelan asked. "I'm out of ideas, sweet-heart."

A knock on the window behind him had Phelan jerking around to find Ramsey and Logan on the deck looking in. Charon motioned them in as Logan opened the sliding glass door and stepped inside.

"What brings the two of you here?" Phelan asked.

Ramsey turned his silver eyes to him. "The girls were worried about Aisley and Laura. And Fallon wanted us to check on the two of you."

"We're fine, as you can see," Charon said.

Logan accepted the tumbler filled with whisky from Charon. "I'd believe you except for the fear I sense coming from your women."

Phelan scratched his jaw after Aisley moved to his side. "What do you expect with Wallace still out there?"

"Which is Fallon's point," Ramsey said. "We'd all be safer at MacLeod Castle."

"Nowhere is safe," Aisley said and turned to walk toward the sofa.

Phelan lived his life battling the *droughs* who had dared to think they could take over the world. Aisley knew first-hand the lengths Wallace would go to ensure no one thought to betray him.

Aisley's parents had been killed by Jason. Aisley herself had been wounded, and still bore the scar, when Wallace thought she might leave. In this last battle Wallace had brought forth an image of what Aisley's daughter, who died just hours after her birth, might look like. That alone had nearly killed Aisley.

What would Wallace try next? Phelan wasn't sure he wanted to find out, but neither could he hide his head in the sand and pretend nothing was going on.

He was a Warrior, and whether the *droughs* who first

dragged up the gods from Hell had known it or not, it would be Warriors who ended the *droughs*.

"Have either of you spoken with Malcolm?" Charon asked.

Phelan growled his frustration and looked away. But not before he saw Ramsey frown.

"Why?" Logan asked.

Charon rolled his eyes. "Can you no' just answer the damned question?"

"That would be too easy," Logan said with a grin. "Besides, I like to rile you."

Ramsey crossed his arms over his chest. "Nay, we have no'. Have either of you?"

"In a way," Charon answered.

Logan grunted in irritation. "What the hell does that mean?"

"It means he answered my text," Phelan stated. He faced the two Warriors to find their gazes locked on him. "I called Malcolm over a week ago when I was with Aisley and trying to figure things out. We were both looking for Wallace, and I checked in with Malcolm on occasion. He did the same."

"And now?" Ramsey asked.

"Now I get a text saying he's fine."

Logan drained the whisky and moved to pour himself another. "That's more than Larena or Fallon have gotten. Consider yourself lucky."

Phelan hoped the topic would be dropped, at least until he knew more of what was going on with Malcolm. But as usual, Ramsey heard more than just the words.

"You're worried for him."

Phelan glanced at Aisley who gave him a small nod. "Aye," he admitted with a sigh. "I want both of you to swear what we say here about Malcolm goes no further."

"Agreed," Ramsey stated.

Logan stared at Phelan for a long moment before he said, "I give my word."

Phelan lowered himself into the nearest chair and braced his elbows on his knees while he plunged his fingers into his hair. "I think Malcolm is distancing himself."

"Larena has suspected that for some time," Logan said. "It's why she and Fallon kept trying to find ways to bring him to the castle."

"It's no' enough now. I saw it in Malcolm's eyes during battle. If he passes that point, there'll be no returning for him."

Ramsey dropped his arms. "Then we find him."

"Easier said than done," Charon said.

"Broc isna the only one who can find someone. His way is easier and quicker, but no' the only way," Ramsey stated.

For the first time in days, Phelan realized there just might be a way to help Malcolm after all. "After we find him, then what?"

"That's the tricky part." Ramsey looked around the room, his gaze meeting each of them. "There was a time Hayden stood on the same knife's edge. He didna know it at the time, but it was Isla who pulled him back."

Logan choked on his whisky. "Are you telling me we need to somehow find Malcolm a woman?"

"There has to be another way," Laura said, a frown marring her forehead.

Phelan lifted his head and grinned. "There is. We make him know he's needed. No' once has he failed to join us in battling the *droughs*. Forget about finding him a woman. Give him something to kill, give him a reason to keep focused on helping us."

"I like it," Logan said. "I doona suppose you have a plan in mind?"

Ramsey took the glass in Logan's hand and tossed back the contents in one swallow before pinning Phelan with his silver eyes. "You want to go after Wallace."

Phelan nodded. "It's the only way."

"Didn't we just talk about this?" Laura asked Charon before looking at Phelan, her English accent getting thicker as her anger rose. "I'm pretty sure we decided that attacking him was wrong, and that trying to set a trap for Jason wouldn't work either. Or was I just dreaming that conversation?"

"Nay, love," Charon said as he took her hand and kissed her fingers. "Though it looks like we may be having that same conversation again. This isna just for Malcolm. Killing Wallace is on top of all our to-do lists."

Phelan's gaze moved to Aisley as it always did. She was his beacon, his safe harbor in the treacherous world they lived in. He needed her support in order for this to work, but he wouldn't push her. She'd already been through too much.

"If we're going to do this, then you're going to need me," she said.

"Aisley—"

"I'm a Phoenix, remember?" she interrupted him.

Ramsey cut his silver eyes to her. "And it's going to come in handy too."

CHAPTER
SEVEN

Malcolm waited for the Druid to retaliate with magic to protect herself. Instead, she simply stared at him with an unblinking clear blue gaze. It was then he realized she was looking at his scars. If only she grasped that but half of them were visible to her.

Normally Malcolm shrugged off the gawks, but he grew uncomfortable under the Druid's stark perusal. He looked for sympathy or pity that inevitably showed in people's eyes. Oddly, there was nothing but frank curiosity and . . . was that pleasure he saw flare in her blue depths?

That couldn't be right. No one so beautiful would look at him in such a way. He was damaged, mutilated—inside and out.

"You doona fear me?" he asked before he could stop himself.

She lifted a shoulder in a half-shrug, careful to keep the blanket covering her. "You said you weren't a Druid."

"So?"

"So . . . it means you can't do anything if I choose to use magic on you."

For several seconds, Malcolm could only ogle the female in wonder. Did she not know of Warriors? Was she so naïve about the ways of their world that she would dare to flaunt her magic?

Or was it that she did know what he was and didn't care, because she knew she could control him if need be?

Malcolm lifted his chin and looked down his nose at her. She was of average height, but she kept eye contact with him, her back against the stones. He saw her hand splayed upon the rocks, most likely listening as they told her all about him.

With one word, she could have him pulled against the stones as they held him prisoner. He'd seen Deirdre do it. While he waited to see what she would do, Malcolm found himself fascinated by a wisp of a Druid who threw him off-kilter more completely than anything else in his life before.

Her clear blue eyes went distant, her head cocked to the side. "Malcolm Munro."

Just as he expected. The stones were telling her who he was, but would they tell her everything? There was no denying the pureness of her magic. She wasn't *drough*—not yet at least. Did the stones know she would leave if she discovered what had happened in the mountain?

He decided to go along and see just how much the rocks told her.

"Aye."

She blinked, focusing on him once more. "All the stones will tell me is your name. They also say I need to make you leave."

"Is that so?"

"You don't seem surprised."

"I'm no'. I knew the last Druid who commanded the stones."

Her eyes grew large with curiosity. "Really? Who was she? What can you tell me about her?"

"Ask the stones."

That drew her up short. "You haven't asked my name."

"I doona need to know it," he lied. To his surprise, he very much wanted her name. Because he did, he didn't ask for it. It was enough that he couldn't stop looking at her or enjoying the wash of her magic over him. She was addictive. "We both need to leave this place."

She shook her head, her damp hair curling becomingly around her face. "I can't. I'm safe here."

"Who are you running from?"

"Maybe you?"

He raised a brow at her question. Something was making her run. Interesting. "Did the stones tell you someone was after you?"

"As if," she said with a roll of her eyes. "They're the ones who told me to come here so I could hide. No one was supposed to know I was here." A frown marred her forehead. "How did you know I was here?"

Malcolm didn't want to let her know too much too soon. The less she knew about him the better. "I felt your magic."

"You can feel my magic? What does it feel like?"

Sunshine. Harmony.

Hope.

Not that he would tell her any of that. Ever.

Instead he said, "Wholesome."

She wrinkled her nose in distaste, her stance becoming more casual and comfortable. "Is that bad?"

"It would be if the feel of your magic made me sick. That would tell me you had black magic. If you were *drough*, I'd kill you."

"You say that as calmly as if you do it every day."

He let his silence be his answer.

The Druid swallowed hard and shifted her feet nervously. "What are you, some kind of Druid Hunter or something?"

"Or something." Malcolm watched the red-orange glow of the torch flicker alluringly over her skin. He remembered how soft her cheek had been, and he found he wanted to test the rest of her body.

Did she know how fetching she looked standing there with the blanket barely covering her and giving him glimpses of her lean legs and feminine curves? Was she trying to tempt him?

His body had been aching since he first held her in his arms. That ache only increased the longer he stood near her.

"Are you intentionally not giving me in-depth answers?"

Malcolm widened his stance and crossed his arms over his chest. "You're just now recognizing that?"

"Ah. Answering a question with a question. That was something my mum did," she mumbled, her voice heavy with sarcasm and anger. Her gaze narrowed on him as she pushed away from the wall. "The stones don't like you."

"The feeling is mutual."

She gave a loud snort. "They're stones. How could you not like them? They didn't do anything to you."

"Really? How do you know? Just because they doona tell you doesna mean it's the truth, Druid."

"Then you tell me."

Malcolm walked right into the trap without realizing it. It was the amazing feel of her magic surrounding him that kept him from focusing properly. Her magic crashed over him like the waves against the cliffs at MacLeod Castle—violent and unforgiving. But beautiful and beckoning all the same.

He wanted to sit back and soak up the wonderful essence of her magic. But he couldn't. It wasn't fair to her.

"You berate the stones for not sharing your past, but you won't do it either?" she asked with a slight shake of her head. "What am I to think?"

"I doona give a rat's arse what you think, Druid."

"Is that so? Do you forget I've magic?"

How could he when it enveloped him so completely? His body roused at the first feel of her magic, and the longer he was around her the more he . . . *yearned*.

There was just a thin blanket blocking the tempting view of bare skin and a turquoise bra and panties. He could yank it away from her. If he dared.

And at the moment, he dared.

"Are you so sure your magic will work on me?"

She let her hand not holding the blanket slap against her thigh. "You're impossible."

"If you're running from something, then you shouldna trust anyone."

"You came here to scare me, and it worked. Now you can leave."

He studied her closely. She might have been afraid of him, but not anymore. Too bad she didn't realize she was tempting a monster whose desire built for her with each breath. "Why do you no' believe I'm the one after you?"

"Because you didn't ask for the one thing they would have."

"I see." With great effort, he turned on his heel and started for the door. Just before he reached it, he paused and looked at her over his shoulder. A dark curl lay just over her breast provocatively, as if begging him to give it a tug . . . then cup her breast. "You put your soul in danger by remaining here, Druid. Do us both a favor. Leave while you can."

"I can't," she whispered.

He met her blue gaze and tried to think what the old him, the man he'd been before he was maimed, would have said to her. He'd have charmed her to get what he wanted, seduced her to his way of thinking.

It was too bad none of that was left in him. There was only coldness, hardness now. He had a beast within him, but worse, he was becoming that monster inside and out.

"That's too bad, Druid."

He walked away from her then. Even as he wanted to stay near her magic, he made himself leave the chamber. But not the mountain.

As much as he wanted to put distance between himself and Cairn Toul, he found himself remaining within the cold, evil structure. Though he couldn't say exactly why. He could call Fallon and have him retrieve the Druid, saving him from continuing the argument or forcing her to leave.

He wound his way through the twists and turns to the chamber he'd been given when he was there with Deirdre. It was two levels below the Druid, but that didn't stop her magic from reaching him.

Malcolm stood in the doorway and looked at the sparse chamber. There was only a bed and a small table. He'd never actually stepped foot in the room.

When Deirdre had given it to him, he hadn't even looked within. He might have had to be in the mountain with her, but that didn't mean he had to sleep there.

Malcolm backed out of the room and shut the door. He wouldn't be sleeping there this time either.

Evie wanted to call Malcolm back. She bit her lip to keep from giving in to the urge. Obviously the infuriatingly gorgeous man didn't like her. Not that she could discern why.

It bugged her that he hadn't asked her name. But more

than that, she was disturbed at the lack of information the stones had given about him.

All they kept repeating—even now—was for her to make him leave. Or kill him.

Evie wasn't a murderer. Malcolm might have frightened her at the start, but he hadn't harmed her. The apathy she glimpsed in his azure gaze left a cold ache in her chest.

There was such desolation in his eyes, such bleakness that it made her want to cry. How could someone be so empty inside? It was as if every emotion had been severed, as if he were dead inside.

Despite that, she knew he meant every word when he said he would make her leave the mountain. Which she couldn't do.

"I could try and explain things. Maybe he'd help."

As soon as she said the words, she knew they weren't true. It was too bad, because she was sure Malcolm with his bulging muscles and hard stare could stop anyone in their tracks.

"No. Make him leave!"

"Why don't you like him?"

For the first time, silence met her question.

Evie took a deep breath and tried again. "Who was the Druid here before me? The one who spoke to you?"

"Deirdre!" The stones spoke in unison, nearly deafening her with their shout.

Deirdre? Who was this Druid? And why did it make Malcolm urge her out of the mountain?

"Tell me of her," she begged the stones.

"Powerful. She was powerful! Shouldn't have died. Was betrayed. She was betrayed!"

"So she was powerful and she was able to speak to you. You cared for her very much."

"She was our mistress."

"What did she use Cairn Toul for?"

"Her home. It was her home."

"So she wasn't safe here."

"She left usssss!"

Once more there was wailing, as if the rocks were mourning this Deirdre. And they weren't happy she left. Evie wanted to know more, but she had a feeling the stones were too far gone in their grief to tell her anything else at the moment.

She climbed back into bed and found her gaze going to the doorway. Where had Malcolm gone? She hoped he was still in the mountain since she had more questions for him.

Plus, she wanted him to ask her name. Why hadn't the blasted man asked her name? It was beyond rude, and yet seemed to fit him.

Evie slid back down on the bed and tugged the covers up to her chin. It was cool within the mountain. Thinking about how it felt to come in contact with Malcolm's muscular chest helped warm her.

She went over their conversation, as maddening as it was. That's when she recalled his mention of Druids. He knew of them. She was going to have to remember to ask him. Because if he knew them, that meant she might not be the last.

Evie glanced at her watch to see it was half past six in the morning. Normally, she would be up and about. But she was far from normal now. She let her lids drift shut as she thought of Deirdre, Druids, azure eyes, and a deep, sexy voice that made her blood heat.

CHAPTER
EIGHT

Malcolm discovered the small tunnel Broc dug while he'd been in Cairn Toul and found the one place he could remain.

For hours, Malcolm sat in the opening and simply gazed at the beauty around him. It was stark and wild, harsh and remote, but there was no other place on earth he would rather be.

The jagged mountains were a stunning sight in any season. The Cairngorm mountain range was also one of Scotland's top destinations, but despite that, Malcolm didn't worry about bumping into anyone.

He grimaced when his phone vibrated for a third time in a matter of minutes. When his mobile vibrated for the fourth time he jerked it out of his back pocket and glared at the screen. Phelan, the bastard, wasn't giving up trying to get a hold of him. The text read: "Call me or I come and find you."

Malcolm knew it wasn't an idle threat. He dialed Phelan. The Warrior answered on the first ring.

"About bloody time," Phelan ground out. "Where have you been?"

"Busy. What do you want?"

"No small talk today, aye?"

"When has there ever been?" He heard Phelan blow out a breath through the phone. "What is it?"

Phelan paused before he said, "I doona want to wait around for Wallace to attack again."

"He's a crafty one for sure. If we give him time, there's no telling what he'll do to the Druids or innocents."

"Precisely," Phelan said.

"Do you have a plan?"

Malcolm could almost see the Warrior shrug as he said, "In a way."

"Meaning you doona."

Phelan chuckled dryly. "It's coming together."

Malcolm started to respond when he heard male voices through the phone. Instantly, he was on guard. Why was Phelan calling him for a battle instead of Fallon? "I know you well enough to know you are no' at the castle. I imagine you're with Charon."

"Aye," he readily agreed.

"Then why are Ramsey and Logan there?"

Malcolm waited as Phelan muttered something and hushed those around him. Then Phelan asked him, "Will you believe anything I say now?"

"Only if it's the truth."

There was a small hesitation before Phelan said, "I'm worried about you. You're pulling away."

Malcolm had asked for honesty, which Phelan had given. There was no reason he couldn't respond in kind. "I am. It's for the best."

"We can help."

"Nay, you can no'. I'm too far gone. It's better for everyone this way."

"And what about Wallace?" Phelan challenged. "You

know we need every Warrior and Druid to battle him. Are you going to leave us in the lurch?"

Malcolm watched a golden eagle soar upon the wind. "We've already taken out two *droughs*, Phelan. Now there's Jason. After him, who will it be?"

"Hopefully no one."

"Aye, but you can no' guarantee that."

"And Larena?"

He knew Phelan would bring up his cousin. "She has Fallon. She'll be all right in the end, and Fallon will move heaven and earth to give her the family she desires. She doesna need me."

"Damn but you're stubborn," Phelan murmured.

"You pot, me kettle."

Phelan's laughter filtered through the phone. "You just made a jest. Perhaps you're no' as far gone as I thought."

Malcolm didn't correct him. It was better if Phelan thought as he did.

"You'd let me know if I was wrong, would you no', Malcolm?"

He sat there for a moment contemplating his answer. Finally he said, "Do you remember when you left Cairn Toul after being imprisoned for over a century?"

"I couldna remember anything of my family since I was taken as a lad. Why?"

"What did you do after Isla freed you?"

"I wandered all over Scotland trying to learn everything. Each day I thought it would be my last. Yet, somehow, every morning I kept going."

Malcolm looked over the edge of the mountain where he sat to the sheer drop below. "Isla told me what she and Deirdre did to you."

"Revenge is what kept me going, if that's what you want to know."

"I've already taken my vengeance on Deirdre. She's dead and gone."

"Do you want to find a way back to us?"

Malcolm thought over Phelan's question but wasn't sure his friend would like the answer. "When you come up with the plan for Wallace, let me know. I'll help if I can."

"Call Larena. She'll want to hear from you."

"Keep your woman safe. Wallace will still be aiming to harm her."

"He can try," Phelan growled.

Malcolm ended the call and tucked his mobile into his pocket once more. He wasn't sure why he kept it. It would be so much easier just to toss it aside and not have to worry about getting calls and texts from the others.

But if he didn't answer, they'd have Broc use his power to find him. Then Malcolm would have to deal with them face to face since Fallon would teleport to wherever he was and confront him.

It was better to keep the annoying mobile phone until such time as it wasn't needed anymore. Which, Malcolm suspected, wouldn't be too much longer.

The Druid's magic suddenly swelled, and instantly his claws sprouted from his fingers to dig into the stone. He closed his eyes, his lungs locked by the crushing desire that slammed into him.

It had taken him most of the night to get his body under control because of the constant feel of her magic. With one wave of it, his cock was hard and aching, his body longing to touch her.

"Nay," he said between clenched teeth.

Malcolm refused to acknowledge the craving that coursed through him. If he admitted it—or even accepted it—he wouldn't be able to stay away from the Druid.

He drew in a deep, ragged breath and forced himself to remain where he was. If he allowed himself to wonder how no woman had stirred his body since before he was scarred, he would begin to ponder what made the Druid so special.

And that couldn't happen.

Even with focusing on his lungs rising and falling, he couldn't get the image of her out of his head. That brief glimpse of her feminine curves, of the patch of turquoise lace between her legs made his balls tighten.

He wanted to yank away the lace at her breast and between her legs. He wanted to lay her on the bed, her glorious curls spread around her as he feasted his eyes upon her body. His hands itched to cup her breasts and feel the weight of them in his hands.

He yearned to know the color of her nipples and hear her breath hitch as he suckled them. The consuming, devastating longing to sink into her until he was buried to the hilt ate away at him.

With his chest heaving, Malcolm tried to pull himself out of his musings, but he was trapped. His lips peeled back as he saw himself sink his hands into the Druid's hair and hold her head as he filled her again and again.

Malcolm palmed his cock, but it wasn't enough. He jerked his pants open to free his aching staff and took himself in hand.

The desire filling him was too raw, too visceral. He wasn't sure if he could survive it. After so long without feeling anything but rage, he didn't know how to leash back such reactions.

His hand began to pump up and down his length as his mind filled with more images of the Druid. Her tempting lips, her expressive eyes. That remarkable body he wouldn't forget in a thousand years.

Malcolm's hand moved faster as he pictured the Druid

bending over him, her lips wrapping around his cock and taking him deep in her mouth.

He jerked as the climax took him, his seed spilling onto his hands and stomach. The release gave him a moment's peace, but it wasn't nearly enough to calm the raging need pounding within him.

Long after he was spent, he sat there trying to figure out what to do. If he stayed in Cairn Toul he would have to face the Druid again. Keeping his desire in check might prove more painful than anything before. If he continued on, he might be able to keep the evil from her.

If he left, his body would once more be his own. Not to mention he wasn't the Druid's keeper. She was an adult who could make her own decisions. If she was foolish enough to believe everything the stones told her, who was he to tell her differently?

Malcolm cleaned himself and rose to button his jeans. He crawled through the small opening and let the cool air wash over him. For long minutes, he stood on the small outcropping trying to decide if he would leave or stay.

The longer he waited, the more he began to wonder why the Druid had left Aviemore to travel during a storm. More importantly, why did she think she would be safe in the mountain?

And just who was after her?

What had she told him? Oh, aye. She knew he wasn't the one looking for her because he hadn't asked for something specific.

There was a chance it could be Wallace after her. Jason Wallace, after all, was a sociopath who seemed to have a backup plan for everything—even death.

Deirdre had done the same thing, but in the end they made sure she was dead once and for all. The same would hold true for Wallace.

Especially for what he'd done to Larena. That was when

Malcolm knew he had to remain with the Druid. Even if it wasn't Wallace after her, she was a *mie* and there were too few of them left in the world for him to walk away so callously.

Admit there is another reason. Admit you like how she makes you feel. Admit you want her, that you need her.

Malcolm squeezed his eyes closed at the sound of his conscience. He refused to admit anything. The Druid was pretty, her magic amazing. That's all it was.

That's all it could be.

He turned and ducked back into the mountain. With sure, confident steps he made his way to Deirdre's—or now the Druid's—chamber.

To his surprise, she was sitting on the sofa in the sitting room with her laptop open and pounding away on the keys. She was so involved with her work that she didn't notice him for several minutes.

Malcolm leaned a shoulder against the doorway and observed her. Her dark curls were pulled away from her face in a queue at the base of her neck, but not even that could tame a few unruly curls that broke free and fell tantalizingly against her cheeks and neck.

She sat with her legs crossed and a pillow cushioning the laptop, her gaze intent and a small frown upon her brow. A notebook sat on the cushion and a pencil lay on the floor where it had fallen.

"Well, damn," she mumbled and leaned her head back to stare at the ceiling. A heartbeat later, she lifted her head in his direction.

As soon as their eyes met, it was like a kick in his stomach. He was sucked into her gaze, enveloped in her magic. It was pleasing, wonderful.

And startling.

His body reacted instantly, urging him to taste her lips, to learn her curves. The need was so overwhelming he found himself almost going to her. Thankfully, he stopped himself in time.

"You're going to get a stiff neck from the way you're sitting and looking down," he told her.

Her clear blue eyes gave away nothing as she shrugged and looked back at her screen. "Why are you staring at me?"

"It hadn't occurred to me to look anywhere else."

"Are you always so rude?"

"Always."

She licked her lips and looked up at him. "Are you here to throw me out?"

"No' yet." Touching her would be a very bad idea. "It may come to that, but I'm hoping your good sense will prevail before then."

She gave a loud snort and typed something without looking at the screen. "Doubtful."

"Who are you hiding from?"

Wariness stole through her eyes. "I'm not sure exactly."

"Then how do you know you need to hide at all?"

"I just know." She sat there for a second, her head tilted to the side, before she asked, "Can I trust you, Malcolm?"

"Nay, Druid. You can no'."

CHAPTER
NINE

Evie wasn't sure if anyone had ever been so honest with her in her life. The stones didn't like Malcolm about. It was obvious he didn't want to be in Cairn Toul either.

She gazed into eyes so blue it almost hurt to look at them. A lock of his golden hair fell over his forehead to tangle in his lashes, but he didn't seem to notice.

With a deep breath, she set her laptop and pillow on the coffee table and folded her hands in her lap. He was one of those rare men she could look at all day. It seemed every time she saw him there was another side of him.

Today he seemed calmer, more intent on approaching her another way to get her to leave. He would learn soon enough she wasn't going to budge. But that didn't mean she wasn't enjoying him being about.

He was gorgeous with a magnificent physique that made her mouth water. To be so attracted to him was baffling. He was aloof, cold even, and his emotionless eyes would be off-putting if she hadn't heard his seductive voice or felt that hard body beneath her palms.

The problem was she had. "I want to know more about Deirdre."

"Why? So you can copy what she's done?"

"No," she said and rolled her eyes. He was always thinking the worst. "I want to know because you can barely stomach to say her name, and the stones think she's the greatest thing since the invention of whisky."

Was it her imagination or had there been a hint of a smile upon Malcolm's lips? By his stoic expression, she had to have imagined it. Which was sad. She'd like to see him smile.

"You're in a bad place, Druid. Is that no' enough for you to know?"

She shook her head and got to her feet. Just as she hoped, Malcolm followed her into the bedchamber. She stopped at the wardrobe and looked over her shoulder to find him leaning against the doorway once more.

Damn him for being so good-looking.

Evie flung open the wardrobe and held out her hand to the garments within. "These clothes look pretty recent. How long ago was Deirdre here?"

"She occupied this mountain for a thousand years. In the seventeenth century she jumped forward in time to present day. She was here a few months before she was killed."

Well. Evie hadn't expected an answer, but she also recognized there was much more Malcolm wasn't telling her. "Thank you. The stones say she was betrayed."

"She was."

"You know by who?"

His nostrils flared. "I do."

"Will you tell me?" she asked, frustration edging her words.

"I doona think you really want to know. Deirdre was evil. She sold her soul to Satan to become *drough*. Is that really someone you want to know?"

Evie softly closed the wardrobe's doors and faced him.

"I don't want to know because I want to emulate her. I want to know so I can make my own decisions about Deirdre, Cairn Toul, and my future. That isn't too much to ask."

It seemed all Evie did was watch for some emotion, some sign that Malcolm felt anything. He was like a wall of stone, immovable and unmoving. What could turn a man so . . . cold?

Somehow the reason for Malcolm's animosity against her being in the mountain was in the telling of Deirdre's story. But would it be enough to make her depart?

"You willna leave no matter what I tell you," he finally said.

Evie looked around her. To some, the granite might seem impersonal and desolate, but not to her. "You can't hear them. The stones, that is. They're alive to me. They whisper of deer on their slopes, of tourists who climb as far up as they dare to take pictures. They will warn me if someone enters. There isn't another place on this earth I would be as safe."

"Safe from whoever you think you're running from. But how protected is your soul?"

She blinked and turned her gaze to him. This was new, but she could see it wasn't a bluff. He truly believed it. "You think my soul is in danger?"

"Malicious debauchery called this place home for a millennium. What do you think? You think evil that deep, that awful wouldna penetrate the stones and the earth?"

Evie rubbed her hands up and down her arms. Even with her sweater, a chill descended upon her she couldn't shake. "I couldn't even begin to answer that. Not without the facts. I'm not asking for anything other than the tale you obviously seem a part of. If you want me gone, the best way to do it is convince me. Start by telling me of Deirdre."

The seconds ticked by without Malcolm showing any inclination that he'd even heard her. Evie shook her head and started back into the sitting room to return to her computer.

Except Malcolm straightened and blocked the doorway. He didn't just block it, he filled the entire thing. Evie was reminded again of the strength she felt when she had tried to push against all those chiseled muscles.

She longed to brush back the lock of hair over his forehead. He stood so rigid, so unyielding that he appeared not to need—or want—anyone's touch. So she kept her hands to herself.

And it was difficult. She longed to run her hands over his chest and wide shoulders to feel his strength and warmth again. That brief instant had been enough to lure her, entice her. Rigid control leashed him, and Evie had a sudden desire to see him break free.

She looked up into unblinking azure eyes and wondered how it would feel to have his lips on hers.

"How long have you known you were a Druid?" he asked.

His question surprised her enough that it took her a second to form a thought. "Since I was old enough to understand what magic was."

"What do you know of the history of Druids?"

Evie grimaced. "That's just it. I don't know anything of Druids other than what my mum taught me before . . . Well, after that my grandmum took over my teaching, little that it was. I know magic enough to defend myself if need be, but I was always taught never to use magic unless it was absolutely necessary."

Without a sound, Malcolm turned on his heel and walked into the sitting room. She hastily followed, thinking he was leaving only to find him standing to the side of one of the chairs, his back to her.

Evie lowered herself onto the sofa and let her eyes soak up more of Malcolm Munro. Danger rolled off him in waves, coming nearer and nearer to her, almost daring her to get close to him.

Despite that, she didn't feel threatened. He set her on edge with his feral attitude and too-sexy body, but it wasn't enough to force her to use magic on him. Not when all she really wanted to do was pull him down for a kiss and to stroke the hard sinew.

"Druids used to be revered and respected." Malcolm's voice filled the small chamber with his silky timber. "They were teachers, healers, and counsel to the clan leaders. It was an honor for a clan to have a Druid in its midst. Every laird did what they had to do to earn the companionship of a Druid."

Evie settled back against the sofa, eager to hear more.

"Those Druids were the *mies*. They were content to channel the magic they were born with."

"There cannot be good without evil," Evie said, repeating something her grandmother had drilled into her.

Malcolm turned to her. "Aye. *Droughs*. They are the Druids who wanted more—more power, more strength, more everything. They were able to delve into the forbidden black magic, but it came with a cost. Their souls."

Evie couldn't suppress a shudder. "Was there a war between them? Is that what happened to all the Druids?"

"Nay," he said with a shake of his golden head. "The *mies* and *droughs* were always fighting amongst themselves, but they had a shared enemy. Rome."

"Rome," Evie whispered as she searched her memories for anything pertaining to Druids and Rome. "Caesar hated the Druids. He had it written that we performed ghastly sacrifices of children and virgins."

She expected Malcolm to show some kind of emotion that he agreed with her, but his silence was deafening.

"The *droughs* . . . did they . . ." She trailed off, unable to complete the question.

"They did."

"Bloody hell."

"Who do you think helped the Celts keep Rome behind Hadrian's Wall? This land belonged to the Druids as well, and they were no' going to stand by and do nothing. After years of constant battles, the Celts were running out of men. They were losing hope. So they once more turned to the *mies* for help.

"The *mies* had given all they could. But the Celts didna despair. They went to the *droughs*. Using black magic, the *droughs* brought up ancient gods long buried in Hell. Those gods filled the bodies of the strongest men who volunteered."

Evie's mind swirled with Malcolm's words. "So Rome didn't leave because they wanted to step away from territories they couldn't sustain. They were pushed out."

"Aye. The men became . . . something else. They didna stop fighting, even when Rome was finally gone. When the *droughs* tried to pull the gods out of the men, the gods refused to release their hold. It took the combined magic of both *mies* and *droughs* to bind the gods. But the gods had the last laugh since they traveled through the bloodline always to the strongest of the line."

"This seems so far-fetched," Evie said softly. "So surreal."

"I doona lie."

She flinched at the iciness of his words. "I didn't mean to imply you did, only that I've never heard this version before." After swallowing to wet her dry throat, she asked, "What happened next? I gather this isn't the end of the story."

Malcolm's azure gaze was riveted on her. "There's more. Are you sure you still want to know?"

"Yes." But she didn't sound as sure as she had a few minutes earlier. Maybe it was because Malcolm told the tale as if things were going to get worse.

He crossed his arms over his chest while his muscles bulged with each movement. "The spells to bind and unbind the gods were supposed to have been destroyed. Except they were no'. Deirdre and her twin were raised with their family who were all *droughs*. Laria was thought to have no magic, but she hid it so she wouldna have to become *drough*. Deirdre, however, killed her family when she discovered the scroll and the spell to unbind the gods."

It was like she was watching a thriller movie play out right before her eyes. They might be Evie's favorite, but this tale had her wanting to cover her eyes and hide beneath a blanket.

"The stones—these stones," Malcolm said with a jerk of his chin, "called Deirdre to them. Here she set about taking over the world."

Evie rose and began to pace before the sofa. "There's no happy ending to this story, is there?"

"The scroll named one clan—MacLeod," Malcolm continued as if she hadn't spoken. "For centuries she kidnapped men from the MacLeod clan in the hopes they were the one she searched for. It was only later through her magic she learned it wasn't one MacLeod she needed to find, but three. Three brothers in fact, who were equally skilled in battle. The god, you see, was split between the three of them."

Evie stopped and looked at Malcolm. There had been something in his voice when he said the MacLeod name. Almost as if he knew them. Which couldn't be correct. This happened eons ago. "What happened next? Did Deirdre find the brothers?"

"Aye. She tricked them in order to capture them."

Evie's legs gave out as she plopped down on the couch.

"Oh, my God. MacLeod. There hasn't been a MacLeod clan in . . ."

"Seven hundred years," he finished for her. "Aye, I know. After Deirdre tricked the brothers, she wiped out the clan. She unbound the god within the brothers, but she didna count on them trying to escape. They got away from her and returned to their burned, ruined castle where they stayed for three hundred years."

"Is that the end of Deirdre?"

She could have sworn Malcolm mumbled something like, "I wish," but she couldn't be sure.

"While the MacLeods were gaining control over their god, Deirdre scoured Scotland for more men who might house gods. But it wasn't just the gods she searched for. She captured Druids—*mies* and *droughs* alike—and killed them in order to take their magic."

Ice filled Evie's veins. The more Malcolm told the story, the more she understood why he wanted her out of the mountain. Yet, she wasn't evil and didn't want to become evil. That should count for something.

"So there's no more Druids," Evie said. "I feared as much."

"I never said that."

Her head jerked around. "There are others? I thought I might be the only one."

His chest expanded as he took a deep breath. "There are others. Over four hundred years ago, a Druid found herself on the brink of death. One of the MacLeods saved her and brought her into the castle. Deirdre attacked the castle to try and gain the Druid, but the brothers held her off. That's when the MacLeods opened the castle to anyone willing to fight against such evil."

"Opened the castle," she repeated with a smile. "Now I know you must be pulling my leg. There's no MacLeod Castle."

He dropped his arms and walked to the doorway. As he reached the corridor he paused and said, "There is, Druid. I've been there. It's hidden by one of the many Druids in residence."

The idea that she wasn't alone sent hope coursing through her. A smile pulled at her lips as she closed her eyes thinking how she could get Malcolm to take her to the castle.

When she opened her eyes, he was gone. There was still more to the tale, and she would eventually get it all out of him. Until then, she would be content with what she knew.

"I'm not alone. There are other Druids out there. I just have to find them," she said to herself.

CHAPTER
TEN

Veronica, better known as Ronnie to her friends, tried not to stare at their resident scientist, Britt Miller. From the anxiety running rampant through the castle, Ronnie knew Britt was feeling the pressure.

By her side, as always, was Aiden MacLeod. His parents, Quinn and Marcail, were staying near in case either Britt or Aiden needed them.

Not that any of them could help Britt. She was working on completing an antidote to the *drough* blood that was adversely affecting Larena.

"The wait is killing me," Tara leaned over and whispered.

Ronnie nodded in agreement. The entire castle seemed to be holding its breath as it waited to hear if Britt could do it.

A strong hand came to rest on Ronnie's waist and dragged her back against a rock-hard chest. She leaned against Arran, grateful for him. He knew when she needed him the most. Which was always.

"She'll do it," Arran whispered in her ear.

Ronnie looked up into his golden eyes and smiled. If there was one thing she'd learned since coming to the castle, it was that they were one big family. Everyone was there for everyone else.

That's why they were all waiting for news regarding Larena. Fallon had taken her off to their chamber until Britt had news. That had been days ago.

Only Fallon emerged for food, and each time his face grew grimmer and grimmer. His brothers, Quinn and Lucan and their wives Marcail and Cara, were making sure anything Larena wanted was seen to.

Britt lifted her blond head and let out a long sigh from looking under the microscope. It was then she noticed the room full of people.

"Nothing like pressure," she teased with a lighthearted laugh.

Aiden rubbed her lower back in slow circles. "They're just anxious."

Marcail, looking as young as Britt thanks to Isla's shield over the castle that kept it hidden and those within from aging, handed Britt a tall glass of iced tea.

Gwynn, a native Texan who had found love with Logan, raised her own glass of sweet tea at Britt. The women exchanged a laugh before drinking.

Ronnie saw Tara wrinkle her nose. Tara didn't understand the cold sweet tea thing, but Gwynn assured her it was an American thing. Just like lemonade that didn't fizz. It just seemed absurd to Tara and the rest of those from Scotland.

"I feel so useless," Danielle said into the silence.

After draining about half the glass, Britt set it aside. "There's nothing any of you can do. I'm working as fast as I can, but I want to make sure I do it right."

"We know," Saffron said.

Ronnie still felt like she needed to pinch herself to be in a place with so many amazing Druids and Warriors who risked their lives to end first Deirdre then Declan, and now Jason.

"Malcolm should be here," Marcail said. "Larena needs him."

Gwynn ran a finger over the condensation on her glass. "Logan and Ramsey will return soon from Ferness. Hopefully Charon and Phelan have an idea of how we can get Malcolm here."

"But he knows," Aiden said. "He knows about Larena and he isna here."

Camdyn said, "Everything Malcolm has done has been for Larena. If he's no' here, it's because he needs to be elsewhere. There are some things only time can heal."

"And some that can never be healed," Quinn said.

No one responded because they all had seen firsthand how close to the edge of losing it all Malcolm had been. The only good thing was that Larena was battling her own goddess and so didn't realize everything else that was going on.

"We'll get through this," Ronnie said. "All of us. We have to."

Too many centuries had passed, too many lives lost, too much blood spilled for those at the castle to lose now.

Arran's fingers entwined with hers. He gave her a squeeze. It was all she needed to face the rest of the day.

Malcolm returned from hunting with a pheasant. As far as he'd seen, there was no food in the mountain. The Druid could use her magic, but if she had told him the truth, she didn't use magic unless she had to.

He stripped the bird of its feathers and made his way to the Druid's chambers. Her magic was mixing with that of the mountains, and he wasn't sure he liked it. He felt her everywhere, in everything.

In a very short amount of time.

He stopped at the entrance of her chamber. It took him a moment of shifting through the magic surrounding him to realize that though he felt her, she wasn't in the room.

Malcolm dropped the bird before he closed his eyes and focused on her magic. His eyes snapped open when he realized where she was.

He used his unnatural speed to rush through the mountain, downward to where he'd hoped to keep her from going. The closer he got, the stronger her magic pulsed against his skin.

With a low growl, he shoved aside the arousal he felt and ran faster. He turned the corner and came to a halt just inside the room.

Only once before had he come this close to the hated room. Even now he could feel the hundreds—the thousands—of Druids who had been murdered for their magic.

He clenched his fists in an effort not to be taken down by the lingering terror from the souls who had died upon the large table in the center of the room.

Malcolm drew in a breath, glad to feel the tightness in his chest lessen. That's when he spotted the Druid running her finger along the grooves cut into the table that sloped to all four corners.

He pulled back his lips and had the Druid up against the wall, his hand around her neck in the next moment. "I could snap your neck with a twist of my wrist."

"Malcolm," she wheezed and grabbed at his hand.

"What are you doing here? Can you no' feel the death of this room? Can you no' sense the anguish from the Druids who were killed here?"

Her gaze darted to the table. With cold calculation he

knew just the amount of pressure to keep against her wind-pipe to let her know how precarious her position was.

"Those grooves you were looking at collected the blood from the slit wrists. The blood would pool at the corners and drip into goblets below. Deirdre would drain the Druid strapped to that table of their magic and their blood. Then she would trap their souls. After it was done, she would drink their blood."

"Pl-please," she rasped.

"If you didna want evil to touch you, you shouldna have come to this chamber."

Clear blue eyes met his. She didn't beg. She stopped clawing at his hand. Malcolm waited for her to throw him against the opposite wall with her magic. Instead, she gazed at him, waiting for . . . what he didn't know.

His gaze dropped to her mouth, her wide pink lips parted to let in air. He bit back a groan when the coldness that had taken him began to fade. To be replaced by a fiery heat that scorched him from the inside out, begging him to kiss her, to take her lips, to taste her.

Her magic was wrapping around his arm and sliding over his body, descending through his skin into his bones. The arousal he'd ignored a short time before returned with a vengeance.

He found himself leaning into her. With his body demanding release, and the source of his yearning in his grasp, Malcolm couldn't find a reason not to kiss her. Then he noticed his hand locked around the slim column of her throat.

Malcolm blinked. Twice.

Anger. That's what had taken hold of him. He relished the rage he let loose during battle, but he'd taken it out on a Druid.

Instantly, he released her and took two steps back. She

drew in a ragged breath and coughed while she held a hand against her throat.

He'd come close to killing her. He realized that now, almost too late. Were his thoughts about ending all Druids bleeding over to reality?

"I didn't know," she said on a wheeze. "I swear. I didn't know."

Malcolm glanced down at this hand, a hand that had nearly taken another life. Somehow he wasn't surprised by that revelation. It seemed all he was good for was dealing out death and betrayal.

And the others wondered why he kept his distance.

He doubted his fellow Warriors would so eagerly welcome him if they knew what he'd nearly done. Malcolm thought of Phelan, who had reached out to him weeks ago.

Malcolm had been told the castle was his home and those within its walls his family. Larena and Fallon made sure of it, but everyone else kept their distance.

Except for Phelan. He was the only one who tried to become a friend. Friends. Malcolm wasn't even sure he knew what that term meant anymore.

"Malcolm?"

He looked up at the Druid, recalling that he wasn't alone. Faint bruises marked her throat yet her clear eyes held a measure of concern. For him.

It was laughable. She should be worried about her safety, not him.

"I went exploring," she said in the silence. She swallowed several times before she continued, "I . . . there was a coldness about this room that frightened me. I wanted to know why. That's all. I swear."

"If you stay, I'll hurt you again. And I can no' leave this place until you do."

She took a step toward him, and it was all it took for him to retreat. Malcolm, the Warrior who was a murderer and betrayer, retreating from a Druid. He was just thankful Deirdre wasn't there to see it.

"You hate this place," she said.

"More than you could possibly understand."

"Help me to understand it then," she urged. "You started the story, but you didn't finish it."

He shook his head, his eyes drawn to the fuchsia-and-gold sweater that hugged her breasts like a second skin. One minute he wanted to be inside the Druid, pounding into her tight body, and the next he wanted to kill her.

"Deirdre was here. She ruled and became overconfident. She was killed, and regenerated her body to come back and wreak more havoc on us. She was transported into the future and betrayed by someone she wasn't expecting. That betrayal allowed her twin, Laria, to kill her."

"Oh," the Druid said with wide eyes.

"Declan stepped in where Deirdre had been. There were many battles and several deaths before he was killed. And as always, there's a new evil to take his place. It's never going to end."

"There can't be good without evil."

It was the second time she'd said the words. He wanted to dismiss them, but he couldn't because he knew they were the truth.

How did he fit into such a world? And did he even want to try? He had attempted it at the castle, but he'd felt confined, imprisoned. If he couldn't become a part of something at the castle, where could he? Where did he belong?

"Somewhere that gives you peace."

He jerked at the Druid's words. He hadn't even realized he'd spoken aloud.

Malcolm took one more look at her tempting lips before he turned on his heel and strode away.

CHAPTER
ELEVEN

Evie's heart still pounded as she watched Malcolm walk away. She shivered as she looked around the chamber. If she'd had any idea just what it was, she never would have ventured into it.

But it wasn't the room that gave her pause. It was Malcolm. During the entire incident, his face had remained impassive, his eyes empty.

It was his voice and actions that gave her an inkling of his wrath. And it had been tremendous. His words had been clipped, harsh, and as icy as winter.

Evie rubbed her neck. Malcolm had moved swiftly to have her against the wall before she even had time to realize what was going on. His hand had been like steel holding her in place.

His fingers had been firm, his hold solid, but not once had he harmed her. Frightened her, yes, but never hurt.

Unable to resist another look, Evie's gaze returned to the massive stone table in the center of the room. Now she understood what the dark stains were.

Blood. How many innocents had died by Deirdre's hand? If Malcolm could be believed, it was thousands.

All to take their magic. Which was something else she hadn't known a Druid could do.

Yet that was black magic. That was delving into an area she had no interest in discovering. She didn't consider herself a saint, but neither did she want to hand over her soul for the sake of using forbidden magic.

Evie walked out of the chamber with shaky legs. She put her hand on the wall. "Is what Malcolm said true about the room? Did Deirdre take the lives of Druids for their magic?"

"Yessss. She was meant to rule the world."

"By killing people?" she asked the stones in horror.

"A necessity only. There was no other choice."

But Evie knew there was. Deirdre could have refused. "I'm not like that. I won't fill the spot Deirdre left."

"Nay. Never," the rocks whispered. *"Too pure."*

Evie held back a snort. Barely. "Pure. Yeah, not what I'd consider myself. If you knew how I made my neighbor Mrs. Finch think she was going daft by sneaking into her house and moving things, you wouldn't call me pure."

"Pure. Too pure."

She rolled her eyes and started toward her chamber when she changed her mind. "Where is Malcolm?"

"Looking. He's always looking, always watching."

"What is he watching?"

"Everything."

"But where in this mountain is he? Above or below me?"

The rocks didn't answer right away, making her think they would rather her not know. *"Below,"* they finally responded.

"Lead me to him," she urged.

Evie followed their instructions, glad the torches continued to light the way with barely a thought from her.

With every step she took toward Malcolm, she wondered if she was going a bit daft herself.

He'd not only told her he couldn't be trusted, but he had pinned her against the wall. The only thing that kept her walking was that he hadn't killed her.

Then there were his words before he stalked away. He hadn't known he'd spoken aloud. The surprise that flickered for the briefest second in his azure gaze had told her that.

Malcolm was like a wounded animal. Something awful had happened to him that scarred his body and broke his soul. Though she'd never been a woman who felt the need to change or heal a man, she felt compelled to go to him.

It was a lot like walking into a cage with a tiger, but onward she went.

The deeper she walked into the mountain, the more she couldn't shake the feeling that she was sinking further and further into a life she both sought and feared.

Evie turned a corner and saw light flare out of the corner of her eye. She instantly turned and frowned at the amount of illumination flickering on the walls.

Ever the curious one, she walked through a doorway and gasped as she found herself on a balcony overlooking a cavern of immense height and width.

Torches hung all around the walls, but it was the large round candelabra hanging from the ceiling that caught her attention.

"Wow," she whispered in awe.

She could only guess that this is where Deirdre had ruled over . . . what? Druids? That didn't seem right since she'd killed them.

"The men whose gods she unbound," Evie said with a nod.

Deirdre had wanted to control them for her use. The

MacLeods had gotten away, but many others must have remained. Where were they now? she wondered.

What kind of woman sought that much power? What had been lacking in her life that it needed to be filled in such a way? Evie was afraid to ask the questions aloud and receive the answers.

That kind of woman was better left unknown, just as those questions were better left unasked.

Evie turned and retraced her steps until she was once more in the corridor and on her way to Malcolm. It was fifteen minutes later that she ducked beneath a low-hanging entrance. There were no torches that lit for her.

She could make out the first few feet in front of her because of the light coming from behind, but only pitch black met her beyond that.

Instead of bolting, she squared her shoulders. The stones wouldn't allow anything to happen to her. She could tell the room was fairly large, but Malcolm could be anywhere.

"You shouldna be here," came his deep timbre that made her stomach quiver in anticipation.

"I don't mean to disturb your privacy. I just wanted . . . I don't know what I wanted. It just felt right to come to you."

"You wouldna say that if you knew the person I was."

"I'm getting an idea of who you are. You're the one who came to warn me about the Druid who lived here before. You're the one who could've killed me and didn't."

"Maybe I'm waiting to kill you."

Evie looked around the darkness and took a tentative step into it. Malcolm was there somewhere. The size of the room prevented her from pinpointing where exactly. "If you wanted me dead, you would've already done it. You're trying too hard to get me to leave."

Silence.

Damn. She'd hoped that would make him see that she knew he was lying. Evie took several more steps, hearing the stones whisper about dips in the floor or boulders she needed to avoid.

"Do you have family?" she asked.

Seconds ticked by. Just as she was about to give up he said, "A cousin."

That was it? All he had in the way of family was a cousin? Well, all she had was Brian. "I have a brother. Half-brother actually. He's an amazing kid, and he's counting on me. If something happens to me, he'll be alone."

"Then stop whatever it is that's making you hide here."

"It's not that simple." But how she wished it was. "My curiosity has always been my worst trait." Evie blew out a deep breath. "What I'm trying to say, very badly I might add, is that I could use a friend."

"You doona want me for a friend. I'm no' a good man."

"Maybe. I'm not exactly a good person either." Evie put her hands on her hips and shook her head. "I think I've gotten myself into something that could put my life in danger. I . . . I'm scared, Malcolm. This place, these stones have allowed me to breathe a little easier. I'm not Deirdre, and I've made sure the stones realize that."

She'd hoped Malcolm might answer her, but it looked like she was wrong. Evie dropped her hands. "You know where to find me. I'd like to hear the rest of that story you've yet to finish."

Malcolm let her soft, sweet voice fill his mind. His eyes remained closed while he kept his body in check against the exotic, brilliant magic.

With her movement, however, his eyes snapped open. He moved directly beside her as she spoke. His brain demanded he keep his distance, but his body—and his god—wanted closer.

He lifted a hand as she spun around. Dark curls slid

over his palm and against his fingers. It was all he dared, all he could risk. But that simple touch left him with a deep, vast longing that would never be filled.

She had come to him. After he threw her against the wall and choked her. She'd come to him. His mind could barely wrap around it.

He watched as she exited the chamber and made her way back to her room. He had the chance to leave when he'd felt her magic grow closer and closer to him.

Malcolm still wasn't sure why he stayed. The Druid had tenacity and courage that surprised him. He frowned then, because he couldn't remember the last time he'd been surprised.

She had asked for a friend. There was no way he could give her that when he couldn't even answer the calls and texts from those at the castle who claimed to be family.

To make matters worse, it had been on the tip of his tongue to tell her aye. Her voice had broken when she'd spoken of her half-brother. The lad meant a lot to her.

Malcolm tapped a claw against the stones behind him and made a decision right then. If the Druid thought she was in danger, he needed to learn what it was. He couldn't be her friend, but he could watch over her and keep anyone away who might want to do her harm.

He understood all about needing a place to breathe easier. Why it had to be Cairn Toul that gave it to her, he didn't know. But did it really matter?

With the strength of her magic, he'd know the instant she turned *drough*. That's all it would take for him to end her life. It would be another way he'd ensure her safety. Because if he could kill her before she sold her soul, then he was saving her.

Malcolm rubbed a hand over his jaw. He would have to hold off giving up the last of his humanity for a few days yet. If he could.

He took out his mobile and held his finger over Phelan's name. Finally he pressed the number and brought the phone to his ear.

"Malcolm," Phelan answered on the second ring. "Is everything all right?"

"It hasna been all right in a long time." He wasn't sure who was more surprised by his honesty, him or Phelan.

"What do you need?"

"I doona know."

"You want me to meet you somewhere?"

The old Malcolm would have smirked at Phelan's less than subtle attempt to get him face to face. This Malcolm, however, simply said, "Nay. I know you're . . . concerned for me. There's no need."

"There's every need," Phelan said.

Malcolm inhaled deeply. "I can no' be the person everyone wants me to be."

"Then doona be. If Deirdre tried to kill me and then unbound my god, I wouldna be the same either. I thought it was better for me if I kept to myself. I didna realize how wrong I was until I met Charon. I wasna looking for a friend, and I made it difficult for him to be one, but that friendship saved me."

"I see the disappointment in Larena's eyes." Malcolm's hand fisted as the words passed his lips. It caused something to move inside him, emotions he didn't want to deal with began to stir.

"She blames herself, you know. Both she and Fallon had every intention of telling you about your god."

"It wouldna have made me remain at the castle. I thought my destiny was to be laird. Instead, I'm . . . this. I killed Duncan."

"You did what you had to do to keep Larena safe. No one blames you for that. Deirdre was a master manipulator. She used you."

"Nay. I think this was always inside me, I just chose to ignore it. Keep your attention on Wallace and no' me."

Malcolm ended the call and dropped his head back against the stones. Why had he called Phelan? It wasn't like him. Then again, he wasn't exactly himself since meeting the beautiful, infuriating, courageous Druid.

CHAPTER
TWELVE

For two days Evie hoped to look up from her computer screen to find Malcolm standing in her doorway once more. And for two days she was disappointed.

She promised herself not to go looking for him after the last time. Malcolm had an off-putting way of letting it be known he didn't wish to be bothered.

"Damn," Evie said and squeezed her tired eyes shut.

There were just a few more finishing touches to put on her new and improved set of walls, traps, and dead ends for anyone brave enough to try and hack her site again.

Between writing new code and a virus to attack any potential hackers, Evie was also doing more research on Druids. Given the story Malcolm told her, she was able to refine her search and include Deirdre's name.

The links that pulled up were mind-boggling. Evie had been to twenty of them before she realized Deirdre was a legend and few actually knew the story.

Yet there were parts that were consistent in each of the sites that mentioned the Druid. The fact that she was missing from history for four centuries was a common thread.

If that part of the story Malcolm told her was true, then the rest had to be as well. It wasn't that she thought he lied. It was just that she had a difficult time processing all she'd learned.

Her phone beeped, drawing her out of her thoughts. Evie reached for the mobile that was always near. She smiled when she saw Brian's text about acing some exam.

She quickly punched the keys to congratulate him. No sooner had she hit send than another text from him popped up asking if he could bring a friend home for the holidays.

Evie stared at the screen for several seconds before she said yes. She didn't stop to think how she would make it work, only that she would. She had to. For Brian. For herself.

There were a few more texts talking about one of his teachers and the amount of work in a class. But Evie's mind was racing.

Once Brian said good night, she gently set her mobile aside and rubbed her temples. Her plan had been to stay hidden until the people wanting her information got tired and left her alone. Obviously, that plan wasn't going to work. She'd have to come up with a new one.

She touched the pendant beneath her shirt. *"Keep it safe always. It's dangerous,"* her grandmother had urged every day from the day she gave it to Evie three years before. They had been her grandmother's last words as well.

In the year after her grandmother's death, Evie had searched for answers, answers her grandmother either hadn't known or refused to share. Evie had begged to know about Druids, but nothing would make her grandmother budge in talking.

Evie set aside her laptop and rose from the sofa. As guilty as she felt for using her magic to put some rugs throughout her chamber, she was glad she had. The cold penetrated the stones, even through her wool socks.

The only thing missing from Cairn Toul was a kitchen. Though she hadn't seen Malcolm, she'd found the food left in her sitting room.

She hadn't known how to cook the pheasant that first night, but magic had taken care of that. It was while she was eating the tasty bird that she began to wonder about food. She decided before bed to use her magic in order to eat. It was a necessity, after all.

But then there had been the bags of groceries. Evie had known they were from Malcolm.

Evie went to the small stock of groceries she'd piled against a wall behind the couch. She grabbed a plastic glass and poured a hefty amount of red wine into it.

She sipped the alcohol and looked from the bed to the wardrobe to the vanity. The sitting area had plenty of furniture as well.

It was obvious Deirdre had either used magic or had the items brought in. There was no reason Evie couldn't do the same with a small fridge and maybe even an electric skillet.

The thought had merit even if she knew she'd have to actively seek out who was searching for her. It would still be days she'd be inside the mountain, mayhap even weeks.

"There's time."

"Time for what?" said a deep voice behind her.

A thrill went through her as she recognized the sultry voice. Evie smiled and slowly turned to face Malcolm. "I didn't think I'd see you again."

"Time for what?" he repeated.

She shrugged and pointed to the groceries. "Thank you for the food, by the way. And I was thinking of getting a small fridge."

"How would it work? You have no electricity here."

"Damn," she said with a frown. She hadn't even thought of that. "I guess that means no coffee."

He raised a blond brow. "If you're that worried about being safe and having your luxuries, go into town and find a place. I'll make sure no one bothers you."

"That's a very kind offer. Unfortunately, it isn't as easy as that."

"Explain it then."

She swirled the dark wine in her glass, amused at how Malcolm didn't think twice about ordering her about. "You offer to keep others away without knowing my name? Odd, if you ask me."

"I'm no' like other men."

"I hadn't noticed," she said and took a drink to hide her smile.

His head cocked to the side. "Are you . . . teasing me?"

"Yes. The fact you had to ask tells me just how dour your life has been. When was the last time you smiled?"

"If you think your questions will make me forget that I've asked you to explain why you can no' live in town, you're mistaken."

It was a try, her shrug said. "I'm a software designer by trade. I made good money at it too. Enough to support me and my brother well."

"Then what's the problem?"

"I had to leave my job. The savings I had dwindled quickly. The little I have left will cover Brian's tuition for another year, but not if I use it."

"Send him to another school."

Evie blew away a curl that kept falling over her eye and sank into a corner of the couch. "I would if it were that simple. Brian was born unable to speak. When I got custody of him we couldn't communicate at all. He was three and couldn't write yet. I had to learn sign language quickly."

"What happened to his mother?"

"She died. Mum walked out on my dad and me when I was very young. I didn't hear from her again until after her death and I got a letter from the solicitors that she'd written me asking me to raise Brian. Not something an eighteen-year-old wants to do."

"But you did it," he said softly.

Evie chuckled as she recalled that fateful day. "I wasn't going to. I went to the solicitor's office to tell them that, and Brian was there. We were both orphans. How could I let someone else do my duty? So, I picked Brian up in my arms and brought him home."

"And now?" he pressed.

"Now Brian has found a school where he feels comfortable. He fits in. There are other mute kids there, but most have some sort of disability. I couldn't bear to tell him he couldn't return." She looked down at her wine, her heart heavy with the decisions she had to make.

If something happened to her, she didn't know where Brian would go or who would take care of him. There wasn't even enough money in her savings to cover the years for the rest of his schooling. How could she do that to him?

"Your car has been towed to Aviemore."

She jerked her head up to look at him. "Are the authorities searching for me?"

"Aye. You might want to let them know you were picked up by a friend."

Evie set aside her wine and immediately reached for her laptop. A few minutes later she hit send to an e-mail to the police in Aviemore. "Hopefully that'll be enough to keep them from looking for me."

"I'll make sure it is."

"Thank you, Malcolm."

His chest rose as he took a deep breath. He wore an olive-green shirt that looked a size too small and had seen too many washes.

As if noticing her scrutiny he shifted his shoulders. "I had to . . . borrow . . . the shirt."

The way he'd paused when he said *borrow* told her he meant stolen. She couldn't help but grin. "Next time when you . . . borrow . . . a shirt, check the size."

"I will." He glanced down before he said, "The rest of the story you want to know. It might be better if you didna."

"Why?"

"Sometimes it's better no' to know what's waiting in the dark."

A shiver ran over her skin. It seemed to do that a lot with Malcolm, or maybe it was the mountain. "Knowledge is power. I'd rather have the information."

"The men who had their god unbound are Warriors."

"Why warrior?"

"Nay. A Warrior," he corrected.

"Okay. They're Warriors. Why?"

"They become immortal, Druid. They hold and use whatever power the god inside them has. There is also the enhanced senses and speed."

There was something else he wasn't telling her. "And?"

"They . . . change. The gods each favor a color. The Warrior's skin will change to that color when he calls forth his god. The Warrior also has claws and fangs."

Evie nodded as he spoke. All she could think about was a rainbow of colors and men walking around with vampire fangs and claws.

"That is if the Warrior has control over his god," Malcolm said.

"What? What do you mean?"

"No' every Warrior is in control of his god. Sometimes the gods take over. The gods are evil, Druid. What do you think happens to the Warriors then?"

"They turn evil," she said in a small voice.

"Aye."

"What about the Warriors who can control the god within them?"

He looked away, his eyes going distant. "The evil is always there, but if a man is good of heart, the evil willna win."

"You're thinking of the MacLeods, aren't you?"

He blinked and focused on her. "There are others besides them. Good men who have fought to keep innocents from Deirdre's wrath."

"But Deirdre is gone."

"Declan brought Deirdre to this time. After she was killed, the focus turned to Declan until he was slain."

"How did that happen?"

Malcolm flexed his hand. "Painfully. Declan used different methods of hurting the Warriors and Druids than Deirdre did. Some Druids were killed. It was the strength of a Warrior who also happened to be half-Druid who eradicated Declan."

"Why then do I get the feeling it's still not safe?"

"Because it isna. There's another Druid out there—Jason. He's used his black magic to hurt my cousin. For that, I will destroy him."

The pieces began to all fall together. "Your cousin is a Druid then?"

"A Warrior."

"Oh. What's his name?"

"*Her* name is Larena."

"But . . . I thought all Warriors were men," she said in exasperation.

Malcolm gave a single shake of his head. "Nay. Larena

holds a goddess within her. As far as we know, she's the only female Warrior, which makes her special."

"How was Larena hurt?"

"A drop of *drough* blood in a Warrior's wound will kill them. Jason altered the *drough* blood he uses. Larena died, but the Druids managed to bring her back. Yet, she's no' the person I knew. She's changed. She's becoming . . . me."

Evie's heart broke at his words, spoken faintly and dispassionately. But she wasn't fooled. Malcolm was affected deeper than he wanted to admit.

In that moment, that barest brief of time and space, she knew he'd do whatever it took to kill Jason as violently and viciously as he could.

And Evie hoped he did.

CHAPTER
THIRTEEN

Ferness

Phelan stood on the second floor and eyed the sleek bright blue Maserati GranTurismo MC Stradale as it pulled up in Charon's private drive at the back of his building.

Behind Phelan, Charon was in his office going over some figures for the flats he leased while Aisley filed papers and Laura worked on the computer.

The door of the Maserati opened and the tall form of Constantine unfurled from the car. He stood and buttoned the jacket of his charcoal-gray and black pinstriped hand-tailored Brioni suit.

Behind the designer sunglasses, Phelan knew Con was letting his gaze leisurely roam the area. He grinned when Con turned his head of blond hair and looked behind him before facing the building once more.

Constantine, the man behind Dreagan Industries, was much more than he appeared. For one, he wasn't human— or mortal. He was a Dragon King. The King of Kings actually.

Dreagan land had been used to stop Wallace once. If it

hadn't been for the help of the dragons, Phelan was certain he wouldn't be alive.

He watched as Con put one hand in his pants pocket and started for the steps. Con ascended the steps like a man who had all the time in the world.

Like a man who owned the world.

Since Con and the other dragons were as old as time itself, there was a reason Con acted that way. It also contributed to his self-assured, arrogant attitude that made Phelan want to see how long it would take to anger the King of Kings.

When Con reached the top, he stared through the sliding glass door at Phelan. A few seconds later, with a smirk he couldn't hide, Phelan slid open the door.

"What brings you here?" Phelan asked as he moved aside.

Con stepped inside and removed his sunglasses, pinning Phelan with his black eyes. "Just stopping by."

"No such thing," Charon said as he exited his office. He extended his hand to Con and they shook. "What can we do for you?"

"Con," Laura said as she came to greet him. "It's always good to see you."

"And you," Con replied with a smile and placed a kiss on each of her cheeks. He then moved past her to greet Aisley in the same manner. "How is the Phoenix today?"

Aisley laughed. "I've got a cranky Warrior to deal with. How do you think?"

Phelan crossed his arms over his chest and stared at Constantine. "Stop flirting with my woman and tell us why you're really here."

"I came to see how things were going."

"Bollocks. You know everything that's going on. What's the real reason?"

A slow smile spread over Con's face. "You're worried

about Malcolm. I'm here to tell you he's been spotted near Cairn Toul."

"Shite," Charon said and ran a hand through his hair.

Even Phelan was unsettled by Con's words. "Are you sure?"

"Rhys knows what he saw."

"So Rhys was taking a little midnight flight," Charon said.

Con nodded.

Phelan dropped his arms. "Malcolm called two nights ago. He . . . well, he seemed lost for a minute. He told me he was all right, but I doona believe him."

"What would bring him back to Cairn Toul?" Con asked.

Charon gave a snort of anger. "No' a damn thing. He hates that place as much as we do."

"But that doesna explain what Rhys saw," Phelan argued.

Con's black eyes studied Phelan. "Perhaps you should try and contact Malcolm again."

"It wouldna do any good. He answers only when he wants to."

Charon shrugged. "Con has a point. It might help."

"Malcolm needs a friend," Con said. "It looks like he turned to you for that."

Phelan felt Aisley's magic and wrapped it around himself. A moment later she was next to him, her hands on his arm. Phelan let her magic calm his racing mind. "If anyone can reach him it would be Larena, if she was able. Since she's no', and Fallon is too preoccupied with her, I'll do what I can. I want it known that I think it's a mistake for me to try and help though."

"You'll do great, babe," Aisley said and rose up to give him a quick kiss.

Con ran a hand over his chin as he glanced out the

window. "Do any of you know of an antiques and collectibles shop in Perth by the name of The Silver Dragon?"

"Nay. Should we have?" Charon asked.

"It's a Dragon King problem. I was just curious if it was something that had drawn your interest."

This piqued Phelan's attention. "You're coming to us to ask something? That's no' normal. No' when you dragons seem to know the goings-on everywhere."

"We're no' all-seeing," Con stated flatly.

"Obviously. Is there something in this antique store you need?"

Charon blew out a breath and rocked back on his heels. "Phelan has a point. Why come to us with this? You're dragons."

Anger sizzled in Con's dark gaze as a muscle jumped in his jaw. "This . . . problem . . . is one that has been around for a verra long time."

"Then remove the problem," Phelan said.

Aisley turned her startled fawn-colored eyes to him. "Phelan," she admonished. "Did you not hear the name of the store? I'm guessing this has something to do with the King of Silvers."

Con put a hand up to stop her. "Forget I said anything."

"As if. Did you come here hoping we'd take care of this . . . problem?" Charon asked, his eyes guarded.

"Never. As I said, I asked in the hopes you might have information."

Laura looked from Charon to Con. "One of us could always drop by and have a look around this store."

"I'm no' sure that's a good idea."

Charon's dark brow lifted as he rocked back on his heels. "Is this problem of yours dangerous?"

Something vicious and primitive flashed in Con's eyes. "No' anymore."

Phelan had a feeling there was much more Con wasn't

telling them. And until he did, there was no way he would allow Aisley anywhere near this . . . problem. "I've seen the way you dragons heal. It's almost instantaneous. Whereas we Warriors take a few moments. Tell me why you doona just go into this store and end this problem?"

Con chuckled, the smile not quite reaching his black gaze. "It's . . . complicated."

"Meaning," Charon said, "that this *problem* is a King and the other Dragon Kings wouldna be pleased."

"To say the least," Con admitted, though by the tightness of his lips, it cost him.

Phelan knew he had to be diplomatic. The Dragon Kings were good allies. They would be lethal enemies. "Perhaps it would be best if we stayed out of the middle of this. For now."

Con's gaze came to rest on him. He stood still as he studied Phelan for several long seconds. "Perhaps."

"You don't happen to have any information on Jason, do you?" Laura hastily changed the subject.

Aisley glanced up at Phelan. "Since we don't want to sit around waiting for Jason to make his next move, anything you have would be great."

"He's at his mansion," Con said and turned to look out the glass door. "Tread carefully. Wallace will be expecting you."

"We're no' going to him," Phelan said.

One side of Con's mouth lifted in a grin as he looked at Phelan. "Wise decision. What are you thinking?"

"Still working on that," Charon said before Phelan could.

Constantine turned back to the small group. "The others from the castle are no' here. You wouldna be thinking of doing this alone, would you?"

Aisley cleared her throat and shrugged. "If we could take Jason unawares, there's a chance we could end it all."

"A chance. A slim chance." Con looked at each of them in turn. "I know each Warrior has been given the serum to combat Jason's *drough* blood, but it hasna been that long since the last battle. If anyone knows just how dangerous Wallace is, it's you, Aisley."

"That's right," she said. "I also know he's brash and egotistical. He can be brought down."

Con bowed his head to her. "If I learn anything new about Wallace, you four will be the first to know."

With those parting words, Con opened the door and left. Phelan slid the door back into place and watched as Con got back into his Maserati and drove away.

"Well. That was interesting."

Charon grunted. "Verra. Should we take a look at this antique shop?"

"Already done," Laura said from her desk. She turned the monitor toward them. "The store doesn't have a Web site, but there is such a place in Perth. It's on King Street."

"Does it say who the owner is?" Aisley asked.

Laura shook her head. Her moss-green eyes met Charon's. "If it is a Dragon King—and with a name like The Silver Dragon I suspect it is—this is who Con is after."

"Agreed," Charon said. "I'm no' sure what to make of this visit. A Dragon King who isna on Dreagan land."

"We do nothing. For the moment." Phelan walked to the couch and sank onto the cushion. "I've got a bad feeling about all of this. Con doesna want the other Dragon Kings to know what he's up to. He expects us to look into this, and I've a feeling this is about Ulrik."

"Ulrik?" Laura repeated with a frown. "What an unusual name, and one I've heard recently."

Aisley nodded. "Remember when Rhys let it slip about one of the Dragon Kings who was on the outs? We didn't hear the entire story."

"Nor will we," Phelan said as he rubbed his chin. "Rhys was quick to change the subject."

Laura shrugged and propped her elbows on her desk. "They did allow us to have that battle on Dreagan land. Not to mention they helped us."

Charon frowned thoughtfully. "All good points, sweetheart. I'm just no' sure it's enough. I doona want to make an enemy of any of the dragons, but if we side with Con on this, we could potentially be stepping in the middle of a minefield."

"Look, I know the Kings have come to your aid before. It's just . . ." Aisley trailed off and bit her lip.

Phelan leaned forward and braced an elbow on his thigh. "Go on, babe. Finish your thought."

Aisley inhaled a breath to speak, then held it a second before releasing it in a rush. "I just . . . I just think it's odd that Con and the others know so much about so very much, but they aren't helping us with Wallace. Why is that?"

"Because it's our problem," Charon said.

"Bugger that," Laura said angrily. "Jason has tried to kill all of us. Repeatedly. What would happen if he succeeded and there were no more Druids to take a stand, or Warriors who could fight him? Where would that leave the great and mighty Dragon Kings then?"

Charon smiled and walked to his wife. He leaned down and kissed her. "I love when that temper of yours comes out."

"She's right though," Phelan said.

Charon straightened and braced a hand on the back of Laura's chair. "Maybe. We battled Deirdre without help from the dragons. Same with Declan. We can take Jason as well."

"Yes, we can," Aisley said with a firm nod of agreement.

Phelan rubbed a hand over the back of his neck, worry niggling in his gut. Even though Aisley was a Phoenix and could come back to life, he wasn't quite ready to test that theory again so soon. He had shattered when she'd died. He'd known then he would never be the same, never look at anything the same after having her in his life.

She'd been returned to him, but those few days had been a worse kind of hell than anything Deirdre had done to him. Aisley was his life, his very reason for continuing. Losing her wasn't an option.

But he saw her need for revenge burning in her fawn-colored depths. Wallace had used her daughter, the infant who had died hours after being born, against her.

Phelan held out his hand, and Aisley eagerly took it. He pulled her into his lap and simply held her. "Tell me of Wallace's weaknesses."

CHAPTER
FOURTEEN

Evie tried to concentrate on her work, work she did to help pass the time. But her thoughts turned again and again to Malcolm.

She'd never met anyone with so much pain and torment bottled within them. If Malcolm didn't release it, he could well explode from the force of it. A person could only stand so much.

He didn't seem the type to want—or need—help, however. All Evie could do was try to be there for him when he opened up a fraction. It wasn't much, but at least he was talking about some of the things that pained him.

There was a depth to Malcolm that staggered her. He was intelligent, yes, but the depth was due to the things that had happened to him.

With his hatred of *droughs* and his cousin being a Warrior, it wasn't far-fetched to think that somehow a Druid had hurt him in the past.

A ding signaling a new e-mail had her clicking over from her work screen to the e-mails. Her heart hammered in her chest when she noticed it was the e-mail corresponding to her site.

The subject read: Fellow Druid.

Evie's hand shook as she opened the e-mail and read it aloud. "Hello. I came across your site and knew instantly that I'd found another Druid. I've been hoping to find another of us. Would love to talk more. Sincerely, J."

Minutes ticked by as Evie sat with her hands on the keyboard trying to decide how to answer. Or if to answer.

She was suspicious of everyone, so she contemplated ignoring the e-mail. At the same time she gloried in the fact she could communicate with a potential Druid. How could she pass that up?

For several minutes she sat there staring at the screen. She hit delete and started to return to her work, when she paused. What could it hurt just to respond to the e-mail? It wasn't as if she was meeting with the unknown person.

Evie bit her lip and went to the Trash file and found the e-mail. She dashed off a quick response telling J that she would love to talk more, but it would have to be through e-mail and hit send before she changed her mind.

But even as the e-mail winged its way through cyberspace, she regretted it.

It was less than a minute after she sent it off that J replied. Evie chuckled to herself at the innocent message that was returned. That's when she realized she was being entirely too paranoid.

She smiled when she read the response asking her how long she'd been practicing magic.

"All my life," she said as she typed and hit send.

That's all it took for the correspondence to begin. For the next hour they communicated. She learned J was a man and lived right there in Scotland. He told her how he'd only just come into his magic a few years ago and was still sorting things out. It was his mention of a book of spells that intrigued her.

Evie really wanted to see that book. J even offered to

let her look at it if she met him for coffee. Which she politely declined.

She was careful not to tell him too much about herself. It would've been better had she told him she lived in America or something, but she was excited to find a Druid so close she hadn't been able to pass up the chance to let him know.

Besides, he was in need of other Druids just as she was. He tried to hide how lonely he was, but she could tell in the way he worded things.

If only she didn't feel the necessity to hide, she'd already have agreed to meet him. Just thinking of all they could be sharing about magic made her excitement bloom.

It was that same exhilaration that had her looking to tell someone. She closed her laptop and stood. "Is Malcolm in the mountain?" she asked the stones.

"*Nay.*"

"Will you bring me to where he's been staying?"

The stones were reluctant, but eventually they set her on the right path. Evie was a little surprised to find she was back in the dark chamber from the other night.

She took a deep breath and caught a whiff of fresh air. It didn't surprise her too much because she knew there were several vents located throughout the mountain. But the breath she'd gotten was filled with fresh air.

Evie cautiously walked forward, the stones guiding her all the while. When she came to a boulder or wall—she couldn't tell which—the shadows began to fade as light filtered in.

As soon as she turned the corner, she caught sight of the opening. It was about three feet high and two feet wide. The light she saw was lightning that lit up the sky.

She walked closer to the opening to kneel down and glanced outside. The rain splashed down on the ledge, causing the water to bounce up on her. When the lightning forked across the sky again she caught sight of just how far up she was and the majestic view of the mountains around her.

"My God," she breathed reverently. She wanted to see the same view during the day.

So this is where Malcolm stayed? Now she understood. Evie stood and took a few steps back. "Make the opening bigger so Malcolm can stand in it without bumping his head or shoulders."

The stones complied instantly. With the mountain shaking beneath her feet, she watched as the opening widened and lengthened.

"Thank you," she told the stones.

Evie gave the stones a pat and turned around. This was Malcolm's place. She didn't want to intrude more than she already had. The fact she wanted to know more about him didn't seem to faze her. The fact he was private and volatile didn't daunt her.

The fact that he caused her blood to sing and her body to throb with desire only pushed her onward.

For whatever reason Malcolm was in her life. She knew he didn't particularly care for her, but that didn't mean she couldn't ogle him whenever he was near. He was a splendid specimen, even with his scars.

She frowned. Not "even with." Because of.

Yes, she was beyond curious to know how he came to have the scars, and why he seemed to have such personal hatred for Deirdre. That wasn't the only reason she wanted to know him.

It was the deadness, the numbness she saw in his beautiful azure eyes that pulled at her heartstrings. There would be no changing a man like Malcolm. He would always do what he wanted to do.

Changing him she didn't want. She just wished to be

near him. If she could somehow help him, then she would gladly do it.

"Why?" the stones asked.

Evie turned and walked out of the chamber. Instead of going left to return to her room, she turned right and found herself descending deeper into the mountain.

"Because," she answered. "He's unusual. And he needs a friend whether he wants to admit it or not."

"He should leave."

"Tell me why none of you like him," she urged.

The stones all answered at once, their voices mixing and ringing in her ears as each shouted to be heard over the other. They were talking over each other so loudly she couldn't hear any of them.

Evie stopped and put her hand over her ears. "Stop!"

Instantly, the stones quieted.

She dropped her hands and waited for her ears to stop ringing from the onslaught. "Obviously there are many reasons. Just give me one."

"Betrayer."

CHAPTER
FIFTEEN

Evie let the stones' word soak in before she started walking again. There had to be more to the story, more to why the stones had such a hatred for Malcolm to call him a betrayer.

Not that either Malcolm or the stones would tell her the truth.

Evie wandered the long corridors without asking the stones anything else about Malcolm. They in turn said no more about him. It was a truce of sorts.

But how she wanted to know more. Regardless of how dangerous she knew it could be, there was something about Malcolm Munro she couldn't leave alone.

It was that curiosity she had been plagued with since birth. It had already gotten her into an awful mess, but Malcolm was . . . different. His scars notwithstanding, he was an enigma she wanted to solve.

She came across many chambers. Most were small with dark stains on the floor. Evie had a distinct feeling those stains were blood. She didn't stay in those rooms long.

Somehow, she made it back to the cavern she'd seen

days before. Except this time she was looking up at the balcony. A look around the spacious area showed her broken tables and benches strewn about.

It looked as if someone had come in and destroyed everything with a wrecking ball. Or something incredibly strong.

"Like Warriors," she whispered.

There was a loud crack behind her. Evie whirled around to see a section of the floor dropping down. She walked to it and looked into what appeared to be caves on either side of a wide area.

"What is this?" she asked the stones.

"The Pit. Veryyyyyyyy useful for Deirdre."

"How?" she asked with a shudder. What light came through wasn't enough to see more than the outline of openings on either wall beneath her.

"It was used to break Warriors to her will."

Well. She'd asked, after all. "Were the MacLeods held here?"

"Aye. Quinn. Marcail ruined it all."

Now that wasn't something she'd expected to hear. "How? How did Marcail ruin things?"

Never mind the fact the stones confirmed a MacLeod brother had been held there. That alone made her heart thud against her ribs.

"Deirdre wanted Quinn for herself. He should've been herssssss."

"Yeah, well, we don't always get what we want. So Quinn and Marcail were together?"

"Yessss. Deirdre tried to kill her. Then the others came for Quinn. They killed Deirdre's Warriors and her wyrran."

Evie straightened and swallowed. "There was a battle here?"

"Fallon and Lucan came for Quinn."

Fallon, Lucan, and Quinn MacLeod. Interesting. "You said Deirdre tried to kill Marcail. So she failed?"

"Barely."

"You enjoy death, don't you?"

"Deirdre was our mistresssssssss."

Evie realized things were getting a bit creepy regarding Deirdre and the connection to the stones. Malcolm's warning ran through her mind, but Evie decided to remain within the mountain. She wasn't Deirdre. Nor was she evil. "What are the wyrran?"

"Creatures Deirdre created," Malcolm said from behind her.

Evie spun around in surprise. Her foot slipped on the edge. She flailed her arms wildly in an effort to keep her balance and not go falling into the Pit.

Suddenly, she was yanked against a chest of solid, unyielding muscle. Evie flattened her hands against his damp shirt and felt the heat of him, the power.

It made her quiver with longing so deep, so intense it took her breath for a moment. She looked up into azure eyes filled with . . . nothing.

Not even that could dampen her attraction to him. He held her securely, gently against him. His wide, full lips were so close. All she had to do was rise up on her toes and fit her mouth against his.

What would he do? Would he push her away? Or would he return her kiss? Evie was tempted to find out. Just as she began to go up on her tiptoes, he spoke.

"You doona want to go into the Pit, Druid. You willna like what you find."

"I know," she said and tried to swallow. "The stones told me Deirdre used it to break Warriors."

She half expected him to jerk her away from him. Evie

found she couldn't move. Malcolm was like a magnet, and she was the answering side of that piece of metal who had no choice but to go to him.

No matter the threat, no matter the risk.

The darkness, the mystery surrounding Malcolm only drew her nearer. It was like she was destined to encounter him, their lives intertwined in ways she couldn't begin to fathom yet.

"Are you all right?" he said in a low voice that sent chills over her skin.

"Yes." In his arms, she realized she was more than all right. She was comfortable, calm. At ease.

"Good," he said and took a step back, releasing her. "Be careful what you find in this mountain, Druid. The stones willna always be there to help you."

She watched him walk away and wanted to stamp her foot in frustration. "Infuriating, irritating man," she murmured.

Malcolm fisted his hands before he flexed them. Damn but he could still feel the Druid's softness and allure. He wanted to rub his chest where her hands had been. It was like he'd been singed his skin burned so hot.

And the devil take him, but his cock was as hard as the granite he walked on. Need, intense and stark, sizzled in his veins.

It burned him, branded him. The need made it difficult to breathe, to form a coherent thought. He was on fire. Every thought centered on a Druid he didn't dare touch, but couldn't keep his hands off of.

A Druid who would be better off if he would leave her now and never look back. But he couldn't. No matter what argument he used, he found himself staying in the hated mountain.

"Malcolm," she called from behind him.

He inwardly winced at the sweet sound of her voice. It slid over him like velvet, inviting and tantalizing. Combined with her magic that kept him in a constant state of yearning, he was surprised he could think at all.

As if she had some pull over him, Malcolm halted and waited for her to catch up. She came even with him while her hands played nervously with the strings hanging from the waist of her fuchsia sweatpants.

He tried not to look at her, but once again he found himself drowning in the depths of her clear eyes. The innocence, the purity he saw reflected there reminded him of the fiend that he was.

"Thank you."

His nod was wooden but words wouldn't come. He looked over her head at the doorway. It was just steps away. If he could get away from her, he could calm his heated body and right his thoughts once more.

"Do you feel anything?"

Her question surprised him enough that he met her eyes. "What?"

"You heard me. Do you clamp down on your emotions to keep them hidden?"

"Nay. I have no emotions."

"Don't be a wanker," she said testily. "Of course you have emotions. It's up to you whether you show them or not."

Malcolm leaned down so that his face was even with hers. He blew out a harsh breath and glimpsed a small ringlet near her face billow out. "Doona pretend to know me, Druid. You know nothing of my life, nothing of what I've done. I'm dead inside."

He straightened and walked around her. Four more steps and he was out the door.

Just as he reached it, she said, "If you didn't feel anything, then you wouldn't be here trying to keep me from becoming what Deirdre was. And you wouldn't have saved me from falling just now."

His steps slowed, but he refused to stop. She was wrong. He knew what was inside him. A hefty measure of nothing.

And desire he couldn't shake.

Malcolm didn't stop until he was in the darkened room that had once been a prison. He threw off the soaking wet shirt and then came to a dead stop when he saw the opening that was now three times the size it had been.

No more did he have to sit in order to view the scenery. He knew exactly who was responsible. The Druid.

But why? He'd been nothing but testy and rude since he first woke her and demanded she leave. He didn't want her kindness. What did a man like him do with kindness?

He'd been hardened by a brutal attack, life-altering debilitation, and a *drough* who made sure his soul was knotted with hers.

Malcolm sighed and walked to the opening before stepping onto the ledge. The storm still raged, the wind lashing him like a whip. Rain pelleted him viciously, obstinately. He lifted his head to the sky and closed his eyes.

Above the storm, he heard the distinctive sound of wings. The beat was long and deep, which meant it wasn't Broc. It was a dragon.

Was the dragon here for him or enjoying the few seconds of freedom he got by taking to the skies? It didn't matter why the dragon was there. Nothing would change.

The Druid.

Malcolm didn't want to be concerned over her, but she was his responsibility. He had been quick to judge her. The others would likely do the same. He'd given her a chance—though a slim one—to change his mind, he wasn't sure if any of the others would.

His decision made, Malcolm released his god and jumped onto the side of the mountain. He used his claws to anchor him to the rocks as he jumped higher and higher up the mountain until he reached the top.

He let loose a bolt of lightning that extended from his hand to the next mountain. That's all it took for the beat of wings to come closer and the form of a dragon to be seen in the clouds.

A heartbeat later and the gleaming scales of a crimson dragon dove from the sky. Malcolm watched, mesmerized, at the ease of the dragon's body cutting through the rain and wind.

He was beginning to wonder if the dragon would spread his wings to land when the beast rolled into a ball as it sped closer and closer to the mountain.

Just before he would've crashed, the form of the dragon shifted and Guy landed with his legs bent and hands upon the ground. He lifted his head and shook the long hair out of his eyes before his gaze pinned Malcolm.

"Guy," he said. "I should've known."

The Dragon King stood, seemingly oblivious to the fact he stood naked in a storm. "I've been charged with babysitting you, Warrior. And I take my responsibilities seriously."

"So I see."

Guy looked around and grimaced. "Cairn Toul. This is unexpected."

"Cut the shite. You've known I've been here."

"So I have." The Dragon King crossed his arms over his chest. "Why are you here, Malcolm?"

"No' to reminisce, if that's what you think."

"Then why?"

Malcolm glanced down at his claws. They looked as dark as blood in the flashes of lightning. He should tamp down his god, but he couldn't think of a reason why. "I'm checking this vile place to make sure there's nothing of Deirdre's that Wallace can get his hands on."

"You think there could be something here?" Guy asked, his brows drawn together.

"With Deirdre, anything is possible. Wallace is already stronger than we expected. I doona want to leave anything to chance."

Guy's chest expanded as he took a breath. "Why no' tell the others? They're concerned for you."

There was no need for Malcolm to answer that, and Guy knew it. Malcolm ran his tongue over his fangs as he regarded the Dragon King. "Who requested I be watched? Con or Fallon?"

"Does it matter?"

"Aye. Who?" he demanded.

"Con."

Malcolm absorbed that for a moment. "Why would he be so interested?"

"The Warriors have always been of interest to us. We kept to ourselves for so long that I think Con is trying to make up for it now."

"By acting like an older brother? We Warriors can take care of ourselves."

"Oh, sod it, Warrior. We know that," Guy said, his voice laced with a thread of anger. "Con didna send me tonight. I needed to take to the skies. I learned you were here and wanted to have a look around."

Malcolm turned to the side and tamped down his god. It didn't matter who spied on him. It was the same as Phelan and Larena calling and texting as they did. Or the way Larena used to.

"Something on your mind, Warrior?" Guy came to stand beside him as he spoke.

Malcolm kept his gaze forward as he said, "You've been alive much longer than I."

"Aye. Do you want to know how to get through the years?"

"Something like that."

Guy held his hand out so that rain could gather in his palm. "Think of the years like this water. Some will stay in your memory forever. Others will be forgotten as soon as they occur. It's knowing which ones to cling to and which ones to let go that's tricky."

"Have you mastered it?"

"Nay. Just as looking at the years stretching ahead can be daunting. There were times I wanted everything to stop. I didna want to be here anymore. I wanted to give up. But I was charged with something important, Malcolm, and I couldna just let go."

"It would be easier if I did."

"Larena needs you."

Malcolm looked at him and comprehended that Guy was trying to be a friend. Odd that he only now realized it. A friend. The Druid asked that of him, but he hadn't given it a second's thought.

"Why?" Malcolm asked Guy. "Why are you trying to help?"

Guy smiled wryly. "Because you remind me of where I had been headed at one time."

"What stopped you?"

"We dragons can sleep for thousands of years. I took that option, and it helped to sort me out."

"I doona have that opportunity."

Guy threw back his head and laughed. "Nay, Warrior, you doona." The laughter stopped as he peered closely at Malcolm. "Something has changed."

Malcolm wasn't going to tell him about the desire or the way the Druid had him feeling things he'd forgotten.

"You can tell me," Guy urged.

"You answer to Con."

"I answer to myself. Con is my King, but I'm a King as well, Warrior. Doona forget that."

Malcolm faced the Dragon King. "No need to get riled on my account."

"You need something kept a secret, then I'll make sure it's done."

For just an instant, Malcolm considered telling Guy about the Druid. As much as he might like Guy, it would be better if no one knew about her existence until she was out of Cairn Toul.

"There's nothing."

Guy made a sound at the back of his throat and leapt into the air. When he did, his body shifted back into dragon form. Rain sluiced over the dark red scales as Guy's huge wings beat against the air to take him up through the clouds and out of sight.

Malcolm made his way back inside the mountain and the chamber. He sat with his back against the stones, staring out through the darkness surrounding him to the storm that raged.

Jason sat at his desk and saw on his tablet that he had a new message from one Evangeline Walker. He couldn't contain his smile as he opened it. Already he was one step closer to fulfilling the prophecy.

He'd known he had her captivated when she answered his second e-mail. Luckily for him she had no contact with anyone from MacLeod Castle. But just in case, he would tell her his name was Jay, or J for now as he signed his e-mails.

The rate at which she answered his messages and her hunger to learn more about magic meant he would have her on the hook soon. After that, it would take nothing to get her to meet him.

He gave her more tidbits about his book of magic.

Jason even sent her a spell she could use. Not once had she hesitated in trusting him. It was almost too effortless. In this day and age to have someone trust so easily was too much.

"Like candy from a baby," he said while typing his next message.

She soaked up his woe-is-me role as he'd expected. Just as he fed her lies about being lonely to make her feel sorry for him.

The one thing he didn't like was how cagey she was about herself. She eagerly corresponded with him when he spoke about himself, but if he asked questions about her family or past, she closed up tight as a clam.

He tapped his desk as he waited for her to respond to his fourth request that they meet. When the reply came, he wasn't shocked at her decline.

Instead of inviting her again, or demanding as he wanted to do, he asked how the spell had gone. Her response had him rethinking things.

"She hasna tried it yet."

This Jason hadn't expected. Perhaps she was more cautious than he'd taken into consideration. Of course, his hacking into her site had frightened her. But it was meant to lead her to him, not away.

Evangeline was meant to fulfill the prophecy, and she could be used as a pawn against the MacLeods. She wasn't supposed to take a long time to convince to join him. If she didn't change her tune soon, he'd have to take more drastic measures to ensure that she did.

Jason shut off the tablet and leaned back in his chair as he propped his feet up on the desk corner and crossed his ankles.

Evangeline Walker was going to be pivotal in his conquering of the world. The destruction of the interfering Warriors and Druids would be an added bonus.

CHAPTER
SIXTEEN

Evie stared at the small refrigerator that sat in her sitting room against the back wall. Next to it was a generator that ran so quietly she almost missed it.

She opened the fridge to find it empty except for a quart of milk and some eggs. Evie laughed as she closed the door and stood.

"And what does he expect me to do with those eggs? Fry them with my magic?"

That's when she looked on the other side of the fridge and saw a coffeemaker and an electric skillet. Evie was so surprised that she could only stare at the gifts as if she were a five-year-old on Christmas morning.

She turned and started to go find Malcolm to thank him when she drew up short. He liked his privacy. It was difficult to remember, but she couldn't intrude upon his sanctuary every time she wished to.

As much as she wanted to thank him, she was going to wait. Evie reached for a plastic cup to pour some milk and found the coffee.

"I'm in heaven," she whispered and hurried to make

some coffee. She'd been caffeine deprived for days and she needed a fix.

Once the coffee was in the cup and the first sip slid down her throat, she let out a contented sigh. Since she enjoyed the comforts of the city life, this was as far as roughing it as she'd gone. It wasn't as bad as she'd thought it would be.

Of course it didn't hurt to have someone as handsome and appealing as Malcolm around. It would be better if he had even a smidgen of charm in him, but then he wouldn't be him.

"At least he could ask my name," she grumbled.

It irked her that he didn't care enough to even want to know. She could just come out and tell him, but she was determined to make him ask. There was a stubborn streak a mile wide within her, and he brought it forth.

"He'll ask for my name. I'll make sure he does. Then I'll decide whether to give it to him or not."

The caffeine chased away the grogginess and made her more alert. Which might not be a good thing for Malcolm since she found she focused on him.

She glanced at the doorway hoping to find him there thanking her for expanding the opening so he could see out better. Even as she knew he wouldn't.

Malcolm didn't seem the thanking sort. By the way he went about his day without so much as a look in her direction, he was used to being on his own.

She was as well, but the difference between them was that she had Brian. Brian needed her. Because of that, she made decisions with him in mind.

Evie glanced at her mobile looking for a text from her little brother. The simple fact of the matter was that he needed her less and less as the years went by. Soon he wouldn't need her at all.

What would she do then? She'd railed against the fates for putting him in her life. Her nights had been spent corralling a youngster when she could have been out partying with her friends.

Looking back she wasn't sure how she survived those first years. Somehow she'd managed to get her degree at university. Those days were one huge blur. Between her classes and trying to find a school that Brian didn't get expelled from had been a nightmare.

There had been a point where Evie expected the government to come in and take Brian away from her. Yet, they had survived it. Somehow they had not only gotten through it all, but grew close in the process.

"Oh, Brian, what have I gotten myself into?" she whispered forlornly.

Suddenly the coffee didn't taste as good as before. Evie glanced at her computer and frowned. She needed something to do, something besides trying to keep hackers out of her Web site.

The walls were closing in on her. She missed her life, her friends, and her favorite restaurants. She missed her job, her boss, and his practical jokes. She missed her flat and having people to talk to.

Evie touched the pendant. She could destroy it. Though she didn't know if it would keep anyone from looking for it. The spell inside had to be important or her family wouldn't have kept it secret for so long.

It might be better if she knew exactly what spell was hidden in the pendant, but somewhere in her family line someone had decided not to pass it along.

How she wished she could go back in time and change the decision about putting up the necklace on her site. That seemed to be what drew everyone. A simple necklace that looked like an heirloom but nothing more.

Evie rose from the couch and walked into the bathroom. A long soak in the tub sounded like just the thing. She said the simple spell for fire and waited as it heated the water stored above the flames.

It was a more primitive way of heating the water from what she'd known, but hot water was hot water.

The stones hollowed out a boulder with enough water that would fill the tub. Once the fire heated it, all Evie had to do was remove a rock the size of her fist that was jammed in a hole. The water poured into the tub while she stripped out of her clothes.

In no time at all, Evie stepped into the water and let out a sigh as she leaned back and let the heat surround her.

The storm dispersed before dawn, but the rain continued in a steady downpour that didn't show signs of letting up anytime soon. Malcolm could feel the restlessness in the Druid's magic. It put him on edge and made him uneasy.

She stayed in her chamber, but it didn't stop the force of her magic from barreling into him as if he were standing next to her.

He then found himself wondering if she had used the coffee machine yet. Before the thought finished running through his mind, he sucked in a breath at the force of her magic.

Malcolm used the wall and climbed to his feet, his teeth gritted together. The only thing that could send that kind of magic was when a Druid did a spell.

Her magic felt too good to even consider. He wanted it around him, needed to feel it against his skin.

And that's what stopped him cold.

To his surprise, it was anger that began to well up. Anger because he didn't want to feel anything, anger because he certainly didn't want to need the Druid.

Malcolm straightened, intent on ignoring the rush her

magic gave him. He stalked from his hideaway to the Druid. Each step closer brought her magic stronger and headier.

His body tingled with the feel of it. With all his blood centering in his cock and his heart drumming in his chest, Malcolm couldn't stop the desire. His mind was screaming nay, but his body pulsed with a longing that wouldn't be denied.

Malcolm's strides ate up the distance separating him from the Druid. Another wave of magic slammed into him, doubling him over it felt so good, so . . . right.

He shook his head to try and clear it, but there was no getting away from such hunger. With a hand on the wall, Malcolm palmed his aching cock to try and give himself some relief.

It wasn't enough. His body wanted the Druid, needed her.

The Druid's chamber was steps away. He could stand before her and have her against the wall as he plundered her mouth with a kiss as fiery as the blood that pumped in his veins.

The thought appealed to him so much that he took a step toward her before he realized it. He drew up short. With a growl, he straightened and turned away. He couldn't remember the last time he felt such desire.

He'd been happy being dead inside. The . . . feelings . . . the Druid stirred only enraged him. If he let himself feel, if he gave in, he'd have to confront everything he'd done. And it would destroy him.

"Malcolm."

He squeezed his eyes closed as he came to a halt. To stay so near her wasn't smart, but he couldn't seem to put any distance between them.

"Thank you," she said. "I had a cup of coffee. I had no

idea I needed the caffeine. I noticed you brought tea as well. Would you like a cup?"

Malcolm remained silent. It was the only choice he had if he wanted to stay in control of his body, even though his god, Daal, raged at him to take the Druid.

"I was getting ready to make a fried egg sandwich. Won't you join me? Please."

He opened his eyes as he shook his head.

"Are you angry that I was in your space yesterday? I thought you might like the opening larger. I'll have the stones return it to the way it was if you'd prefer."

Did she have to be so damned nice? Malcolm took a deep breath and slowly released it. "It's fine."

He hardly recognized his voice. It came out hoarse and croaky. Malcolm willed her to return to her chamber and leave him in peace. The irony didn't go unnoticed by him. As long as he stayed in Cairn Toul, he'd never know peace from her—or the ghosts that remained.

He looked down at his hand. Twice he'd touched her, and twice she'd been branded upon him. Her softness, her femininity called to him. Her allure beckoned like a siren.

Malcolm lifted his gaze to find her standing in front of him. When had she moved? That's when he discovered he'd been the one to turn and walk to her.

"Are you hungry?" she asked.

He was famished, but it wasn't food he wanted. It was her. Her lips soft and open beneath his, her hands clutching him. Her curves pressed against his body, her moans of pleasure filling his ears.

Her body cushioning him as he filled her again and again.

The images only made his desire ratchet up several notches until sweat popped out on his forehead. His gaze dropped to her mouth when her tongue peeked out to moisten her lips.

His muscles seized to keep him in place and not drag her against him.

"I'm going to start breakfast. You're welcome to join me," she said slowly before she walked back into her rooms.

Malcolm watched the sway of her hips in her jeans that clung to her legs. Unable to help himself, he followed. He stayed by the door as she listened to Linkin Park coming through her laptop.

She didn't seem bothered by the lack of necessities most took for granted. He hated to admit it, but perhaps she did belong in Cairn Toul. There was no denying her connection to the stones.

His gaze never left her as she went about cracking the eggs on the electric skillet and began to fry them. She glanced up at him, a smile in her eyes.

Malcolm was too busy noticing how her black sweater dipped into a V, giving him just a glimpse of the swells of her breasts. She looked fresh as a summer's rain and as innocent as the dawn.

She was temptation and excitement, enticement and seduction. She was beauty and pleasure.

And she could never be his.

"How does this generator work? I've never heard one so quiet."

He shrugged. "It's a new design." She didn't need to know that it was the power of his lightning that would keep it running for years before he had to zap it again.

"You're an amazing man, Malcolm Munro," she said as she glanced at him. "I've been thinking. Do you know who betrayed Deirdre? The stones know who it is, but they refuse to tell me."

Malcolm found that curious. The stones hated him,

so why not just tell the Druid he was to blame? "Does it matter?"

"Why won't anyone tell me?" the Druid said with a roll of her blue eyes. "It's not like I'm asking for the crown jewels."

"Leave it, Druid."

She threw down the plastic fork and faced him, anger sparking in her eyes. "Why? What's the big deal? It's just a name."

"It's more than that."

"Bollocks."

Malcolm wanted distance from her, and he now had the perfect reason. He took a step toward her. "You really want to know who betrayed that evil bitch? It was me, Druid."

CHAPTER
SEVENTEEN

It was me, Druid.

His words echoed over and over in Evie's mind long after he left. She could only stare at the doorway in shock. Everything began to make sense now.

Why he'd been so adamant about her leaving the mountain, why he hadn't wanted to share the story of what happened to Deirdre, and why he hated the stones so much.

But most especially why he feared she would turn *drough*.

It was the burning smell that reminded her of the eggs. Evie quickly saved as much of them as she could before putting them on a piece of bread she'd toasted on the same skillet.

She ate her breakfast without tasting it. Her mind was too full of Malcolm. As usual his face had been barren of any emotion. His voice, however, conveyed what his face could not—satisfaction and anger.

After the meal, Evie busied herself with cleaning. It didn't take long, and before she knew it, she stood in front of Deirdre's wardrobe.

Evie flung open the doors and began to yank down the

clothes that hung there. She gathered them in a pile and walked out of her rooms into another one farther down the hall. Evie used her magic to build a fire and tossed Deirdre's clothes on the flames.

She watched them burn down to ash. She returned to her room and hung up her clothes. There was no need to live out of a suitcase anymore.

A scant fifteen minutes later, and she was done. Evie let out a long breath. She'd been so wound up when she woke that she had dared to try the spell J sent her.

It was a simple spell to clear her mind, but it hadn't worked. All she could think about was Cairn Toul. Images of a woman of uncommon beauty with eerie white eyes and white hair that hung to the ground filled her mind. Evil laughter had then reverberated in her mind.

That's when she stopped the spell and decided to go for a walk. Only to find Malcolm in the corridor. He'd looked to be in pain.

Evie needed to lose herself for a while. Anything to get Malcolm out of her mind as well as the woman she'd seen from the spell. She opened her laptop and pulled up the code for a new software idea she had.

Within minutes she was focused solely on the coding.

Malcolm shed his shirt and ran through the opening of his chamber outside the mountain. He jumped, the air whooshing around him as he fell. When he landed, he immediately jumped across the valley onto the opposite mountain.

He pushed his body hard, running faster, climbing higher, jumping longer. The more distance he put between himself and the Druid didn't ease his jumbled mind. If anything, it made it worse.

After hours of punishing himself, Malcolm turned back to Cairn Toul. He stared at the imposing mountain for several minutes. If anyone had told him he'd want to return there one day he'd have called them a liar.

But the truth was he wanted to return. For the Druid. She needed protecting from herself. Her curiosity was going to get her killed, especially in that mountain.

His gaze then turned east toward MacLeod Castle and Larena. Some emotion he couldn't quite name niggled at him. He pushed back his wet hair and blinked through the rain. It was then he realized what that emotion was—guilt.

A memory of him and Larena hundreds of years before sitting in the forest after he watched her train suddenly sprung up. He'd been but a lad of twelve and he'd known the importance of a vow. He made Larena a promise that day to always watch over her. She'd smiled, her smoky blue eyes filling with tears as she thanked him.

He broke that vow when he walked away from MacLeod Castle. Each time he left Larena, he broke it. Malcolm could just imagine the stern look of disapproval his father would give him if he were standing there.

Malcolm faced Cairn Toul. He'd made another promise to a Druid. Larena was a Warrior. She could take care of herself. Not to mention she had Fallon.

The Druid had only him.

His decision made, Malcolm started back to the mountain. The sun couldn't break through the dense clouds, which bathed the land in a wet, gloomy atmosphere that fit his mood.

By the time he stood in the entrance of his chamber, over half a day had passed. He sought out the Druid's magic to make sure she wasn't hurt. Then he breathed a sigh when he realized she was in her room.

He tried to sit in the dark, but memories he hoped never to revisit wouldn't leave him. Over and over he saw Logan's face flash surprise when Deirdre ordered Malcolm to take Duncan's head. Worse was Duncan's fury over Malcolm's betrayal right before he killed Duncan.

Betrayer.

Murderer.

That's what he was. He'd betrayed those at the castle, regardless of his reasons. Then he'd deceived Deidre.

Malcolm walked to the opening and out onto the ledge to let the rain fall upon him. He hung his head, shame and remorse making it difficult for him to breathe his chest was so tight.

Duncan had been a friend. He'd been there when Malcolm needed him, and in return Malcolm killed him. Then there was Ian, Duncan's twin. Ian had forgiven him because Malcolm had done it to protect Larena.

That wasn't an excuse. Ian should've exacted his revenge and taken his head, not called him friend.

Malcolm had disgraced his family, his clan, and himself. He'd done the very thing his father had told him never to do. *Never betray a friend, my son.*

The scenery blurred, and Malcolm blinked. That was when he felt something besides the rain drop onto his cheek.

Evie was going to regret it, she knew, but she had to see Malcolm. She wanted him to know she didn't care that he'd betrayed Deirdre. From all he'd told her, Deirdre deserved what she'd gotten.

She slowly walked into the darkened room with a torch in her hand and waited for Malcolm's bellow for her to leave. When that didn't come, she continued onward until she came to the opening.

Very little light came through with the low-hanging clouds and the rain, but it was enough for her to see the silhouette of a man.

Malcolm.

She stood looking at him for a moment before she crept

closer. His head hung down to his chest, his blond hair hiding his face.

The glow of the torch cast his skin in a golden flush. She set the torch on a rock and took in the scars on Malcolm's right shoulder and down his back and side.

Scar tissue so thick it appeared mangled met her gaze. It looked as if someone had taken a blade and cut strips from his neck, down his back, and onto his side.

She couldn't imagine the pain he'd suffered. Without thinking, she reached out and touched him.

He moved so quickly that it took her a second to realize he had her wrist in an iron grip while droplets of cool rain fell upon her from his hair and body.

"Doona," he ground out.

Evie swallowed and lifted her chin. She met his blue gaze, surprised to find they no longer looked at her dispassionately. There was anger there now.

For reasons she'd probably never understand, she wanted to touch his scars. She wanted him to know they only enhanced the man he was. Evie had never been able to say what people needed to hear. But in this, she could show Malcolm.

She tried to lift her hand to his face, but he held her fast, almost daring her to try again. She did. And this time he allowed it.

Slowly, she traced the pad of her finger down a scar that went the length of his cheek to his bearded jaw and then to his neck.

All the while, she kept her gaze locked with his. The anger faded, replaced with . . . desire.

Her heart began a slow steady drumming as his head gradually lowered. The rain that covered him was at odds with the heat coming off him.

She swept her fingers along his beard when one of his hands came to rest at her waist. His eyes lowered as he pulled her hips against him. Her lungs seized when his lips met hers.

The kiss was fleeting, but heady. Before she could open her eyes, his mouth was on hers again. A low moan rumbled in his chest before she found herself between a wall and Malcolm.

He kissed as he did everything—full throttle. He plundered her mouth, his tongue dueling with hers. He stole her breath and made her ache for more. She shook from the impact of his kiss, of the passion he allowed her to see.

With just a kiss he took, he claimed.

He conquered.

A moan left her when he deepened the kiss until she didn't know where he ended and she began. Heat infused her when his hips rocked against her and she felt his arousal.

Evie lifted a leg and wrapped it around his. Malcolm's large hand grabbed her thigh and lifted her leg higher at the same time he rocked his hard length into her sex.

She clutched his thick shoulders as hunger nestled low in her belly. His beard scraped her face as he kissed her harder, but she didn't care. Evie wound her arms around his neck trying to get as close to him as she could.

The kiss had begun fiery. It had gone beyond that to sizzling. And she never wanted it to end.

His hand tightened on her leg as his hips continued to tease her with his large cock. When his hips rotated against her, Evie felt a rush of moisture between her legs.

She'd never been so close to orgasm from a simple kiss before. And if she were like this with a kiss, what would it be like to make love to Malcolm?

The kiss ended as suddenly as it began. Evie blinked up at Malcolm. His breathing was as ragged as her own, his eyes burning with a longing that made her heart miss a beat.

He still held her leg and slowly ground against her. Evie's eyes slid closed as pleasure filled her. She leaned her head against the stones, their coolness doing nothing to ease the heat infusing her.

Malcolm's other hand lifted the hem of her sweater and touched her stomach. Evie hissed in a breath when his thumb caressed the underside of her breast.

Her breasts instantly swelled, her bra becoming too tight and confining. She wanted out of her clothes. She wanted Malcolm out of his.

Her body was fully aroused, and she needed relief. She was helpless to stop her hips from seeking him out.

He cupped a breast through the lace of her bra then lightly thumbed her nipple. She cried out, her knee giving out on her.

Malcolm released her leg and propped one of his between her. Her eyes flew open when his fingers touched her sex. She hadn't even known he'd unbuttoned her pants or pushed them down. His gaze studied her as he slid a finger inside her.

Evie let out a low moan. In and out his finger moved, teasing her, learning her. She had to grab hold of him when his thumb flicked over her clitoris.

Then he was kissing her again, his tongue moving in time with his finger. Evie's body was his to do with as he wanted, and he proved it by taking her higher and higher. He added a second finger and stroked her.

She tried to hold off the orgasm, but he wouldn't allow it. He pushed her, demanding more. Her body wound tighter and tighter, the world falling away, until she shattered.

Waves of ecstasy seized her, took her, leaving her floating on a tide of mind-boggling bliss.

CHAPTER
EIGHTEEN

Malcolm's body throbbed and pulsed—not just from his need, but from witnessing the Druid's pleasure and feeling it through her magic. It magnified his own need, intensifying his desire until she became the center of his universe and nothing else mattered.

He'd never known anything like that was possible.

Her eyes gradually opened. It took her a second to focus her clear blue eyes on him, and then her slow, satisfied smile nearly snapped the thin thread that was left of his control.

She seemed to glow she was so luminous. Her hips shifted, and he was reminded of his fingers still deep inside her. A pleasure-filled groan met his ears. Dimly, he realized it had come from him.

He could lay her down and have his way with her right then. It's what she wanted. It was what he wanted.

Her head leaned to the side causing her dark curls to fall over his arm, their silky mass tempting him to plunge his fingers into the thickness and grab a handful as he held her head and plundered her sweet lips once more.

Malcolm pulled his fingers from inside her tight body. He tried to step away, but he couldn't. The Druid had awoken more than just his desires. She'd stirred the emotions he thought long dead.

Emotions he wasn't equipped to handle.

"Malcolm," she whispered irresistibly, a slight frown marring her forehead.

His gaze lowered to her mouth to find her lips still wet and swollen from his kisses. He wasn't sure why he'd pleasured her, only that he wanted to be able to bring something other than death and betrayal to someone.

The Druid reached for the waist of his jeans and unbuttoned them before he knew what she was about. He grabbed her wrists to halt her actions even as his balls tightened when her fingers grazed the tip of his cock.

He craved her hands on him. His mouth went dry just thinking of her lips sliding over his rod and taking him deep within her mouth.

"I know you want me," she said. "I felt how hard you are. Why then did you stop?"

He didn't have an answer, or at least not one that wouldn't bring more questions.

With her hands trapped, she ground her hips against him. His control was slipping. Malcolm's eyes briefly closed as pleasure swarmed over him from the contact. He was powerless to stop himself from rocking into her softness.

"You want me," she whispered, her voice a siren's call. "So take me."

"Nay," he managed past his tightening throat.

She rose up on her toes and slowly slid her body down his, her breasts against him, her sex rubbing along his cock. It was too much. After feeling nothing for so long, he was about to explode from the need driving him.

"Yes."

He shook his head even as he leaned into her for another kiss. Daal laughed, the sound loud in his head, but it was a reminder of what he really was.

Like a bucket of ice water dumped on him, Malcolm was snapped out of the irresistible desire. He released her and took a step back. "You doona understand, Druid."

Her body listed forward and she had to quickly gain her balance. "I'm not a . . . I don't do this, Malcolm. I don't allow men I barely know to touch me as you did. But I don't regret it either. I've never felt anything like that before. I want to feel it again."

All he could do was stare at her and the emotions crossing her face.

"I know you need release. If you don't want to be with me, at least let me pleasure you," she offered.

"I can no'."

Hurt clouded her clear blue eyes, chasing away all the warmth and desire he'd given her. "Fine," she said and pulled her pants up and fastened them. She turned and grabbed the torch as she walked away.

Malcolm flexed his fingers, fingers that had been inside her, stroking her to a fever pitch. Her heat, her moisture had been heaven.

Just before the Druid exited the chamber she halted and turned to him. "Tell me why you don't want me."

"I never said I didna want you."

"You didn't have to. You made it perfectly clear just now."

"There are things you doona understand."

She lifted her chin, daring him with her eyes. "Try me."

Malcolm opened his mouth only to close it again. In all the months he'd wandered after betraying Deirdre, he'd kept away from people. There hadn't been a need to interact with those he didn't know. It hadn't been a problem until the Druid.

She had smiled at him, asked him to be her friend, and she looked and touched his scars with awe. There had been no revulsion or pity in her eyes.

"You . . ." He paused and started again. "I've no' felt anything in a verra long time. I've been dead inside. It's how things need to be."

"Because you betrayed Deirdre?" came her softly spoken question.

Malcolm looked away from her probing gaze. "I was dead inside before that. I've forgotten what it was to have any feeling. Until you. You have . . . roused what I thought was dead and gone."

"Why is this a bad thing?" she asked and started walking toward him.

"Because I've forgotten how to handle them. As it is, my skin feels too tight with trying to hold it all in."

"And making love would only complicate all of it," she finished with a nod. "Will you tell me why you were dead inside?"

"Deirdre unbound my god."

The Druid's mouth dropped open as her eyes widened in astonishment and accusation. "Bloody hell. So . . . you're a Warrior?"

Malcolm watched her take an involuntary step backward. "I was born in 1579."

"That means you're . . . Oh, shit." She swallowed nervously and took another few steps back.

"Do you fear me now, Druid?" he asked angrily. "You wanted to know. Shall I tell you the long, ugly truth of it?"

She shook her head. "No."

"I'd spent years as a mortal helping Larena track down the MacLeods. We finally found the eldest brother, Fallon. As I hoped, Larena and Fallon fell in love. I was on my way to see them when Deirdre sent Warriors to kill me." Malcolm turned his face so the light of the torch shone on his scarred side. "This is what they did."

"Stop," she murmured, her face stricken by what she was hearing.

"They tried to rip my arm from my body, using their claws to do it." Fury built inside Malcolm so quickly he couldn't contain it—and didn't try to. He released his god and grimaced when he heard the Druid's gasp. He held up his long maroon claws. "Claws like these. To this day I can still remember how it felt to have them ripping through my skin and muscle as they scraped to the bone. The Warriors could've yanked my arm off in a second, but they wanted me to suffer."

The Druid took in an unsteady breath. "I don't want to know any more."

"Ah, but you asked," he stated cruelly as the memories returned. "Broc came upon us and killed the others before taking me back to MacLeod Castle where the Druids did their best to heal me." His chest ached as he remembered learning he didn't have the use of his right arm.

The humiliation and frustration had been almost as bad as the helpless feeling that hadn't released its hold on him yet. He roared his fury and plunged his claws into the rocks.

He didn't want to remember any of the awful memories. The pain of it, the powerlessness he felt came rushing back as if it had just happened to him.

"They should've let me die. Why didna Larena let me go?" Malcolm hung his head, wishing he could go back to that fateful day and make Broc finish what the Warriors had begun.

"If Larena is all that you have, then you're all the family she has. She didn't want to lose you."

"I was to be laird, Druid. I couldna return to my clan half a man who didna have the use of his sword arm. It wouldna have mattered to them that I was able to wield a sword with my left. To them, I wasna whole. So I stayed with the MacLeods. Mortal. Feeble. Helpless."

He nearly choked on the resentment as he recalled being relegated with the Druids when Deirdre attacked. He was half a man, after all. He hadn't been able to make a stand with the Warriors.

That had cut him deeper than anything Deirdre had ever done to him. It didn't matter that Malcolm knew his friends had been trying to protect him. They hadn't allowed him to be the Highlander he was.

"I stayed until I couldna remain any longer," Malcolm continued. "I snuck away from the castle during one of Deirdre's attacks. A few days later she found me and unbound my god. I promised to do anything she asked as long as she left Larena alone."

Malcolm pulled his claws from the stones and faced the Druid. "I've killed in Deirdre's name. I became a monster. And, aye, I betrayed her!"

His voice echoed in the chamber, making the Druid wince, but Malcolm didn't care. He was too caught up in the raw emotions running rampant through him.

"Look at me," he demanded of the Druid when she gazed at the floor. "Look at what I am. A Warrior, a man with a god inside him. You allowed me close and asked me to be your friend. You're too trusting, Druid. It's going to get you killed."

Her eyes narrowed on him. "Perhaps I am too trusting. It's better to be trusting than emotionally dead as you've been. You don't feel anything. You didn't even care enough to want to know my name despite promising to watch over me." She shook her hand slowly as her ire mixed with her magic. "Every time I talk with you, you're someone different. You want to scare me by showing me you're a Warrior? Well bravo, asshole, because you did it."

All the rage deflated from Malcolm as the Druid stalked away. Each of her words had been like a punch in his gut. He had wanted to frighten her so she wouldn't ask him to make love to her. But now that he'd done it, he keenly regretted it.

Malcolm slumped against the wall. Who was he? He couldn't begin to answer that question. He wasn't the idealistic man who had been waiting to step into his father's shoes as laird. He certainly wasn't the easygoing person who had watched Larena with curiosity and jealousy.

The only thing he knew for certain was that he was a murderer and a betrayer. He didn't deserve any of the friendships that had been offered by those at the castle, Guy, or the Druid.

He hadn't realized not asking her name bothered her so much. He'd done it in an effort to keep his distance from her so she wouldn't be tainted by who he was.

That had been blown out of the water when he began to lust after her. Then he kissed her. That amazing, glorious kiss had rocked him to his black soul.

In her kiss, he found desire, passion, and . . . tranquility. For those few precious moments he kissed and pleasured her, he forgot the fiend he was. For those minutes he'd become someone else, someone that had a soul.

Malcolm ran a hand through his hair. Whatever he'd found in the Druid's arms was lost forever. It was time he called Phelan and told him of the Druid. Let Aisley help the Druid in her plight.

He pushed away from the wall and walked to the opening of the mountain. The rain had tapered to a drizzle. The mist was rolling down from the mountains to cover all that was in sight. A perfect place to hide.

Malcolm looked over his shoulder and briefly thought of telling the Druid farewell. He'd scared her though, and he would be the last person she wanted to see.

The taste of her was still on his tongue, her scent still clung to his body. Both of which would forever be etched upon him.

"Good luck, Druid," he said before he jumped.

CHAPTER
NINETEEN

Jason slammed his hand on his desk. Evangeline was cagier than he'd thought. She hadn't responded to one of his e-mails in over a day.

He'd thought he had her right where he wanted her. Now he wasn't so sure. He could force her with his magic, but he needed to have more finesse than that.

She had to willingly come to his side. He wanted her to know he had every intention of turning her *drough*, but that came later. First, he had to get her to his house and show her what it meant to have another Druid as her friend.

Once she was *drough*, it would take nothing to have Malcolm take her to his bed. Jason would love to use magic to help her get pregnant, but if he wished to fulfill the prophecy he couldn't.

"Show me Malcolm and Evangeline again."

Instantly, an image of Malcolm kissing the Druid formed on his desk about twelve inches high and in 3-D.

"I knew he wouldna be able to resist her. The attraction is palpable."

The image shifted, and Jason watched as Evangeline

walked away angrily. Jason frowned as he saw all the rocks.

"Where are they?"

Colors blurred as the image changed and drew back to show none other than Cairn Toul.

"Priceless," Jason said with a satisfied grin.

That grin faltered when the picture shifted and showed Malcolm jumping out of an opening in the mountain and sprinting away from Evangeline.

"This willna do. I need them together." He drummed his fingers on the arm of his chair as he tried to think of a way to get Malcolm back to Evangeline. Or the Druid to him.

Jason sat up straight and said, "Show me anyone close to Evangeline."

The image of a teenage boy with dark hair and dark eyes popped up. Jason leaned in close to the likeness and drummed his fingers on the desktop.

"Who are you, lad?"

Colors blurred as the image faded and another took its place. This picture was of a file folder from a private school with the name Brian Smyth.

Jason leaned back in his chair and considered this new evidence. How was this Brian connected to Evangeline? He was too old to be her son.

"Show me the connection to Evangeline."

In the next image the file folder was open and focused on two lines of a form.

"Guardian," Jason read, "Evangeline Walker. Relationship: half-sister." He smiled and rubbed his hands together. "Oh, sweet Evangeline, looks like I've found the perfect way to send you straight to me. And Malcolm straight to you."

Jason rose from his chair and walked around his desk. He hurried to his Jaguar XF and slid behind the wheel.

The school was only a few hours' drive. He'd be there and have the kid in his dungeon before dinner.

He started the engine and drove down his long driveway wishing the spell he'd found to teleport would work. For some reason the spell did nothing for him. Every other spell he'd tried worked without much effort. The teleportation was an entirely different matter.

But he would master it as he had everything else. He just needed more time, which was in great supply. Once Evangeline was *drough,* she would convince Malcolm to stay near her. The child would come about soon after.

Then all hell would break loose. There would be nothing the Warriors and Druids could do to stop it either.

Jason couldn't stop smiling as he drove toward the school.

Evie dried off after her bath and changed into yoga pants and an oversized sweatshirt. Her body was still languid from the pleasure Malcolm had given her.

She couldn't believe he'd been able to touch her so expertly and bring her to orgasm as quickly as he had. Not once had she felt such decadent sensuality from a man before. He'd taken her to heights of pleasure she hadn't known existed.

She touched her lips where they still tingled from his kisses. He had the body of chiseled marble, each muscle hard and powerful. Yet, to touch him was to find molten heat. He looked at the world with an azure gaze that was as barren as a desert.

But he caressed her as a man driven by desire and need. She felt his desperation and hunger, his need and longing in his kisses, knew pleasure from his deft fingers.

Malcolm Munro was a contradiction. She wanted to hate him or fear him, but she could do neither. He'd told her part of his story and it ripped at her heart.

Deirdre had tried to have him killed. In the end, she maimed him in such a way that Malcolm thought he could never return to his clan. Since Highlanders prized strength, he'd known his clan might accept him back in, but he'd never be laird.

Evie pulled her hair into a ponytail and sighed. He'd been groomed to be a leader. He'd gone from having a future as laird to simply . . . existing. That would be a blow to any man, but one that could destroy someone like Malcolm.

She walked to the sitting room and stared at her laptop. There was no sense trying to work when her mind was filled with him. Even when he wasn't near, he occupied every inch of available space.

"He's a Warrior."

She'd never even considered it. A Druid, maybe, but never a Warrior. He had scared her witless when he'd transformed, but he hadn't come near her. If he really wanted to put the fear of God in her, all he needed to do was move toward her.

A Warrior. She recalled how the torchlight had shone upon his skin that turned the deepest maroon. The claws he'd held up were long and deadly. The fangs gave him a fearsome look.

She'd thought it all some trick until she looked into his eyes expecting to see his beautiful azure gaze and found herself mirrored in maroon eyes.

The stones had yelled at her to run, but she couldn't. The raw emotion reflected in his maroon eyes kept her rooted to the spot. She saw grief, remorse, and self-loathing.

Inwardly, she winced when she recalled how he'd plunged his claws into the stones. The stones themselves had screamed in pain, nearly drowning out the growls coming from Malcolm.

Every word Malcolm uttered held a wealth of emotions.

They battered him endlessly, ceaselessly tugging feelings he was desperately trying to keep locked away.

But those emotions were breaking free.

Evie didn't know how to help him. If he even wanted her help. And that was a big if. Malcolm pushed her away at every opportunity.

Had she left Cairn Toul that first night he arrived, she was sure she'd never have seen him again. He might infuriate her by not answering her questions fully, or annoy her by not being able to read his emotions.

Yet, the idea of not knowing him or his story didn't seem right. It was as if she was meant to stumble across Malcolm and learn the history of her ancestors and Deirdre.

When her mind turned to Deirdre, she recalled the images that had assaulted her after the last spell she'd performed. Who was the woman with the long white hair and white eyes?

There was one person she knew could tell her what Deirdre looked like. Malcolm. And if the woman's image who now filled her mind wasn't Deirdre, then Evie wanted to know who she was.

Evie began to rise from the sofa when there was a ding from her laptop announcing a new e-mail. She was going to ignore it when she saw it was from J.

She'd meant to return his message earlier but had gotten sidetracked with Malcolm. No doubt J was thinking she didn't want to hear from him again. Quite the opposite really.

"Except for the spell."

There was something about the spell he'd given her. If it was supposed to relax her, why had it done the opposite? Unless she had messed it up. Or he wrote it down wrong in the e-mail. Whatever the reason, she needed to give him a second chance.

He was the only other Druid she knew, after all.

She clicked on the e-mail to find three simple words: "How are you?"

Now she felt really bad for not answering him. Evie quickly wrote a note to let him know she was busy and apologized for taking so long to get back with him. She hoped it was enough to keep him sending the e-mails.

Before she could set her laptop aside, J answered her. She blew out a frustrated breath. He wanted to know how the spell had gone.

Evie bit her bottom lip as she tried to decide if she should lie to him. She finally settled on the truth. It would be good to know if she'd done something wrong with the spell. Especially now since she could really use some relaxation after her last run-in with Malcolm.

She was holding out hope that J would be able to tell her what she'd done wrong. Yet, he assured her that he'd written the spell correctly. Which meant she was the one who'd screwed it up.

"I'll have to give it another go," Evie said as she signed off the e-mails.

Her mind was too jumbled with Malcolm, desire, and the image of that woman. If she could just clear her head for a bit, she'd be able to figure everything out.

Evie read over J's spell and instructions twice more. Then she set her laptop on the coffee table and moved to sit cross-legged on the floor.

She took a deep breath and slowly read the words of the spell over and over until she knew them by heart. With her eyes closed and her thoughts centered on her magic, Evie kept repeating the spell.

Time ceased to exist as she felt her mind clearing itself of everything. She took a deep breath and simply let her magic surround her.

Evie didn't know how long she stayed like that until

the evil laughter sounded as if it came from right beside her. She tried to open her eyes and break out of the spell, but there were hands grabbing her from behind and keeping her from moving.

Strands of long white hair suddenly wrapped around each wrist. Evie tried to scream. She even tried to call out for Malcolm, but it was like her body was no longer her own.

Her heart raced, her blood turned to ice. Panic set in until she remembered she was the one with magic. Evie gathered her magic close and waited.

She wanted to know who the woman was and why she kept showing up when Evie did this spell. Her eyes opened then. Evie had to stop herself from using her magic when she found white eyes staring at her.

"Who are you?"

The woman simply smiled, the action chilling Evie to her bones because of the malice and evil she glimpsed.

White hair curled around Evie's throat and began to choke her. Evie let loose her magic into one powerful blast at the woman.

Immediately, the hair was gone. Evie fell to the side and coughed as she dragged in huge gulps of air. She looked to where the woman had been, but she was no longer there.

The eerie trepidation that settled around her like a warm coat hadn't departed with the apparition, however. Whatever was going on with the spell, Evie had no plans of trying it again.

Twice was more than enough.

Evie climbed to her feet and went to get some water. She downed two full glasses before her heart ceased to race. Though her knees kept knocking together.

She looked at the clock to discover almost five hours had passed. Surely it had only been an hour at the most. But her watch, iPhone, and computer all read the same time.

There was no denying that the spell had taken her far longer than she had expected.

Evie realized belatedly that there hadn't been a text from Brian after school finished for the day. With her laptop battery dead, she couldn't work or watch a movie.

"Luckily Malcolm solved the issue of recharging for me," she said as she dug out her power cord and plugged it into the generator.

She put on some shoes and walked into the hallway. "Show me the dungeon," she told the stones.

It was no surprise when she found herself walking lower into the mountain. The air became cooler and staler the deeper she went. When she came to a door, she opened it and saw the compartments with walls of rock separating them. The front of each cell was also rock fashioned like iron bars.

"This is where Deirdre kept the Warriors?"

"This dungeon was for the Druidssssss."

Evie shivered. Malcolm had said Deirdre killed Druids for their magic. Had Deirdre been so powerful that none could fight against her? It was another question she had for Malcolm.

She walked out of the dungeon and leaned her hand against the stones to find them wet. Water trickled down from the ceiling in a steady flow that looked as if it hadn't stopped in hundreds of years.

Evie wiped her hand on her pants and took two steps when her mobile rang. She hurriedly dug it out of her sweatshirt pocket expecting to see a text from Brian.

Instead, it was from an unknown number. Evie read the message twice, thinking it was a practical joke. But as she read how her brother had been kidnapped, she knew it was no jest. She gasped and covered her mouth with her hand when a second message popped up, this one a picture of Brian with his hands tied behind his back.

"Oh, God," Evie murmured.

Her fingers shook as she tried to type. It took her four tries before she was able to ask what the kidnappers wanted.

"You know," she read their response aloud.

The necklace. They wanted the necklace in exchange for Brian.

Her legs gave out as she crumpled to the ground. How had they found Brian? It was bad enough they had been after her. It had never entered her mind they would seek out her brother.

The first instinct was to rescue him. Then she held the pendant in her hand. The spell housed in the necklace was important and could be deadly to some. That much she knew from her grandmother.

Could Evie trade it so easily and be responsible for thousands of deaths? Could she live with that?

There was no way. Nor could she leave her brother in the hands of the kidnappers who showed they were willing to do whatever it took to get the necklace.

She dropped her head in her hands and squeezed her eyes shut. Whatever decision she made would have repercussions that rippled outward.

Evie tried to convince herself that the necklace could hold nothing but a simple spell that did no harm.

That was quickly shot out of the water as her conscience pointed out that no one would resort to kidnapping for a simple spell.

"Oh, God," she said as she lifted her head. "Brian or the necklace. What do I do?"

She couldn't let the kidnappers think she was going to leave her brother with them. With shaking fingers, she typed: "When and where?"

Evie tried to swallow around her tightening throat when the next text appeared telling her they'd be in touch.

"Malcolm!" she yelled. "Malcolm, I need you!"

She stood and raced through the mountain shouting his name until her throat was raw. Only then did she hear the stones screaming that Malcolm was gone.

Evie's legs gave out as she collapsed in the corridor and let the tears fall.

CHAPTER
TWENTY

"I know you can no' talk," Jason said as he drove away from the school with Brian bound in the backseat of his Jaguar. He glanced in the rearview mirror to find Brian glaring at him. "But you can listen."

It had taken very little magic to get the schoolmaster to turn Brian over to his care. The teenager, however, had been another matter.

Jason had wanted to knock him out, but the picture he sent Evangeline with Brian awake had been perfect. The only thing that would've made it better was if he had been there to see her reaction.

"I've no intention of harming you," Jason continued. "That is, unless you give me a reason. I'm after your sister. Once I have her, I'll let you go."

If looks could kill, Brian's dark gaze would have smote Jason on the spot.

"Anger is good, lad. It's what got me through the darkest years of my life. And look at me now. No one would dare to tangle with me."

Jason smiled as he thought back to what a wanker he'd been. He'd been afraid of his own shadow. Magic changed all of that. Magic and money. The family name helped as well.

Brian leaned forward. The seat belt Jason had spelled to keep him in place jerked Brian backward. The lad grunted as he fought against the restraints.

"I think I proved that no matter how you fight me, I'm going to win." Jason drove around a bend in the road and continued on to Wallace Mansion. "You can stop worrying. I doona want to hurt your or your sister. She's no' responding to me as I wish her to, so I've taken you to hurry her along."

Jason turned up the radio as Brian continued to strain and make the guttural sounds in the backseat. He didn't care what the lad did. Evangeline would soon come to him.

And this time there wouldn't be any Warriors from MacLeod Castle to come to her rescue.

Malcolm jerked to a halt. He was hours away from Cairn Toul, but there was no denying the spike of terror that viciously slammed into him from the Druid's magic.

He turned to look at the way he'd come. There was no way he should have been able to feel the Druid's magic from such a distance. It was too far. It's why he'd run so fast. The farther away he was from her, the better off she'd be.

Yet he knew in his gut that it was the Druid he felt. Without another thought, Malcolm started back to Cairn Toul. He used the incredible speed of his god as he raced to her.

She could be hurt, or something in the mountain left by Deirdre could have harmed her. All Malcolm could think about was everything that could have happened.

The worse his imaginings got, the faster he ran.

With every step he berated himself for leaving. All

because he hadn't been able to keep his hands off her. And his damned emotions.

He hated them, hated how they ruled every second as long as he allowed them. Malcolm wasn't used to the panic pumping through him. He didn't like the apprehension that caused his chest to tighten every time he thought of the Druid hurt.

Daal bellowed inside him, urging him faster. Malcolm let his chest rumble with a growl. He didn't need his god to tell him to hurry. He knew by the feel of the Druid's magic that something had gone terribly wrong.

"Hold on, Druid," he whispered as he leapt over a large boulder.

With Malcolm gone, Evie didn't have anyone else she could turn to. That was when she thought about J. He'd been nice and supportive, as well as easy to talk with. There was a possibility he would know of a way to use magic to find her brother.

Still shaking, Evie picked herself up and stumbled her way back to her chamber. She wiped at her eyes to try and dry the tears. It wouldn't be tears that got Brian back safely. It would be strength and magic.

Evie grabbed her laptop and quickly shot off an e-mail to J asking for his help. He responded within ten minutes talking about a set of standing stones that were kept in a secret spot near Ullapool and a spell she needed to recite that would increase her magic so she could fight the kidnappers.

"Increase my magic how?" she said aloud as she typed.

Five minutes ticked by with no answer. Each second was a knife plunged in her heart as she thought of Brian.

Finally, the e-mail popped up with a simple sentence: "You'll need black magic to succeed."

"Become a *drough*? He can't be serious."

But she knew he was. It was revenge she was seeking, retribution for hurting someone she loved. No matter how she looked at it, it would be black magic she called forth.

That kind of anger, that kind of resentment would bring nothing but disaster to her door. She would lose her soul.

Evie closed the laptop and jerked off her yoga pants and sweatshirt so she could put on the black corduroy skinnies, a cream sweater, and black boots before grabbing her coat and fedora hat to keep the rain out of her eyes.

She still didn't know what she was going to do, but she knew she had to leave the mountain to do it.

"I'll be back," Evie promised the stones when they began to wail. "I need to somehow save my brother. When I do, I'll return. I promise."

She strode to the door through which she'd first come into the mountain. The great stone slab opened as she drew closer. Evie huddled in her jacket when a blast of cold air hit her. The rain had stopped for the moment, but judging by the thick, dark clouds above her, it would return.

Evie adjusted her hat so it fit more snugly, and then she started down the mountain. The stones led her through the safest—and quickest—path in the dark.

She kept her head down and walked as fast as she could, sending a prayer that Brian was safe and unharmed. Evie kept her mind focused on the decisions she had to make, because if she didn't, she would fall apart.

Brian. He was family. Blood was thicker than any magic she possessed. Nothing should matter but getting him back.

The pendant heated against her skin, reminding her of its importance and how diligently her family had kept it hidden. Until her.

"I'm such a bloody idiot," she mumbled.

All her troubles had begun the moment she'd put up her site.

Malcolm was so intent on reaching Cairn Toul Mountain that it took him a second to realize the Druid was no longer inside.

He let out a growl and punched one of the boulders in irritation. The anger that simmered just beneath his skin jerked him out of his haze so that he could get himself under control.

With his eyes closed, Malcolm concentrated on the Druid. He felt the brush of her magic to his left and found himself gazing toward Aviemore.

"What made you leave?" he asked.

The Druid wasn't that far ahead of him. He started running again, leaping down the mountain and rushing through the forest. Malcolm didn't slow until he caught sight of her brown plaid coat as she walked in the woods just a few feet from the road.

Her strides were long and quick. She was in a hurry, but why? She'd told him she feared for her life, which was why she was in the mountain.

He had to know what drew her out. Malcolm decided to follow her. If she got into trouble, he'd be there to help. There was much about the Druid he didn't know, and maybe it was time he found out.

It was the feelings she stirred that made him forget he should be fielding her for answers. Instead, his desire had grown while he told her stories of Deirdre and the Warriors.

Shite, but he even told her how he'd become a Warrior.

By the time they reached Aviemore, Malcolm was in a fine temper. He was furious at himself for letting the Druid's beauty, appeal, and vulnerability get to him like a lad with his first crush.

It was pitiful and irresponsible, disgraceful and embarrassing.

He was glad he hadn't made the call to Phelan regarding the Druid yet. Malcolm could well imagine the questions Phelan would have that he couldn't answer.

Malcolm wanted to think the Druid was innocent. Her sweet magic said as much. But she was drawn to an evil place. There was no good that could come from her being in Cairn Toul.

He hid behind a car as the Druid walked to the bus station and sank onto a bench. Indecision warred plainly upon her face, which was pale and strained. After a half hour she rose and purchased a ticket. Malcolm's enhanced hearing allowed him to hear the destination—Inverness.

Just what had the Druid coming out of hiding?

CHAPTER
TWENTY-ONE

Evie counted out the money and paid for the ticket. Her stomach rumbled with hunger, but she ignored it. Food would have to wait. Her mind was too full of sorting through the consequences of choosing to save her brother, handing over the necklace, becoming *drough,* or doing nothing.

She tucked her ticket into her purse and looked at her phone again. Adrenaline pumped like ice through her veins and her heart hammered so hard it was beating against her chest. All because she had yet to hear when the exchange was supposed to take place.

Evie resumed her seat on the bench and shivered. Her clothes were soaked through, but she barely paid any notice. Her world was falling apart, and she was facing it all alone.

There was no one to talk over her options with, no one who might give her an idea of what she should do. Brian expected her to come for him. Every fiber of her being told her she should.

The burden of a family's vow, however, weighed heavily

upon her shoulders. It pushed her down, submerged her in promises given and assurances guaranteed.

The necklace was dangerous, a potential source of magic that could hurt many. Which is why the pendant had been changed and hundreds of spells put on it so others couldn't find it.

And she had handed it to them on a silver platter.

If that wasn't enough to agonize over, she had the option of becoming a *drough*. She would lose her soul, but she would have black magic to kill those who threatened Brian as well as protecting the pendant.

Thirty minutes later when she got on the bus she was no closer to making any kind of decision.

Evie settled in her seat and recalled from a recent movie that she should ask for proof of life. With shaky fingers she typed in a quick text stating she wanted proof Brian was alive.

Once more minutes went by with no response. She rested her head back against the seat and closed her eyes. Brian was supposed to have been safe at the school. Who had gotten in and kidnapped him?

She rubbed her eyes and dug in her purse for a mint she'd picked up from a restaurant a month or so back. She bit into the chocolate and mint hoping it would silence her grumbling stomach for a little while.

The question of how Brian had been taken from the school prompted her to call. They seemed surprised to hear from her since apparently she had authorized Brian to leave with his uncle.

Evie ended the call and held back a scream of frustration. She didn't want to do this alone. She wasn't prepared to go up against whoever this was. And she suspected she knew exactly who it was—another Druid.

She'd never been so scared. To make matters worse,

she had pulled Brian into her nightmare because she was too damn curious—a fault her father had often said would get her into trouble.

If Brian died because of her recklessness, she would never forgive herself. Evie wiped at a tear that escaped and wished for the hundredth time that Malcolm were with her. He'd know what to do.

By the time the train arrived in Inverness, she had a full-on stress headache that was making the base of her neck feel as if a jackhammer was pounding. She looked left then right as she stepped off the train and proceeded down the walkway.

She was steps away from the door when someone bumped into her shoulder, sending her spinning around. Evie was instantly on guard. Without her even realizing it, she called forth her magic, prepared to use it.

"Pardon me," a teenage girl said as she rushed to the train.

Evie squeezed the bridge of her nose with her thumb and forefinger. She had to calm down or there was no telling who she might hurt.

Her mobile chimed, announcing she had a new text. She let out a relieved breath when she saw a video was attached to the blank text.

As soon as she pressed play and watched her brother look into the phone and give a nod of his head, the tears started all over again. She wished his hands weren't tied behind his back so he might be able to tell her who it was that kidnapped him.

She wiped at her eyes and sniffed as she sat on the bench beneath the streetlamp and darkening sky and waited for the bus to Ullapool. Instead of thinking about what she was going to find at the secret standing stones, she watched the video again.

After a quarter of an hour, she discovered she'd missed the bus by watching the video of Brian for the tenth time and would have to either wait or walk.

The longer she sat and waited, the more her mind pulled her in a million different directions. She had to *do* something. The only thing she could do was find the stone circle. What she would do once she was there, however, she would decide later.

Evie touched the necklace beneath her sweater and gathered her magic close. She closed her eyes and listened. All around her the stones spoke, but she was searching for a stone circle northwest of Inverness that Druids had gone to for centuries to increase their power by becoming *droughs*.

She ignored the rocks closest to her that urged her to come to them and concentrated on the ones in the direction of Ullapool. Then she heard a loud, deep call filled with magic that rang above the rest of the stones.

"The stone circle," she whispered and opened her eyes.

Evie started walking.

Malcolm sunk his claws into the building's brick in an effort to stay where he was and not go to the Druid and kiss her senseless. The feel of her magic brushing over him with a soft, seductive lover's touch was driving him mad with need and yearning. It was made worse because he knew what she felt like in his arms, knew the taste of her kiss, knew the sound of her cries of pleasure.

His cock was hard and aching to be inside her. How he wished he had taken her offer back in Cairn Toul. But would once with her be enough?

Would he be able to stop at having her just one time?

The Druid was indescribably exquisite, her magic hauntingly divine.

Her touch compellingly, evocatively poignant.

He wanted her with a fierceness that should startle him, but it only made him more resilient to everything else. She was a guiding light in his soulless life.

And he wasn't going to leave her again.

He looked around the corner and saw her walking away from the station. Malcolm ground his teeth together and started to follow when he felt the air stir around him.

When he turned it was to find Guy watching him. The Dragon King had his arms crossed over his chest and a shoulder leaning against the building. The light of the lamppost behind him cast him in shadows. Not that it hindered Malcolm's ability to see the grin on his face.

"A woman, aye?" Guy said.

"Sod off."

Guy tsked. "And testy as well. No' a good sign, Warrior. Surely you've had a taste of her lips by now."

Malcolm blew out a harsh breath before he asked, "What do you want?"

"Do I need to want something to talk?"

"Aye."

"That's where your problems begin, mate," Guy said as he pushed away from the building and dropped his arms to his sides. "You need to learn to have a conversation."

"I'm busy. Get on with what you need from me."

The smile from Guy's face dropped. "I doona need anything. I saw you and stopped. Elena and I came for a night out."

Malcolm frowned and turned his face away. The Dragons were annoying, but he'd never felt such anger toward any of them before. It wasn't a good sign if he was ready to pounce on Guy just for stopping him from following the Druid.

"Something has definitely changed."

"Always stating the obvious," Malcolm said, then cringed as he heard the sarcasm in his own voice. He looked back at Guy. "Something *has* changed. I feel . . . *everything*. Every single emotion. I can no' get them under control."

"The Druid did this to you?" Guy asked, a frown marring his forehead.

Malcolm shook his head. "Nay. Or if she did, it wasna on purpose."

"Who is she?"

It was Guy's interest that brought up Malcolm's protective instincts. "She's mine to deal with. Are we clear?"

"Crystal." Guy observed him for a moment. "You shouldna be going through this alone."

Malcolm understood in that instant that Guy knew everything about his past. The Dragon Kings made it their business to know the goings-on with those at MacLeod Castle. They hadn't interfered or made themselves known until recently, however.

"I'm better alone."

Guy lifted a light brown brow. "No one is better alone. If you willna allow your friends, or me, to help, then go to the Druid. At least with her, you willna be by yourself."

"And if she is doing this to me?"

"I've no doubt she is the cause of this, but no' in the way you think." With that, Guy turned on his heel and walked to an Aston Martin DB9 in a beautiful reddish-bronze parked on the side of the street.

Malcolm waited for Guy to climb inside and drive away before he turned back to where the Druid had been. Malcolm started following her immediately.

He stayed far enough behind so that she didn't see him while in the midst of the city. But once Inverness fell behind and she started across the bridge, Malcolm decided to scale his way under the bridge rather than have her see him.

When she was safely across and several hundred yards

ahead of him, Malcolm emerged from beneath the bridge and continued to follow her.

Her steps were quick and purposeful. Her shoulders were back, but her face was lined with worry. He knew just how frightened she'd been when she told him she had to stay in Cairn Toul.

Malcolm flattened himself on the ground when the Druid suddenly stopped and turned to look behind her. The headlights from the cars flashed over him, but her gaze wasn't on the ground, so she never saw him.

A few minutes later, she turned around and continued on. Malcolm jumped to his feet, ready to confront her when the Druid turned from the road and started walking through a field occupied by cattle.

For the next forty minutes, she walked across pastures, climbed over fences, and ran through private property. Through it all, Malcolm stayed close to her, ready to spring into action should something dare to harm her.

He was so intent on the Druid, it took him a moment to feel the magic. It was starkly ancient, utterly dominant. And ferociously potent.

The fact the Druid was heading straight to it put him instantly on alert. Not because there was a place of magic, but because there was a place of magic that he hadn't known existed.

He wasn't the only one who felt its existence. The Druid paused for a moment before she took off at a jog up the hill. He watched as she reached the top and came to a halt.

Malcolm closed his eyes as he felt the excitement in her magic. Was this what she had been searching for? Was this place what had drawn her out of the mountain?

As soon as he sensed her magic moving away, his eyes snapped open and he hurried to the top of the hill. He reached the crest when he spotted her halfway down the other side.

That was when Malcolm saw the stone circle. There were twelve megaliths in a perfect circle in the middle of the field. It was as if time hadn't touched the area.

The valley pulsed with ancient magic that seemed to draw the Druid like a moth to a flame. She stood outside of the circle, her head leaning one way and then the other.

With the clouds hiding the moon and the valley bathed in darkness, Malcolm knew it was the magic the Druid had been lured to.

Any Druid knew the standing stones were for them. They had been constructed eons ago by Druids to use in rituals and to help grow their magic.

Malcolm had been around many standing stones, but this was the only one that gave him pause. Enough that in two leaps down the hill he landed softly behind the Druid.

He straightened and touched her arm. There was a soft gasp before she turned around and sent a blast of magic at him. Malcolm ducked the blast, but the edge of it caught him, sending him flipping through the air.

With a growl, he landed on his feet and stalked back to the Druid. "Enough."

"Malcolm?" she asked, her hands raised and ready to send another blast at him.

"Aye."

She sighed and dropped her hands so they smacked her legs. "Did it ever occur to you that it's pitch black out here and I can't see?"

"I know."

"Well, that's nice. Now go away."

"Nay."

Her lips flatted in anger. "Please."

"No' happening, Druid."

"What do you want then?" she asked as her voice pitched higher.

He glanced at the huge standing stone next to her. "I'm no' certain you should be here."

"It's you who shouldn't be here. I thought you left. When I . . ." She trailed off and cleared her throat. "Go away."

He wanted to push her to finish the sentence. There was something wrong. He could see it in the way she held herself so rigidly, but he could also hear it in her voice. But he knew how stubborn she could be. No amount of pushing would get her to reveal anything now. He'd have to wait until later.

"I'm no' going. It's dark and late, Druid. If you persist, I'll walk away until you can no' see me, but I'll remain."

"Ugh," she said and rolled her eyes. "Why do you have to be so bloody difficult?"

Suddenly he felt like smiling. Smiling! What was wrong with him?

Instead, Malcolm focused on the woman. He noticed the way she kept shifting from one foot to the other. Her tall boots might look good, but they weren't made for the kind of walking she'd done.

"You need to rest."

The fact she didn't respond told him how exhausted she was. "Just . . . go away."

"Go away?" After she'd tried so hard to get him to talk while at Cairn Toul? "No' likely."

"I didn't realize it would take me so long to get here."

He gently tugged on one curl that fell over her shoulder and lay along her breast. It was all he allowed himself, because if he touched her, if he gave in to the driving need, he would take her right there. "Why did you come here?"

"I had to." She shoved the curl out of her face. "You wouldn't understand."

Malcolm looked around for a place he could set her up for the night when he spotted the house on the next hill. "Stay here. I'll be back."

"Yeah. Sure. Leave again," she said sarcastically as he ran toward the house.

Malcolm stopped and slowly turned to the Druid. She let out a long sigh and pressed her forehead against one of the stones. There was a look of defeat about her that made him want to hurt whoever had done that to her.

That was when he realized that someone could very well be him.

CHAPTER
TWENTY-TWO

MacLeod Castle

Britt straightened from the microscope and looked at her latest test. She'd checked the results a dozen times, and they all said the same thing—that she'd done it.

Over the table, Aiden met her gaze. A moment later his deep green eyes widened as he slid off his stool and walked to her.

"Baby?" he asked.

She glanced around the room to see the Druids who had remained were asleep while their husbands read, listened to their iPods, or sat with their eyes closed. She wasn't deceived however. The Warriors didn't have to sleep, and most likely weren't deep in dreamland, not when what she worked on was so important.

Britt swallowed and swiveled her stool so that she faced Aiden. "I found it."

The man who had stolen her heart, only to give her his own, slowly smiled. "I never had any doubt."

"I did. Heaps of it," she said with an exhausted bark of laughter.

There was a creak as Ramsey rose from the sofa. "You found what you needed to help Larena?"

"She did," Aiden said and pulled Britt into his arms.

Britt gave in to the precious few moments with Aiden. Her back ached, her head felt like mush, and her limbs seemed to be weighted down with Mack trucks, but she still had lots of work to do.

She pulled out of Aiden's strong arms, liking how he kept one arm around her waist. "I've tested it several times. It should work."

"Your other serum worked," Arran said as he pulled his headphones off his ears and turned off his iPod. "This should as well."

Britt was staggered by their confidence. "Well, only testing it will tell."

"I'll get Fallon," Logan said as he headed toward the door.

A few minutes later Fallon's form filled the doorway followed closely by his brothers, Lucan and Quinn. "Did you do it?" Fallon asked expectantly.

The hope shining in his green eyes so similar to Aiden's made her heart ache. "I believe so."

"What are we waiting on then?" Quinn demanded, the lines of worry bracketing his mouth.

Britt licked her lips as she looked from Quinn to Aiden to Fallon. "I'd like to test it on someone before Larena. I don't want to get her hopes up, and then have it not work."

Lucan grunted from his place at the door. "I agree. The best one would be Malcolm, but he willna come willingly."

"Then we bring him," Aiden said.

Ramsey shook his head, his silver eyes pinning Fallon. "Forcing Malcolm here willna solve anything. It could only make things worse with him."

"This is for my wife!" Fallon bellowed. "I'll no' stand by and watch her suffer another minute if I doona have to."

"There's always Charon," Arran added.

When Fallon didn't immediately call Charon, Lucan dialed the Warrior's number himself. A few words later, Lucan ended the call and looked to Fallon. "Charon is waiting."

While the men had been talking, the women had awoken. It was Gwynn who rose and walked to Fallon. "The sooner you go, the sooner you can return to Larena."

That seemed to snap Fallon out of his indignation. He gave a nod, which was all Britt needed to gather her stuff. In the next instant, Fallon disappeared.

Before she could fill the syringe with 50cc of the serum, Fallon returned with Charon. Britt met the brown eyes of the Warrior before she slid off her stool and walked to him.

The entire room seemed to collectively hold its breath when she rubbed a cotton ball soaked with alcohol over his bicep.

"You needn't do that," he said in his deep voice.

Britt shrugged, anxiety making her stomach turn into a ball of knots. "Habit. Ready?"

"Aye, lass."

She took a deep breath and briefly met Aiden's gaze before she pressed the end of the needle into Charon's arm and pushed the syringe, releasing the serum into his bloodstream.

When it was emptied, she pulled the syringe out and capped the needle. "The pain from the wound is still plaguing you?"

He gave a slight nod. "There are times it feels as if the blade is still inside me."

Britt set aside the used needle and nervously popped her knuckles. Minutes ticked by. She straightened papers on the table and moved glass bottles from one angle to another. She found all her pencils and stacked them in a pile. Then she turned vials so that all the labels were facing in the same direction.

"This could take days," she said as she braced her hands on the edge of the table.

"Or no'," Charon said.

Britt's head jerked up as she turned to him. "What?"

"I doona feel the pain as I used to. Whatever you did is working."

She frowned while the others were patting her on the back. "But you still feel some of the pain? It's not all gone?"

"No' yet. Give it time, lass. You figured it out." Charon turned to Fallon. "As much as I'd like to stay and see how Larena fares, I need to return to Laura."

"Be ready," Fallon told Britt before he placed his hand on Charon's shoulder and teleported away.

Britt woodenly turned and reached for another syringe. "Maybe I should give Larena more."

"You can always give her a second dose," Aiden said near her ear. "Trust yourself."

Britt looked over Aiden's shoulder to find Fallon had already returned. He stood waiting, his face lined with apprehension and fatigue, when she grabbed a new syringe. Without a word, she followed the eldest MacLeod out of her tower and down the stairs to the master chamber.

No one had been allowed into the room other than Fallon since Larena locked herself in. Everything looked as if the room had never been used, which seemed odd for a couple who hadn't left it in weeks.

Behind Britt, Aiden squeezed her hand. She looked over her shoulder at him to find Lucan and Cara and Quinn and Marcail in the doorway. The others remained behind to await the news.

"Britt," Larena's voice came from a darkened corner of the chamber.

There was a clicking noise as Larena reached over and

turned on the lamp next to her. Golden light reached her, and Britt was surprised to see what toll had been taken on Larena's body as she fought against Wallace's *drough* blood.

"I look terrible, I know," Larena said and tried to smile. "Fallon keeps telling me I look the same, but I've caught a look at myself in the mirror a time or two."

Britt smiled while Fallon walked around the back of the chair and placed his hands on Larena's shoulders before leaning down to kiss her head.

"I've found the antidote," Britt said. "I've tested it on Charon, but it might take several doses for you."

"You've pushed yourself too hard," Larena said. "I think the dark circles under your eyes are almost as bad as mine."

Britt found herself laughing. Larena was trying hard not to let the melancholy get to her. "I admit, I'm eager for about a week of sleep."

"Sleep?" Aiden said with a snort. "There willna be sleeping, love."

With the mood less stilted, Britt walked to the female Warrior. Larena's golden hair was dull and limp, her smoky blue eyes muted.

Larena pushed up the sleeve of her white shirt and looked at the floor while Britt rubbed the alcohol on her arm before giving her the antidote.

When Britt was finished, she stood and walked back to Aiden. "I think we should leave and give them some privacy. I'll have another syringe ready and waiting just in case."

"I agree," Quinn said and ushered everyone out.

Just before the door closed, Britt saw Fallon lift Larena into his arms and carry her to the bed. Britt hastily blinked the tears that gathered. She wasn't a crier, but there was something about that scene that pulled at her heart like nothing before.

"You did good," Marcail said.

Britt licked her lips while Marcail rubbed a hand up and down her back. "We shall see."

"You've done what no one else could," Cara said. "Not even with magic."

Lucan gave her a wide smile. "Exactly. We'll stay near in case Fallon or Larena needs you. Until then, Aiden, take your woman somewhere she can rest."

Britt wanted to protest being treated like an object, but she knew Lucan didn't mean anything Neanderthal about it. It was just a Highlander's way, a way she'd come to like quite a lot.

Aiden didn't give her time to say anything as he steered her down a flight a stairs to their room. He sat her on the bed and removed her shoes and socks. Then he gave her a slight push to her shoulders to lay her back on the bed and covered her with a blanket.

Britt's eyes slid closed on their own. She briefly heard Aiden say something about food, but before she could respond, sleep claimed her.

Larena knew how much Fallon was counting on Britt's antidote to make things better, but she feared the *drough* blood had done too much damage and she would never be the same person she'd been.

She didn't have the heart to tell him that however. She also didn't press him about Malcolm. It all became clear how much Malcolm had suffered—how he was suffering still.

There was an emptiness inside her she imagined was the same for her cousin. The difference between her and Malcolm was the way her goddess was trying to take control.

"Stop thinking about it," Fallon said.

She snuggled against him. He always had an uncanny

way of knowing exactly what she was thinking. "You know you're the only reason I've not given in to Lelomai. If you hadn't been with me, I would've granted her control long ago."

"Had you no' been with me, you wouldna be in this predicament."

Larena lifted her head to look at her husband. "Don't you dare do that. This isn't your fault, Fallon MacLeod. What happened to me could've happened to any of us. I'm lucky enough to have you by my side to help in all of it."

"It's a fact I doona like feeling so damned helpless. I can only sit and watch you bear something I can no' even begin to imagine."

A teasing comment sprang to mind. As Larena opened her mouth to say it, she stopped, surprise making her body jerk.

"What is it?" Fallon asked, concern filling his green eyes.

For several seconds she could only stare at her husband, the words locked in her throat. Finally she ran her fingers through his dark hair and said, "It's working."

She laughed as she cried. Fallon smiled, his own eyes filling with tears as he kissed her. Larena parted her lips and welcomed his kisses. The voice of her goddess lessened, and it no longer felt as if she was being crushed by the weight of the world.

It was Fallon who pulled back, his breathing ragged and his eyes dilated. "Has the antidote worked completely?"

"I feel as if I've just come into the rays of the sun after a lengthy illness. As Britt said, I may need more than one dose."

"But it's working."

Larena nodded, then laughed when Fallon leaped from the bed and threw open their door.

"It's working!" he shouted from their doorway.

Cara and Marcail rushed past Fallon who tried to keep them out, but Lucan and Quinn diverted his attention. The Druids climbed on the bed, both women talking at once. Larena looked to Fallon to find him staring at her while listening to his brothers.

They shared a secret smile.

Larena, having stayed in the chamber for too long, rose from the bed and walked through the door onto the balcony. She looked over her shoulder at Fallon and held out her hand.

He didn't say a word to his brothers as he strode to her. Together, hand in hand, they leapt from their balcony onto the cliffs below.

"Well," Lucan said as he looked at the now empty balcony. "I'd say they want some time alone."

"I think they have a great idea," Quinn said as he took Marcail's hand and pulled her out of the room.

Cara laughed and rose from the bed to walk to her husband. "You're not going to take my hand?"

"I rather thought you might want to take the lead this time," he said with a teasing light in his green eyes.

"Oh. I like that. Tara gave me a pair of fuzzy handcuffs. I think we should try those tonight."

Lucan groaned as desire shot through him. "Lead the way, wife. I'm all yours."

CHAPTER
TWENTY-THREE

Malcolm watched from behind the rose bushes at the back of the house. He spotted the man and woman through the window. The woman was rushing through the lower floor calling out names as she did. There was an answering shout from the second floor, and then a teenage girl with short, spiky red hair came bounding down the stairs with a bag over her shoulder.

When the man came outside, Malcolm's attention was diverted to him as he opened the back of the SUV and began stuffing luggage in.

"We're going to be late!" he shouted.

The woman called out names again as she grabbed her purse and ran through the kitchen door outside. Malcolm watched two younger boys with identical ginger hair and freckles pushing each other as each tried to reach the bottom first.

"Hurry, you two!" the mother shouted.

The boys tossed their bags at the father and fought to get in the SUV first. The man slammed the back hatch closed before he closed the house door.

"We're never going to make the flight," he mumbled as

he walked past Malcolm to get in the SUV. "Twenty-five hours on a plane. To see my in-laws. In Australia. Bloody hell."

He didn't try to hide his groan from his wife as he got in the vehicle and drove away.

Malcolm watched their fading taillights. When he was sure they wouldn't return, he came out from behind the roses and ran back to the Druid.

He found her just as he'd left her, though she now had both hands flat against the stones. Her eyes were closed and her head turned so that one ear was close to the megalith.

"What are they saying?"

She jumped, her eyes flying open. "I thought you left."

"Nay."

"Where did you go?"

"To find a place for you to get out of the weather."

She glanced at the sky. "They're only clouds. We have them all the time. Besides, the storm is past."

"There's another coming. I can smell it in the air."

She rolled her eyes in response.

"You doona believe me." He shouldn't have been surprised by the revelation, but he was. And hurt as well. He hadn't lied to her once.

The Druid faced him, her gaze narrowed. "It's pitch black out here. How can you see me?"

"I'm a Warrior."

Evie bit back a sigh. Malcolm could be so frustrating at times. She wished she could see his face, but all she could make out was his silhouette somewhat. "That doesn't explain everything."

"The god inside me . . . enhances my senses."

"All of them?"

"All of them."

She took that in. "Just how well can you see in the dark?"

"As well as in the light."

Evie let out a low whistle. "Impressive. So now that you have an unfair advantage and can see me, why are you still here?"

There was a long pause as if he were debating what to say. Finally, he said, "I felt the terror in your magic. I returned to Cairn Toul to find you gone."

"I see." Evie wanted to sit. Her legs hurt, but it didn't come close to the pain in her feet. She'd thought the boots would be decent to walk in. And maybe for a day meandering around a city they would, but certainly not hiking all over Scotland.

"We'll talk about this later. You're about to collapse."

"I'm not," she said defensively, even though he was right.

A shot of something electric and needful raced through her when his hand wrapped around her wrist. His touch was firm without hurting. By the way he tugged her to follow him, she knew there would be no getting away.

Not that she wanted to get away. Malcolm was with her once more. The strength he carried and displayed was within reach, and she wanted to lay her head upon those wide shoulders of his and let her burdens fall away.

His warm hand didn't just give her a measure of calm, it reminded her of how skillful those hands had been on her body, how easily he had brought her to orgasm.

Evie winced when she stumbled over an indentation in the earth. She righted herself only to feel Malcolm's hard body against hers as he lifted her in his arms.

She could feel his eyes on her, and she wished she could see him. Was there any emotion on his face or in his azure eyes now? Was that lock of blond hair in his eyes once more? How she wished she could see him and get the answers to her questions.

"I can walk," she said around the need being so close to him caused.

He made a sound at the back of his throat that she wasn't sure meant that he agreed or not. Evie decided it was easier not to talk.

His warmth soaked through her jacket and sweater into her aching muscles. As she relaxed in his strong arms, she recalled why she was out in the middle of nowhere. It was thoughts of Brian that made the backs of her eyes prick with tears again.

"I'm going to need a car," she said.

"It'd be better than you walking Scotland. I'll find one."

She frowned. "You don't want to know why?"

Evie felt him shrug when he lifted his shoulders. "My concern is for your safety."

Evie looked back in the direction of the stones. She wanted to see them. They were calling to her. Not just the stones—but their magic. The answer to keeping the necklace and having Brian returned was in the center of those stones if she dared to take the answer.

If she did, she would be the only one to pay the price for her stupidity. If she didn't, Brian could be hurt, or worse, thousands of innocents. Neither of which she could live with.

She didn't want to give up her soul, but it seemed only fair that she be the one to pay the price for her screw up.

"Take me back to the stone circle."

"No' now. You need to rest. Whatever you want with it can wait."

"Actually, it can't."

Malcolm stopped walking. She could feel his gaze on her. Evie could well imagine his blue eyes intent and fierce as they stared at her. She had seen desire in them once.

In that instant she decided Malcolm couldn't know of her plans to become *drough*. He hated them, and he would try and stop her.

"Explain," he demanded.

Evie blew out a breath. "Someone has kidnapped my brother."

"And you think the answer to your problem is in the circle?"

"Yes."

"This is what sent you racing from Cairn Toul?"

She nodded and fiddled with her purse strap. "It is."

"You doona want my help?"

Evie squeezed her eyes shut. The hurt she heard in his voice was nearly her undoing. "I didn't say that."

There was no response as he began walking again. Evie opened her eyes when a light appeared from over the top of the rise. A few steps later and she spotted the house. It was a decent sized house made of brown stone and brick. The back of the house had a large sunroom that over-looked the stones.

"Whose house is this?" she asked when he set her down by the back door, light flooding them from the lamp above.

"They've gone on an extended trip. You'll be safe here tonight."

"And where will you be?"

She wished she could have hidden the desperation in her voice, but she was barely hanging on to her sanity. Malcolm's strength gave her strength whether he knew it or not.

He asked how he could help, and he'd been doing it without even knowing.

Evie looked up into Malcolm's face to find him watching

her. His eyes were in shadows, and his face once more unreadable. His hands, however, were still touching her. Warmth spread through her, settling low in her belly as desire flared and spread.

"I shouldna have left you," he said slowly. "You'd be better with someone else watching over you."

"You're here now. Don't leave. Please." She wouldn't make it if she had to do it alone.

His hands fell away from her. "I willna."

He turned away to open the door. Evie stepped inside to find a homey kitchen that reminded her of her grandmother's. There was an old iron stove and a beautiful tea set visible in a glass cabinet.

Rows of plates sat in their places in a rack next to the sink while pots hung on hooks near the stove. On the far side of the kitchen was a fireplace and next to it a round table and five chairs.

Evie sank onto a chair and pulled off her boots. She rose and started for the stove to make some tea when she spotted Malcolm rummaging in the fridge.

By the time she had the kettle on, Malcolm had set out a tray of cold chicken, several blocks of cheese, and a loaf of bread. He cut up the chicken and cheese as she found two cups and poured them tea.

They ate in silence, their fingers touching occasionally. Each time a little shock went through her, making her want to touch him more. Malcolm made sure her plate was never empty. Evie was caught off guard by his chivalry. She tried to catch his gaze to thank him, but he refused to look at her.

He offered her the last piece of chicken, which she declined. "I'm stuffed."

Evie reached for the now empty plate only to have Malcolm's large hand graze hers again. She shivered at the way her blood heated and her heart pounded whenever they touched.

She must be the only one who felt it though, because he rose and began cleaning the kitchen without so much as a look in her direction. Evie stood and wandered the house looking at pictures of the family while trying to tamp down the desire.

It seemed odd to be in someone's house, but she was out of the chilly weather. She glanced out the window to see rain running down the glass.

So Malcolm had been right. There was another storm. Evie was glad not to be in it, but the longer she held off gaining black magic, the longer Brian was in danger.

She pulled out her phone from her pocket and checked the texts. The kidnappers still hadn't told her when they were supposed to meet. She started to demand her brother back right then, but she paused, her fingers over the keys.

If she went for Brian now, then she'd lose the necklace, and most likely Brian. The odds of getting her brother back were slim. She understood that, which was why she had to have more magic. The kidnappers would never see what she had in store for them.

She watched the video of Brian again, afraid of texting the kidnappers and them harming her brother. Her throat tightened when she saw the frightened look in Brian's eyes. He was trying to tell her something, but the brief view she had of his face wasn't enough to give her anything.

Her phone vibrated in her hand, making her jump. Evie looked down to find a text from the kidnappers demanding to meet at Urquhart Castle the next day at noon.

She had only a little while until she'd get Brian back. Only a short time to gain a tremendous amount of magic and learn how to use it.

Evie looked out the window again. The rain was coming down hard. It wasn't the weather that kept her inside, but Malcolm. She didn't want him to see what she was going to do. J had said the stone circle was a private place for Druids only.

But it was more than that. There was a chance Malcolm would kill her. His hatred of *droughs* ran that deep.

She would wait until Malcolm was asleep, and then she would sneak out and do the ceremony. With her decision made, Evie continued her exploration of the house.

The house had three bedrooms and two baths. Evie couldn't resist the master bathroom when she walked in and saw the large shower. She stripped and turned on the water.

Just before she stepped in, she looked at the door wondering what Malcolm was doing and if he would stay as he'd promised.

She thought of her brother and the people who had dared to kidnap him. Evie sent up a prayer that Brian was being treated fairly, and that somehow both of them would come out of everything alive.

Evie removed her necklace and held the pendant in front of her. The knotwork etched into the silver cross was breathtaking, harking back to a different time. She vividly remembered tracing the knotwork while her grandmother had worn the necklace.

It had been given to her for safekeeping because she was a Druid. And because of her stupidity and foolishness, Brian was in danger and the necklace was being sought.

"I'm so sorry, Grandmum. I made you a promise to keep the pendant safe, and I've not done that. I've really made a muck of things."

But she was going to straighten it out.

If she did lose the pendant, she'd get it back. No matter

how long it took or what she had to do, she would wear it once more.

The sound of Malcolm's boot heels sounded on the wood floor as he walked the living room. An image of him in Warrior form flashed in her mind.

He was starkly beautiful, dangerously wild. Completely menacing.

And wonderfully, utterly male.

He stood solemnly against the world, boldly daring it to take him on, for anyone courageous enough to try. He defied the magical world he was part of and shunned the mortal one.

He was alone, a solitary Highlander who was as fierce and tempestuous as the land he belonged to. Fate dealt him cruel blow after blow, and still he remained standing, valiant and bold.

She closed her eyes as she stepped beneath the water. If only Malcolm was with her, if only he would give in to the need she saw glimpses of every now and then.

If only he wanted her as much as she wanted him.

CHAPTER
TWENTY-FOUR

Brian walked the length and breadth of his cell. He wanted to scream his exasperation, but it would do no good. No one could hear him.

He slammed his open palm against the metal bars holding him. Not even the pain of that could dampen his rage. The maniac who had taken him was going about his business as if he abducted people all the time.

And for all Brian knew, he did.

Brian got a glimpse of the wealth of the mansion when he was summarily ushered through the front door and then down into the dungeon.

The fact the man was all alone didn't go unnoticed by Brian. His kidnapper managed to convince everyone at the school that Brian had to go with him.

Then there was the issue that he'd subdued Brian without any effort.

Brian flexed his hand. He could bench 250 pounds. For two years after being ganged up on by a group of guys, he spent every spare minute of his time in the school's weight room.

No longer did anyone pick on him. He filled out his shirts with arms that were thick and strong instead of skinny and useless.

He regularly got into the ring at the village's boxing club, because there was only so much muscle could do unless someone knew how to wield their body into a weapon.

Brian had become that weapon. Or so he thought until he met his capture. The man had taken him easily. Too bloody easily.

"What would you be saying, I wonder," came a voice behind him.

Brian whirled around to find his abductor. The man was tall and thin. He had thin blond hair and cold, calculating blue eyes. His nose was hawkish, and his face too thin and angular. Not even the fit of his tailored suit could make him meagerly good-looking.

He sneered at the man and rushed the metal bars separating them. Brian wrapped his hands around two of the bars and bared his teeth.

"Doona worry, lad. Your sister will be along shortly. I've made sure of it, you see."

Brian felt sick to his stomach. Why did the man want Evie?

"Jason Wallace is the name," the man said. "I might have failed to give you my name earlier."

Brian narrowed his gaze and stilled. There was only one reason for a criminal to show his face or give his prisoner his name. And that was because he planned to kill Brian.

"Oh, no," Jason said as he shook his head. "I'm no' going to kill you, lad. There willna be a need once Evangeline arrives. You see, she's important to me. She's going to fulfill a prophecy that will unleash an evil this world has never seen."

Brian released the bars and took several steps away from Jason. He shook his head, not wanting to hear more—or believe any of it.

"It's true," Jason continued. "She's a Druid, lad. Did you know that? Your sister holds magic, and it's that magic that is going to help me. Right now she's a simple *mie*. But it willna be long now until she gives her soul to Satan and becomes *drough*."

Brian let out a sound as close to a scream as he could get. Evie was all that he had left in the world. He might give her hell sometimes, but he would do anything for her.

He also knew that she'd do whatever it took to get him freed. Brian dropped his chin to his chest and silently raged at his inability to do anything.

"How is it, Brian, that your sister has magic, but you doona?" Jason asked.

Brian fisted his hands and slowly raised his gaze to Jason. He let every ounce of hate and fury show through his eyes. When Jason chuckled, it only made his rage grow.

"You didna know your sister was a Druid."

Brian let the bastard think what he wanted. In truth, he knew all about Evie's magic. It was one secret that had been shared. He, however, had a secret of his own.

"It's too bad you doona have any magic," Jason said with a smirk. "I could turn you as well. I'm ever amazed at the bonds people share. It's those bonds that make them do whatever it is I want."

Jason came closer to the bars and peered at Brian. "Did you know there are monsters out there? There is one with your sister now. He's doing all sorts of things to her. By the time he's done, I wonder how much will be left."

Brian didn't want to believe him, but how could he not? He tuned out Jason and let his mind wander. Evie had always been independent and headstrong. She was also highly intelligent and rarely reckless.

If anyone could look out for themselves, Brian knew it was her.

He made himself relax and sit on the narrow cot that served as his bed. It had a thin mattress, a blanket, and a pillow. There was a pot in the corner for him to relieve himself. That was it in the square room he'd been confined to.

Nothing to use as a weapon, unless he wanted to throw piss at Jason.

Brian bit back a grin as he imagined Jason's outrage.

Suddenly Brian was slammed back against the stones that made up the back wall of the cell, his head banging hard. Something warm and wet trickled down the back of his neck.

"You're no' listening to me," Jason said through clenched teeth.

Brian blinked twice until his vision cleared and he saw Jason standing outside the cell. It hadn't taken much to rile him.

Pain throbbed in his head and neck, but Brian refused to let Jason know. He returned Jason's stare and simply waited.

"Ah. So no' like most lads your age, are you?" Jason smiled coolly and rubbed his chin with his thumb and forefinger. "I could make you my slave if I wanted."

Brian's blood turned cold at the thought. He had underestimated Jason. He couldn't—wouldn't—do that again. Now that he had a hint of how much magic Jason had, he'd be able to tell Evie.

He just had to make sure he was still in control of his own mind and body when Evie got there. Then she would be able to take Jason on and get them both out.

Malcolm walked into the master bedroom intent on looking through the man's closet for a shirt. When he heard the water from the shower, he stopped and stared at the door.

Just on the other side of a slim piece of wood was the Druid. Naked.

Water rushing over her skin, soap sliding seductively, slowly down her body. That long, lovely hair of hers wet and thick as she rinsed the shampoo out.

Breathing became difficult as all his blood rushed to his cock. Malcolm remembered the weight of her breast, recalled the feel of her slick walls as he pushed a finger inside her.

He didn't know how long he stood there thinking of the last time the Druid was in his arms, of how right it had felt, how absolutely wonderful. It could have been seconds or hours.

The door to the bathroom opened and the Druid emerged with a towel wrapped around her. Her skin was still dewy, her wet hair already beginning to curl as strands clung to her.

Malcolm knew he should leave. By being this close he tempted himself in ways he couldn't overcome. No matter what his brain told him to do, his body was in control. And he wanted to stay.

Clear blue eyes met his. Her lips parted, but no words were spoken. They stared at each other, locked in silence, passion and desire growing with each breath.

There were only six steps separating them. It would be so easy to close the distance and take her in his arms, and Malcolm knew how good she tasted, knew how incredible she felt in his arms.

He'd managed to walk away once. He wouldn't be able to do it again.

Her fist clutched the fluffy purple towel at her breasts. In another life Malcolm would have charmed his way into the Druid's bed. But he no longer knew how to be charming or anything else.

For years, he simply existed. Now, emotions he didn't want ruled him every second. And, right then, it was desire and need that had a firm hold of him.

Malcolm swallowed thickly when the Druid took a step toward him, the towel parting to reveal a long, shapely leg. With each step the towel drifted open more, until he caught a glimpse of her bare hip.

His heart pounded in his chest as if he'd run a thousand miles. Malcolm lifted his gaze to her face and inwardly groaned. He hungered for her—with a desperation that made him want to toss her on the bed and take her right then.

"Leave," he told her.

The Druid shook her head before her slender arm reached up and her fingers ran through her hair. Large, wet curls a deep, rich brown fell about her face and shoulders.

Her allure was palpable.

Her seduction irresistible.

Malcolm feared what he would do to her if he took her. It had been too long since his body had had release. And he was a beast. He could hurt her.

"Leave," he urged again.

The corners of her lips lifted. And then she released her hold on the towel.

All the breath left Malcolm as the towel landed with a soft *whoosh* around her feet. His gaze raked over her body leisurely, noting her small but full breasts and her dark, dusky nipples.

His gaze lowered to her waist, down her navel to her flared hips. And then down to the triangle of dark curls. He got his first look at her lean legs and couldn't wait to have them wrapped around his waist.

"You doona know what you're doing teasing me like this, Druid." He didn't recognize the rough voice coming from his body, but then again, he'd never felt such aching, insistent desire before.

"Touch me," she urged.

He had to make her understand that she needed someone else. Not him, not the fiend that he was. His hunger was too strong, his yearning too intense to attempt to restrain.

"Doona tease me."

"I'm not. I'm offering myself to you."

The last shred of Malcolm's control snapped. In the next heartbeat he had her on the bed, his body covering hers as he took her mouth in a kiss meant to claim.

A kiss meant to possess.

CHAPTER
TWENTY-FIVE

The feel of Malcolm on top of her froze Evie's lungs. His heat, his weight spurred her passion into a frenzy. He was solid, firm.

Powerful and fierce.

And it made her burn.

Evie sighed into his kisses. His mouth seized, captured. His hands caressed, stroked.

Everywhere he touched he seared her skin, raising her desire to new heights each time.

She plunged her hands into his silky locks and delighted in the feel of the golden strands through her fingers. A moan tore from her throat when his hand cupped her breast and squeezed.

Her nipples hardened and her breasts swelled. She clutched at the thick sinew on his shoulders. Her back arched when he pinched her nipple, sending a flood of wetness between her legs.

She lifted her hips to grind against him. A deep, guttural groan rumbled from his chest. His lips left hers to travel down her neck before clamping over her aching nipple.

His tongue flicked back and forth over the tiny nub, shooting pleasure through her body. Evie's body went taut, the desire beginning to tighten low in her stomach.

He moved from one breast to the other, teasing her, arousing her until her body quivered. Only then did he kiss down her stomach to settle between her legs.

A cry of pleasure tore from her at the first touch of his tongue on her sex. He licked, he laved, he teased. Each flick of his tongue ignited a yearning that consumed her.

The pleasure was too formidable, too intense. She tried to hold her body back, but Malcolm refused to allow it. He demanded all of her.

And she was powerless to deny him.

The climax struck without warning, the power transporting her. She screamed his name as the rush of pleasure claimed her. He continued to lick her, prolonging her orgasm until she was thrashing her head from side to side and begging him to stop or continue. She wasn't sure which.

When he rose up over her, Evie reached for him, needing to feel his muscles and heat beneath her palms. Malcolm's azure eyes clashed with hers, desire blazing in his blue depths. Her heart missed a beat at the pure, unadulterated longing she saw there.

Her hands grasped the waist of his jeans and unbuttoned them. In a matter of seconds he discarded his clothes and loomed over her.

The light coming from the bathroom bathed him in a soft glow. Evie ran her hands up his arms and over his shoulders. The raised skin of his scars didn't diminish her desire or take away from the perfection that was Malcolm.

Suddenly, he grabbed her wrists in one hand and pulled them over her head. She caught sight of his arousal and all the moisture of her body pooled between her legs.

He held her arms securely, but gently. The savage look in his eyes told her he had lost himself in his need. It made her flesh sizzle with anticipation, excitement.

She didn't want soft and gentle. She wanted hard and quick. She wanted all that was Malcolm, all that he had to give.

Her breath came faster and faster when she saw his eyes flicker from azure to maroon several times. It wasn't fear that took her but . . . delight.

"Don't you dare stop," she whispered.

"Too much," he rasped.

Evie wrapped her legs around his hips and tugged him closer until the thick, blunt head of his arousal met her entrance. A muscle ticked in his jaw and his body began to shake.

When she couldn't pull him closer, she lifted her hips until the tip of him entered her.

The moan that was pulled from him made her heart skip a beat. It was as if whatever had been holding him back snapped. He gave one hard thrust and filled her.

Her body jerked at the feel of his length filling her, stretching her. Several seconds ticked by as he remained still. Evie had never been so aroused, never been so close to orgasm after having one just a few minutes earlier.

But there was something about Malcolm that affected her as no other man could.

She tried to move, but he gripped her hip with his free hand. His lips were pinched as he struggled to hold back. Just the opposite of what she wanted.

"Please," she begged, needing the release that was building again. "Don't hold back. I need this. I need you."

His eyes scorched her with his desire. He pulled out of her and began to move. With his face inches from hers, she couldn't look away, couldn't do anything but feel the incredible sensations each stroke of his cock gave her.

His hips jerked as he drove into her relentlessly, merci-lessly. Her body silently reached for him, yearning for more, craving him.

Her heart pounded in her ears. Her blood was molten heat.

Her entire universe revolved around the mysterious, gorgeous man who was taking her body to places she hadn't known existed.

She yearned to touch him, but he had control of her. And there would be no escape from him. Not now.

Not ever.

The desire tightened and twisted until she couldn't take it anymore. Each thrust sent her spiraling toward bliss, and just when she thought she could give in, Malcolm would push her further.

"No' yet," he growled.

Evie tried to yank her arms loose, but he held tight. She tried to twist her body away so she could wait as he demanded, but he refused to give her an inch.

"Malcolm!" she screamed. "I can't!"

He shifted her hips higher and drove into her deeper, harder. "No' yet," he demanded.

Evie tried to hold back the climax, but how could she when he felt so good? No matter what she did, her body was barreling toward release and there was nothing she could do to stop it.

"Now. Come for me, Druid," Malcolm whispered.

As if on cue, her body exploded in an orgasm so intense white lights flashed behind her eyes. His thrusts grew quick and shallow as he wrested every drop from her before he gave a shout and stilled.

The feel of him pulsating inside her sent Evie to yet an-other climax before the previous one ended. She opened her magic and let it wrap around them, holding them, en-veloping them in a cocoon of paradise.

For long moments they stayed as they were before she opened her eyes to find him gazing down at her with what looked like wonder.

With her body fully sated, Evie found herself relaxed and sleep pulling at her. She smiled as he released her hands and gently pulled out of her.

Her eyes closed on their own, and she could've sworn he ran a hand down her cheek. He said something in a language she didn't understand.

She told herself to remember to ask him when she woke.

Malcolm stared down at the Druid long after she went to sleep. He couldn't believe he'd given into his need. But more than that, he couldn't believe the Druid hadn't run.

Instead she had urged him on.

He had lost control and not harmed her, as he'd feared. It seemed too good to be true. He took one of her big curls and wrapped it around his finger.

He stroked the cool strand and contemplated the Druid. Foolishly, he'd thought he could forget her. He should've known better.

After one kiss, she'd gotten in his blood. Now, after having her, tasting her, she had somehow found what was left of his soul and claimed it.

Malcolm pulled the covers over her so she wouldn't get chilled before he lay back on the pillow. With one hand under his head, he kept the other with her curl around his finger.

It was dangerous for the Druid if he stayed. Yet he couldn't leave. He'd known it when he ran from her at Cairn Toul.

His chest tightened as he thought of the Druid's accusing eyes when he returned. She had every right to be angry with him. His vow to protect her had come in second as he worried for himself.

And it had cost him because something had happened to her. He wasn't sure if she'd ever tell him either. She didn't trust him now, if she ever had to begin with.

Trust. Did he even deserve it? She knew he had betrayed Deirdre, and according to Larena that was more than acceptable since Deirdre had been evil.

But what of Duncan? What of the rest of those at the castle? He'd betrayed each and every one of them when he killed Duncan.

Malcolm pushed away the memories that kept replaying in his mind—of Duncan joking with him, trying to make him laugh, of Duncan trying to get him to take his side against something he and Ian had been arguing over, of Duncan covering his plate when Galen tried to steal his food.

But the one that never left him was Duncan's furious gaze right before Malcolm killed him.

Shame and self-loathing consumed him. He didn't merit friends, he didn't warrant trust. And he certainly didn't deserve the pleasure given to him by the Druid.

He wanted to know her name. She'd been right. He should have asked for it. He'd wanted to keep her at a distance, and thought he could do that by not knowing her name.

Just another of his mistakes.

Malcolm knew the only reason he was still welcome at MacLeod Castle was Larena, and he'd treated her badly. *Family,* she'd said, *it's family no matter what.*

Was that the only reason she kept in touch with him? Malcolm hoped it wasn't. He needed Larena now, now that it was probably too late.

The fact he had no idea how Larena was faring in her battle against the *drough* blood didn't speak well of him. There was no excuse for him turning his back on her.

Malcolm hated himself even more. He should call Larena, but then he didn't know what to say. The others didn't need to know of the Druid. They would want to know where he was and what he was doing. He didn't want to lie to them anymore. It was better if he held off talking to them.

He turned his head on the pillow to look at the Druid. But for how long could he hold off? He'd done the worst job imaginable in gaining the Druid's trust, and he doubted she would tell him anything for months to come.

And what if the others called for him to battle Wallace again?

Malcolm was eager for another try at the bastard but leaving the Druid wasn't an option after what had happened last time. Nor could he bring her with him.

The Druid turned on her side, facing him, as one of her hands came to rest on his chest. Malcolm stilled, afraid to move for fear that she would stop touching him.

Slowly, he pulled his arm from behind his head and gently placed his hand atop her small one. Her chest rose and fell evenly as she slept the sleep of the innocent.

"You'd have been better off with one of the other Warriors. I'm no' good for you," he whispered.

They were words he'd never be able to say if she were awake, but they needed to be said. She was a good person who was now tainted because of him.

"I'm no' good for anyone."

Not for the first time he thought of asking one of the Dragon Kings to take his head. Larena and Fallon would no longer have to worry about him. And perhaps his death might make up for some of the atrocities he'd committed in Deirdre's name.

He had so much to make up for, so much to answer for. How he wished he could go back to feeling nothing, because the constant emotions were sending him an ever-changing landscape that he never quite got his footing on.

Malcolm closed his eyes and tried to find some semblance of quiet in his mind. He wanted just a few minutes in order to get his equilibrium back.

He was going to need all the help he could get regarding the Druid. Once she woke, he had some explaining to do. Firstly, she needed to know who he really was.

Then he could try and learn what had sent her running from Cairn Toul to a circle of stones he hadn't known existed. How she knew of them was on the agenda as well.

Thinking of the Druid helped to calm his mind. The more he thought of her and felt her magic, the further away the memories that hounded him went.

Malcolm let out a deep breath and rubbed his thumb on the back of the Druid's hand. Tomorrow would be a new day in more ways than one.

CHAPTER
TWENTY-SIX

Evie came awake with a start. She'd heard her name whispered in her mind. Gradually, she pulled her hand from under Malcolm's and sat up so she could look out the window to the standing stones.

They were calling for her. Just as Cairn Toul was.

But whereas the rocks of Cairn Toul wanted her to return, the stone circle wanted her to do what she'd come for.

Evie looked at Malcolm to find his eyes closed. She wasn't sure if he was asleep or not. A glance at the clock on the bedside table said she'd slept for almost two hours.

She still had a little time before she had to meet the kidnappers, but the more time she wasted, the more anxious she became. The only thing she could do was get out of the bed and see if Malcolm woke.

Evie crawled out of the bed at such a slow pace a snail could have passed her. By the time she was standing by the bed looking down at Malcolm, she wanted a drink to calm her nerves.

As quietly as she could, Evie gathered her clothes from the bathroom and hurried into the dining room to change.

She pulled one of the chairs out in order to place her clothes down.

No sooner had her clothes left her hand than she was jerked around against a hard chest. She looked up into Malcolm's azure gaze and her heart raced when she saw his desire.

"You thought to leave the bed without telling me," he whispered in a deep, husky voice that sent chills of anticipation over her skin.

"You can't make love to a lass like that and not expect her to get hungry," she said as she quickly came up with the fib.

Evie's stomach fluttered when he traced a finger along her jawline to her chin before tipping up her face to his. Some deep emotion moved across his gaze.

"It's madness," he whispered. "Madness for you. I tried to deny it, and even tried to run from it. But I can no'. What have you done to me?"

Her lips parted at his words. The honesty reflected in his gaze surprised her. Malcolm had been many things in the short time she'd known him, but the man standing before her now with the raw emotions made her fall a little in love with him.

"Your name, Druid. What is it?"

She blinked back the tears and swallowed. "Evie. Evie Walker."

"Evie."

He said the name like a caress. Her knees went weak, and she had to grab his arms to stay upright. The fact both were naked didn't go unnoticed.

She used the time to run her hands up his chest to revel in his hard muscles. There was the smallest jerk from him when she touched his scarred shoulder.

The skin was smooth there, but also raised and puckered. She then stroked a finger down one of the scars running the length of his side.

He moved so quickly she wasn't prepared for it. When she next looked up, he had her on the table, one of his arms hooked beneath her knee. She urged him toward her and reached down to grab his engorged staff.

Malcolm almost spilled right then. Her soft hands knew just how to touch him. He hadn't meant to take her again, but he'd made the mistake of touching her.

He bent and took one of her turgid nipples in his mouth and suckled until she cried out. The harder he sucked, the faster her hands stroked him.

Malcolm found her clit and began to move his thumb back and forth slowly, lightly. Her soft cries grew louder as he felt her body begin to stiffen. But he wasn't yet ready for her to climax.

He moved to her other nipple and softly bit down as he pushed a finger inside her. Evie moaned and lifted her hips for more.

When he removed his hand, she guided his cock to her curls. Malcolm slid inside with a groan. She was as hot and tight as before. Her slick walls drew him in deep.

Malcolm lifted his head to look down at her heavy-lidded eyes and parted lips. She was stunning all laid out on the table.

He began to move slowly within her, pulling out until the head of him remained before filling her once more. Her soft cries of ecstasy were his undoing. He couldn't remember the last time he'd given a woman pleasure. It was like there was no one before her, before Evie.

Malcolm straightened and flattened his hand on her stomach as he rotated his hips. Her eyes pinned him, looking deep as if she peered straight into his black soul.

Her other leg came up and wrapped around his waist,

urging him faster. He complied, eager to hear his name upon her lips again as she peaked.

The faster he pumped within her, the louder her cries came. Sweat glistened over her skin while his thumb circled her clit. The walls of her sex clamped down, sending his desire spiraling.

Malcolm leaned over and took her lips in a fierce kiss, their tongues moving in time with their bodies. Her nails dug into his back as her legs tightened. He thrust harder, deeper to send them down a chasm of hedonism.

They climaxed together, the pleasure blending and melding until it erupted into a fiery storm of decadence so blinding, so consuming that neither would ever be the same.

Malcolm ended the kiss and looked down at the amazing woman who had touched him like no other. He wasn't entirely sure what to make of her, but he knew he wasn't ready to be parted from her just yet.

There was no need for words as he pulled out of her and carried her back to bed. As he lay her down, she took his hand and tugged him beside her. She turned on her side away from him, and Malcolm found himself molding to her back, his arm thrown over her waist.

For the first time in what seemed like an eternity, he smiled.

And then he found sleep pulling at him. He hadn't done more than rest for a few minutes at a time since becoming a Warrior, yet being with Evie changed everything.

Malcolm didn't fight the sleep. He let his eyes fall closed as he held Evie in his arms.

Evie struggled to remain awake for the next two hours. Malcolm had rolled onto his back and was lightly snoring. It was the only way she knew for sure that he was asleep.

It was the only reason she got out of bed once more

and hurried back into the dining room to dress. Since the rain was still falling, she looked in the coat closet and found a rain jacket and boots.

She paused at the back door and looked down the hallway to where Malcolm slept. Hopefully she would be back before he woke and she wouldn't have to tell him anything.

Evie quietly closed the door behind her and pulled up the hood on her jacket before she started toward the stones. They hadn't stopped calling to her since she'd arrived.

She slipped on the wet ground as she started down the hill and lost her footing. Evie landed hard on her bum and slid all the way to the bottom.

"Well, that's one way of getting down," she said as she stood and shifted in her wet and muddy jeans. "Ugh."

Evie forgot about her jeans as she ran to the standing stones. Once she reached them, she placed her hand on one and sighed.

"I'm here."

She'd forgotten to look at the spell again, and her phone was back at the house. Evie dropped her forehead and wanted to scream in frustration.

"We know it," the standing stones said.

Evie's head jerked up. "Tell me then, please."

"Come inssssside the ring."

She didn't hesitate to do as they asked. The stones had never lied or led her astray before. There was no reason for her not to trust them.

Malcolm hadn't seemed to like them, however. Then again, he hadn't liked Cairn Toul either. With that, she didn't give it another thought.

The rain came down in torrents and lightning was her only source of light. She sighed when, in a bright array, lightning forked across the sky and showed her the circle was made up of two rings of stones.

Evie walked through the first ring. The second ring of stones stood closer together. She paused beside one and placed her hand upon it. It vibrated slightly. She tried another stone to find it did the same.

She looked up, blinking through the rain and wished she could see the stones in the daylight. Then she laughed at herself.

"I'm a Druid. I have magic."

Evie walked through the second ring of stones and used her magic to create small fires in between each of the stones in the outer ring.

She gasped when she saw the sheer size of the megaliths. They were enormous, towering over her as if she were no taller than an ant.

All over the stones were Celtic symbols carved into them. The second ring of stones stood a little over five feet apart. When she looked in the middle of the ring she found a large flat stone set atop a wide boulder on one side.

On the other was a long, skinny megalith that looked as if it had been purposefully laid flat.

Evie walked into the middle and closed her eyes. She could imagine the Druids who had once stood where she was. How many hundreds of years had Druids touched these very stones?

Now, she was one of them.

"I was never alone, was I?"

"Nay. We are alwayssss with you, Druid."

If only she'd known this before she put up that damned site. But the entire site was coming down as soon as she could get to a computer. It had caused her enough grief.

"What do I do?"

"Kneel before the small altar."

Evie walked to the stone that was laid flat and knelt before it. Upon closer inspection she noticed that the megalith wasn't smooth like the others, but was conclave with more symbols etched into it.

Except these symbols weren't any that Evie recognized. She ran her hand along the stone and felt a jolt of magic go through her. She jerked her hand back, fear replacing her enthusiasm.

"Thisssss is ancient black magic, Druid. Proceed with caution."

"Good to know," she said sarcastically.

Why they couldn't have told her that before, she wasn't sure. Then again, she should've been smart enough to know to be careful with any kind of black magic.

"Now what?"

"Repeat after ussssssss . . ."

Evie began the spell, and with each word the air grew heavy, the pressure around her forcing her down. She felt as if it pressed upon her body, making it impossible for her to rise from her knees.

She struggled to breathe, and the words grew more and more difficult to say. Evie had to place her hands on the ground just to remain upright.

"I can't finish," she said when she realized the wind and rain were howling around her as fiercely as a tornado.

"Finish it!" the stones demanded.

Evie wasn't sure if she should. Then an image of Brian flashed in her mind, and she knew she'd do whatever it took to get him back.

She took a deep breath and repeated the words the stones told her. There were six more lines she said before she felt something in her hand and looked down to find a dagger.

The handle was made of onyx, and the blade was long and curved. Fear began to build because she knew she hadn't held a weapon before she walked into the circles.

"Slice both wrists and hold them over the altar. Five drops from each must touch the stone."

Evie rose up on her knees and held her left arm over the altar with the blade against her skin. "I willingly give my soul for black magic."

She sliced her wrist and counted the five drops before she switched the weapon to her other hand.

Malcolm shot out of the bed as he felt the *drough* magic begin to rise up. He knew without looking that Evie wasn't in the bed with him.

He raced from the house toward the feel of the black magic. With every step he prayed that Wallace hadn't gotten to Evie.

Because both Evie's magic and the *drough* magic were coming from the standing stones.

He released his god as he approached the circle. With a roar, he jumped over the two circles of stones to land in the middle. When he stood, he found Evie kneeling before an altar as she cut her wrist.

For a second, he stood rooted to the spot. She was becoming *drough*. Why would she willingly give up her soul? What would push her to do something so violent after she swore to him she wasn't Deirdre, wasn't evil?

Malcolm didn't know whether to stop her or allow her to continue. He didn't have all the facts. If he stopped her, he didn't know what could happen. If he didn't stop her, he knew exactly what he could be forced to do.

A *drough* with the same magic as Deirdre, living in Cairn Toul? The coincidences were too great to ignore.

Evie had freely given her body to him, eagerly plunged into the bliss of their lovemaking. All the while knowing she was coming to do the spell.

"Nay!" he bellowed and raced toward her.

Malcolm tried to grab the last drop of blood before it

hit the altar, but the wind and rain made it impossible. He clenched his teeth and raged as the black smoke rose from the stone and started for Evie.

He wrapped an arm around her stomach and tossed her away from the smoke as an evil laugh reverberated through the megaliths.

Malcolm rose to his feet and stalked toward Evie who backed away on her hands and bottom until she hit a stone. She used the stone to gain her feet.

"Why?" Malcolm yelled. "Why did you do it?"

"Because I must!" she shouted over the rain. She pushed back the hood of her jacket and wiped at her face.

"You didna need to become *drough*. All you had to do was ask me!"

She blinked, her face going pale. "You weren't there. I had to make decisions on my own!"

"You're a *drough* now! I was here, Evie. All you had to do was talk to me."

Her face crumpled. "No one else will suffer for what I did to put us in this situation."

"You can no' possibly comprehend what you've done. What do you think that black smoke was? It was Satan, and you've given him your blood—and your soul. He owns you now."

CHAPTER
TWENTY-SEVEN

Malcolm watched Evie slide down the stone to slump on the ground. He tamped down his god and fell to his knees beside her.

"Why?" he asked her again.

Her throat moved as she swallowed. "They kidnapped Brian. This was my only choice so that no one else was harmed."

"Nay. Only you've lost your soul."

He wanted to get the information out of her right then. Malcolm sighed. He knew all about doing awful things in order to save family.

The label of murderer and betrayer was his to shoulder for eternity because he had protected Larena. How could he fault Evie for doing something for her brother?

Malcolm's skin sizzled as magic began to gather. It wasn't Evie, so that left the stone circle. They weren't happy he'd interfered, though they had gotten what they wanted. Another *drough*.

"Evie, we need to leave this place."

Her eyes were dilated and unfocused. "I can feel it inside me," she whispered. "It's a dark menace, coiling and slithering through me."

Malcolm should be repulsed by her now being *drough*. Instead, all he wanted to do was help her. There would be no getting through to her now, however. Malcolm gathered her in his arms and stalked from the circle, daring the stones to do anything.

Once inside the house, he set Evie on her feet by the back door and stripped off her clothes. Just before he wrapped the blanket around her, he noticed the necklace that had been hidden beneath her clothes. It looked old, ancient even. He pushed it from his mind and wrapped her in the covers before carrying her into the bathroom. After sitting her on the toilet, he turned on the water.

While the tub filled, Malcolm squatted before Evie and took one of her hands in his. Her skin was like ice. He rubbed his hands along her arm vigorously, trying not to notice the cuts on her wrists that had already stopped bleeding.

As soon as the water was high enough, Malcolm shoved aside the blanket and lowered Evie into the water. He sat there feeling helpless and useless as she tried to wrap her head around what she had become.

Her clear blue eyes suddenly turned to him as large tears gathered. "I'm evil now. I can feel it."

"Nay," he said sternly. "You choose what you do with the magic given to you. Use it for good or use it for evil, but it's your decision."

"When I die, I'm going to Hell."

How Malcolm wanted to lie to her, but it was better if she faced it all as soon as she could. "Aye."

"Oh, God," she whispered and wiped at a tear.

He watched her hand drop into the water as steam rose around her. The desire to hold her was overwhelming. He wanted to offer his support, but he also craved her touch. "You did this for your brother. Just as I did . . . things for Larena. I made that choice. I killed a friend and betrayed those I called family. All to protect Larena. Those were my choices. I must live with them."

Her head swiveled to him as a frown marred her brow. "You killed?"

"The correct label is murdered." Malcolm shifted so that he sat on the edge of the tub. "When Deirdre unbound my god she promised me that as long as I did her bidding she would ensure Larena was never harmed. Larena was all the family I had. How could I refuse the offer?"

"I'd have done the same."

Malcolm gave a soft snort. "No' if you knew the person Deirdre truly was. I understood by agreeing to do whatever she wanted that my soul wouldna survive. Her first test was when she captured two Warriors who were my friends. She ordered me to kill Duncan. And I did. Every time I close my eyes, I see his face.

"I can no' go back and undo what happened. Duncan's twin, Ian, forgave me. Everyone said it was Deirdre's doing no' mine since they discovered my pact with Deirdre. I doona deserve their absolution," he said as he turned his head to look at her. "I could've refused. I could've fought her. But I didna."

Evie sniffed and drew her knees up to her chest to wrap her arms around her legs. "If I take this new potent magic inside me and use it to kill those who dared to threaten my brother, I'm evil. It'll be my decision to kill. It wasn't your decision to murder Duncan."

"But I did it."

"Yes, you did. That will never change." She placed a hand on his back. "You said she captured the two Warriors. Could she have stopped you had you tried to fight her?"

Malcolm frowned. "Aye, and I know what you're doing. Larena and the others did the same. They showed me how I wouldna have been able to win against Deirdre, and I could've died as well. I know all of that, but it doesna change anything."

"It changes everything. Would you have killed Duncan had it just been the two of you?"

Malcolm looked into her eyes and shook his head. "I'd have tried to find a way for him to survive."

"Was there anything Deirdre ordered you to do that you didn't?"

"Aye," he said softly as he leaned forward so that his forearms could rest on his knees. "It was after we'd been pulled into the future. She found a Druid she wanted to take her power from. The Druid, Tara, was a teacher. Deirdre wanted me to kill the children so the Druid would know no' to fight me."

Water sloshed over the side of the tub when Evie rose and wrapped her arms around him from behind. She laid her head on his shoulder and said, "But you didn't kill those children."

"I couldna. Larena and Fallon arrived and thankfully prevented me from getting ahold of the Druid. I might have bypassed the murder of children, but I did other things. Horrible things."

Her arms tightened around him. Malcolm's throat constricted. He'd expected Evie to push him away, not console him. That was for those who earned it.

"I told you all of this no' so you'd feel sorry for me, but so you would understand that just because you're *drough* doesna mean you're evil."

"I didn't think it would feel so . . . evil," she whispered. He felt her eyelash tickle his skin as she closed her eyes. "He told me what I would become."

"Who?" Malcolm asked, his muscles tensed as he waited for the answer.

"He only signed his e-mails as J."

"Jay?"

"No, just the letter J. I looked into his e-mail account. I thought he checked out."

Malcolm turned so that he faced her. He smoothed away a wet curl that stuck to her face. "I suspect the J you know is Jason Wallace. We've been fighting him for some time now. He's more powerful than Deirdre ever was, and more cunning."

Evie stood and reached for a towel. She quickly dried off as she asked, "Is there any way the *drough* ceremony can be reversed?"

"Nay."

"I didn't think so," she said as she straightened and squared her shoulders. "Then I will do what I must for Brian."

Malcolm stood between Evie and the door. "Tell me what happened."

"He was kidnapped."

"What do they want? Money?"

She laughed dryly. "No. They want . . ."

He tried not to show his agitation as she hesitated. Malcolm understood that she was determining whether to trust him or not. He inwardly sighed when her shoulders slumped.

"They want this," she said and touched the necklace.

Malcolm ran the pads of his fingers over it and felt a pulse of magic. "Because it's magical?"

"Yes. As I told you, I thought I was the only Druid. I put up that site and got hacked, but what I didn't tell you is that I think I was hacked because I put up a picture of this necklace."

"What does the necklace do?"

She shrugged. "I don't know exactly. My grandmum gave it to me to keep hidden. It's been in our family for as many generations as I know. We've always had it, and always hidden it." She cleared her throat as her gaze drifted over his body. "You have mud all over you."

"I woke to the feel of *drough* magic. I didna think of clothes as I went looking for you."

"You were willing to fight naked?"

He shrugged. "Clothes doona matter in battle."

"Well, I'm cold and tired of being in the buff. Get cleaned up while I find my clothes."

"They're no' fit to wear."

"Guess I'll have to try out my new magic, won't I?" she asked with a dour expression as she walked around him.

Malcolm wasn't finished getting answers from her. He hurriedly cleaned up and put on his clothes before he found her in the kitchen sitting at the bar staring at nothing.

He paused when he saw her jeans were dry and free of mud, just as her sweater was.

She looked at him and shrugged. "I may never do laundry again."

Malcolm grinned despite himself. The smile faded however, when he took the stool next to her and said, "Now, tell me what happened to Brian."

"I received a text." She shoved the phone at him so he could read over everything. "They made it clear I am to do as they asked or they'd hurt Brian. I looked for you, but you were gone, so I asked J if there was anything I could do. He told me of the stones and that if I turned *drough* I could defeat my enemies. He said I'd hear the stones long before I saw them. Something about how they recognized when a Druid was near and called out to them."

"Did they?"

"Yes."

"What else did this J tell you about the circle? Did he tell you what to do?"

She perched her elbow on the bar and leaned her head against her hand. "Yep. I didn't memorize the spell though. It was the stones that told me what to say."

"Shite," he mumbled and quickly read the texts. "Noon, aye? What were you going to do?"

"I couldn't leave Brain, and I can't turn over the necklace. There is a spell hidden in the pendant."

"What kind of spell?" he asked.

She shrugged. "Unfortunately, I don't know. It was important enough that my family not only hid the necklace, but changed its look and put dozens of spells on it to keep it hidden. Then, they stopped handing down the information on the spell. I think to keep it safe. Whatever spell the necklace houses can be dangerous in the wrong hands. I can't have innocent deaths on my head."

"And you couldna allow Brian to die," Malcolm said with a nod. "You felt your only choice was to become *drough*."

"It wasn't an easy choice," she said defensively. "You think I want to go to Hell?"

He held her gaze and slowly shook his head. "Nay. What is your plan?"

"I don't know." She blew out a harsh breath. "I can't give up the necklace, but I have to get Brian back."

"I'll make sure you do. We're going to have to come up with a plan."

She sat up and shook her head. "Did you not read the texts? I can't bring anyone with me."

He gave her a droll look. "Do you really think I'd allow myself to be seen? Besides, I can sense magic. I'll know if you're dealing with Druids or not."

"You mean you'll know if it's Jason Wallace."

He raised a brow. "Aye. This sounds like something he would do. You've no' had any dealings with the likes of Wallace. You didna battle Deirdre or Declan. You've no' seen how easily they take innocent lives and destroy everything in their paths."

"And you've seen too much." She paused as her eyes softened. "My main concern is Brian. I want to make sure he's not hurt."

"You can worry over Brian. Let me worry about getting the both of you out alive. Because I guarantee whoever is meeting you tomorrow willna come alone. They're going to want you, Evie. You *and* the necklace."

"Bloody hell," she said and banged her hand on the bar. "I never thought of that."

He lifted one shoulder in a shrug. "The place you're meeting is going to be filled with people. You willna be able to use magic without being seen."

"I get your point," she said testily. "I didn't think any of this through."

"Then let me help," he urged.

Her clear blue eyes were filled with fear and hope. "Please do. I need you, Malcolm."

His chest constricted at her words, words he never thought to hear from anyone—much less her.

CHAPTER
TWENTY-EIGHT

MacLeod Castle

"I'm no' kidding when I say I'm about to toss that laptop in the ocean," Logan growled from across the table.

Gwynn looked over the screen at her husband and grinned. "You can try, sweetie."

"You've been on the wretched thing all night."

"What's the matter, Logan?" Hayden asked as he sauntered into the great hall from the kitchen. "You can no' keep your wife in bed."

Isla elbowed Hayden in the ribs. "I wouldn't go there if I were you."

Hayden laughed and tossed Isla up and over his shoulders. "Let me show you how it's done, Logan."

"Hayden Campbell, put me down now," Isla said with a squeal.

Gwynn couldn't contain her smile. "Isla, that might be effective if you weren't smiling and rubbing his bum while you said it."

"You all need a real man to show you how it's done," Galen said as he sat beside Logan and speared two sausages from Logan's plate before dumping them onto his own.

Reaghan gave a loud snort as she walked from the kitchen. "Oh, you mean how you fell asleep watching *The Wedding Date* last night?"

"Baby, that's no' a real movie," Galen said around a bite of sausage. "I need action."

Gwynn exchanged a look with Isla who had taken the seat beside her after Hayden set her down. "Which I bet you might have gotten had you not fallen asleep."

Everyone laughed, including Galen who raised his glass of juice to salute her. Gwynn looked around at her family. The gloom had been lifted from MacLeod Castle with Larena's recovery, but there was still a cloud hanging over them.

"What is it?" Logan whispered.

Gwynn met his hazel eyes. "Evangeline Walker. The Web site she had talking about Druids and the necklace. Well . . . I'm not the only one who hacked it."

"What?" Tara asked, rubbing her eyes as she walked down the stairs with Ramsey at her heels. "How do you know someone else hacked in?"

Gwynn shrugged. "It's difficult to explain. It's just things you see in the keystrokes logged in between this time and the last time I hacked it."

Cara, Sonya, and Dani walked into the hall with large platters of food while Marcail and Saffron held pitchers of coffee and tea.

Roni walked to Tara and handed her a Coke. "Do you know who hacked the site?"

Gwynn shook her head as she caught sight of the others coming into the hall. "I've tried to see, but they covered their tracks well. Too well, in fact."

"Which means what exactly?" Lucan asked.

Gwynn sighed and stretched her shoulders. "What it

means is that whoever hacked into the site is a genius who makes no mistakes, or I'm not as good as I thought I was."

If it was the latter, Gwynn had some work to do. She hadn't started out as a hacker. In fact, it had come as a surprise, but the more she learned, the easier it was to do.

While some people could sing or draw or dance, she knew computer code. Her magic never came into place with her hacking, not that she wasn't above using it if the occasion arose.

"You're that good," Logan stated, as if daring her to argue.

She mouthed "I love you" to the man who had brought her into a world of magic and given her everything she could have ever dreamed of.

"Aye, you are that good," Quinn seconded. "How many geniuses are out there anyway?"

"Less than a handful. I can't imagine this site would've caught their eye," Gwynn said. She bit her lip as she stared at the screen full of code. "I can't help thinking this hack was too neat."

Cara cleared her throat, her chestnut hair pulled over one shoulder in a braid. "What she means is that Gwynn studies other hackers. She knows their moves. No two hackers gain access to a site in the same way."

Ian rubbed his chin as he peered over Gwynn's shoulder at the screen. "I'm no' sure how you can read anything, but we trust you. If it seems odd, then it most likely is."

"I hate to say it," Saffron said as she dumped sugar in her coffee, her tawny eyes meeting Gwynn's. "But could magic have played a part? Evangeline's site is about Druids. She wanted attention, and it looks as if she's gotten it."

Gwynn considered the code she was reviewing. "I can see where Evangeline has gone in and strengthened her firewalls and set traps. I've gotten past them, but I did it through a back door that would hide most of what I've done. If Evangeline looks, she'll see I've come in."

"And?" Sonya urged.

Gwynn looked around the table and shrugged. "And the other hacker did it with finesse that leaves me scratching my head. I didn't think about magic being used before, but now I can see that it might have."

"Wonderful," Camdyn said sardonically.

Dani passed the teapot to Ian and asked Gwynn, "Is there anything you can do to check to see if it was magic?"

"I've not tried before."

Broc dished out some jam onto his plate and frowned. "Let's assume it was magic. Does that mean it's Wallace?"

"Most likely," Logan said. "Who else would go after Evangeline?"

"Just because she put up a Web site?" Gwynn asked. She scrunched up her face. "I don't see it."

"What about the necklace?" Sonya asked.

Gwynn switched screen tabs so she could see the page Evangeline had taken down about the necklace. "It was taken down, but I was able to find it in the deleted files. The necklace is old. It could be just a family heirloom that she posted to draw interest."

"That she took down after being hacked? No' likely. I say we talk to her. We've done enough poking around her site," Lucan said.

Ramsey nodded. "Whether that necklace really is the one we've been searching for or no', the Druid needs to take down the site."

"Finding Evangeline might be more difficult than we thought," Broc said with his hands fisted on the table as aggravation came off him in waves. "I can no' locate her."

"Oh shit," Gwynn mumbled.

The few times Broc hadn't been able to use his Warrior

power of finding anyone, anywhere were when magic had been involved—specifically *drough* magic.

In other words, it was very bad.

"Has anyone contacted Malcolm to let him know about Larena?" Saffron asked.

Marcail set her fork down. "We were leaving it to Larena to do, but she and Fallon have been . . . occupied."

"A well-deserved holiday those two needed," Ian said.

"Where are Britt and Aiden?" Reaghan asked.

Quinn looked up the stairs and grinned. "Another couple who needed a . . . holiday. Is that what we're calling it now?"

Laughter sounded around the table once again. Until Broc got to his feet slowly, his face lined with anger . . . and unease. The entire great hall stopped and looked at him.

"I can no' locate Malcolm either," Broc stated tersely.

As one, Lucan and Quinn stood. The other Warriors quickly followed. Gwynn closed her laptop. Evangeline, the Web site, and the hacker would have to wait. For now, Malcolm was their priority.

"Can you still no' find Wallace?" Hayden asked.

Broc shook his head of long blond hair. "He's hidden from me as always. I doona have a good feeling about this. Any of this."

"Me neither," Logan said and reached across the table for Gwynn's hand.

She gave it a squeeze before he walked away with the other Warriors. When the men were gone to find Larena and Fallon, the Druids gathered at the table.

"What are we thinking?" Tara asked.

Sonya smoothed a hand down her face, her short red curls a riot around her. "I wish I knew."

"I think we prepare," Cara said. "It's all we can do right now."

Isla's ice-blue eyes narrowed. "Whether it is Jason who is stopping Broc from seeing Malcolm or Evangeline, we will be doing something about it. If it's Jason, then there will be another battle."

"And if it's someone else?" Ronnie asked.

Gwynn smiled coldly. "They'll never know what hit them."

Evie sat in the front seat of the stolen car and kept hoping and praying that no one found them as she gazed at the early morning sky still a muted gray. Her magic stirred, dark and tempting, and she tried not to dwell on the fact that she was *drough*. She expected to feel like a superhero after receiving the type of powerful magic Malcolm spoke of. She did feel different, just not in a good way.

It had to be the shock. Why did she feel as if she had been duped, conned, hoodwinked into becoming *drough*?

"Who came up with that word, I wonder?" Malcolm said.

Evie looked at him with a frown. "What word?"

"Hoodwinked. It's rather a silly word for such a serious definition."

She blinked at him as he glanced at her. "Did I say that last bit out loud?"

He gave a single nod.

"I'm losing my mind." She rubbed her palms on her thighs and wondered if someone could know they were going insane.

"You're no' going daft. You've just had a rough morning."

"Rough? It's the mother of all bombshells, Malcolm. I feel this awful and powerful magic within me. I can't wait to use it on the bastards who threaten my brother. And I can't wrap my head around the fact that I'm going to Hell and Satan now owns my soul."

She drew in a ragged breath when his hand reached over and took hers.

"First things first," he said. "We're going to get Brian. Then I'm going to discover who took him."

"I want to know who it is."

"Nay. Let me deal with them."

Evie turned her hand over and laced her fingers with his. "Why? Because you think your soul is already lost?"

"I know it is. There's no need to dirty yours."

"Decisions, remember? You told me they were mine to make."

A muscle ticked in his jaw as he steered around a corner in the road. "Evie, please. You'll no' survive the weight of taking another's life on your conscience."

"And you don't need another life to add to the ones you carry."

She studied his profile for several minutes as he drove in silence. Evie wasn't foolish enough to believe she'd won the argument. Malcolm was a Highlander in every sense of the word. He would do everything in his power to keep her from anything bad.

"We have hours before we're to meet. Why are we going so early?" she asked.

"I want to have a look around. I need to know all that exists and what to expect if there's a large crowd or no'."

"I won't allow them to take me."

His faced hardened as he glanced at her. "Nay, they willna take you. I'll no' permit it."

She couldn't help but grin. "You have all the answers, don't you?"

"I doona. I'm just trying to keep you and Brian safe."

Evie looked out her window surprised to see the storm clouds were drifting away. "If they've hurt Brian, I'm not sure what I'm going to do."

"One thing at a time."

Her mind drifted, the passing scenery became a blur. Evie had no idea how long she sat there lamenting the fact she was now evil.

She started when he put the car in park and she found them outside of a quaint inn. With her stomach in knots, Evie opened the door and stepped into the cool air.

In no time at all, Malcolm had secured them a room. He left her to find breakfast and ordered her to relax. When he refused to leave the room until she was lying on the bed, she had no choice but to do as he wanted.

"I'm not tired," she argued. Not that it did any good.

Malcolm was as stubborn as they came.

CHAPTER
TWENTY-NINE

Malcolm sat by the bed and watched Evie slumbering. He'd purposefully left her alone in the hopes that exhaustion would win out and she would sleep.

He spent the last hour and a half scoping out Urquhart Castle. Malcolm wasn't sure why the kidnappers wanted to meet at that particular castle. Or why a castle at all.

As a visitor, there was only one way in and out of the castle. He found three more points of entry used by the staff that worked at the ancient castle.

But as a Warrior, there were infinite ways he could gain access.

Malcolm held his mobile in his hand and debated about calling in reinforcements. His finger hovered over Phelan's number before he changed his mind at the last minute and dialed another.

The phone rang three times before a perturbed voice answered, "This had better be good, Warrior."

"Are you up for some action in saving a lad, helping a damsel, and possibly keeping hundreds of innocents alive?"

"Where are you?" Guy demanded.

Malcolm let out a breath he'd been holding. After the way he'd dismissed Guy the last time, he hadn't been sure the Dragon King would help. "Loch Ness."

"Who is it?" Malcolm heard Elena's sleepy voice through the phone.

"I'll be there in fifteen minutes," Guy said and ended the call.

Malcolm set down his mobile and glanced at the sky. The sun would be up in less than an hour. The darkness would give Guy the cover he needed if he was arriving in dragon form.

He left the small room and walked outside the hotel to await Guy. Malcolm stood looking over the loch for several minutes just watching the way the deep, dark water moved. Memories of the first time he'd seen the loch washed over him.

His parents had gone to visit friends, and Malcolm had been allowed to tag along. The loch had been as dark and impressive then as it was now.

While they rode along the water's edge in the carriage, his father had told him stories of a giant beast that was believed to live in the loch. The memory was a pleasant one.

"You're smiling. That's a good sign, aye?"

Malcolm cleared his throat and looked over his shoulder to see Guy buttoning a shirt that barely fit over his large chest. Malcolm raised a brow when he took notice of the jeans bunched around his hips by the belt that held them in place.

Guy gave him a droll look. "It's no' like I can carry my own clothes while in dragon form. I had to make do."

"Obviously." Malcolm glanced away. "I didna think you'd come."

It was Guy's turn to lift a brow. "I said I'd be here. I doona go back on my word."

"Aye. I'm just . . . surprised you came."

Guy came to stand beside him and sighed. "We all do idiotic things. I meant it when I said to let me know if you needed anything. I'm glad you took me up on the offer. So, tell me why I'm here."

Malcolm parted his lips when the sound of a motor approaching halted him. He turned and saw a red Ferrari FF pulling to a stop. The doors opened, and two men stepped out.

"I thought we might need reinforcements," Guy said. "Since you contacted me, I had a feeling you didna call the other Warriors. And more eyes are always better."

Malcolm nodded to the dark-haired Dragon King. "Rhys."

"Malcolm," Rhys replied with a lopsided smirk. "I was glad to get Guy's call. I've been a bit . . . well, let's just say bored."

"You're always bored," Hal said as he stepped around Rhys and held out his hand to Malcolm. "Good to see you again."

Malcolm shook his hand and met Hal's moonlight blue eyes. "I wasna expecting the two of you."

"Someone has to keep Rhys in line," Hal said as he cut his eyes to a smiling Rhys. "Banan was otherwise occupied, so I volunteered. Cassie is a bit irritated with me at the moment anyway."

Guy chuckled. "What now?" Hal refused to answer, which only made Guy laugh harder. "You might as well tell me because Cassie will tell Elena, and I'll find out anyway."

"Let's just say I lost my cool with her wanker of a brother."

Malcolm watched the exchange with interest. The camaraderie between the Kings was very much like the

Warriors, and it made him long to return to MacLeod Castle.

"Tell us why we're here," Rhys urged.

Malcolm looked at the hotel and the window to Evie's room. "I met an unusual Druid. She was under the impression there might no' be any more of her kind so she set up a site hoping to find others. She did."

Guy crossed his arms over his chest as he widened his stance. "It isna Wallace, is it?"

"I can no' know for sure. She's been exchanging e-mails with a person who calls himself by the letter J. I doona believe in coincidence. To make matters worse, Evie's brother was kidnapped."

"Bloody hell," Hal muttered.

"There's more." Malcolm ran a hand through his hair. "Brian is mute, and Evie's been his guardian and only family since she was eighteen and he a small lad."

Rhys's lips flattened. "Let me guess. This J told her how he could help."

"In a manner. He told her how she could strengthen her magic by going to a stone circle and performing a ceremony."

Guy followed Malcolm's gaze to the inn. "She's *drough*?"

"She wasna until a few hours ago," Malcolm said. "She couldna leave Brian in the kidnappers' hands, nor can she turn over what the kidnappers want."

"Which is?" Rhys asked.

"A necklace that holds a spell her family has been protecting for generations. They even stopped passing down the information on the spell, so she doesna know what she's protecting. Only that it could be dangerous in the wrong hands."

Guy rocked back on his heels. "So she chose to become *drough*."

Hal shook his head and stuffed his hands in the front pockets of his jeans. "It has to be Wallace."

"My thoughts exactly." Malcolm's skin felt too tight over his body as he itched to take his anger out on Jason Wallace. "I suspect Wallace is involved in the kidnapping, and I also believe he wants the necklace Evie has."

Guy's hands fell to his sides as he frowned. "This just gets better and better. Anything else?"

"The kidnappers want to trade Brian for the necklace at noon today at the castle," Malcolm said and pointed to Urquhart.

Hal clapped his hands together and nodded. "It looks like we'll get to play the part of tourists."

"No' all of us," Guy said. "Two out in the open. Two hidden."

Malcolm grinned at the Kings. "Aye. I've already had an up-close look at the castle an hour ago."

"Sun's coming up," Rhys said. "There willna be time for us to have a look."

Malcolm squatted in the loose rocks and grabbed a thin stick. "No need. Rhys, I want you here," he said as he drew a quick diagram of the castle layout and put a stone in the tower. Next he put a stone on the east side by the castle wall. "Hal, that's you."

"And me?" Guy asked.

Malcolm put a stone in the courtyard. "Here. I want you as close to Evie as possible."

"Why are you no' taking that position?" Rhys asked.

Hal bent over to look at the sketch. "Because he fears what he might do to the kidnappers."

Malcolm blew out a breath and stood. "Hal's right. I'm no' in control of my emotions. I doona know if I can remain levelheaded if something goes wrong."

"Something always goes wrong," Guy said. "It's inevitable. But we'll be prepared."

"If it is Wallace, he's mine." Malcolm waited for the Kings to argue, but they simply nodded in understanding.

Hal rubbed his chin. "If it is Wallace, we willna be able to help you. But we'll get the innocents out."

"And look after Evie and Brian," Guy added.

Malcolm agreed, and after confirming the meeting at noon, Hal and Rhys drove away. Malcolm looked back over the loch and tried to draw the feel of Evie's magic closer around him.

"What's changed with you?" Guy asked.

"The Druid. I knew it as soon as I came across her. She's . . . different."

"And now a *drough*."

Malcolm inwardly winced. "Just one reason I didna call the Warriors."

"What are the other reasons?"

He turned to glare at the Dragon King, refusing to state the reasons. "You're nosy."

"I usually am with my friends."

Malcolm jerked as if punched. "Friend?"

"Aye. Doona look so surprised," Guy said with a crooked grin. "Well, maybe you should since I didna want to think of you as a friend at first. You're too obstinate and careless." His smile faded. "But I saw your pain. You did a good job of hiding it from your fellow Warriors, but no' from me."

"I've no right to ask, but will you look after Evie and Brian for me?"

Guy's brows lowered over his eyes as he took a step closer, understanding dawning. "You doona plan to come out of this alive."

It wasn't a question, and Malcolm didn't treat it as one. "If it's Wallace, I'll no' stand by and allow him to get away."

"Deliberately putting yourself in his path with no one to help you is foolish. What will Evie think?"

Malcolm's hands clenched as he thought of holding her in his arms again. "She'll understand. Just keep her away from Wallace. I doona know what his plans for her are, but they can no' be good."

"I'm in agreement there. And of course we'll watch over her and her brother. She belongs with the others at MacLeod Castle."

"Nay," Malcolm said angrily and immediately took a step back to calm himself. "She's *drough*, Guy. They may no' believe her when she tells them why she did it."

"Then you be there to tell them."

"I doona know why she came into my life. I hate the constant feelings that bombard me incessantly. Just when I think I can get a handle on one, another arrives. I'm undeserving of her soft touch and giving heart. If she remains near me, she'll get hurt. It's what always happens. I can no' walk away from her, but she can leave me."

"If she will." Guy stared at him for several seconds. "I think you're making a mistake in this."

"I'm no'. Trust me. For once, I'm doing the right thing."

"No' if she's the one bringing back your feelings. You were a cold bastard before. I often wondered if there was any humanity left in you."

"There was," Malcolm said with a shrug. "It wouldna have fit in a thimble, but somehow Evie found it."

Guy smiled wryly. "She sounds like a remarkable woman."

"She is. She'll no' know you. Evie is already concerned by the fact that I'll be there. If you have to take her and Brian away, tell her I sent you."

"If she's anything like Elena, she'll no' want to leave you behind."

Malcolm knew that wouldn't be an issue. "She'll have Brian to concern herself with. He's her only family."

"So you mean nothing to her?"

"I protected her when she needed it. That's all it is."

"On her part," Guy said as he pinned him with a stare. "And you?"

Malcolm turned to the inn. "Me? I'd like to say that I doona crave the feel of her magic. I'd like to tell you that I could walk away and forget her kisses or the way she feels in my arms. But I'd be lying. Evie found my soul, and in the process touched my heart."

CHAPTER THIRTY

Dreagan Distillery

Constantine replaced the receiver on the phone atop his intricately carved desk and leaned back in his chair. "Well, that was interesting."

Banan sat forward in his chair across the desk. "I gather that was Warriors from the castle."

"Aye. Looking for Malcolm."

Banan met Con's gaze. "You didna tell them what we know. Why?"

"I'm no' sure." Con rose and turned to one of the large windows behind his desk looking over his land. "Fallon told me Broc wasna able to use his power to locate Malcolm. They think Wallace may have him."

"You could've told them Malcolm was all right."

Con rolled up the sleeves to his starched dress shirt. "There's a reason Malcolm called Guy and no' those at MacLeod Castle. I doona know that reason yet, but I feel it's important."

"You're the one who didna want to get us involved with the Warriors in the first place. But we have. To deliberately keep information from Fallon could be contrived as a betrayal."

"Could be. I'm no' worried about it."

"Are you no' troubled with why Malcolm asked for Guy's help?"

Con turned and looked at Banan. Banan was loyal and a great King to his Blues. Con never stopped his Kings from questioning his decisions or motives. They hadn't been chosen as Kings for nothing.

"Guy, Rhys, and Hal know they can no' show their true form to humans. I'm no' concerned with that possibility. We've remained hidden from humans for thousands of millennia, Banan. Tell me what's truly bothering you."

Banan slowly stood. "You're making a mistake no' telling Fallon about Malcolm. Malcolm could very well need them in the end since, as you say, the dragons with him willna be much help."

"If it comes to that, I'll no' hesitate to inform Fallon."

"Good. I like the Warriors. I doona want them to become our enemies. We have enough of them as it is."

Con walked back to his desk and resumed his seat. "We were here since the beginning of time. We tried to keep the peace with the humans, and when we couldna we sent our dragons away. The humans will always hate and fear us."

"I'm no' talking about the humans," Banan said, his voice lowering in anger. "I'm talking about the damned threat to us we still have no' discovered. I'm talking about Ulrik and if he's involved. And let's no' forget the Fae who have taken an interest again."

Con snorted and shook his head. "It's just Rhi. Forget the Fae. Their interest lies in Phelan since he's a descendant. The Fae willna be bothering us."

"Allies are good. We may only be killed by one of our

own, but it's happened before. Things are changing, Con. Be prepared for them."

"Are you saying I'm no'?" he asked, quietly belying the anger simmering.

Banan suddenly smiled. "I know you too well, old friend. There's no need to hide your rage from me. And aye, you can think we're above many things. We tried to warn you about Ulrik and his human woman."

"A woman who betrayed him!" Con bellowed as he jumped to his feet. He leaned his hands on his desk and regained his composure. When he spoke again, his voice was once more calm and low. "A decision had to be made regarding that traitor. The woman got what was coming to her."

"And we made Ulrik an enemy for life. He's one of us, a King. It may take him another five thousand millennia, but he *will* get his revenge. I've no doubt of that."

Con watched him walk out of his office. He wanted to forget everything Banan said, but Con knew he was right. Ulrik would one day take his revenge.

What Banan had wrong was that they needed allies. They were Dragon Kings. They had ruled the skies, the land, and the waters of Earth since it was formed. They were masters.

They kept who they were a secret so the war between dragons and humans wouldn't erupt again. Perhaps it was time to rethink a few things.

Evie couldn't be angry at Malcolm no matter how hard she tried. She hadn't wanted sleep, but her body needed it. With those few hours of rest, her mind was refreshed and more focused.

She finished her sandwich and tossed the paper away. Malcolm sat in the only chair while she remained on the bed. "All right, I admit it. I needed sleep."

His lopsided, boyish grin made her heart flutter in her chest. "There are still two hours before the meeting."

Evie wiped her mouth before setting the napkin aside. "Did it hurt when Deirdre released your god?"

"Verra much. Have you had a broken bone?"

"My arm."

"Imagine every bone in your body breaking and your muscles shredding before everything healed."

She winced. "That sounds painful."

"It was."

"If you don't want to talk about it—"

"Ask your questions," he interrupted her gently.

Evie picked at her nails, and took a deep breath before asking, "You mentioned that Warriors have powers. What are yours?"

"I only have one. I control lightning."

"Control it," she repeated in awe. "How exactly?"

He held out his hand palm up and a soft ball of light appeared. Evie gasped in surprise when she saw the lightning running from finger to finger.

"Doesn't it hurt?"

"I doona feel it," he said and made the lightning disappear. "It's a part of me."

"What are some of the other powers Warriors have?"

His azure eyes smiled at her. "Teleporting, fire, water, snow and ice, shadows, talking to animals, and the ground are a few. There is one who is able to find anyone, anywhere."

"That's amazing."

"You talk to rocks. How is anything I just told you more astonishing than that?"

She laughed and shrugged. "I don't know. I guess maybe because I thought I was the only one who could do something like that."

"Does Brian have magic?"

She tucked her hair behind her ear. "Sadly, no. I wished he did. What is your god's name?"

"Daal. He's called the Devourer."

"That sounds ominous."

"Because he is. He's verra powerful, and no' one who likes to be trifled with."

"Do you enjoy the power he gives you?" she asked, hoping not to offend him.

There was a slight pause as if Malcolm was considering her words. "I do. It allows me to protect the ones I care about. If I had been a Warrior when I was attacked, I wouldna be scarred nor would I have lost the use of my arm."

"You use your arm now."

"Only because of Daal. The gods make us immortal, Evie. If I'm wounded, I heal quickly."

"Immortal," she mused. "You could potentially live forever."

He shrugged. "I suppose. There are ways the Druids have figured out how to remain alive through the centuries to be with their men."

The idea that she would die while he lived on had been like a kick in the stomach. Was Malcolm telling her how the other Druids remained alive so they could be together? She hoped so, because she wasn't yet ready to be parted from him. "That's good. Do you like being a Warrior?"

"If the spell to bind our gods is found as those at MacLeod Castle wish it to be, I would once more return to being a man with the use of only one arm. Given that choice, I'd rather remain a Warrior."

His voice was level, but she saw the distress in his magnificent azure eyes. "There are worse things than having the use of only one arm."

"In a world of magic and immortals, do you really believe that?"

She swallowed, unable to answer him. Evie looked away, thinking over his words. All the questions she wanted to ask about his god were gone. Malcolm put everything into perspective with just a few words.

"What will you and Brian do after all this is over?"

Evie was taken aback by the quick change in subject. She licked her lips and looked down at her hands folded in her lap. "I haven't thought that far ahead yet."

"It's obvious your hackers are the ones who took Brian. Once he's back and your necklace is safe, you know they'll no' bother you again."

"Yeah," she mumbled. It also meant Malcolm wouldn't be in her life.

The thought of that made her sick to her stomach. She'd gotten used to Malcolm's intense stare and his steely resolve. Even with everything he was suffering, he'd been there for her last night when she gave her soul to the Devil.

"What will you do?" she asked.

He shrugged but didn't answer.

"You should go to Larena. You need to talk to her, and I know she would want to see you."

Malcolm looked out the window. "I've considered it."

They fell into silence. Worry began to eat away at Evie the longer she sat there. Worry about Brian, about keeping the necklace, but also about being able to use her new, stronger magic.

Evie called to her magic and let it gather around her. It spun around her, growing until she could feel it through every inch of her body.

She lifted her gaze to find Malcolm sitting with his forearms braced on his thighs and his hands in tight fists.

His skin flashed maroon as he kept his head down and his face turned away from her.

"Malcolm?"

His head gradually lifted until she was staring into his azure eyes. "Doona. Stop."

"Stop?" she asked in confusion.

"Your magic. Doona stop."

Realization dawned as she remembered he could feel her magic. She rose from the bed and walked to him. Evie knelt before him so that she was looking up into his face.

"Does it hurt you, my magic?"

He shook his head. "Never."

Evie swallowed and gathered magic in one palm before she placed that hand on his shoulder. A low growl rose up from his chest as his gaze speared her.

Desire and excitement raced through her. Her chest heaved, just as Malcolm's did.

"More," he demanded.

Evie moved closer, situating herself between his legs. She used her other hand and placed it on his face.

She sucked in a breath when she saw his eyes close and pleasure wash over him. There was no doubt he not only felt her magic, but enjoyed it.

His eyes snapped open as his hands grabbed her shoulders. He pulled her against him, the heat of him searing her. Evie wound her arms around his neck.

She took a breath, allowing her magic to fill her even more. Then she expanded it so her magic surrounded Malcolm as well.

He cupped one side of her face and rubbed his thumb along her lower lip. Desire and need were reflected in his eyes. There was sadness there also.

Before she could ask him about it, his lips captured hers in a scorching, all-encompassing kiss that left her gasping for air.

And yearning for more.

He dragged her up from the floor so that she straddled him. His thick arousal pressed against her as she clung to him.

A storm of longing raged around them. Malcolm was her anchor, the rock she cleaved to so she wouldn't be swept away by the rampant need.

They tore at each other's clothes, discarding them one by one until they were flesh to flesh.

Evie let out a sigh and sunk her fingers in his cool gold locks. His fingers bit into her hips as he lifted her over him. With their gazes tangled, he slowly lowered her onto his thick cock.

Her body trembled at the feel of him once more filling her. She let out an unsteady breath when she was fully seated. Then he rocked her hips forward with his hands.

Evie bit her lip at the exquisite sensation. She dropped her head back and continued to rock her hips. Malcolm's hand braced against her back as he bent her farther.

She moaned when he flicked his tongue over her nipple before wrapping his mouth around the turgid peak. A cry was wrenched from her when he lightly bit down on her nipple.

Her hips moved faster and faster as she continued to wind her magic around them.

"Can no' hold back," Malcolm rasped.

"Don't." She lifted her head and smiled.

He slid a hand between them and swirled a thumb around her clit. That's all it took to send her over the edge.

Evie screamed her pleasure as they peaked together, their passion colliding, swelling. Until it coalesced into a brilliant flame that blazed hotter than the sun—and brighter than the moon.

CHAPTER
THIRTY-ONE

Rhys tapped his finger with a slow rhythm on the hood of Hal's Ferrari as he stared across the loch to the inn where Malcolm and Evie stayed.

"What is it?" Guy asked.

Rhys turned his head over his shoulder to Guy who was pulling his long, light brown hair back in a queue at the base of his neck. "Malcolm is different."

"Aye. We've already agreed on that."

Rhys shifted so that he leaned his forearms on the hood and stared across it to his friend. "You know more."

"Why does it matter?"

"It doesna. You know I'll help. I like the Warriors. But Malcolm has the look of a man who is about to do something stupid."

"I'll be sure to tell him you said that," Guy said irritably.

Rhys narrowed his gaze, his assumptions proven correct. "So he is."

"He thinks he is," Guy said with a sigh. "I'm no' going to sit by and allow it though. Malcolm believes he has a debt to pay that only his life will do as payment."

"As I said. Stupid." Rhys straightened and drummed his fingers on the car once more as he thought about Malcolm.

Guy scratched his jaw where a shadow of a beard had begun. "If it's Wallace who shows, as Malcolm suspects, we'll have our hands full getting the tourists away. Any given day there are hundreds of people touring those ruins."

"It would make life easier if we could be in dragon form," Rhys said with a grin.

"Doona even tease about that," Hal said as he walked up. He replaced his mobile phone in his pocket. "If Con heard you, he'd have your arse."

"He could try," Rhys said, his jaw tight as anger built. "Con may be the King of Kings, but that doesna mean he's always right."

Guy snorted. "And you wanting to show the humans dragons do exist is right?"

Rhys wiggled his eyebrows. "Nay. But it would be fun."

"Too much fun," Hal said with a smile as he slapped Rhys on the shoulder.

Rhys lifted his face to the sky. He yearned to take to the heavens and spread his wings, to feel the currents rush along his body.

"There are times it seems just a dream that we once ruled," he said. "I long to have the Yellows back. I miss the days when we were free."

"We all do," Guy said.

Silence filled the air before Hal asked, "Do you ever wish we'd gone with our dragons?"

"Every damned day," Rhys answered without hesitation.

Guy's lips twisted. "If you'd asked me before I met Elena, I would've agreed with you, Rhys. Now, I have her. I want my Reds back. I want to see dragons fill the skies again, but I fear it will never happen."

Rhys couldn't begin to understand Hal's, Guy's, or Banan's need for their women. He was happy his friends had found their mates, but he was glad he'd not been touched by such madness.

"So who is going to get Evie away?" he asked. "She'll be a handful once she discovers what Malcolm plans."

Guy crossed his arms over his chest, his expression one of disquiet. "I'll get Evie. Rhys, you'll need to grab the brother."

"And I'll help Malcolm," Hal said.

Rhys shook his head in aggravation. "We could take out Wallace once and for all. I'll get Brian out and protect the humans, but I'm no' leaving Malcolm to die."

"Nay," Guy said, his voice laden with determination and resolve. "We're no'."

Rhys smiled and rubbed his hands together. "We've less than an hour. Time to get in place."

"You'll be all right," Malcolm said. He stood with Evie at the door to their room. She was dressed and ready to face the kidnappers, but her pallor and rapid breathing caused him concern. "I'll be there, hidden, but keeping watch over you. We'll bring Brian home today."

She nodded and forced a smile. "I know."

"Do you?" When her face crumpled, it tore at him. Malcolm pulled her against his chest and held her. "I remember when I found Larena dying. Deirdre sent Warriors for her, but one of them didna like the idea of a female Warrior, so he stabbed her with a blade covered in *drough* blood."

Evie pulled back to look at him. "What do you mean? What does *drough* blood do?"

"One drop will kill us."

"Oh. You saved her, obviously."

Malcolm tugged at one of her curls. "I was merely a

man. I found Fallon. He was able to jump Larena to Mac-Leod Castle and Druids who could help her."

"Jump? You mean you can do that?"

"Nay. I meant he teleported. That's Fallon's power. He got her to his castle in time and she was saved. The point is that I understand how you're feeling. Larena didna get kidnapped, but she was dying. Right in front of me. Then Fallon took her, and I didna know what happened."

"So you went after her," she said softly.

Malcolm touched his scarred shoulder. "Aye."

"I know I won't get hurt, Malcolm, and not just because I have magic. I won't get hurt because you'll be there."

He stared down into her clear blue eyes, amazed that anyone could look at him with such confidence. His fingers caressed her jaw. "You're beautiful."

A genuine smile pulled at her lips as she glanced away, the embarrassment evident. "Flattery, Malcolm Munro, will get you everywhere."

He wanted to tell her how she had changed his life and made him feel again. He wanted her to know how much he owed her for believing in him when no one else had. But more than anything he wanted her to know how much he was going to miss her.

"I need to get moving," she said and rose up to place a quick kiss on his lips. "I know we're going to come out of this because you'll be there. Thank you."

He let her pull out of his grasp as she turned toward the door. Just before she went through it, she paused and looked back at him with another smile.

"I'll meet you back here. I can't wait to introduce you to Brian."

Malcolm swallowed the words he had been about to say and nodded. Once the door shut behind her, he turned to the window and the ruins of Urquhart Castle through the trees.

He walked to the window and waited until he saw the little rusted Nissan he'd stolen drive away before he strode from the inn. Malcolm walked along the road until he came to a section of the loch that was hidden from view. There he discarded his shirt and shoes and dove into the dark waters of Loch Ness.

Evie's hands shook as she drove to the famous castle. The narrow road took her up the mountain before she had to turn off and drive down into the parking area of Urquhart Castle.

She parked the car and turned off the ignition. "I can do this," she told herself. "I'm going to get Brian back no matter what."

Her hand touched the necklace through her sweater. Malcolm had warned her she might have to give it up. They had come up with a plan to get it back if that should happen.

She was ready to use her magic in whatever way was necessary, even if it meant killing. It was her brother's life at stake.

Evie took a deep breath and climbed out of the car. She settled her purse strap on her shoulder and walked to the window to purchase her ticket.

She was there twenty minutes early, but she wanted a look around herself. Apprehension prickled her skin as she waited in line behind a large group.

When she was finally inside and descending the stairs down to the museum and gift shop, she passed dozens of people.

It wasn't until she went through the gift shop and stepped outside once more that she spotted the group of schoolkids led by three teachers as they spoke about the history of Urquhart.

All those children gave her pause. What if she used her

black magic and it hurt them? What if she didn't use her magic and Brian was killed?

She felt sick to her stomach. Brian was her family, her only family. She was responsible for him. It had been her curiosity that had gotten him into this mess.

But to injure or kill a child on purpose or by accident to save her brother?

I'm going to Hell anyway.

She squeezed her eyes shut. Malcolm had warned her she would have difficult choices to make. This would be the first of many.

Her steps were awkward and wooden as she walked the gently sloping steps that took her down to the level of the ruins. She passed through the gatehouse of the castle and gasped as a gust of wind struck her.

She noticed the dark clouds gathering above. Would she be lucky enough that the approaching storm might send everyone inside? But no one took notice. Not even when large, fat drops of rain began to fall.

"Can't I catch a break?" she mumbled.

Two squealing young girls came running into the gatehouse area out of the rain, their giggles and laughter reminding Evie of innocence and youth.

That could be shattered if magic—black magic—was used at the castle. How many would die? How many mentally scarred for life?

But Brian's chances at remaining alive had risen now that she had black magic.

She prayed Brian had been treated well, because though she might not want to kill anyone, she wasn't sure how she would react if her brother showed any physical signs of abuse.

Evie stepped into the rain. She opted against the main castle since it was jam-packed with people and instead went to the right where there was a small tower that would offer her protection from the rain and more privacy to keep a lookout for Brian.

She hurried to the stone building unmindful of the rain. Just as she stepped inside, she ran into someone. Evie looked up into the palest blue eyes and stopped short. The man was gorgeous. Heart-stopping material actually.

He grinned and ran a hand through his black hair. "Excuse me, lass. I didna see where I was going."

Evie nodded. She watched him walk into the rain, his camera in his hand. A month ago she might have flirted with him, but not after a night in Malcolm's arms.

Her gaze searched for any hint of Brian, but she also looked for Malcolm. Without a doubt, she knew he would be there. She just wished she knew where.

He'd told her it was for her protection because she might glance his way if something went wrong. That would lead the kidnappers to know she wasn't alone. Or so Malcolm had said.

Evie wanted to think she knew better than to look at him, but then again, she wasn't sure of anything anymore. She'd never been in such a situation before.

Her blood pounded in her ears and her stomach was so tied in knots she feared she might lose what breakfast she'd managed to get down.

Evie bit back a giggle as she imagined what the kidnappers would do if she vomited all over them. She covered her mouth to hide the laughter that wouldn't be contained.

If it would throw the kidnappers off, she might be willing to get sick in public.

She took a deep breath when the giggles subsided. It was delirium. She knew that. Fear, apprehension, foreboding, and a multitude of other emotions were her constant companions. A person could only take so much before they broke.

Apparently her breaking point was thinking of vomiting on someone.

Evie smiled again, but it quickly died as she saw a group of people walking from the gift shop toward the castle. A glance at her watch showed it was ten minutes until noon. Brian could be in that group.

She rose up on tiptoes, leaning her body one way and the other looking for some sign of him. Just as she was about to give up, she spotted his tall frame that had begun to fill out with muscles over the last year.

His head turned and she saw his face. Evie let out a relieved breath. It was Brian. She was closer than ever to getting him back.

Nothing would stand in her way now.

CHAPTER
THIRTY-TWO

Malcolm broke the surface of the water and began to climb the rocks to Urquhart. He'd felt Evie's magic the entire swim to the ruins, and now that he was closer, he could pinpoint where she was on the grounds.

He breathed a sigh of relief that somehow she'd put herself close to Hal. Hopefully, the Dragon King would stay near her.

Malcolm peered over the rocks and saw the sheer number of tourists. He clenched his jaw. It was going to be difficult to get everyone out safely, if his worst fears came to pass and it was Wallace after Evie.

The steps leading up and out of the castle were wide, but there were many, and the fact there was a group of children didn't bode well for anyone.

The rain was helping to keep a large number of tourists in the large gift shop and café. A few more were making their way inside as he watched.

Malcolm paused when he felt his god roar in approval right before there was a crack of lightning. It was always the same in a storm. Daal craved the lightning.

And now, so did Malcolm.

Electrical currents rushed along his arms and pooled in his palms, waiting to be released. He refused to give in to the thrill of shooting the lightning from his hands as he normally did. Instead, he focused on Evie.

He continued up the rocks until they merged with the stones of the ruins and he was on top of the small tower where Evie was. He stretched himself out on his stomach and let his gaze wander the area when he felt the first nauseating strings of *drough* magic.

Malcolm knew the feel of that particular magic. It was Jason Wallace. Just as he'd suspected. Electrical currents crackled in his palms, vibrating the tower as he fought not to attack the bastard.

"Easy," came a voice to Malcolm's left.

He recognized it as Hal's and knew the dragon was trying to help. "Wallace is here," he whispered, knowing the King had hearing as good as his own.

"Fuck," came the muffled reply.

In the distance, bells began to chime from a nearby church, signaling noon. Malcolm struggled against leaving his hidden position and going to Evie. She might be a *drough* now, but she didn't stand a chance against someone like Wallace.

Not only did he have more potent magic, but she was too tenderhearted and had too much of a conscience to do the unspeakable things Wallace was capable of.

Malcolm's claws shot from his fingers and punctured the roofing when he spotted Evie as she emerged from the tower and walked away from him.

"Nay," he whispered.

If he went after her, there was a chance she would lose Brian, possibly forever. She'd never forgive him for that.

But if he remained where he was, Malcolm knew Wallace would try and take her. Malcolm would never forgive himself if that happened.

"Give her time," Hal cautioned.

Malcolm looked over the side of the tower to find Hal facing away from Evie and pretending to take pictures. Hal kept turning his body and clicking the camera until he had his back to the water.

It was killing Malcolm to wait, but he knew the dragon was right. He had to give her time to try and make the exchange.

His body tensed when she stopped walking and grabbed her mobile. Anger and fear spiked in her magic as she slowly lowered the phone and turned to a bench.

When she sat, Malcolm watched anyone who came near her, waiting to see if it was Wallace or some lackey. The fact Malcolm could feel Wallace's magic but not find him only made it more difficult to linger where he was.

Malcolm's god bellowed in warning when a teacher called a group of kids together behind Evie's bench. A woman sat beside Evie, and just when Malcolm thought she might be the lackey, a man called out to her and she rose to go to him.

Evie was once more alone. She sat stiffly, her gaze alighting on everyone. Seconds ticked by until a man in a trench coat and plaid cap pulled low sat beside her.

As soon as Evie's head swiveled to the man, Malcolm knew she was about to make the trade for Brian.

"You came alone. Good."

Evie's heart beat a slow, sickening thud in her chest. She clutched her purse and looked to her right where the man sat. "Where's Brian?"

"Oh, he's around. Doona concern yourself with him."

Evie tried to see something of the man's face, but with his hat low and the collar of his coat up, she had no luck catching sight of anything but his thin lips and the ever-present smirk.

"I'm not giving you the necklace until I see my brother," she said in a voice she didn't recognize.

"Hmm. Maybe you have some gumption after all. You should've been smarter to begin with and no' put up a picture of that lovely necklace of yours. Do you even know what it is?"

"Yes," she said. It wasn't an outright lie. She knew the necklace held a spell, she just didn't know what the spell was. "Enough stalling. My brother. Now."

The man stretched out both arms on the back of the bench. "Now, Miss Walker, you need to mind your manners. I'm the one calling the shots today."

Evie made herself remain still when she wanted to send a blast of magic straight at his head. "The longer you hold off returning Brian, the longer you'll wait to get the necklace."

"There's no need for that. Give me the necklace now."

"Do you think I'm that naïve?" she asked with a snort.

"Give me the necklace now, or you'll never see your brother again."

Evie couldn't feel her legs, but somehow she got to her feet. "You could've already killed him for all I know. I'm not handing you the necklace until I know he's alive."

"Did you ever stop to wonder how I got your brother away from the highly skilled security at his school? Maybe you should think about that before you threaten me."

"It's not a threat. It's a promise. And you might think you're skilled enough to hack into my system and somehow get to my brother, but trust me when I say if I don't get Brian back today, you'll never get your hands on the necklace."

The man's head shifted upward, but the shadows still concealed his face. "You and I would make a fine team, Miss Walker. If you ever decide to join those of us using black magic, let me know."

"Brian. Now."

He put his hands on his legs before he rose to his feet. "In a few seconds you'll see Brian come through the gate-house. Leave the necklace in the tower under the left window. If you try to trick me, trust me when *I* say neither you nor your brother will leave alive. And if you're thinking of using magic, know that I have no problem killing everyone here."

Evie blinked through the rain and nodded. "Fine. Just get out of my sight and send Brian."

The man gave a bow of his head and turned on his heel. He faded into the crowd as lightning struck behind her. She jumped, startled by the vibrations in the ground. Evie briefly wondered if it was Malcolm, but those thoughts scattered as she caught sight of Brian coming through the gatehouse.

"Brian!" she hollered and waved her arms even as she wondered if she could give the necklace to a man who was obviously evil.

Malcolm watched the tall, lanky teenager start toward Evie. He was several inches taller than she, and already he'd begun to fill out. Malcolm suspected the lad would reach his full height soon.

He wanted to observe Evie and Brian's reunion, but he focused instead on the man who had approached Evie. His voice didn't match Wallace's, but that was something easily changed with magic.

The only thing that kept Malcolm hidden was that he caught sight of both Hal and Guy closing in behind Evie. Malcolm rolled to the side and off the roof, landing on his feet behind a couple huddled under an umbrella.

They never heard him come within inches of them. Malcolm turned and started after the man, making himself as invisible as he could.

An older woman whistled when he passed her, but he didn't slow his stride. He was almost upon the man when Evie's magic, full of shock and fury, stopped him cold.

Malcolm stood straight and slowly turned to his right where Evie was.

Evie shook her head at the boy before her. She noticed something odd about him when he'd drawn close, but she was so happy to see Brian she hadn't given it much thought. But the longer she looked at him, the more she knew.

This wasn't Brian.

"Who are you?"

The boy scrunched up his face and shrugged.

"No," she said and fought tears. "You're not my brother."

The boy suddenly smiled and reached for her. Before Evie could react, he somehow got ahold of her necklace and gave a vicious jerk. The chains bit into her neck, cutting her before they broke and he took off running with her necklace.

"Stop!" she yelled and sent a blast of magic at him.

As soon as her magic hit the boy, there was nothing but smoke. It was as if he disappeared.

Evie's legs buckled when someone grabbed her arms and kept her upright.

"You need to come with me, Evie," the man said urgently. "I'm a friend of Malcolm's. He asked me to look out for you while he tended to things."

Evie turned her head and looked at the man with the startling pale brown eyes ringed with black. His hair was shoved away from his face and was as soaked as his clothes.

"I'm Guy. A friend," he repeated more slowly as he stared into her eyes. "I'll bring you to Malcolm, but we have to go. Now."

"Aye, now," said another man who ran ahead of them.

Evie recognized him as the one she'd bumped into earlier. She touched her neck, but there was no comforting presence of the necklace anymore. "They got the necklace. And they still have Brian."

"Leave that to Malcolm for now."

Guy began to tug her after him, and that was when Evie noticed everyone running toward the gatehouse to try and leave the ruins.

Hundreds of screams suddenly filled her ears before a crack of lightning landed somewhere behind her. She jerked her arm out of Guy's grasp and turned to find Malcolm standing in the middle of a grassy section with his arms out to his sides and lightning blazing around him, from him.

Through him.

It was a glorious, impressive sight to behold. Malcolm's power was evident in his ferocity and unleashed fury. He stood bare chested, his skin colored maroon as he became one with the lightning.

"Oh," she whispered.

"Evie, Malcolm will have my head if I doona get you out of here."

She looked over her shoulder at Guy. "I can't leave him. I'm a . . . I have magic."

"I know." Guy's lips flattened briefly. "I want to help him as well, but if he's right—and he has been so far—whoever took your brother and the necklace will be coming for you next."

She let him pull her farther away from Malcolm. "But why? They have everything now."

"No' hardly," said the second man. "You know how to work the necklace, lass."

They reached the gatehouse, and Evie took one last look at Malcolm as another man approached him. A bolt of lightning struck the man, but a second later Malcolm went flying backward to land with a thud against some ruins.

"Bloody hell," Guy said.

Evie screamed Malcolm's name, but Guy lifted her in his arms and started running.

CHAPTER
THIRTY-THREE

Malcolm's head exploded with agony as it slammed back against the ancient stones before his body crashed to the ground. Blood oozed down his neck in thick rivulets.

He picked himself up and faced Wallace. "I knew it was you."

Jason Wallace threw off his hat and smiled. "You knew and you didna come prepared to fight? Come on, Malcolm, we both know you're no match for me."

Out of the corner of his eye, Malcolm saw Guy carry Evie away. The hold on his heart eased once he knew she was safe. Now, he could turn his full attention to the *drough* that wouldn't die.

"You're worse than a roach, Wallace. How can you claim to be so smart, yet no' know when you're no' wanted?"

"The people doona know they need me. Yet. But they will. They will. Perhaps I'll keep you alive long enough to see it."

"I hear insanity runs in the family."

Wallace merely leered. "No. I think I'll make you watch as I turn your Druid into a killing machine."

Rage, bright and hot, scorched through Malcolm at such a rate that he was powerless to contain it. Lightning built in his hands, waiting to be discharged.

"You'll never get your hands on her."

"Want to bet?" Jason asked much too confidently for Malcolm's pleasure.

Malcolm threw both his hands forward, his palms facing Wallace as dozens of lightning bolts sailed across the distance and slammed into the *drough*.

Again and again Malcolm hit him with the currents, but Malcolm knew it was going to take more than that to kill Wallace. He wanted to be the one to do it, wanted to be the one to end it all. But it wouldn't be him.

All he was doing was giving Guy and the other Kings enough time to get Evie away.

There was a loud bellow before a heavy dose of black magic came at him. Malcolm blocked most of it with his lightning, but he couldn't stop all of it.

The heaving, sickening feel of it encircled him. It enfolded him, besieging him at every turn until even Daal was telling him to flee. But Malcolm knew his time of reckoning had come.

He was prepared.

The *drough* magic weighed him down until he dropped to one knee, his lips peeled back over clenched fangs. His body strained against the assault, his power surging through him to give him added strength.

Guy exchanged a glance with Hal and Rhys as they ran up after ensuring everyone had gotten out of the castle safely. Guy looked at the battle going on below.

It wasn't in his nature—or any of the Kings'—to leave a friend in trouble. He knew when he'd promised Malcolm that he would take Evie that it might very well come to this.

"We're no' seriously leaving him," Rhys said angrily.

Guy licked his lips and glanced at Evie who stood against the car with tears running down her face. "I made a promise. I have to get Evie away."

"We doona," Hal said.

Guy nodded, a plan taking form. He walked to Evie and bent so that she had to look at him. "I need you to use your magic and prevent anyone from seeing the battle."

"What?" Evie asked and tried to pull away from him. "I don't know that spell. How can I do that?"

Rhys stalked to her and pointed to the few who lingered to stare at the odd array of lightning coming from below them at the ruins. "Take a look around, Druid. People are noticing. Once they think they're no' in danger they'll want a closer look. Do you really want them to see Malcolm? Do you know what will happen if they do?"

"I . . ." She paused and gave a little shake of her head. "They can't see Malcolm. They can't know."

"Then do something," Hal urged.

Guy watched as Evie pushed away from the car and walked between him and Rhys. She stopped before she got to the stone wall separating the parking lot from the ruins below.

"Doona worry about a spell," Guy said. "Just think of blocking out Malcolm and his opponent from view."

Just as Guy expected, it took Evie but a few minutes before her magic was able to hide Malcolm and Wallace from view.

"Let's go help Malcolm," Evie said when she faced him.

Hal opened the passenger door to his Ferrari. "Malcolm's opponent is no match for him. Besides, Malcolm will do his best fighting once he knows you're no' here to get hurt."

"I can't leave."

"He's down there for you," Guy argued. "To make sure you get away. Doona make what he's doing for nothing."

She wiped at a tear and walked to the car. She paused with one foot in the car and said, "Don't let anything happen to him. Please."

"You'll be seeing him soon." Hal closed the door once she was seated.

Guy gave a nod to his fellow dragons and walked to the driver's side. He slid behind the wheel and started the engine. As he drove away, he prayed they hadn't just lied to Evie.

Malcolm felt more blood run down his abdomen as his chest was sliced open. He shifted his shoulders to try and deflect the next hit of magic, but Wallace was too fast.

"You're supposed to be a Warrior," Jason taunted. "I see a slow, wounded animal in front of me, no' the immortal beasts I usually fight."

Malcolm roared his fury. He threw a bolt of lightning at Wallace as he leapt toward him. Malcolm smiled when he caught Jason by surprise and landed on his chest, pinning him to the ground.

He wrapped a hand around Wallace's neck and squeezed. "We found a way to kill Deirdre. We'll find a way to kill you."

"We?" Wallace laughed and touched Malcolm's arm holding his throat.

Malcolm bit back a bellow of anger as fire raced up his skin, scorching him. He refused to release Jason though. He sank his claws into Wallace's neck and smiled when his blood flowed. "You *will* die."

A massive blast of magic hit Malcolm squarely in the chest and sent him somersaulting through the air. He shifted in the air to land on his feet and spotted Wallace standing.

"I've already died, you miserable fuck! You can no' kill me. No one can."

"Want to bet?" Malcolm threw his words back at him. "I've had enough of this."

Malcolm let his lightning fly around him, hitting anything and everything. He wanted Wallace dazed when he ripped out his heart.

But Malcolm never got that chance. He knew Wallace's magic had increased, but he wasn't prepared for the full force of it that had him pinned against the tower unable even to pull a breath into his lungs.

Jason walked to him as the lightning died away. "This was . . . entertaining to say the least. I have plans for you, Malcolm. You just proved everything I needed to know."

Pain blinded Malcolm as he felt his scarred shoulder begin to twist at an odd angle. Bone popped, muscle shredded, and ligaments broke. Skin was torn, sliced as more cuts covered him.

All the while he was powerless to fight. It was worse than when Deirdre had sent her Warriors after him. At least then he'd been able to defend himself. It had been a poor attempt, but it was better than what he was enduring now.

He tried to call up his power, but Wallace had even put a halt to that. Malcolm had endured pain before. He would again. Anything for Evie.

Because despite Wallace still having Brian and now Evie's necklace, he didn't have her. It was the one thing Malcolm had done right. He knew without a doubt the Dragon Kings would make sure Wallace never touched her.

He also suspected the Kings would do what they could to get Brian back, even if that included bringing the other Warriors in on it.

Inwardly, Malcolm yelled as his arm was torn, leaving

it hanging from his body by a thin strip of flesh. Wallace wasn't going to allow him to live, which is what he'd expected.

Malcolm just wished he'd have taken a few minutes and called Larena. He'd put his cousin through too much already. With his death, maybe she could get on with her life instead of worrying over him.

"That looks like it hurt," Wallace said as he peered at Malcolm's damaged arm. "Let's see if I can make the other hurt worse."

It felt like white-hot pokers were thrust into his shoulder. Malcolm's gaze was locked on Wallace. The *drough*'s magic seemed to be unstoppable and never ending. With mere thoughts, he could do whatever he wanted.

Jason's smile, full of satisfaction and delight, made Malcolm sick. Wallace enjoyed making people suffer. He savored the shouts of pain and cries for mercy.

It was too bad Malcolm wouldn't be the one to bring the asshole down.

Malcolm's gut clenched when he felt his shoulder shatter into pieces. If he hadn't been held by Wallace's magic, he knew he would be doubled over from the pain.

"Did that no' hurt?" Wallace asked in confusion. "I know that must've hurt. Yet you didna cry out, Malcolm. I suppose I need to inflict more pain."

Malcolm thought of ways he could kill Wallace, of how he'd skin him inch by inch. Malcolm imagined the thousands of different methods that could make Jason suffer.

All the while, Wallace used his magic to continue to torture him in varying ways.

Malcolm was suddenly pulled away from the tower, only to find Wallace with a deranged smile on his face as he sent Malcolm crashing back into it. Time and again.

Malcolm heard the stones crack under the assault, felt

the bones in his body break one by one. His nose and jaw were crushed as Wallace sent him face-first into the tower.

When the stones finally shattered and Malcolm crashed into the next wall, an image of Evie's face filled his mind. He drifted away from the agony and concentrated on the one thing in his life that had given him happiness.

Evie.

"It's time," Wallace's voice sounded in his ear.

He knew what Jason was going to do next. What Wallace didn't know was that Malcolm, along with everyone at MacLeod Castle, benefited from Britt's serum, which would counteract the *drough* blood.

Malcolm tried to smile, but he couldn't manage it. In the next instant, Malcolm's body jerked as *drough* blood was dropped into one of his many wounds.

He ground his teeth together, not understanding why the serum wasn't protecting him. Then he realized why— magic. Malcolm didn't know how long it took for Wallace to use his body as a battering ram to break through the tower's outer wall. None of it mattered as one by one, his organs began to shut down.

One moment he was smashed against the stones, and the next Malcolm was sailing through the air, the dark waters of Loch Ness rising to meet him.

Rhys let out a shout when he and Hal raced through the gatehouse to see Malcolm's body being rammed against the tower again and again.

Wallace turned to them, ready to fight, just as Rhys shifted into dragon form. That's all it took for Wallace to use his magic and disappear.

Rhys flew over the now-crumbling tower and tucked his wings to dive into the water. Just before he hit, he shifted back into human form.

Seconds after he dove into the water, Hal followed.

They followed Malcolm's still form as it floated downward into the loch.

Rhys was the first to reach him. He took hold of Malcolm's arm and started to pull when he saw the damage. With a curse, Rhys swam deeper and locked an arm around Malcolm's chest as blood continued to seep from his wounds.

Time was of the essence. Rhys shifted into dragon form with Malcolm carefully clutched in one of his claws before he broke the surface of the water and flew to the clouds and turned toward Dreagan.

CHAPTER
THIRTY-FOUR

Evie had imagined how her afternoon would be, but not once had she thought Brian wouldn't be beside her and that she would leave Malcolm behind to fight some unknown foe.

She'd never felt so helpless, defenseless. So . . . incapable.

A tear dropped on her cheek and she hastily swiped it away. How she hated that she couldn't even get her emotions under control.

"You know it's no' your fault," Guy said.

She glanced at him before focusing her gaze back on the road. "Of course it is. I put up the Web site. I went looking for Druids. I'm the imbecile who posted the picture of the necklace. I'm the one who chose to become *drough*."

"Perhaps, lass, but you were no' the one who set out to betray you."

Evie shuddered as she remembered the man's voice. "You know who it was Malcolm was fighting, don't you?"

The only indication she got that Guy had actually heard

her was the slight whitening of his knuckles as he gripped the steering wheel tighter.

"Who is he?" she prodded.

Guy put his blinker on before he turned off the main road. "Malcolm should be the one to answer that."

"He's not here with me now. You are, and I asked a question. I still don't have my brother, my necklace was stolen, and I left Malcolm behind. You can answer this."

"Wallace. Jason Wallace is his name," came the grumbled reply.

Evie closed her eyes and refused to shed any more tears. "Dear God. Malcolm told me it was him. I kept hoping Malcolm was wrong, but he wasn't."

Her eyes snapped open when a mobile began to ring. Guy quickly pulled over and dug the phone out of his pocket. "Aye," he answered.

Evie looked down at her hand to see a broken thumb nail that went all the way to the quick. When had that happened? She didn't remember feeling any kind of pain.

"Shite. We're on our way," Guy said and tossed aside the phone before stomping on the accelerator, the Ferrari spinning out before it roared to life and raced down the road.

A feeling of dread descended. Evie gripped her hands together in her lap. "Tell me that wasn't about Malcolm. Please, Guy, I need some good news."

Guy's eyes briefly met hers before he focused on the road, weaving the red supercar in and out of traffic as he sped down the road.

"No. No, no, no, no. This can't be happening. Get me to him now!" Evie shouted.

Phelan smiled when Aisley gave him the other half of her sandwich. "How'd you know I was still hungry?"

"You're always hungry," she said with a roll of her eyes.

"You know it." He gave her a wink and pulled her into his lap.

Aisley tucked her hair behind her ears and pretended that Charon and Laura weren't watching. "You were satisfied this morning."

"TMI," Laura said and laughed. "I've got my hands full with Charon. I don't need to know about the two of you."

Charon shrugged and set aside his napkin. "What? You know I never get enough of you."

Phelan opened his mouth to tease Aisley more when a form filled the doorway. He recognized Hal instantly. The fact the Dragon King wore Phelan's newly bought jeans that had been folded on the couch seconds ago didn't go unnoticed.

"I'm sorry to barge in," Hal said and looked from Charon to Phelan. "I've come for you."

"Come for me?" Phelan repeated. He walked to the window and looked down from the third story of Charon's building into the back parking area to see only his and Charon's vehicles. "As in you flew here? As a dragon?"

Hal nodded solemnly. "It's an emergency."

"What kind of emergency would make you risk being seen?" Charon asked.

Hal briefly shut his eyes and shook his head. "It's Malcolm. He fought Wallace."

Phelan welcomed Aisley's comfort when she walked to him and took his hand. "Where is Malcolm?"

"At Dreagan. Rhys took him. There's no' a lot of time, Phelan. We have to go now."

"We'll never make it by car."

Hal stared at him, his moonlight blue eyes telling them

without words how precarious the situation was. "I'll be flying you."

Phelan gave Aisley a kiss and walked to Hal. "Let's get going."

Charon, Laura, and Aisley rushed for the stairs. "We'll meet you there," Charon called.

Phelan followed Hal to the sliding glass door and walked outside.

"I need to climb high and fast. I'll no' let you fall though."

Phelan grunted. "Just get me to Malcolm."

The words had barely left his mouth before a dragon the color of emeralds was hovering above him. Phelan leaped into the air, and Hal's large claw came around him. And then they were flying straight up into the clouds.

Phelan might have enjoyed how fast Hal flew, his massive wings eating miles in one flap, but his worry over Malcolm was too great.

"Were you with Malcolm?" Phelan yelled up at Hal.

Hal's great head gave a nod, which caused Phelan to curse. If they needed him for Malcolm, it was because Wallace had used *drough* blood and the serum hadn't worked. It was Phelan's blood, his Fae blood, that allowed him to heal anyone of anything.

The only thing he couldn't do was bring someone back from the dead.

The clouds began to thin. Phelan caught sight of Dreagan on the horizon. In no time at all, the mansion was in view. Hal dove from the sky and released Phelan.

Phelan landed with his legs bent and rolled. He immediately came to his feet to find Constantine, the King of Kings standing at the front door to the mansion with bloodstains on his white dress shirt.

"Follow me," Con said brusquely.

Phelan hurried after Con, dusting off his clothes as he did. He was taken to the third floor of the mansion and down a long corridor to a back bedroom.

He looked into the room and saw Malcolm lying still—too still—on the large bed.

"I got him here as fast as I could," Rhys said from the corner.

Phelan took a look at the dragon's gaze and knew whatever had happened to Malcolm, Wallace had enjoyed it.

It wasn't until Phelan stood by the bed and saw the damage to his friend that he grabbed the headboard to keep himself on his feet. "Son of a bitch," he ground out.

"I've paused the *drough* blood inside him," Con said as he walked to the other side of the bed. "It's odd that I can no' heal him completely. We're hoping you can."

Phelan raked a hand down his face knowing he would forever see the image of Malcolm's right arm almost completely torn from his body and his entire front, including his face, so cut up he was unrecognizable.

"It's been the same for me," Phelan finally managed to get out. "Wallace has done something to his blood. A serum was created to block whatever Wallace did, but it must no' be working. I can slow what the *drough* blood does to a Warrior, but I can no' heal it as I used to."

Con removed his cuff links and rolled up his sleeves. "Looks like it's going to take both of us."

"I'm no' going to lose him," Phelan said. "I'll do whatever it takes, contact whoever it takes."

Con raised a blond brow. "Meaning you'll send a message to Rhi?"

"If I have to." It was Rhi, a Fae, who had first found him. She was elusive and came only when she wanted, but he'd never asked her for a favor. He just hoped that she would understand it was an emergency if he called for her.

Con shrugged. "If I have to have a Fae on Dreagan, she's the least offensive."

Phelan let a gold claw elongate from his right hand. He held his arm over Malcolm and used his talon to slice a long cut down the length of his forearm.

His blood gushed out and onto Malcolm's many wounds. Normally it would take just a drop or two of his blood to begin healing, but with Wallace's new *drough* blood, things were different.

While Phelan continued to pour his blood into Malcolm, Constantine simply touched Malcolm. That's all it took for Phelan to experience the unusual dragon magic possessed by all the Kings.

"Why is it no' working?" Rhys demanded.

Phelan met the dragon's gaze and heard the unmistakable rattle of death in Malcolm's chest.

It was another thirty minutes before Phelan let out a slow breath. "He's improving."

"No' by much," Con said flatly. "Just what did Wallace do to the *drough* blood?"

Phelan cut his arm again and held the wound over Malcolm's damaged right arm. "He died and came back. I fear he's indestructible now."

"That's shite," Hal said from the doorway. "Everything can be killed. It's just finding a way to do it."

Phelan nodded as he saw one of Malcolm's smaller cuts begin to slowly knit together. "We'll kill Wallace. Doona worry about that."

Rhys walked into the connecting bathroom and grabbed some towels. "Guy will arrive with Evie soon. She can no' see Malcolm like this."

"Damn," Hal said and hurried to help.

Phelan caught Con's gaze. "What the hell happened?"

"I'm no' sure I should be telling you."

"That's no' what I asked." Phelan fisted his hand. He was ready to punch Con, regardless of who he was.

Con removed his hand from Malcolm. "That's all we can do for him now. He's healing, but slowly."

"Constantine."

Black eyes met Phelan's, and he saw determination and a shadow of regret. "Malcolm found a Druid but didna want to tell any of you. Her brother was kidnapped, and he helped her try and get him back."

"It was Wallace who took the Druid's brother?"

Rhys came to stand beside Con and looked down at Malcolm. "He knew it was. It's why he called Guy for help. Guy asked me and Hal to tag along in case there was trouble."

"I see none of you are injured. Did you no' join in the fight?" Phelan asked. Though he knew the answer. The Kings were good allies, but Con wanted them kept secret and out of any skirmishes.

It was Hal who said, "Rhys was to take Brian and Guy was in charge of Evie once the exchange happened. We vowed to get them and the innocent tourists out no matter what."

"Malcolm knew it was Wallace from the beginning," Rhys said as he wiped up more blood. "Then Wallace tricked Evie by not bringing her brother, and all hell broke loose. We did as promised and got everyone out."

"It was during all of that when the fight between Malcolm and Wallace began." Hal rubbed the back of his neck, his gaze on the floor.

Rhys moved the wet towel from one hand to another. "Guy got Evie to hide Malcolm and Wallace from view so no one would see anything."

"As soon as Evie was gone, Rhys and I went to help Malcolm."

"But it was too late. Wallace disappeared, and I had to

dive into the loch for Malcolm," Rhys finished and cleared his throat.

Phelan pulled the chair from the corner closer to the bed and sank into it. He was taking it all in, more troubled than ever that Malcolm hadn't called him. More than that was Malcolm pitting himself against Wallace. "Malcolm knew he wouldna survive fighting Wallace alone."

"He did indeed."

Phelan turned his head to find Guy standing in the doorway with a petite brunette by his side wearing a shell-shocked expression in her blue eyes.

"Malcolm," she whispered in a shaky voice and walked to the bed.

Con and Rhys immediately got out of the way to give her room. Her hand shook as she reached out to smooth a lock of Malcolm's blond hair from his forehead.

Phelan then understood why Malcolm had kept the Druid secret as he felt her curious magic that had an unmistakable feel of *drough* mixed in.

CHAPTER
THIRTY-FIVE

Evie couldn't look away from the blood that coated Malcolm. Some of it darkened as it dried on his flesh, but more of it was bright red as his wounds continued to bleed.

"Why isn't he healed?" she asked the room at large. "He's immortal."

"Normally he would be all but healed by now," replied the man who watched her with blue-gray eyes as he sat next to the bed opposite her.

Guy came to stand beside her. "Wallace wanted him to suffer."

Evie blinked and turned her head to Guy. "Jason used *drough* blood, didn't he?"

Guy looked away, but it was the man in the chair who answered, "Aye."

"Are you Malcolm's friend?" she asked.

"I am. The name is Phelan."

She fisted her hand before she touched Malcolm's arm. The need to feel him was strong, but she feared hurting him. "Thank you, everyone, for helping him. I didn't know . . . he didn't tell me that he . . ."

Evie couldn't finish the sentence. Now she understood

Malcolm's urgency when they'd made love the last time. He'd been saying good-bye with his body and touch rather than words.

Her gaze went to his scarred shoulder that was torn to bits. She gagged and covered her mouth with her hand. "What kind of monster is Wallace to do this?"

"The worst kind," Rhys said from behind her.

Malcolm's handsome face was destroyed, his chest shredded with so many cuts she couldn't begin to count them. "Will he recover?" She lifted her gaze to look at the five men around her. "He has to be all right."

"He's mending," said the tall, golden-haired man with the black eyes. "It's slow, but he's fighting the effects of the *drough* blood, with our help and a serum he took before. He should pull through. I'm Constantine, by the way. Welcome to Dreagan. Guy, Rhys, and Hal will see to anything you need while you're with us."

Her mobile chimed then with a message. She pulled it out of her purse and read the message. Her stomach dropped to her feet when she saw it was from the kidnapper—or Jason Wallace as she now knew.

"Evie?" Guy asked, concern lacing his voice.

She handed him her mobile and reached for the headboard to keep herself upright. "It's Jason. He's offered me Brian's return if I go to him now."

Phelan stood and grabbed her mobile from Guy before she finished talking. After reading the message, he handed the phone to Hal. "We wait for Malcolm to wake before any decisions are made."

Evie bristled at his tone. It was obvious he blamed her for what happened by the anger in his voice. She lifted her chin, but didn't bother to argue.

The only person she would talk to about this was Malcolm. Or maybe Guy, but certainly not Phelan. It was her brother's life on the line.

"I never wanted Malcolm to get hurt," she told Phelan.

Phelan cut his gaze to her. "Then you should've never involved him. He's a good man. Of course he was going to help you. You knew he would."

Had she? Evie looked back down at Malcolm. Had she brought him to the brink of death?

"Sit," Guy urged while putting pressure on her shoulders.

Evie sank into the chair and put her hand on Malcolm's thigh, one of the only spots not covered in blood.

Phelan reluctantly followed Con and the others into the hall. He watched Evie closely as she sat beside Malcolm.

"You doona trust her," Constantine stated.

Phelan shrugged and found Guy staring at him. "Nay, I doona. She's *drough*."

"Wallace didna give her a choice," Guy said. "She did it knowing she would lose her soul, but to save innocents and her brother."

Rhys crossed his arms over his chest. "Malcolm told us all about it. Malcolm tried to stop her, but didna get there in time. Evie has a spell Wallace wants, and she was trying to keep it from him and get her brother back."

"He didna call me because she turned *drough*." Phelan sighed loudly. "I'd been through all of that with Aisley. He should've contacted me."

Hal raised a black brow. "Did you let the others know about Aisley? Nay. You kept her existence a secret until you had no choice. Malcolm was making the same decision."

"I was protecting Aisley," Phelan ground out in a low voice.

Guy's forehead furrowed. "And what do you think Malcolm was doing with Evie?"

Phelan didn't want to hear this. It would be easier to hate Evie and place the blame squarely on her shoulders. But the Kings were right. Malcolm had been protecting her, which meant he cared. How deeply, was the question.

"Point taken," Phelan grumbled.

Guy leaned a shoulder against the door frame. "Malcolm asked that we protect Evie in his absence."

Phelan wanted to argue the point. It was the Warriors, after all, who gave sanctuary to all Druids. Malcolm had sought aid elsewhere, and as much as it irked Phelan, he would go with Malcolm's wishes. "I think we should call Fallon and have him bring more of it for Malcolm."

Banan walked up then and glanced at Con. "I agree. Fallon was looking for Malcolm."

The tension between Con and Banan was evident. But that was Dragon King business and didn't involve Phelan. Though he was immensely curious, which meant there was no way he was keeping his mouth shut.

"So Fallon called looking for Malcolm?" Phelan asked.

Con slowly pulled his gaze away from Banan. "Before Rhys arrived with Malcolm, aye."

"You've dealt with *drough* blood inside you," Rhys said as if to change the subject. "Can you no' figure out what it is Wallace has done to change it?"

Phelan looked into the room and saw Evie use her ger to measure the length of a cut on Malcolm's arm. concern was evident, as was her caring. Maybe he'd be too hard on her.

Then again, she was *drough*. By choice.

Phelan cleared his throat as he looked at the Kings. He lowered his voice and said, "I sensed death when trying to heal Malcolm. It's nagged me ever since. Death has a certain feel to it. It's no' something I'd mistake, no' after all the battles I've been in."

"Wallace did die," Banan pointed out.

Phelan wanted to punch something. "Fuck. How did we all miss it? How did we all overlook something so obvious?"

"Because it was too obvious," Hal said with a twist of his lips.

Guy shook his head. "With Wallace having come back from the dead, he brought Death back with him. It's inside him, so it would be in his blood."

"And now inside Malcolm," Phelan said, hatred for Wallace rising to new heights.

"There is one who could help," Hal said into the silence.

Con's gaze whipped to him, fury coming off him in waves. "Doona even dare bring it up. Ulrik's power is gone. Now leave it, Hal."

Phelan watched Con stalk away. Ulrik's name again? It wasn't the first time Phelan had heard his name, and it probably wouldn't be the last.

By the way the four remaining Kings exchanged looks, Ulrik was a cause of discontent through the ranks of the dragons.

"It was worth a try," Guy said and clapped Hal on the shoulder.

Banan jerked his chin to Phelan. "I think it's time you called Fallon."

But Phelan wasn't so sure. "Why didna Con tell him where Malcolm was? I gather Con knew Guy and the others had gone to help."

"Aye," Banan said tightly. "Con didna give me a reason for lying to Fallon. He just said to leave it."

Rhys raked a hand through his hair. "Con doesna do anything without a purpose. If he didna tell Fallon, there was a good cause for it."

"I doona know Con as you all, but I was thinking the same thing. He's helped us before. Why would he stop now?" Phelan asked, more to himself than the others.

But it was Hal who asked, "What are you thinking?"

Phelan met his gaze and sighed. "I'm thinking I wait to contact Fallon."

"And if Charon does it?"

"He willna," Phelan said. "No' yet anyway."

Guy pushed away from the wall. "You said Charon was given a serum. Why did he need it?"

"When he took a blade meant for Arran, my blood couldna heal him immediately either. He was left with the feel of that blade in him for weeks after. Larena suffered even more. No Druid magic could stop her death, though I do think they brought her back somehow."

Banan frowned, his head cocked to the side. "Brought her back? Are you telling me she died?"

Phelan nodded. "She returned different. Larena struggled to remain in control of her goddess. She wanted to let it all go and give in. Had Fallon no' been there, I believe she would've."

All five of them turned their heads to look at Malcolm's still form. Phelan knew how close to that edge Malcolm already walked. What would happen if he woke just as Larena did?

Phelan didn't want to have to hunt his friend and kill him. Malcolm could be a cold son of a bitch, but he was still part of the MacLeod family. He deserved better.

"Malcolm was changing," Guy said.

Phelan looked at him and asked, "What do you mean?"

"He was beginning to feel again."

Rhys nodded. "His emotions were all over the place. He couldna get a handle on them most of the time, but he's no longer indifferent to things."

"Cold. That's what I heard Quinn call him," Banan said. "The last time I saw Malcolm he was detached and, aye, apathetic."

Hal scratched his check. "No' the Malcolm I spoke with today."

"He said Evie did it," Guy explained. "She's what made him begin to feel again. It's why he was so adamant about her being protected and no' harmed."

Guy suddenly smiled wearily and pushed past him. Phelan turned to see Elena, Guy's wife, walk up. She wrapped her arms around Guy and held him for several seconds.

When she pulled back, her sage green gaze locked on Phelan. "It's good to see you. I wish it were under better circumstances."

"Aye," Phelan said and watched as Guy gave a slight tug to the dark blond locks of her ponytail.

"Con said Evie might need this," Elena said and held out a bottle of Dreagan scotch.

Rhys was the one to take it. "We all do. Thanks, Elena."

"I'll bring something up for her to eat," Elena said as she peered around Phelan to look inside. Her face went pale as she caught sight of Malcolm. "Dear God."

Guy pulled her away from the door. "We're going to make sure he survives. Charon, Laura, and Aisley are on their way. Will you show them up when they arrive?"

Phelan didn't hear what she said as he took the bottle of whisky and strode into the room where some glasses were set on a table. He took one and filled it with the amber liquid before setting the bottle aside.

He walked to Evie and squatted beside her chair. "You look like you could use this."

Her devastated expression hit him squarely in the chest. Phelan knew in that instant that somehow Malcolm and Evie had found a connection. She'd reached a part of Malcolm everyone had thought dead.

For that, he owed her a debt.

But he wouldn't hesitate to kill her if she used her black magic for evil.

CHAPTER
THIRTY-SIX

Evie accepted the glass, and without asking what it was, drained it. She covered her mouth with the back of her hand and coughed as the whisky burned her throat.

"Sipping it might have been better, lass," Rhys said as he came into the room.

She licked her lips as the warmth of the alcohol settled in her stomach. "I need him to wake up. I have to know he's all right."

"I'll make sure he is," Phelan said as he rose and walked to the other side of the bed.

She gaped when a gold claw extended from Phelan's finger and he cut his arm, letting his blood flow onto Malcolm. "Um . . . that's unsanitary."

"Warriors are no' like mortals," Guy said.

Phelan cut himself several more times, the blood flowing quickly. "Another Warrior's blood will normally reverse the effects of *drough* blood."

"But?" she asked when she recognized there was more. "I hear a 'but' in there."

"But . . . Wallace changed the game by altering his

blood. No' even the Druids can heal a Warrior infected with *drough* blood now."

She clutched the glass in both hands as her stomach clenched in dread. "You're not giving up trying. Thank you."

"My blood is . . . different," Phelan said. "I can heal anything."

Guy leaned his hands on the dark wood of the footboard. "I doona see much change in Malcolm."

Evie put her forefinger along one of the cuts on his arm. It had started out a half inch longer than her finger. It was now almost to her nail. "He is healing. This cut was longer before."

"Keep fighting, Malcolm," Phelan whispered.

She looked at Phelan to find his gaze steady on Malcolm's face, as if he were mentally trying to make Malcolm wake. Evie wished he could. She had to know he was going to be fine before she went to Jason.

There was no need to talk to anyone about Jason Wallace and his offer. She knew what she had to do. Malcolm paid the price for trying to help her. No one else needed to be hurt. It was her fault this entire mess was created. She would be the one to clean it up.

One way or another.

Another ten minutes went by before Phelan halted pouring his blood into Malcolm. Evie had been watching Phelan's wounds and saw how quickly they disappeared.

Her chest tightened as she realized Malcolm should be healing that quickly as well. He'd known Brian's kidnapper was Jason Wallace. Malcolm had also understood that Jason would try and take her.

It was Malcolm's quick thinking in asking Rhys, Guy, and Hal to help that allowed her to get away. The price, however, could very well be Malcolm's life.

Evie was thankful when the men left her alone with him. The door to the room wasn't shut, and Phelan was never far, but she let out a deep breath all the same.

Phelan didn't trust her, and she couldn't blame him. She was a menace. Look at the giant mess she'd caused because she'd wanted to know if there were other Druids out in the world.

"Oh, Malcolm," she whispered and dropped her forehead to the mattress.

He hadn't moved an inch. His chest continued to rise and fall, but it was slow. Too slow. She put her hand on his thigh and fought against a fresh wave of tears.

Crying wouldn't help him. Evie wasn't sure if anything could.

Then she remembered how he liked the feel of her magic. Phelan had also mentioned that Druids used magic to heal. She'd never tried it before, but she knew her grandmother had used a healing spell or two.

Evie lamented the fact she didn't have those spells when she recalled how she had used her magic at Urquhart without a spell. She had done it then for Malcolm.

And if she did it once, she could do it again.

It had always been easy for her to call up her magic, and it was no different now, though it was darker, heavier. It rushed through her like a tidal wave. The power of it staggered her. Evie let it surround her until only she, her magic, and Malcolm existed.

Then, she began to methodically push her magic into him while she pictured his wounds healing. Evie had never used her magic thus, and she was surprised at how quickly her body drained of energy.

She refused to give up, however. A smile formed when she heard the drums and chanting her grandmother had taught her to seek in the times she needed guidance.

Evie let herself draw closer to the chanting, but it wasn't just the ancients with her. There was something dark, something sinister lurking on the fringes of her mind.

It beckoned her with shadowy fingers, urging her closer. Wickedness surrounded the entity. Like a black cloud of gloom, it waited patiently.

Evie turned her attention away from it and concentrated on the chants and drums, but again and again she found herself looking to the shadow figure. And then the shadows faded and she was able to see.

A wall of flames suddenly appeared, their edges licking high into the sky. And then she saw the figure. It danced in a large circle to a provocative, bewitching beat that lulled her, pulled her.

The person, neither man nor woman, was clothed in solid back. Even its head was masked by material that kept every inch of skin from being revealed.

Evie couldn't stop herself from moving. She began to sway with the figure. It was captivating, hypnotizing. It knew exactly what she wanted. Without words, the figure promised to heal Malcolm, pledged to get Brian back. It vowed magic potent enough to wipe out Jason Wallace once and for all.

All the figure asked for in return was . . . her.

Evie forgot about the ancients as she focused on the figure. All her problems could be solved if she just gave in. All she had to do was go to the figure, to say yes.

She jerked as it took her hands and began to twirl her around, holding her securely in its embrace. It wooed her, enticed her.

Tempted her.

Strong, violent magic raced through her veins. She could feel herself changing, becoming dark . . . dangerous. The magic was addictive, enslaving. Dominating.

Evie tried one feeble attempt to turn away from it, but the black magic had her in its grip. As if overjoyed, the figure spun her around faster and faster.

All around them flames danced, reaching higher and higher. Her eyes became heavy, her limbs weighty. The more she danced, the harder it was for her to remember why she was using her magic at all.

The flames licked at her, touching her skin without burning. She laughed as she weaved in and out of the blaze. Dimly, she realized the figure was now watching her instead of dancing with her. There were no eyes, no mouth, no nose—but she knew the figure approved.

Malcolm.

The name was a shout in her mind. She halted instantly, her mind remembering Malcolm and his injuries. The figure began dancing again, drawing nearer and nearer, as it once more tried to enchant her.

The hold the figure had on her was gone. She remembered Malcolm, remembered why she was using her magic to help him. Her stomach heaved at what she had nearly forgotten, and the people who counted on her. Evie tried to walk away, but the flames that hadn't harmed her before now burned her.

"No!" she shouted.

She strained to hear the chanting of the drums, but there was nothing but the crackle of the fire. Evie covered her ears with her hands and bent over.

"Malcolm!"

The figure took her hand, but she yanked it away. She had to get back to Malcolm, had to return her magic to helping him. Evie ran through the fires, heedless of the flames that scorched her skin and clothes.

She ran for what felt like miles, pushing her body well past its limit, before she found herself in a room devoid of any light. Her legs gave out as she slumped to the ground.

Malcolm said she would have to make choices—impossible choices, tempting and alluring choices.

Evie pushed the dark figure from her mind and concentrated on the ancients. It was with them that she could pull the poison of the *drough* blood from Malcolm.

"Please," she whispered.

"You turned from us," the ancients said, their voices surrounding her and echoing until her ears ached.

"I had no choice. I was only trying to help my brother."

"You should've come to us."

Evie hung her head. "Punish me in any way you want, but please help me save Malcolm."

"He's a traitor to his friends, a murderer."

"Everything he did was for his family. He's dying because of me!"

The ancients were silent for a moment before they said, *"You want to use your magic to kill."*

Evie wanted to deny it, but it was useless. In this dreamlike world of the ancients, they could peer into a Druid's mind with ease. They saw the truth of every thought, every wish. Every desire.

"Yes. Jason Wallace is evil. He needs to die."

"The drough *cannot be killed."*

Evie felt as if she'd been kicked in the ribs. "There has to be something that can stop him."

"There is."

"What?" she demanded when they fell silent. "Tell me!"

But there was no answer. The ancients left her with no hope of healing Malcolm and no answer regarding Jason Wallace.

She started running again, but it was as if she were standing in place. Nothing moved, no light could be found. She was lost, lost in the dark and all her fears closing in around her.

"Evie!"

Her eyes flew open to find Rhys leaning over her as she lay on the floor. A heartbeat later, fierce, debilitating agony ripped through her. The pain was so great she couldn't take a breath. Every bit of skin felt as if it had been flayed from her body inch by inch.

She tried to shrink away from the torment, but there was no distancing herself from it. All around her she could hear voices but couldn't think enough to understand what they were saying. She tried to reach out her hand and get back to Malcolm. Her magic could help him, she was sure of it. She just had to find a way past the pain to him.

"No' now, lass," Guy said from her other side. His voice was insistent, his tone low. There was a mewling sound she only then realized was coming from her. "You need to rest. We'll look after Malcolm."

Evie screamed as a new wave of anguish slammed into her when someone touched her arm.

"Con!" someone bellowed.

Evie closed her eyes and retreated into her mind, anything to get away from the pain. It felt as if she'd fallen into a fire. Even her face hurt.

"Slow, even breaths, Evie," Rhys urged from beside her.

She tried to tell him it hurt to breathe, but she couldn't get the words past her lips.

"I can help."

Evie recognized Phelan's voice. She didn't want his help, but it wasn't as if she could tell him no. Just when she thought the pain might truly kill her, something warm dropped onto her skin, and the agony immediately began to subside.

"I leave for five minutes and come back to see Evie covered in burns. What the hell happened?" Phelan demanded.

Evie opened her eyes to find Phelan staring angrily at Rhys and Guy.

"I doona know," Guy said.

Rhys ran a hand down his face and let out a breath. "One minute she was sitting on the chair, the next she was on the floor as burns covered her and scorched through her clothing."

Evie took a deep breath, which gained her everyone's attention. The pain was diminishing to just a memory, but with it came the realization of just how close to death she had come. Con came running into the room at that moment.

"What happened?" he asked, his brow furrowed deeply.

Evie winced as she sat up and looked down at her arms to find large holes burned through her black sweater. "I tried to use my magic to heal Malcolm."

"It was working too," Rhys said.

"I was with the ancients, and then . . . I wasn't." Evie looked up at Con, and then to Phelan as a shudder went through her. "There was something else with me."

"What was it?" Constantine asked tersely.

She shrugged, wishing she could forget, but knowing what transpired would be with her until the end of her days. "A person, a thing? I don't know. It was just there. It was so tempting that I couldn't help myself. I went to it, but when I tried to leave the flames wouldn't let me."

"As soon as she began to burn, all the healing she'd done for Malcolm reversed," Guy said.

Evie lifted a shaking hand to her forehead. "I just wanted to help Malcolm, but now the ancients won't aid me. They called me a traitor."

"Rest, and then try again later," Phelan said as he took her hand and pulled her to her feet. "The ancients may just need some time."

Evie had one last thing to tell them. She resumed her seat in the chair and said, "Wait," when Con and Guy began to leave. "There's more."

"More?" Phelan asked, a frown marring his forehead.

"I asked the ancients if there was some way to end Jason Wallace. They said there was."

"Well? What is it?" Guy asked.

Evie swallowed past the lump in her throat. "They refused to tell me."

CHAPTER
THIRTY-SEVEN

Phelan stared out the large windows in the sitting room not seeing the rolling green pastures of Dreagan before him. His thoughts were centered on the Druid upstairs.

He hadn't been able to convince Evie to leave Malcolm's side. Phelan wanted to think it was because she cared for Malcolm, but he knew how deceptive *droughs* could be.

A wave of exquisite, seductive magic washed over him, instantly making his cock harden. He turned on his heel and stalked to the front door to greet Aisley. As he opened it, Charon parked his Mercedes CL65 AMG Coupe and Aisley climbed out of the back and rushed to him.

"What happened?" she asked once she had her arms wrapped tightly around him.

Phelan squeezed her, his gaze meeting Charon's. "Malcolm isna doing well. Neither Con nor I have been able to heal him as we should've."

"No' what I wanted to hear," Charon said as he walked up with Laura.

Aisley pulled out of Phelan's arms and cupped his cheek. "What do you need from me?"

"Actually, there is something you and Laura might be able to help me with."

He walked them into the manor and told them everything that had happened after he'd reached Dreagan, as well as why Malcolm had been helping Evie.

"Evie," Laura repeated the name and frowned. "What's her surname?"

Phelan shrugged. "I didna ask. Why?"

"Just thinking," Laura said and shrugged it off.

Charon took his wife's hand in his. "I'm more concerned with how Evie and Malcolm met."

"That's no' a part of the story I learned," Phelan said as they started up the stairs.

"You're hurt he didn't contact you," Aisley said, knowing him better than anyone else.

Phelan couldn't deny it. "Aye. Guy reckons it's because of Evie."

"Is she *drough*?" Charon asked. "I doona feel *drough* magic as I should."

"It's . . ." Phelan hesitated. "It's difficult to explain. I sense *drough* magic in her, but it's no' overwhelming like with others."

Laura reached the first landing and said, "Maybe it takes some time for the black magic to build up and be sensed by a Warrior."

Aisley shook her head. "I'm sorry, but that's not how it works. Once the ceremony is completed, you're *drough*. There's no waiting period, no buildup. The force of the black magic is there waiting to be used."

"Guy did say Malcolm tried to stop the ceremony but was too late." Phelan put his hand on Aisley's lower back and guided her up to the third level.

Charon's lips twisted in frustration. "Obviously Malcolm failed if I can feel any part of *drough* magic."

Aisley stopped at the third-floor landing and faced the

three of them. "If Evie really had no choice, we should give her a chance. Malcolm saw something in her. We need to do the same."

"Precisely," Laura said. "Jason has a way of twisting the truth to suit his needs. We have no idea what he told Evie to get her to perform the ceremony."

"He used her brother," Phelan said. "Brian is all Evie has."

Charon blew out a breath. "Just as Larena is all Malcolm has left. Perhaps that's what drew Malcolm to Evie."

"Which we won't know until he wakes." Aisley gave a reassuring smile to Phelan and turned to the hallway.

Phelan led the group to where Malcolm and Evie were. Rhys stood at the door, his arms crossed over his chest and his expression bleak.

"She's no' said a word," he told Phelan as they approached. "She's no' eaten either."

Aisley smiled a greeting at Rhys before she walked into the room, Laura right on her heels. Phelan and Charon took positions across from the doorway so they could watch what happened inside.

"You're wrong no' to trust her," Rhys said.

Charon turned his gaze to the Dragon King. "After all the run-ins with *droughs*, it's hard no' to distrust them."

"What of Isla? What of Aisley? Both are *droughs*."

"No' Aisley anymore," Phelan interjected.

Rhys dropped his arms to his sides. "So there are exceptions, just no' for Evie."

"Why are you defending her?" Charon asked.

Rhys turned his head to glance into the room. "You two were no' there. You didna hear Malcolm talk of Evie, and you didna see her stand up to Wallace. It took Guy, Hal, and me to get her away from Urquhart as Malcolm asked. She wanted to get back to him."

"You can no' believe everything a *drough* says."

Rhys's aqua-colored eyes landed on Charon with deadly intent. "I've been around long enough, Warrior, to recognize when a human is lying. They are no' that good at it. Evie wasna faking anything."

"Maybe, Dragon, but we've been dealing with *droughs* for many centuries. We can no' help but be skeptical," Phelan calmly stated.

Phelan met Charon's guarded gaze. Malcolm had known how Warriors would react to Evie. It all made sense now why he'd contacted the dragons. The Dragon Kings had seen what Malcolm hadn't wanted the Warriors to see—himself.

Evie stood when she saw the two women come into the room. It was on impulse that she took a stance to guard Malcolm.

"We're friends," said the one with the long, wavy black hair and fawn-colored eyes. "I'm Aisley. And this is Laura." She motioned to the woman beside her. "We're Druids."

Evie nodded to Aisley before turning her gaze to Laura and her unusual moss-green eyes. "I spent many years of my life thinking I was the only Druid. Now, within days I've encountered three."

"You look dead on your feet," Laura said in her English accent and motioned to the chair.

Evie sat once more and rubbed her eyes. "Are you from MacLeod Castle?"

"How do you know of the castle?" Aisley asked.

She glanced at Malcolm. "He told me. I thought I knew all there was to know of Druids, but either my grandmother didn't know, or chose not to tell me."

Laura squatted beside her. Her dark brown hair was pulled back in a low ponytail, the end of it draping over her shoulder. "We don't live at MacLeod Castle, but we are part of the group of Druids."

"We heard you had an encounter with Jason," Aisley said. "He's my cousin, Evie. A nastier man never lived. I'm sorry he's hurt you."

Evie couldn't look at the Druids anymore. She focused on Malcolm and tried not to feel the hatred for Jason that threatened to consume her. "He kidnapped my brother. Brian is mute. I thought he was safe from everything in school. It never crossed my mind that someone would go after him."

"He's doing it to get to you."

Laura said, "Aisley's right. Jason wants you for something, Evie, and he won't stop until he has you."

"He's waiting for me at his mansion."

"What?" Aisley and Laura said in unison.

Evie closed her eyes and placed her hand on Malcolm's leg. "Jason said he'd release Brian if I came to him."

The sound of footfalls moving from the rug onto the hardwood floor and then onto another rug sounded as Aisley walked around the other side of the bed. "You can't be seriously considering going to him."

"What choice do I have?" Evie opened her eyes to look at Aisley. "If I wait, he could kill Brian, or do this," she said and motioned to Malcolm with her other hand. "The only reason I'm holding it together as I am is because I know Malcolm has a chance to pull through. Brian won't."

Laura rubbed her hand up and down Evie's back. "It'll be all right. Trust us, Evie. Aisley and I have each had confrontations with Jason."

"And it's never pretty," Aisley mumbled angrily.

Evie felt her eyes prickle, but there were no more tears to shed. "You know I'm now a . . . a . . ."

"Drough," Laura supplied. "Yes, we know."

Aisley gave a frustrated shake of her head. "Jason has a plan for you. It's why he forced you into doing the ceremony. I just wish I knew what that plan was so we could try and stay a step ahead of him."

"I expected you two to distrust me as Phelan has."

Aisley's head jerked to her. "He didn't," she said in a low, dangerous voice.

Evie glanced at Laura and shrugged. "It's understandable. His friend was hurt. I'm to blame."

Aisley stalked out of the room. Evie watched as she grabbed Phelan's arm and dragged him out of sight.

"Up until a few weeks ago, Aisley was *drough*," Laura said.

Evie's eyebrows shot up. "Really? So is there a way to reverse it? Malcolm said there wasn't."

"There isn't," Laura said sadly. "I'm sorry."

"Then how?"

Laura rose and leaned against the footboard. "Aisley betrayed Jason to Phelan and the others. So, Jason wanted Phelan to think she betrayed him. It almost worked. There was a large battle, and Jason was winning. Except Aisley stepped between Jason and Phelan and took a hit of magic meant for Phelan. It killed her."

Evie gave a choked half-laugh. "But she's alive."

"Magic," Laura said with a grin. "Turns out Aisley is a Phoenix. It's something passed down through her family line and hasn't been seen in ages. She's able to regenerate like a mythical phoenix."

"That's truly amazing. I didn't know such a thing existed."

"Every Druid and Warrior from MacLeod Castle has had an encounter with Deirdre, Declan, or Jason. It's been a constant battle against these powerful *droughs* that seems to never end."

"It can end. At least with Jason."

Laura licked her lips slowly. "Phelan told me what happened with the ancients. Have you tried to talk to them again?"

"No." And Evie wasn't keen on trying anytime soon. She feared the figure might show once more. Yet, she knew she would have to attempt it again.

For Brian.

For Malcolm.

"Perhaps Aisley and I can try as well," Laura offered. "One of us should be able to learn how to kill Jason. We've asked before, but none of us has gotten the information you have."

"I think they were just really pissed at me," Evie said with a lift of her shoulder.

Laura turned and softly walked around the bed until she took the chair Phelan had occupied earlier. She caught Evie's gaze. "Rhys and Malcolm are convinced you are a good person despite now being *drough*. There is a Druid, Reaghan, who can look into your eyes and determine if you're lying or not. I don't have that kind of magic."

She paused and took a deep breath. "You see, Evie, the Warriors and Druids at the castle are my family. Many have died in these battles, and I don't want to see anyone else killed. So I need to know, did you want to use black magic?"

Evie rubbed her thumb along the tattered remains of Malcolm's jeans. "You know, Malcolm spoke of you all. He carries such guilt for what he's done that he doesn't think he belongs at the castle. I disagree with him. There's no other place for a man such as him." Evie stared into Laura's moss green eyes and said, "No, Laura, I don't want Satan to own my soul, but yes, I wanted the black magic to use on the person or people responsible for taking Brian. I wanted it to protect the spell Jason is adamant about getting, a spell that could be dangerous or even deadly to all. How could I have deaths on my conscience? Deaths that I could prevent by giving up my soul?"

She let her gaze fall to Malcolm's face and sat forward to move the lock of golden hair that kept falling over his forehead.

"Sometimes we want things to be simple," Evie said. "But they rarely are. Nothing is really black and white. There are many shades of gray. Am I evil? No. But I am *drough*."

CHAPTER
THIRTY-EIGHT

Malcolm was trapped in Hell.

There were no windows, no doors. Only mind-numbing blackness and the ever-present shadow figure that slashed his flesh again and again.

Malcolm wanted to fight the figure, but it was as if his limbs were stuck in honey. He couldn't move them quickly enough to do any damage to the individual.

Not even Malcolm's enhanced sight allowed him to see what was attacking him. It melded with the darkness as if it were part of it, controlling it.

Malcolm bellowed in fury as his back was cut. His leg buckled and he fell to one knee. Blood poured down his back and his chest. His hands were covered in it, which made it impossible for him to grab hold of anything.

His entire body hurt. It wasn't just the slashes. It was inside. His bones, his muscles . . . everything felt as if it were dying.

He threw back his head, his arms out to the side, as he called up Daal. But his god didn't answer.

It was as if Daal had ceased to exist.

Malcolm braced his left hand on the ground since his

right arm refused to work. His mind turned to Evie. She was safe, safe with the Dragon Kings. No matter what hell he had to endure, at least Wallace wouldn't get his hands on her.

Malcolm's chest ached as his lungs struggled to drag in air. He thought of Evie's clear blue eyes, of her soft touch and her smile.

Suddenly, off to his right, he could've sworn he caught a glimpse of her running past him, her curls trailing behind her as if ensnared in the wind.

He knew it was either his mind playing tricks on him or the figure's idea of torture. If it was the figure, it'd found the perfect way to torment him. To have Evie so close, yet not have her.

And then she was there standing before him. She looked around as if she couldn't see anything.

Malcolm called out to her, but she was so far away. He could see her standing there, an unseen wind whipping around her and molding her long, thin skirt to her legs.

Her beautiful curls hung around her face and danced in the wind. She was talking with someone, but he couldn't hear her words.

Malcolm blinked as if in slow motion. Evie moved to the side, toward someone or something. He roared his fury when he saw the shadowy figure dancing around her, but no sound came out.

No matter how many times Malcolm tried to go to her, he couldn't take a step. His feet felt as if they were bogged down in tar.

The longer he stared at Evie and the figure, the angrier he became. Yet, the aches of his body began to dissipate.

Malcolm looked down at his hands, and then at Evie. Somehow she was doing this. She was taking away his pain.

"No," he whispered.

He didn't want her trapped as he was. If she didn't leave soon that's exactly what would happen.

"Evie! Evie, you have to leave!"

She never heard him. Whatever the shadowy figure was doing, it had her well in its clutches. Malcolm watched in horror as Evie began to dance with the fiend. Slowly, sensuously.

It was the worst thing Malcolm had ever had to watch. His Evie was changing right before his eyes. He'd warned her there would be choices, and he feared he was watching her make one. And it was one that would forever alter her life.

Malcolm clenched his fists, his arms bent as he leaned over and bellowed his fury and helplessness. This couldn't be happening.

He looked up to find Evie dancing alone to music only she could hear. The shadowy figure stood near her, as if orchestrating everything. There seemed to be nothing Malcolm could do. The deeper into the figure's clutches she went, the better Malcolm felt.

"No' for me, Evie. You need to save Brian. He's the one who warrants it."

She stopped dancing and looked around her. Hope blossomed in Malcolm's chest. Had she heard him? Had he finally gotten through somehow?

Evie tried to run from the figure, but it wasn't that easy. As soon as she turned away from the shadowy character, every one of Malcolm's injuries opened, the blood pouring down him once more as Evie screamed in agony.

Her pain was his final straw. Malcolm roared, the sound deep and furious. It was the sound of a Warrior, the voice of a god.

And it got the figure's attention.

In a blink, it stood before Malcolm once more and proceeded to reach into Malcolm's chest and wrap a hand around his heart.

And squeezed.

MacLeod Castle

"I need better answers," Fallon demanded as he paced the great hall.

Ramsey shrugged. "I've nothing to give. We can no' attack Wallace's mansion. It would be suicide."

"Is he really that powerful now?" Reaghan asked.

Ramsey nodded and pushed away from the wall. "We were lucky in the last battle with him. He was one against all of us, and Aisley paid the ultimate price. Had she no' been a Phoenix, Phelan would've lost his woman."

"And I'm no' keen on losing mine," Lucan said.

Cara smiled sadly and leaned into Lucan. "Nor do I want to lose you."

"If we can't attack, then what?" Saffron asked.

Ronnie tossed aside the pen she'd been fiddling with. "Well, we sure as hell can't set a trap for him."

"I don't know about y'all, but I'm not at all interested in waiting around for him to get to us," Gwynn stated in her thick Texas accent.

Logan shook his head. "Gwynn's right. There has to be some way we can get to Wallace."

"I'm more concerned with Malcolm," Larena said.

Ramsey noticed she sat quietly during much of their talk. Fallon stopped his pacing and went to her. The old Larena was returning, but Ramsey still saw traces of the *drough* blood lingering. Larena was fighting it, and Britt's serum was working.

Larena rose from her seat on the steps. "If Broc can't find Malcolm, then Wallace is to blame. He has something in store for my cousin, and I simply can't sit by and wait to discover what that is."

"We found a way to kill Deirdre and Delcan," Marcail said from her spot near the hearth. "We'll do the same for Jason."

Ramsey looked at Gwynn as she rested her hand on her closed laptop. "Gwynn, we could use the aid of all the Druids we can find. Why no' see if Evangeline Walker might be willing to join us?"

"Is that wise?" Broc asked.

"What do we have to lose?"

Larena stood beside Fallon. "Exactly. We've fought battles before. Jason brought us a war. It's time to end it."

Evie moved her food around on her plate with her fork. She'd left Malcolm and ventured down into the manor's kitchen only because Laura and Aisley hadn't given her a choice.

That's when she met Cassie, Elena, and Jane, the wives of Hal, Guy, and Banan.

"If you don't like that, I can fix something else," Jane said.

Evie looked into her kind amber eyes and shook her head. "I don't have much of an appetite, thanks."

The three women, along with Aisley and Laura, carried on a conversation, but Evie didn't pay attention. Her mind kept going over what had happened when she had gone toward the chanting and drums.

The shadowy figure had never been there before. Was it evil trying to take over? Or was it something else? The only one she felt as if she could discuss this with was Malcolm, but that was impossible now.

Evie sent up another silent prayer to keep Malcolm out of Wallace's clutches until he was healed. If Jason came for Malcolm now, Evie feared what might happen.

She also dreaded going to the ancients again. They hadn't been in the mood to listen last time, and she suspected it would be the same if she tried again. Though she didn't have a choice.

There was Brian to consider. Evie knew if she went to Jason, she would be lost. It was a price she was willing to pay if it meant she could get Brian free and possibly kill Jason.

She realized how rude she was being and pulled out of her musings to hear the women whispering. Evie kept her gaze out the window but listened to them.

"Does she know?" Aisley whispered.

Out of the corner of her eye, she saw Cassie shake her head of brunette hair. The American said, "I don't think so."

Elena, another American, leaned over the table and said in a low voice, "She's been too wrapped up with Malcolm. Besides, the guys were careful not to say or do anything that she could see."

"Should we tell her?" Laura asked.

Evie turned her head to Laura. "Tell me what? What is it that I've apparently missed and no one wants me to know?"

Jane wouldn't meet her gaze, but Elena did. "You didn't seem at all curious about how Malcolm got here ahead of you."

"What?" Evie set down her fork carefully. "Malcolm told me there was a Warrior who could teleport. I assumed he's the one who brought him here. Where is Fallon anyway?"

Laura set down her cucumber sandwich. "Not here."

"Did he leave already? When Malcolm needs him?"

Evie didn't want to talk about Fallon. She wanted to concentrate on Malcolm, Brian, and Jason.

Aisley said, "Fallon was never here. It was Rhys who brought Malcolm."

"He can teleport as well?"

Cassie shook her head. "No."

Evie rolled her eyes and scooted back her chair as she got to her feet. "I've had a very traumatic day. I've got a friend who's barely hanging onto life, and a brother I may never see again. Oh, and let's not forget the sociopath who has some kind of plan for me. So, forgive me if I'm not catching on as I should, but if you all have something to say, just say it."

"Evie, please," Jane beseeched. "We didn't mean any harm, really. It's just that normally people begin to ask questions."

Laura got to her feet. "We're sorry. You're right, of course. You've had quite the day. We've stuffed up. Please sit."

Evie hated it when she wanted to be mad but people were nice to her. It took the wind right out of her sails. She sat back down and looked at her plate.

"A good night's sleep will help," Elena said. "You'll want to be close to Malcolm so we can have the room next to his readied for you."

Evie lifted her head to smile her thanks. Her gaze was drawn to the sky that was colored in vivid orange and gold as it sank behind the mountain.

"It seems wrong for the world to look so beautiful when things are falling apart around you."

A roar that rattled the windows sounded into the silence following her words. Evie sat up straight in her chair and noticed Jane looked away while Elena and Cassie watched her carefully.

"What is going on?" Evie asked warily. The sound was

louder than anything she'd heard from Malcolm, even when he'd been fighting Wallace.

The roar sounded again. A moment later she saw a large shape out of the corner of her eye. When she turned her head to look out the window, she saw the massive amber-colored dragon flying low over the ground and scattering sheep in every direction.

"What the hell?" she asked as she nearly fell out of her chair.

Elena reached for the teapot, and said matter-of-factly, "That's what we've been wondering if you knew. The men here at Dreagan are really dragons."

CHAPTER
THIRTY-NINE

Dragons.

Evie wouldn't have believed it had she not seen the dragon with her own eyes. If she weren't so wrapped up in her own world, she would've thought to ask Rhys how he and Hal had gotten to Dreagan so quickly.

Her system had taken its share of shocks over the last few days to last four lifetimes.

As Evie walked woodenly from the kitchen, she really looked at the Dreagan manor. Dragons were everywhere. Some were evident, some almost hidden.

The wall sconces were iron dragons that lunged from the wall, one of their claws holding the dangling lights. The dining room table that could easily seat twenty or more had legs resembling those of dragons. The designer had carved it so it looked as if the dragons were carrying the weight of the table on their shoulders. Even the newel post at the base of the stairs was a dragon winding around the thick wooden post.

When Evie walked up the stairs her eyes landed on the large pictures dominating the area, and in each and every one of them, there was a dragon.

By the time she reached the third floor, she had numerous questions—all of which would have to wait. She walked to Rhys who once more stood sentry at Malcolm's room.

"So. A dragon, huh?"

He frowned before his face turned hard. "It's no' information you can share, lass."

"As if I'll be going around telling everyone of Malcolm or Jason Wallace. Give me some credit," she mumbled and looked to Malcolm.

Only to find Con and Phelan standing on either side of the bed. Phelan was giving Malcolm more blood, and Con was touching Malcolm, his eyes closed as if all his concentration was on him.

"He's going to get better," Rhys whispered. "You'll come in here to find him up and about as if nothing happened."

"You've no idea how much I want that. I'm more scared of losing him than I am of facing Jason."

Rhys shifted so he leaned a shoulder against the wall. "You care deeply for him then."

"I do. From the moment I first met him I knew instinctively that he would change my life. He's helped me from the beginning, even when I didn't want it. Malcolm deserves better than what I've led him to."

"You didna lead him to anything. You need to remember that," Rhys said in a cold, hard voice. "Wallace would've taken you. Malcolm did what he had to do in order to see you safe."

Evie looked into Rhys's aqua eyes made even more brilliant by the dark hair surrounding his face. "He doesn't deserve to be on that bed fighting for his life."

"He's a Warrior and a Highlander. What else do you expect?" he asked with a lopsided grin.

Evie licked her lips and looked at Malcolm. "If I had only listened to him from the start he might not be hurt."

"Och. No use going down that road, lass. What's done is done. Look to the future, no' the past."

Evie remained in the doorway as the minutes stretched on. No matter how much blood Phelan gave or how much magic Con used, there was no change in Malcolm.

She recalled how much pain she had been in after her run-in with the figure. Just a few drops of Phelan's blood had healed her entire body instantly. And yet it wasn't making a dent in Malcolm's.

A hand suddenly took her arm and turned her away. "You need to rest," Laura told her as she led her to where Jane stood at the next doorway.

Jane smiled and motioned her inside. "You should have everything you need. If you don't, please let us know."

"Guy said you didn't have any clothes with you," Elena said as she came out of the connected bathroom. "I can send him to get them if you like."

Evie quickly shook her head. There was no way any of them would trust her if they knew where she had been staying. "I'll make do."

"Nonsense. You can borrow anything we have," Jane said.

Evie was then left alone. She walked to the wall separating her from Malcolm. Yes, she felt responsible for him being injured, but it was more than that.

She liked him. A lot.

He was reserved, aloof, and stubborn. Then he would turn those azure eyes on her, and she melted. He made her so angry she could scream, then he kissed her.

Malcolm touched her as no one else ever had. Her body had seemed to be waiting for him her entire life. In his arms, she felt things more strongly, experienced everything more clearly.

She knew it was Malcolm and not the black magic that

now occupied her body. He'd kissed her, touched her before she'd done that stupid ceremony.

Evie sat on the edge of the bed and stared at the wall. She knew she had to go to Jason Wallace. There was no other alternative. The only problem was that no one at Dreagan would allow her to go if they discovered what she planned.

Magic sizzled through her, reminding her of what she sacrificed to have such power. In order for her to have a chance at rescuing Brian, Evie was going to have to give in to the black magic.

Choices, Malcolm had said. Here was another choice she was making.

Evie took out her mobile and dashed off a quick text before she rose and headed to the shower. She was going to need to be on top of her game.

In all ways.

Malcolm yearned for the sun. The total darkness was a torture unto itself. He yanked against unseen bindings that held him in place, both on his wrists and ankles.

He was a Warrior, immortal and powerful. Yet, he couldn't break free.

It wasn't magic that held him, but something else. Something powerful and formidable. It frightened Malcolm as nothing else had since his attack by Warriors as a mortal.

He would be resigned to his fate if it weren't for Evie. Wallace had her brother, and if he knew Evie, she would somehow get Brian free. With—or without—anyone's help.

She was just tenacious enough not to ask for assistance.

Malcolm gritted his teeth. His right shoulder ached. He could hardly lift his arm at all. The one time he'd dared to touch it, he'd felt something sticky and warm on his fingers.

Blood.

He knew without looking that his old wounds had re-opened as well as new ones. If he was going to fight his way out of this place, he was going to have to do it with one arm.

And without Daal.

His god refused to answer any of his calls. There hadn't been a peep from Daal since Malcolm had woken in this hellish place.

He tugged his left arm, hoping to get some slack on his invisible bonds, but they held steady. Malcolm took a deep breath as Evie's image filled his mind.

Everything he had focused on her. Her smooth skin, her silky hair. Her full lips, her clear blue eyes. Her pert breasts, her long legs.

Her smile.

Her voice, soft and sweet.

She had gentled him. Somehow, someway she had done what no one else could.

A strange, new emotion filled him. It caused his heart to constrict, his chest to tighten. Malcolm couldn't put a name to what it was. All he knew was that he had to get back to her.

"Evie," he whispered.

Evie quietly walked into Malcolm's room after her shower. When she came out of the bathroom there had been several pairs of jeans and four different sweaters for her to choose from. The jeans were a little long, but the hunter-green sweater fit perfectly.

Rhys hadn't stopped her when she entered the room. Thankfully there was no one else inside. Evie didn't want to leave Malcolm yet, but she didn't have a choice.

He was improving. Slowly. Phelan and Con continued to heal him, but it could take weeks. And Jason wasn't going to wait that long.

"I wish you'd wake up," Evie said in a low voice as she sat beside the bed. She noticed that much of the dried blood covering Malcolm had been removed.

So had his boots and soiled jeans. He now lay with the covers up to his hips. Evie remembered when she'd ran her hands over his magnificent chest feeling the thick muscles beneath his skin. Now his chest was mangled and bloody.

"I need you. And not just to fight Jason. The future hadn't seemed so scary with you beside me. I'm terrified, Malcolm."

She licked her lips, hesitating a second before she pushed her magic into him. If she couldn't heal him, maybe she could relieve some of his pain. It was a long shot. She had no idea what her magic could do to him, but he'd said he liked the feel of it.

"I don't know what's inside you, but you must fight it," she urged. "You survived so much. Don't let this take you. If you do, then Jason will have won. He's like Deirdre. He needs to be killed."

Evie took his right hand in her own, careful not to disturb his arm. "I always thought your scars made you even more handsome. You're too damn good-looking. Those scars are something to be proud of. You survived evil. That's the Highlander in you."

She stopped, unsure if she could continue and not break down. There might not be any more tears to shed, but the emotion was clogging her throat.

"When you wake up—because you *will* wake up—you need to go back to MacLeod Castle. I've seen your friends. They care a great deal about you. Go to Larena and be with your family. Maybe one day we'll see each other again."

She leaned over him and gently placed her lips on his. Evie hesitated, unwilling to pull away. "Farewell, Malcolm Munro. May life pave you a good road."

Evie straightened and stepped away from the bed before she broke down and crawled in beside him. She walked to the door and paused. Every fiber of her being screamed for her to go back to him, but what she had to face, she had to face alone.

She walked through the doorway and nodded to Rhys, never seeing Malcolm's fingers move on the bed.

CHAPTER
FORTY

Jason Wallace reclined on his Chesterfield sofa and sipped his fifty-year-old Dreagan whisky. The day hadn't gone completely to plan, but by the time the sun rose on the new day, he would have what he wanted.

By now, Malcolm would be fighting the effects of the *drough* blood while the others scrambled to try and heal him. While their attention was on Malcolm, Evie's mind had been on her brother.

Jason smiled as he thought of Brian. The lad had some gumption. He was afraid, but Brian did a good job of hiding it. Jason was impressed with the teenager. It was too bad he didn't have any magic. He'd have liked an apprentice.

A glance at his watch showed that Malcolm had been tormented for hours now. He could die there, but Jason knew the Warriors and dragons wouldn't let him.

The dragons. They'd been the one wrench in his plans he hadn't counted on. Malcolm was a loner. It should've only been Malcolm and Evie at Urquhart. Instead, the damn dragons had been there and nearly ruined everything.

Apparently, he was going to have to deal with the interfering dragons, but they shouldn't be any more difficult than the Warriors and Druids.

Jason leaned forward and placed his glass on the coffee table as he stared into the flames burning in the hearth. Why hadn't he known of the dragons until recently? How had they managed to stay hidden? And if there were dragons he hadn't known about, what else was out there?

He smiled, feeling suddenly happy at the thought of conquering all the creatures of Earth—mortal and magical.

"It's going to be quite the thing," he said to himself as he gained his feet and walked out of his office into the foyer to the doorway leading below the house.

Jason flicked on the lights and heard the scramble of shoes against the ground as Brian got to his feet. The lad didn't like to be caught sitting or lying down.

He turned the corner and walked down the short hallway before coming to the dungeon. It wasn't as fine a dungeon as the ancient castles that littered his land, but it came close.

It was just as damp, and just as cold during the winter months. Not a ray of sun found its way inside. Jason made sure the entire feel of the dungeon was desolate so that hopelessness fed upon itself.

"Your sister should be arriving soon," Jason said as he approached Brian's cell. "You're going to help me win her over."

Brian vigorously shook his head.

Jason just smiled. "Ah, lad, but you will. Shall I tell you why? Because you love Evangeline. There's no need to worry, however, you'll do everything I need you to do because I'm going to make you. Magic, you'll learn, has its uses."

There was a rapid motion of Brian's hands with sign language that Jason didn't even look at.

"Doona bother, lad. See, I doona trust you. Because I

doona trust you, I'll use magic. It's imperative that Evangeline embrace the black magic inside herself." Jason leaned back against the wall and crossed one ankle over the other while he watched Brian pace back and forth. "Your sister willna be our only visitor. There will be one other. He'll come to see things my way as well."

Jason lifted a brow when Brian flipped him off. "That's crude and beneath you. It's also testing the limits to my goodwill."

Brian then put his fingers beneath his chin and jerked his hand forward.

Jason didn't need to know sign language to know what that meant. He straightened from the wall and sneered at Brian. "Remember your sister well, lad, because by the time I'm done with her, there will be nothing left of the one you knew. She'll bear a child, and that child will hold evil. That child will be the key to my ruling of this planet. So I'd be careful what you say to me."

He turned and walked away before his temper did snap. Jason was in too good of a mood for Brian to ruin it. Hours before he'd been ready to kill Brian on the spot at having lost Evangeline.

But something cautioned Jason to wait.

Now he was glad he had since Evangeline was coming to him. What sister could turn away from a brother in need? It was so trite, but it was that predictability that allowed Jason to gain the upper hand.

He chuckled as he walked into the foyer and closed the door behind him. Let the Warriors and Druids fret over what he would do next. Let them worry about the ways he was plotting to kill them.

While they were preoccupied, he had set the chessboard in motion. By the time they caught on to what he was doing, it would be too late. Already he was several moves ahead.

There was no way they could catch up. They would try to stop him, but it would be to no avail. And once the child was born, there would be nothing they could do to halt him.

That's when he would make them pay for everything they had done. He had something special planned for Phelan and Aisley. Those two would know an eternity of pain they couldn't even begin to fathom.

"Soon," he murmured. "Verra soon."

No one stopped Evie as she walked out of the manor. She was ready with the excuse that she needed some air, but she was glad she hadn't needed to use it.

She made her way to the parking area and saw a red convertible. Evie hurried to the sleek two-door Jaguar F-type and found the door unlocked. And the keys inside.

"Did someone know I was planning to leave?" she asked as she slid behind the wheel.

Evie didn't want to wait around and find out. She started the car and put it in reverse. There was enough lighting from the outside lights to see where the drive was.

Only when she was driving away did she pray that her night blindness didn't get in the way again.

"Ugh. What am I thinking?" she berated herself. "I'm a *drough*, right? I've got enough magic to fix that."

Through the windshield, everything was dark and blurry. She concentrated on her magic to fix her eyes, and within minutes she could see clearly.

"I'll be damned," she mumbled and pressed on the accelerator of the sports car.

Maybe there really was a chance for her to get Brian free.

The binds holding Malcolm didn't seem as tight as before. He could hear Evie's voice, hear her calling to him.

"Evie!" he shouted. "Evie, where are you?"

There was no answer, but he knew she was near. He jerked against his bonds with his left arm again and again. The shadow figure was watching. Malcolm could feel his eyes on him, but he didn't stop.

"Evie!"

The figure was suddenly before him. Malcolm fell to his knees as blades sank into either side of his neck. Blood poured down him, weakening him.

"Eeeeeeevieeeeeeeeeee!"

He climbed to his feet as sweat covered his body. His right arm was jerked behind him. Malcolm gave a shout as he felt muscle tear.

"Evie!"

Malcolm wasn't going to give up. He'd either get out of this hell or die trying. With the agony of his arm pushed aside, he demanded Daal rise up and give him the strength he needed to break free.

Daal gave a growl deep in his mind, and something snapped.

One second Malcolm was standing, and the next he was on his back and a hand was choking him.

Guy looked into Malcolm's room expecting to see Evie. When he didn't see her, he moved to the next doorway and gave a light tap with his knuckles.

He waited for a response. The fact that there wasn't one was what gave him the nudge to open the door. A quick glance showed the room was empty.

"What is it?" Rhys asked.

Guy closed the door and faced his friend. "Have you seen Evie?"

"Aye. She went in to see Malcolm for a few minutes then went downstairs. I figured she grew hungry."

Guy shook his head. "It was like pulling teeth to get her to eat the first time. Why would she willingly go now?"

"Shite," Rhys said with a sigh. "She wouldna."

"Stay here," Guy said as he ran down the hallway and the stairs to the media room. "Is she here?" he asked the Warriors.

Phelan frowned as a sleeping Aisley stirred against his chest while a movie played. "Who are you talking about?"

"Evie," Charon said with a frown. "She's no' here."

Guy slammed his fist into the back of a chair, smashing it. "She's gone. And I've got a bad feeling as to where."

"Wallace," Phelan said. He leaned Aisley onto the arm of the sofa and got to his feet. "We need to stop her before she gets there."

Laura yawned and reached over to nudge Aisley awake. "You three don't seriously think to have a conversation like this in front of us and want us to stay asleep, do you?"

"Is it too much to ask?" Charon said with a grin.

Aisley rubbed her eyes and glared at Phelan. "Explain."

"Evie's gone," Guy said angrily. "We think to Wallace's."

Aisley was instantly on her feet and alert. "We need to stop her."

"Aye," Charon said as he too stood. "There's no telling what she and Wallace will do together."

Laura rose and crossed her arms over her chest as she stared Charon down. "Really? That's what you think? Did you not see her with Malcolm? There is something there."

"And she's a *drough*."

"Because she had to!" Laura let out a loud sigh and shook her head. "Shades of gray, Charon. Remember that."

Guy threw up his hands. "Whatever the reasons, we need to stop Evie. I gave Malcolm my word that I'd keep her safe. She's far from it with Wallace. And I doona want to have to explain what happened when Malcolm wakes."

"If he wakes," Phelan said.

Con stepped into the doorway, his hands in his pockets. "He'll wake soon. I suggest if you don't want to see a Warrior go off the edge, you get Evie back here posthaste."

Before any of them could move, Rhys let out a shout for them. As one, the group rushed up the stairs.

Malcolm's fury knew no bounds. Daal wouldn't help him, the bastard. The only outlet now for Malcolm was death. And he just couldn't believe it.

And then, Daal shifted in his mind, his growl feral and furious. The god had finally responded.

The pain of Malcolm's injuries began to fade as strength returned. With a roar, Malcolm shoved the figure off him and stood.

"Evie!" he shouted and jerked free of the bonds. "Evie!"

She was slipping away from him. Malcolm could feel it as surely as he knew she was the reason he'd found the will to live.

"Evie!"

As the darkness began to fade, the figure came at Malcolm once more. Malcolm released his god and leaped at the figure, only to be met with air. He was falling, his arms and legs flailing to catch hold of something, anything. But there was only darkness . . .

Malcolm's eyes snapped open to find himself in a room lying on a bed. He stayed still and took stock of his body.

"He's awake."

The recognition of that voice caused Malcolm to turn his head and find Phelan beside the bed. He looked around to find Aisley, Charon, Laura, Constantine, Guy, Hal, and Rhys standing around him.

There was just one person missing.

"Evie," he croaked. His throat felt raw, as if he'd been shouting for days.

Phelan held a glass of water. "Drink."

Malcolm shoved aside his hand and stood. The room tipped as the floor rushed up at him. He caught hold of the footboard before he fell flat on his face. What the hell had happened to him?

"Evie?" he called.

"Take it easy," Aisley said as she grabbed his arm to steady him. "You've been through a lot."

Malcolm turned to Guy. His leg gave out in that moment. There was a gasp from Aisley as he began to fall. Malcolm pushed her out of the way and landed heavily on his right side.

Blinding, white-hot pain flared through him. He closed his eyes and ground his teeth together to keep from shouting.

"Easy," Con said. "Concentrate on your breathing. It'll help with the pain."

Malcolm wanted to tell them all to go to hell, but at the moment it would cost him too much. He did as Con recommended because the pain was too great. It reminded Malcolm all too clearly of being ripped to shreds by Wallace.

When he could take a deep breath and not feel like he was about to pass out, he rolled onto his back. Daal was raging inside him, but Malcolm had never felt so weak before. He hated every second of it.

Eventually the throbbing subsided so that he could open his eyes. Con still leaned over him, his face lined with worry. Unease rippled through Malcolm.

"What happened?" he asked the King of Kings.

Con glanced away. "You've been out for a while. We've been trying to heal you, but as you've probably guessed, Wallace's blood has something new added to it. Death."

"Is that what I was fighting?" he asked. Death. He would never have guessed that.

Phelan squatted beside him. "You're here now. You can tell us all about what the bastard looks like."

"A shadow." Malcolm would never forget the feeling of that blackness surrounding him. "I thought Evie was there."

"I think she was," Rhys said.

Malcolm slowly sat up and realized he was naked. Aisley and Laura were gone, leaving just the Warriors and Dragons in the room. That uneasy feeling washed over Malcolm again. "I'm going to ask only one more time. Where is Evie?"

"We think she went to Wallace," Guy said reluctantly.

Malcolm shoved hands out of his way as he painfully climbed to his feet. "I need clothes. Now."

CHAPTER
FORTY-ONE

Evie bit back the nausea that threatened at somehow knowing where Jason Wallace lived. She wasn't sure what she'd expected to find, but it wasn't the impressive manor house she glimpsed as she drove through the large iron gate and past tall hedges.

Lights flickered around the rock-lined turnaround drive made to look like the fire lamps of old. Evie brought the Jaguar to a stop and shut off the engine.

She didn't want to do this alone, but it was her muck-up. She would fix it. After a deep, fortifying breath, she got out of the car and stared at the house. It was constructed of white stone and had impeccable landscaping.

Evie shut the door and walked around the back of the car. She glanced at the fountain in the middle of the parking area. Water trickled into the bottom of the fountain with an air of tranquility that Evie knew she'd never feel again.

Her boots crunched on the rock as she walked to the front door. The steps leading to the double doors looked as innocent as everything else around her, but she'd learned her lesson about Jason Wallace.

Nothing was as it seemed.

Evie reached the second step when one of the double doors opened. She hesitated, expecting to see Jason fill the doorway. When no one appeared, she ascended the stairs and stopped at the threshold.

She wanted to think that there was still time for her to turn around and wait for Malcolm. But it was a silly notion. The time for her to have turned back was before she did the ceremony to become *drough*.

Since then, she was well and truly on whatever path Jason had set in motion for her.

"Bastard," she mumbled.

Hate filled her. She'd never felt such loathing for someone, and she'd certainly never found herself entertaining how to kill someone before. In answer, the black magic within her coiled, waiting and ready.

Jason Wallace had done this to her. He was to blame.

Or was he?

Evie wasn't sure anymore. There was an argument the blame lay with her. She didn't deny it. She was the one to make the decision, no matter that Jason pushed her to it. She could have refused.

It was so easy to say that now, but even as she tried, she knew no matter how things might have gone differently, she would have still walked down the same road.

As awful as it was to feel the black magic within her and know her soul was bound for Hell, it was better than watching Brian die, or thousands of innocents being killed.

"Working it all out, I see."

She lifted her eyes to find a man dressed in navy slacks and a light green dress shirt as he leaned an arm atop the newel post at the base of the stairs. In his other hand, he held a glass with a splash of what she suspected was whisky.

His blond hair was combed back and the blue eyes staring at her were cold and dead. His face was narrow with unflattering angles. He had the look of a predator, of a man who knew just how powerful he was and wanted everyone else to know it as well.

"Jason Wallace," she said.

"At your disposal," he replied with a cocky grin and a small bow of his head. "Come inside, Evangeline. We've much to discuss."

She remained where she was. "Tell me how I knew where to find you."

"There is much you can do with magic. I planted my location in your mind when we met at Urquhart. You just didn't realize it until I needed you to."

"You know I loathe you. What do you want with me?"

Jason straightened and grinned fiendishly. "Sweet Evangeline, we'll get to that in time. For now, I think you'd like to see your brother, would you no'?"

All it took was the mention of Brian, and Evie crossed the threshold. "Did you harm him?"

"No' too much. You might want to discuss his use of profanity, however. He has quite a tongue on him. Oh," Jason said and chuckled. "I should say, he has quite a hand on him."

Evie had never cared for mute jokes, and she certainly didn't want to hear them from Jason. "Let me see Brian."

"In good time. Come with me," he said and walked through an open set of heavy oak doors.

She followed him with her eyes and saw into the room. It looked like an office. A good enough place to conduct business. And it was close to the front doors.

Evie gradually followed until she stood just inside the office. She found Jason to her left pouring himself another whisky from a crystal decanter.

He lifted the decanter to her, and she shook her head. Her nerves were already shot. She didn't need to add alcohol into the mix.

"Have a seat in front of the fire, Evangeline. You look as though you could use the heat."

She was chilled to the bone, but from fear and hatred, not because of the temperature. "You wanted me to turn *drough*. Why?"

He laughed as he walked around his mahogany desk and sat. It was the typical large, ornate wooden desk that men with money owned. It was large to show they dominated the room, and ornate to prove they had money.

All of which was evident from the house itself. Evie wanted to tell him he had gone overboard with the desk, but somehow managed to keep her mouth shut.

Jason took a drink of his whisky. "I'm no' in the habit of sharing my reasons with anyone. Why should I with you?"

"You went to a lot of trouble to make sure I was *drough* and bring me here."

"All true. It was your Web site, Evangeline. It was so easy to read your need to find other Druids between all the mundane text you wrote. And that necklace." He smiled slowly, maliciously. "It was too sweet to pass up."

She walked to the fire and stood with her back to it and her hands clasped behind her. Her fingers hurt they were so cold. If there was going to be a battle for Brian, she had to be ready.

"All of this for a necklace?"

"No," was his only answer.

She looked at him with disdain. "That's all the answer I get?"

"For now."

Evie wanted to roll her eyes at his theatrics. Jason Wallace really was running a show, and there was nothing she could do but go along with it and wait for her chance to strike.

"You wanted me here, Jason, and I'm here. I'd like to see my brother. Please."

Saying please to someone she hated as much as Jason was one of the hardest things she had ever done. Evie suspected that she would be facing many such obstacles in the very near future.

Or at least as long as Jason was alive.

"Your eyes betray you, Evangeline," Jason said off-handedly. "Every emotion you feel, I can see. You want to kill me." He shrugged and swirled his whisky. "I can understand that, but there's something you should know. I was dead once."

Evie swallowed and tried to hide her shock.

"Oh, yes," Jason said with a smile. "Well and truly dead. However, I set things in motion to prevent my staying that way. I returned to the land of the living stronger and more powerful than ever before. So you can try to think of ways to kill me, but it'll never happen. I'm as immortal as they come."

The room began to spin, but Evie refused to faint. It would be a show of weakness. Which couldn't happen. She somehow stayed on her feet and righted the room so that it no longer spun around her.

Evie swallowed. "You want to frighten me into never trying to turn against you."

"Well of course. I'd like to save you any pain. No matter what I say, however, you'll try to do me harm." His lips twisted. "You'll learn soon enough, Evangeline, that I always have the upper hand. For every harm you attempt on me, I'll make you pay in ten times the pain."

Evie cleared her throat. "Now that you've informed me of that, how about Brian?"

One side of Jason's cruel mouth lifted in a sardonic grin. "You're no' going to let up, are you?"

"You'll find that I'm easier to deal with once I've seen Brian."

Jason lowered his glass and gave a nod. "Brian, you may come up now."

Evie's heart thumped with hope and dread. She didn't trust Jason. Based on all she'd learned of him, it didn't go beyond him to have used magic on Brian.

Her worst fears were confirmed when Brian came to stand in the entry of the office. His eyes were blank as they stared straight ahead.

She refused to shed a single tear. Not for Brian, for Malcolm, or even for herself and how well and truly she'd stuffed things up for everyone.

"What did you do to him?" she demanded.

Jason's chair squeaked as he leaned forward. "He may have been born without a voice, but the lad wouldna cooperate. I needed him . . . malleable. I'll release him of magic and even my home."

Evie turned her head to Jason. "On what condition?"

Jason smiled coldly before he lifted the glass to sip the whisky.

Malcolm wished he was the one with wings. The dragons had taken their sweet time in agreeing to bring him to Wallace's. Con was against it, but it was Rhys who stepped in and agreed to do it.

Every second that ticked by and Evie got farther from him was like a dagger twisting in Malcolm's gut. She meant . . . He shook his head. He couldn't allow himself to think about what she meant to him, not yet. He had to concentrate on how he would get her free of Wallace.

Malcolm looked to his left and caught sight of a red

dragon. A glance to his right showed there was a blue dragon. There was no doubt he owed the Dragon Kings a great debt now—one he knew would be called upon in the future.

They hadn't had to help him, but they did. It was unexpected. Especially after how he had treated them before. The Dragons, much like the Warriors, didn't seem to hold that against him.

Malcolm winced as he thought of the argument he had with Phelan and Charon before he left. They'd wanted him to wait for the others, but Malcolm seemed to be the only one who understood that time was of the essence in getting to Evie.

But then again, he'd seen the look in Phelan's eyes. Phelan thought Evie was already in Wallace's clutches. Even Aisley had cautioned Malcolm on what he might find once he reached Wallace's mansion.

Malcolm was all too aware of what Wallace had done to get Evie. And Evie, all she wanted was Brian returned safe and unharmed.

He knew exactly what she would do for Brian—anything. It's how he felt about Larena—and now Evie. He had killed, betrayed, and turned against the very ones who were his family.

Evie would do that and more for Brian.

Malcolm would make sure she didn't go through it alone. He would stand beside her and commit the acts that would take her soul. His was already damned. He wouldn't have hers as well.

Rhys suddenly went into a dive, the wind rushing around him loudly. Malcolm released his god as the ground came toward him at a mind-boggling rate. Just before he hit, Rhys's large yellow claw released him and Malcolm ducked his head to roll several times before he stopped and came to his feet.

Malcolm looked to the sky just in time to see Rhys's dragon form disappear behind a cloud.

"Thank you, my friend," Malcolm said and turned to face Wallace Mansion and the evil that lived there.

It would be up to him alone to rescue Evie. Destiny had never rested so heavily on his shoulders as it did now, especially when Evie's soul was at stake.

CHAPTER
FORTY-TWO

Malcolm knew there was precious little time to reach Evie before the Warriors and Druids arrived. He wasn't sure they would take the time to listen to Evie explain anything.

And he wouldn't have her hurt.

His only choice was to somehow get her away from Wallace and far from the mansion before any of them got there.

Malcolm spread his fingers, his claws eager for Wallace's blood, and walked toward the tall iron gates blocking access to the mansion. He was ready to jump them when they suddenly opened.

"This willna be good," he mumbled as he walked through the gates.

Wallace had nearly killed him just hours ago. Malcolm's body was still healing and weak from the ordeal. He would use his last breath to get Evie free if he had to.

Malcolm didn't try to hide his approach to the front entrance that stood open. Wallace obviously knew he was there. What Malcolm didn't know was why Wallace allowed him in.

Was the bastard so sure of his magic that he no longer feared anything?

If that was the case, they were all well and truly fucked.

Malcolm flexed his hands again. He couldn't remember the last time he had been so eager to sink his claws into Wallace's body and shed blood as he walked through the doors and heard voices to his left.

He recognized both Jason and Evie instantly. A teenage boy stood in the office entry. He had the same dark hair as Evie. It was long, grazing the top of his collar. Whereas Evie's hair hung in large curls, Brian's hair held only a hint of a wave.

"Let's invite our new guest inside," Wallace said.

Immediately, Brian shifted into profile. Malcolm's gaze met Wallace's to see the cocky bastard grinning in triumph. Malcolm stalked cautiously into the office and spotted Evie standing before the fire, her eyes wide and skin pale.

Wallace had frightened her. For that Malcolm wanted to rip his head off. Instead, he looked at Wallace and lifted a brow, waiting for the conversation to continue.

"Doona let me stop the two of you," Malcolm said.

Wallace motioned to the table full of decanters of liquor. "Pick your pleasure."

"That would be seeing you dead."

"As I just explained to the lovely Evangeline, that's impossible."

Malcolm returned his cool smile. "Ah, but then I know what you doona, Wallace. Everything can be killed. *Everything*. Even you."

"I came back from the dead, Malcolm," Wallace said with a chuckle.

"So did Deirdre. She was killed. Spectacularly, too, I might add."

Wallace leaned back in his chair. "Deirdre lost sight of what she was meant for. I doona have such a problem.

Now," he said with a quick intake of breath. "You've lost friends, have you no'? Killed one, as well. I can promise that I'll no' touch another Warrior or Druid."

"I've heard such promises before. You willna do anything. You'll trick or threaten Evie, Brian, or even me to do the work for you. That way, you doona break your so-called promise."

Wallace's smile widened. "Ah, but you do know me well."

"I've known others like you. Deirdre and Declan, to be precise. They're dead now. Think on that."

"Oh, I'm no' the one who will have thinking to do, Malcolm. I let you in because I wanted you here. Just as I wanted Brian and Evie."

"Tell me something I doona know," Malcolm stated flatly.

Wallace considered him a moment. "You've changed. You're no' the same cold, unfeeling Warrior I've seen. Could it be what I did to you? Nay," he said thoughtfully. "I believe the source is the lovely blue-eyed Druid in this verra room."

"Whatever you want with her, I'll take her place," Malcolm said.

"Always so eager to defend those you care about. It got you into all sorts of trouble with Deirdre. Are you sure you want to repeat things?"

Malcolm gave a single nod. He couldn't look at Evie, couldn't think of the hell he'd gone through with Deirdre. He had to keep focusing on righting what Wallace was doing to Evie and her brother.

"Perfect," Wallace said, his smile a little too bright.

Foreboding ripped through Malcolm. Too late, he realized he'd played right into Wallace's hand. Malcolm's head turned so he looked at Evie.

She returned his stare with one of sorrow and regret.

Malcolm looked back at Wallace to find the *drough*'s smile made him ill.

"Tell me, Malcolm, do you remember why Deirdre went to so much trouble to trap Quinn MacLeod in Cairn Toul?" Wallace asked.

"The prophecy. It's said a *drough* and a Warrior will create a child."

And then it hit him. Wallace had set Evie on a path that led to becoming *drough*. He was a Warrior.

They had already shared a night of passion.

"Ah," Wallace said. "I see you're putting it all together."

Malcolm clenched his hands into fists and bared his fangs as he growled. All he wanted to do was attack Wallace and inflict as much pain as he could. But to even try it would mean putting Evie and Brian at risk as well as showing Wallace he was still weak from their last run-in.

"Everything that has happened I've put in motion," Wallace said as he got to his feet. "Brian's kidnapping, Evangeline becoming *drough*, and even your recent near-death experience. I knew while you lay fighting for your life, Evangeline's mind would be on how she could get to Brian. I also knew once you woke and found her gone that you would come for her."

Malcolm didn't take his eyes off Wallace as he walked from behind his desk to Evie's side. She stiffened, but didn't move away when Wallace put his hand on her stomach.

"Already she carries your child, Malcolm. The child of the prophecy. Thanks to the two of you, a child of pure evil will be born and will help me conquer the world."

A single tear rolled down Evie's face, and it shattered Malcolm as nothing else could. He hadn't been able to stop her from becoming *drough*, and thanks to desires he couldn't control, they'd played right into Wallace's hands.

"Doona even think of trying to rid your body of the babe growing inside you," Wallace said as he moved aside

Evie's curls to whisper in her ear while his gaze was locked with Malcolm's. "If you do, Brian will die an instant and horrible death."

"You can't expect me to go along with this," Evie said as she jerked away from him.

Malcolm took a step toward her, but one look from Wallace stopped him.

"You will, because you want your brother to live," Jason said. "All you need to do is carry that baby to term. The babe will be born in this house, and then it'll be mine. I'll be done with all of you then."

"You mean you'll kill us," Malcolm said.

Wallace shrugged. "Perhaps. If you make yourselves useful and prove I can trust you, I might keep you alive."

"If you're going to kill us, why should I do anything you want?" Evie said, her face a mask of anger.

Malcolm called her name, but it was too late. A choking sound came from Brian as he bent over, his face turning red as he struggled to breathe.

Evie rushed to Brian. She looked at Jason. "You've made your point. Stop this!"

Just as quickly as Brian had begun to choke, it stopped. He dragged in a breath, his eyes briefly meeting Malcolm's, before he straightened to the silent guard he'd been before.

Malcolm walked to Evie and gently pulled her against him. "I know your kind, Wallace. You'll no' be content with us just allowing the babe to grow. What else do you want?"

"You're going to kill all the Warriors."

He said it as if he'd been reciting the menu for the night. Malcolm's soul, that had begun to flourish once more, withered.

"For Evie's safety, of course," Wallace continued. "After all, once your so-called friends learn what is growing inside her, they'll try to execute her. And you."

Malcolm knew it was the truth, but that didn't mean he

would be able to slay those he called friends, family. "And if I doona?"

"You'll never see Evie again." Wallace clasped his hands behind his back, a satisfied look upon his face. "You may know me, Warrior, but I know you. You think if you can get Evie and Brian out of my home that you might be able to somehow stop whatever I have in play. That's no' going to happen, because I'm no' allowing Brian to leave."

Evie jerked in Malcolm's arms as if she'd been shot. Her chest heaved and she shook with rage.

"Try it," she dared Wallace. "Try and keep Brian here, and I'll abort this baby with my magic right this instant."

Wallace blinked, the smile wiped from his face. "You do that, and I kill Brian."

"He'll be dead anyway. We all will. If you want us to carry through with this elaborate plan of yours, then we all leave. Or it ends now."

There was a pause before Jason said, "You wouldna dare."

"Try me."

Malcolm squeezed Evie's shoulder, careful his claws didn't cut her. He wanted her to know he supported her in whatever decision she made. They could walk out of the mansion, or they could all die inside.

Either way Malcolm would make sure that whatever Jason Wallace wanted didn't come to fruition.

"You have everything you want," Malcolm said. "Brian comes with us."

Wallace rocked back on his heels and gave a slight nod. "I'll agree if Evie kills the dragons."

"What?" Evie shouted.

"Agreed," Malcolm said over her before she could protest more. He didn't know how much Evie knew of the Dragon Kings, but it was evident Wallace hadn't done his research on them or he'd know the only one who could kill a Dragon King was another Dragon King.

Wallace rubbed his hands together. "I think it's all worked out marvelously. Just remember. I'll be watching the three of you."

"And what if I lose the baby by nothing I've done?" Evie asked. "It does happen all the time."

Wallace looked from her to Malcolm. "Then you get pregnant again. I doona think either of you will mind that ordeal."

Malcolm tamped down his god and turned Evie to the door. He grasped Brian's arm to find the lad's eyes were locked on him.

For a moment Malcolm thought Wallace didn't have control of the teen as he imagined, but just as quickly, the emotionless look returned.

Malcolm watched the lad carefully. Had he looked so . . . lifeless when he hadn't been able to feel anything? If so it was no wonder people called him stony and impersonal.

"Come," Malcolm urged Brian as the three walked out of Wallace's mansion to Evie's car.

He put Brian in the Jaguar, and had Evie behind the wheel with the top down in a matter of moments. "Keep it together for just a little longer, Evie," he urged. "I'll be right behind you."

Her hand gripped the door, her knuckles white. "What have I done?"

"It's no' you," he said as he reached past her and pushed the button to start the car. "It was all Wallace. You heard him. He planned all of this."

"He didn't have me put up the Web site. That was all me."

"It's just a site. There was nothing malicious or evil about what you did. You can no' say the same about Wallace."

She looked over at him. "I'm carrying your child. A child that's supposed to be evil."

He shook his head. "That's no' going to happen. I'll no' let it."

Malcolm prayed he could keep that promise as he closed the door and watched her drive out of the gates as he used his speed and ran behind them, making sure Wallace kept his word.

CHAPTER
FORTY-THREE

Evie placed her hand on her stomach as she drove the two-seater. Pregnant. She still couldn't believe there was a life growing inside her. A life Jason wanted to corrupt.

A life she didn't want to be responsible for.

It wasn't that she didn't want kids of her own. It was just that she had been raising Brian for ten years, and she'd wanted to experience those wild early-twenty years all her friends had.

How could she do that now with a baby? A baby she might have to one day kill in order to save the world?

When she was several miles away from Wallace Mansion, she pulled off the road to try and calm herself. Before she put it in park Malcolm opened the door, unbuckled her seat belt, and pulled her out of the car.

"Evie?"

"I can't do this," she said. "I can't be responsible for giving birth to a child of evil."

"You are no' in this alone. We have each other."

"Jason will kill us."

"We have nine months to sort it out. We'll think of something."

She looked to see his jaw clenched. He was worried, but he was trying to hide it from her. Most of the men she knew would have walked away from her and the situation.

But not Malcolm. He was steady, solid. A pillar of strength and determination she knew she could lean on no matter what. It was only his presence that kept her from completely losing it.

Evie looked at her brother. "Brian? Is that you? Are you with us?"

There was no smile, just stark anger in his dark eyes. She watched his rapid hand movements as he told her he was fine and unharmed.

Before she could answer, Malcolm growled and stalked around the car to head into the trees.

"I'm going to kill him," Malcolm said through clenched teeth.

Evie glanced at Brian. "Stay here," she told him as she followed Malcolm.

Her sweater wasn't enough to keep her warm in the cold night air, but she ignored it as she pushed through the tall grass toward a stand of trees. Evie was breathing hard when she finally reached Malcolm.

"Have you lost your damned mind, Dragon?" Malcolm said.

"I wasna going to just leave you two in there if something went wrong."

Evie tried to see around Malcolm's thick shoulders to Rhys, but he wouldn't let her. Finally, she ducked under his arms and caught sight of a nude male with an impressive dragon tattoo on his chest with the dragon's tail wrapping around his left arm and ending at his elbow.

She had a split second before Malcolm stepped in front of her, a frown directed at her. "What?" she asked. "As if I knew he was going to be in the buff."

"You should've waited in the car."

"If you've forgotten since we left that maniac's house, I'm well and truly in this, Malcolm Munro. You're not going to leave me out of anything."

"Guess she told you," Rhys said from behind Malcolm, a smile in his voice.

"Sod off, Dragon," Malcolm said over his shoulder. He then grasped Evie's arms. "I've no intention of leaving you out of anything. We're in a bind, Evie."

"Because of the baby?"

There was a choking sound before Rhys said, "The *what*?"

Malcolm ignored him as he sighed. "That's part of it. I willna bring you to MacLeod Castle. I'm no' sure of the reception either of us would receive."

"Return to Dreagan," Rhys said.

Malcolm turned his head to the side and said, "I'm no' so certain Con would appreciate being put in the middle of this."

"Con can bugger off. He's always said Dreagan was open to you whenever you needed it. I say you and Evie definitely need it."

"And Brian," she added. "We have my brother."

"Brian as well," Rhys added.

Evie put her hands on Malcolm's chest. "I don't know what to do, so I'll follow your lead in this."

"No' sure that's a good idea. I've mucked things up pretty wretchedly."

She rose up on her tiptoes and placed her lips on his. "No. You've managed to keep me alive and helped me after becoming *drough*. I wouldn't want anyone else by my side."

"Had there been someone else, you wouldna be carrying the child."

"Our child," she corrected him. "I don't care what

Jason says. I'm not ready to give up just yet. I need to wrap my head around everything first, but we have time."

Malcolm nodded and pulled her against him. As soon as her arms wrapped around him, she closed her eyes and enjoyed the feel of him being close.

"Return to your brother," he urged as he pulled back. "I'm sure Brian has questions. Let me talk to Rhys for a moment, and then we'll decide what to do."

She nodded and turned on her heel. The inside light of the car was on, and she spotted Brian standing with the passenger door open waiting for her.

Malcolm watched until Evie reached Brian before he turned to Rhys. The Dragon's aqua eyes were intense as they stared at him.

"Aye, Evie is carrying my child. It seems both of us unwillingly walked right into Wallace's plan to bring about the prophecy Deirdre first tried to fulfill."

"Unbelievable." Rhys ran a hand through his dark hair and shook his head. "Why did he let you three leave?"

"Evie. She threatened to use her magic to abort the babe unless we were allowed to leave. Wallace didna want to test her."

Rhys crossed his arms over his bare chest. "Now that you're free, why no' abort it now?"

"No' an option. His magic is linked to Brian. If we try to do anything to the babe, Brian dies. Wallace made it verra clear."

"He's just going to allow you and Evie to live wherever you want until the babe comes?" Rhys asked incredulously.

Malcolm gave a nod of his head. "Or so he says."

"And when the babe arrives?"

"He plans to take it immediately and raise it as his own."

"Fuck." Rhys's arms dropped as he paced. "We can no' let any of this happen."

Malcolm lifted a brow. "I'm so glad you thought of that, because I hadna."

Rhys gave him a flat look. "Point taken. What do you need from me?"

"I doona know." Malcolm rubbed his eyes with his thumb and forefinger. "Evie isna taking this news well. She was barely holding it together after discovering she was *drough*."

"You think she'll do something?"

Malcolm frowned. "No' at all. That's no' like her to harm herself. Nay, I'm more worried about Wallace doing this to send her deeper into her black magic."

"And thereby closer to him."

"Precisely. Wallace set all of this in motion. It's as if he's thought of every action we could take and planned for that."

"Even Evie's threat to get all three of you out of his home?"

Malcolm nodded angrily. "Even that."

Rhys's lips flatted into a line. "You're in a fix, mate. Are you really concerned with what the Warriors will do?"

"Aye. You saw how Phelan reacted to Evie. I'll no' put her in a situation where she feels everyone is against her, no' when we need to get ahead of whatever Wallace has planned."

"Nay, I agree. But I thought those at MacLeod Castle were your friends."

Malcolm shrugged. "I thought so as well. After what Phelan just went through with Aisley, I wouldna have expected he would act as he did, but I was wrong."

"Then come back to Dreagan. Evie will be better there with friends who can help her."

"Do you think any of your dragon magic could benefit her?"

Rhys's mouth twisted in a frown. "I doona know. Return with me, and we'll see."

"Just be careful no' to be spotted. I'd rather no' have Con on my arse because you were seen."

Rhys's face suddenly split into a smile. "It does Con good to be rattled every once in a while."

In the next instant, Rhys launched himself into the air and instantly shifted into the form of a dragon, his yellow scales muted in the darkness.

Malcolm turned on his heel and walked back to Evie and Brian. One look told him that brother and sister hadn't shared more than two words with each other.

"Everything all right?" he asked Evie.

She gave a small shake of her head, but refused to speak of it. "So, Dreagan?"

"Dreagan," he said with a nod.

"Do you think that's the best place for us?"

He glanced at her and sighed. "I doona know at this point, but I think it's a good start. The Dragons will do their part to protect you and Brian."

"And you."

One side of his mouth lifted in a smile. "I'm more concerned with you."

"And I want to be sure you're safe as well."

"I'm a Warrior, Evie. I'll be all right."

"But you weren't," she argued, her voice rising. "I saw you lying on that bed covered in blood with wounds that weren't healing no matter what Phelan and Con did."

Malcolm pulled on one of her curls. "I'm here now. I'll no' lie and say it was easy. I felt like I was in Hell."

"How did you get out?"

He considered not telling her. Since he still wasn't sure

of what he felt for her, Malcolm didn't want to put her into a position where she felt she had to be with him.

But then he remembered how he'd handled things when he had woken and Evie wasn't there.

"You," he said. "It was the thought of you."

To his surprise she leaned forward to place a kiss on his cheek. "I'm so glad you found me in Cairn Toul."

"Actually, it was before that."

Her brows lowered as she cocked her head to the side. "When exactly?"

"I saw you in Aviemore, and then I was the one who pulled you out of your car when you wrecked."

"I knew someone was there. Why didn't you show yourself?"

"Because I knew then that you were better off no' knowing me."

"Yet you couldn't stay away," she said in a low voice.

Malcolm felt a constriction release around his heart as he admitted what he couldn't have before. "I couldna stay away. I only meant to make sure you left Cairn Toul, but after talking to you, I didna want to leave."

"I'm glad you didn't."

"Are you? Look where you are now."

She put her hand on his chest over his heart. "I'm here with my brother because of you. If you hadn't been there after the *drough* ceremony I'd have given in to all the dark urges I had."

"Aye, but you wouldna be carrying the child of prophecy. You would well and truly be *drough*, but I almost think that would be a better fate than the one given you now."

Brian's hand hit the car with a loud bang to get their attention. Malcolm watched as he used sign language to talk. A few minutes later and Evie turned to him, her face pale.

"What did he say?" Malcolm asked.

She swallowed before she looked at him. "He said that one way or another Jason Wallace would have put us in this situation."

Malcolm ushered them into the car. The faster they could get to Dreagan, the faster they could come up with some way to end this nightmare they were in.

CHAPTER
FORTY-FOUR

They reached Dreagan in record time. Evie parked the car as Malcolm ran up behind them. But he hesitated in following them to the door.

"Malcolm?" Evie asked as she and Brian stood near the hood of the car, her arm wrapped around her brother. "What is it?"

Malcolm frowned as he stared hard at the front door to Dreagan Manor. He felt magic, Druid magic. The amount of magic seemed to be more than just Aisley and Laura, but the dragons' magic made everything difficult to decipher.

The only magic he felt strongly was Evie's. He glanced at her to see her worry growing.

"It's nothing. Let's get you two inside," he said as he put his hand on Evie's back and guided her to the door.

Guy opened the door before they reached it. "I'm glad you two returned. And with Brian, I see," he said with a welcoming smile. "Rhys filled me in."

But Malcolm wasn't fooled. Guy's demeanor was too nice. The underlying current, however, said that something had gone pear shaped.

Malcolm stepped inside the manor, but didn't go any farther. He turned on Guy as he closed the door. "What's going on?"

Guy sighed. "I had no idea Phelan did it, Malcolm. You need to understand that. No King did."

Those three little words said what Guy could not. Unease rippled through Malcolm. His instinct was to grab Evie and Brian and start running. Where to go, was the problem. There was nowhere else. He would have to face those from the castle.

"Malcolm," Evie said, her voice wavering.

He turned around to find the Warriors and Druids from MacLeod Castle spilling into the foyer from the sitting room. Malcolm quickly moved to stand between them and Evie.

"Phelan told us what happened," Fallon said, his green eyes hard.

"I bet he did." Malcolm cut a look at Phelan. "I doona remember you running to the castle when you were trying to keep them from knowing about Aisley."

Fallon cut his hand through the air. "This is Warrior business, Malcolm."

"This is my business!" Malcolm yelled, his teeth bared in anger. He welcomed that fury, took it and let it slide through him until Daal was purring with it. "I didna go to you for this exact reason. Instead of coming alone, you brought everyone. Shall I tell you what that shows me?"

Evie's hand touched Malcolm's arm. "They're your family. Listen to them."

"Nay. Coming en masse tells me the time for talking is over."

Aisley pushed her way past Phelan and moved to stand in front of Fallon. "Malcolm, please. Phelan was doing what he thought was best."

"Strange how he didna feel the same about letting them know of you, Jason's cousin and the one who shot Larena."

Aisley licked her lips and glanced back at Phelan. Her forehead puckered. "It's true. He didn't, but—"

"This is different?" Malcolm finished for her. He didn't hide the sarcasm and ire from his voice.

"Enough!" Constantine said as he strode into the foyer, his jaw set and his fathomless black eyes pinning Fallon.

Malcolm watched Phelan pull Aisley back to his side and whisper something in her ear. Then his gaze moved to Con who looked from him to Fallon.

"Malcolm, Evie, and Brian have been offered sanctuary," Con announced. "The only way they leave is if they want to."

A muscle ticked in Fallon's jaw. "You're overstepping your bounds, Dragon."

"I'm helping a friend," Con said tightly. He looked from Fallon to the other Warriors gathered. "There are things that happened tonight none of you are aware of. Perhaps you should learn all the facts before you react."

Malcolm breathed easier when Evie put her hand in his. When he looked down at her it was to find Rhys, Hal, Guy, Banan, and several other Dragons he hadn't met standing behind him.

"You were offered sanctuary as well, Phelan," Rhys said. "It wasna that long ago all you cared about was keeping Aisley's identity from everyone, including Charon."

Brian touched Malcolm on the back to get his attention. Malcolm turned and focused on Brian's hands. It didn't take long for Daal to help Malcolm learn sign language.

"No," Malcolm said. "No one else is going to hurt Evie. Or you for that matter."

Fallon started to say something but was stopped by Larena as she moved to stand beside him. Malcolm focused on his cousin, hiding his shock at seeing the woman look-ing so vibrant and alive once more.

"Hello, cousin," she said with a smile.

Malcolm gave her a half grin. "Hello, cousin. You're looking better."

"I am better. The effects of the *drough* blood are leav-ing me. I hoped you'd return to the castle."

He looked at Evie and squeezed her hand. "I had no intention of ever returning."

"And now?" Larena urged.

Malcolm looked into her smoky blue eyes and shrugged. "I think it's better if we remain here."

"Why?" she entreated.

At one time Malcolm would have done anything for Larena. He still would, but things were different. Evie was his focus now. Evie, the babe she carried, and Brian.

There was movement though the group of Warriors as Gwynn pushed her way through while Logan tried to yank her back. Gwynn's violet eyes looked first at Malcolm and then to Evie.

"Would your name be Evie Walker?" Gwynn asked.

Brian slapped his hands together to get Evie's attention. She looked from Brian to Gwynn in confusion. Brian was telling her not to tell them anything more.

Malcolm frowned. How much did Brian know, and more importantly, how much control did Wallace still have over him?

"Yes," Evie answered Gwynn then winced when Brian's hands moved faster in his agitation. "Why?"

"You're the one with the site. When you get a second, can you tell me about the necklace?"

Malcolm felt Evie's fear as she recoiled. He grabbed her to steady her, and when she looked up at him with clear blue eyes filled with terror, he lifted her into his arms.

She had withstood too much already. Evie looked ready to buckle beneath it all.

"I've got you," he whispered.

He glared at Gwynn before he stared at the Warriors he had called family, daring any of them to try and stop him from walking out.

Rhys came to stand on his right while Guy moved to his left. Rhys gave him a nod. "Remember, Warriors, you are here because we extended an invitation. You've no idea how many Dragon Kings are still sleeping in the mountains."

"Or how many are out patrolling," Constantine said. "Doona start a war."

Fallon turned his green eyes to Con. "I'm no' the one starting the war."

"What do you call this?" Guy asked. "You come here as a group to confront Malcolm to make him do whatever it is you wanted. None of you have given him a second thought or even seen the man he is now. All you see is the man he was. Take a closer look."

Phelan snorted. "We're worried about him. He was easily sucked into Deirdre's world."

"So I would so easily fall into Wallace's?" Malcolm asked. "I was wrong to think of you as family. Guy's right. You're no' seeing me."

"We stood by you," Hayden said.

Ian nodded. "And forgave you."

Malcolm smiled, though it felt as if he had a dagger in his back. "You've no more forgiven me for killing Duncan than I've forgiven myself. Each of you has said you understood why I aligned with Deirdre, but I think it was all shite."

"It wasn't for me," Larena said and walked to him. Her smoky blue eyes pleaded with him. "Please, Malcolm.

Return with us. Bring Evie and her brother. We'll sort it all out at MacLeod Castle."

Malcolm shook his head sadly. "You ask me that now. I wonder if the offer will remain when you learn everything."

He turned away from Larena and walked around the group of Warriors and Druids, refusing to look at any of them. Malcolm hadn't expected the show of solidarity from the Dragons, but he was grateful for what they had done.

They would remain for one night, maybe two, and then he would take Evie and Brian and move on. The Warriors and Kings needed to remain allies, not enemies.

"I'm so sorry," Evie said.

Malcolm looked at her and sighed. He had his woman back in his arms safe. For now, that was good enough for him. "All will be well."

Constantine followed Malcolm with his eyes until the Warrior disappeared from view. Rhys and Guy trailed behind Brian, and Con knew his men would see all three settled comfortably.

"For someone who didna want us to know of you, you've certainly taken a stand," Fallon said, his voice rough with indignation.

Con took a deep breath and faced the leader of the Warriors. Hal and Banan stood on either side of him while other Kings fanned out around the foyer and around the manor. There wouldn't be a battle with the Warriors, but Con was making a point, and he wanted it brought home effectively.

"What did you expect me to do?" Con asked.

"No' give him refuge."

Con adjusted his silver cuff link at his left wrist. "As Malcolm mentioned, things happened tonight."

"Like what?" Larena questioned.

Banan shook his head of short dark hair. "I'm no' sure we're the ones who should be doing the telling."

"I have to agree," Con said. "Malcolm and Evie, and even Brian, are going to need all the friends they can get in the coming weeks and months. You've just shown Malcolm he couldna count on you, the verra people he called family."

Aisley gasped, her hand covering her mouth as her eyes went wide. "He didn't. Tell me Jason didn't do it."

Con shifted his gaze to the dark-haired Druid and watched her intently. If anyone knew what Wallace was capable of, it was Aisley. "What do you think he did?"

Aisley glanced at Phelan and slowly lowered a shaking hand to her side. "The prophecy. He found a Warrior and a *drough* to complete it."

"Aye," Hal said, his lips twisted in disgust and anger. "Wallace used Evie and Malcolm to achieve his plans."

Larena let out a loud breath. "And we all came to confront them." She turned to Fallon. "I begged you to keep it just the two of us until we spoke with him. I might have lost Malcolm forever now."

"What would that have done?" Fallon asked.

"No' made him turn from us," Lucan stated.

Quinn nodded and looked at the stairs. "There's more that you are no' telling us, aye, Con?"

"Aye," Hal said, a finality in his words.

Con watched the play of emotions on the Warriors' faces. He wasn't sure why Fallon had brought everyone, but there had to be a good reason.

Fallon had done everything in his power to save his Warriors, most especially Malcolm. Why would he ruin all of that in one night?

There was more at play here, and Con was beginning to suspect that Wallace was somehow to blame. He'd set up an elaborate plan and patiently waited for it to unfold.

It was Ramsey who stepped forward. "I'd like to talk to Malcolm."

"Perhaps tomorrow." Con knew Malcolm needed but a small push to send him over the edge, and now wasn't the time for it. "He and Evie need some time alone."

Ramsey bowed his head. "I'll return then. Fallon. It's time we went home."

Fallon didn't say another word as he began teleporting everyone back to MacLeod Castle. When the last of them were gone, Con turned to his men.

"I want guards out at all times patrolling our perimeter. Pay attention to every hint of magic no matter how small."

"You're expecting we'll have a visitor?" Banan asked.

Con looked at the ceiling above him. "I suspect Wallace will want to ensure Evie and Malcolm do as he's demanded. I doona want that foul stench of a Druid on Dreagan land ever again."

Hal smiled, his moonlight blue eyes alight with delight. "I look forward for the bastard to try and come at us."

"Oh, he will, Hal, he will," Con said.

Banan looked at the other Dragon Kings and grinned. "He can try. He doesna know who he'll be tangling with."

Con returned the smile. He might have wanted to stay out of the Warriors' business, but now that he was in it, he and the other Kings would do their part.

"Just make sure he doesna discover the Silvers," Con cautioned.

For if Wallace managed to wake the dangerous Silver dragons, then the war he and the other Kings had ended with the humans would return once more.

CHAPTER
FORTY-FIVE

Malcolm strode down the corridor until he came to a room. He thrust his chin at it and said to Brian, "You can sleep there. We'll be next door."

But when Malcolm continued on to the room he had been in after the confrontation with Wallace, Brian followed. Malcolm turned into the room and walked to one of the chairs were he carefully set Evie.

"I'm not going to break, you know," she said with a grin.

He met her clear blue eyes, ever amazed that she had given herself to him. "I know your strength, Druid."

"Do you?" she asked, her smile gone as seriousness took over. "Because I don't. My world is shattered. In a matter of hours my soul belongs to Satan, and I have a child of pure evil growing inside me." She looked away, blinking rapidly. "Strength? No. I was making a joke to alleviate my own fears. I'm scared to face the coming months, much less the next few hours."

Malcolm put a finger against her jaw and turned her face to his. "We'll weather this together. Your quick thinking got Brian returned to you, and we have the shelter of the dragons."

"Right," she said with a snort. "As if Jason really let us go so easily."

"Whatever the reason, he did."

"Yet you lost your family."

"They were never mine to begin with. What happened tonight proved it."

"Really? Have you known Fallon to ever do anything like this before?"

Malcolm sat back on his heels and sighed. "Nay."

"Then there had to be a reason, and you can't tell me that all of them are against you."

"They stand as one, Evie. They always have, always will. That's how they've won against evil time and again."

She put her hand on his cheek. "But you aren't evil."

"Neither are you. Decisions, remember?"

After she gave a nod, Malcolm rose to his feet and turned to Brian. He stared at the teen for long moments wondering how to broach the subject. Finally, Malcolm decided the direct approach was best.

"Does Evie know?" he asked.

Brian's lips thinned and his nostrils flared as he glared at him. Malcolm patiently waited.

"Do I know what?" Evie asked.

Malcolm kept his gaze locked on the youth. "I wasna sure at first. It took me a moment, but you gave it away when you looked at me while we were at Wallace's. Then I knew for sure once we were away from Wallace and I could feel you."

Brian grunted and shook his head before signing, "She doesn't know."

"I don't know what?" Evie repeated, her voice rising.

Malcolm crossed his arms over his chest. "Your brother has magic."

Evie looked from Malcolm to Brian and back to Malcolm, her forehead creased in a frown. "That's not possible. Brian would have told me." She turned her gaze to her brother. "You would've told me, right?"

"I heard Grandmother talking to you about it," Brian signed with his hands. "I kept waiting for you to talk to me, and when you didn't, I thought you didn't want me to tell you."

Evie was up and enfolding Brian in a fierce hug. "Never. I thought if you had magic you'd mention it. What a mess."

Malcolm dropped his arms, pleased with the outcome. He hadn't been sure how Brian would react to being confronted. With one issue dealt with, that left a thousand more.

Evie sniffed and stepped away from her brother, but not before she gave him a bright smile and pushed his hair back from his face. "Does Jason know you have magic?"

"I doona believe so," Malcolm answered for the lad. "If he did, Jason would've turned Brian *drough* as well just to ensure you did as he wanted. What I want to know is how Brian was able to withstand Wallace's magic."

Brian shrugged, causing his tee to pull at the seams. When Evie raised a brow, Brian sighed and once more used his hands to say, "I imagined a wall between me and that bastard. For some reason, none of his magic touched me. He was stupid and told me what the magic he was using would do, so I just acted as if I was under his control."

"Quick thinking, lad," Malcolm said in approval.

Evie beamed. "That was brilliant. Though I wish I could erect a mental wall between me and him."

"Have Brian teach you. The fact Brian can do that without any training means the magic in your family is strong. There's no reason you can no' do it as well," Malcolm said.

Evie bit her lip nervously. "There isn't much I can't do with this black magic inside me."

Brian slapped his hands together to get their attention before he signed, "What is going on? I want to know all of it. And what are you, Malcolm?"

Malcolm sank onto the newly made bed and waited for Evie to begin. When she backed away and resumed her seat in the chair, Malcolm drew in a deep breath. "How much do you know of Druids?"

Brian shrugged, which is what Malcolm had assumed. Malcolm relayed the telling of Rome and the Druids. The youth listened intently, his gaze focused squarely on Malcolm.

"You're a Warrior?" Brian asked with his hands.

Malcolm nodded. "That's what you saw when I first came into Wallace's office."

"Tell him of your god," Evie said.

Malcolm looked down at his arms. It was the scars on his right arm that caught his attention. Odd how when he was with Evie that he forgot about them.

"My god's name is Daal. He was known as the Devourer. He has always controlled lightning, which is my power."

"Daal," Evie repeated. "And do you speak with him?"

Malcolm lifted one shoulder. "I can hear him in my mind, but we doona carry on conversations."

"Can you kill Wallace?" Brian signed.

Malcolm braced his hands on his knees. "We've killed two *droughs* before him. There has to be a way to kill him."

"There is," Evie said. "The ancients told me. They just didn't tell me what it was."

"Then we find it."

"You're always so confident."

Malcolm felt anything but confident.

"The rest of the story," Brian quickly signed before Malcolm could respond.

Evie took over then, telling Brian about the site and someone hacking in, and her being on the run. When she came to the part of living in Cairn Toul, Malcolm saw Brian's eyes narrow for a fraction of a second.

"You talk to rocks?" Brian asked with his hands.

Evie nodded. "I've always heard them."

"And Cairn Toul is where Deirdre lived? Was that wise?"

Malcolm grunted. "Those were my exact thoughts, which is why I followed her to the mountain and confronted her."

Evie held up her hand when Brian began to sign again. "Let me finish the story quickly, then you can ask your questions."

When Brian gave a quick nod and leaned back against the wall, his hands shoved into the front pockets of his jeans, Evie continued.

Malcolm saw her hands tighten into fists when she spoke of doing the ceremony to become *drough*. She skipped over the part of them making love, much to Malcolm's relief.

"Which brings us to tonight," Evie said. "You know the rest."

Brian ran a hand down his face. "You're really pregnant?"

"It's still a few weeks before I'd have guessed," Evie said. "But there's definitely a chance."

Malcolm rubbed his jaw. "Wallace seemed awfully sure of it. Use your magic to check."

"No," Evie said hastily. "I don't want to hurt the babe with the black magic if I am carrying a child."

Malcolm opened his mouth to answer when there was a knock at the door. Brian pushed away from the wall and opened it. Malcolm wasn't surprised to find Guy and his wife, Elena.

"We thought you three might be hungry," Elena said as

she placed a tray on the table. "We're glad you're back, Evie."

Evie's smile was weak. "I seem to bring turmoil wherever I go. I don't think I should remain."

"Aye, you should," Guy said. He turned his gaze to Malcolm. "Know that all of you are welcome to stay for as long as you need."

"I'm no' sure that's wise." Malcolm stood and faced Guy. "You and the others have done enough. The longer we stay, the more likely it is that Wallace will come."

Elena shrugged. "Let Jason come. Anyone who thinks to fight the Dragon Kings is a fool, and he'll learn that soon enough."

"Aye, but trying to harm you and letting your secret out are two different things," Malcolm said. "We'll stay tonight and leave in the morning."

Guy took Elena's hand. "Where will you go?"

Malcolm met Evie's gaze. "The only other place we can—Cairn Toul."

"Are you sure that's a good idea?" Guy asked. "I know Con wants to talk to you three. After you've eaten and rested, come downstairs."

Malcolm nodded and softly shut the door behind the couple. When he turned around, Evie was wringing her hands. "What is it?"

"I don't think I can go back to Cairn Toul."

"You didna mind it before."

"I wasn't a *drough* before. You said it yourself, evil was there. I don't want to chance anything."

Malcolm glanced at Brian to see his gaze was on the floor. "Then we'll go somewhere else."

No more was said as they sat around the tiny table and ate. All Malcolm could think about was the babe growing inside Evie. His child, a child he thought he'd never have.

He couldn't turn it over to Wallace, nor could he allow a child of pure evil to enter the world. There had to be a way to change the outcome.

Evie suddenly set down her fork. "If Brian was able to stop Wallace's magic from controlling him, does that also mean Jason can't hurt him if something happens to the baby?"

Malcolm stopped mid-chew and looked at Brian. The lad shrugged in response. Malcolm finished chewing and swallowing before he said, "A Druid might be able to tell if Wallace's magic is attached to Brian."

"I could try, but I think you already have a Druid in mind."

He inwardly winced. "I do, but I doona want to reach out to her."

"Who is it?"

"Dani, Ian's wife."

Evie's hand came to rest atop his. "Ian was Duncan's twin."

"He's no' forgiven me, and I doona blame him."

"Everyone was angry last night, Malcolm. Don't hold them to words spoken during a heightened time." She sat back and wiped her mouth. "Besides, I want to talk to the Druid who asked me if I was Evie Walker. She knows about my site. I want to know why."

"That was Gwynn," Malcolm said. "I think she asked because she hacked into your site. That's what Gwynn does. She's a master at it too."

Evie nodded. "Ah. That makes sense. I had a feeling I was hacked by two different people. Now I know."

"What now?" Brian signed.

Malcolm sat back in the chair. "Good question. We need to figure out what will kill Wallace, protect you, and keep the bairn from being born evil."

"So, not a lot then," Evie said with a wink. "We should be able to take care of that by morning."

Malcolm found himself smiling. How could someone with a soul as bright as Evie's be with him? But he knew it was because of her that he had changed, that he was feeling.

That he had hope again.

CHAPTER
FORTY-SIX

Larena was in the last bunch Fallon jumped back to Mac-
Leod Castle. She was still reeling from seeing Malcolm—
who looked almost like the man she'd known before the
attack that had taken the use of his arm.

"I warned you," she told Fallon as she paced the great
hall. The others remained, each finding places at the long
table, near the hearth, or just leaning against the walls. "I
told you it wasn't wise to confront Malcolm with everyone."

"I did what I thought was best."

Larena whirled around to face her husband. She bit back
the angry retort because of her frustration. Instead, she
took a deep breath and counted to ten. "You've backed him
into a corner. None of us reacts well to that, and you pushed
him. Why?"

"I'd like to know that as well," Quinn said.

Lucan folded his arms over his chest and looked at his
elder brother. "I think we all would. You can no' tell me
you didna see a difference in him, Fallon."

Fallon ran a hand through his hair. "Phelan said he didna
trust Evie."

"And Phelan should've trusted Malcolm," Aisley said before she leaned over and kissed Phelan from their spot at the table. "I'm sorry, but I don't think you did the right thing. You kept knowledge of me from everyone."

"I had a reason," Phelan argued.

Larena turned her gaze to the couple. "And Malcolm didn't? Did you see how he protected Evie? Can you tell me you wouldn't have done the same had we shown up as a group to confront you and Aisley?"

Phelan slammed his hand on the table. "I was trying to help a friend."

"He willna thank you for it," Ramsey said.

Charon propped an arm on the back of Laura's chair from their place near the hearth. "I agreed with Phelan on calling Fallon, and though I hate to admit it, but maybe we shouldna have been so hasty. The Kings were looking at Evie with impartiality."

"And we weren't?" Marcail asked.

Isla shook her head of black hair. "No, we weren't. Phelan said she became *drough*, and we reacted. We should've listened. After what happened to me and Aisley, we should've waited to hear their side."

"I just wanted Malcolm here," Fallon said. "He belongs with us."

Larena walked to her husband and took his hand. "I know. We're a family. Families make mistakes. What we need to do now is show Malcolm we're behind him."

"Then we need to know what happened tonight at Jason's," Ronnie said. She leaned her head back against Arran's chest, her forehead furrowed. "Whatever it was had to have been devastating. Evie looked as if the world was coming to an end."

"And Malcolm looked as if he shouldered the world," Camdyn said.

"Let's no' forget Evie's brother in all of this," Ian said.

"He was just a lad and as white as a ghost. There's no telling what Wallace did to him."

"I'm sorry," Fallon said as he pulled Larena against him. "I thought if we all went we could make him come back with us."

Larena squeezed her eyes closed. "I need to go to him."

"I'll jump you and Ramsey in the morning."

She nodded, hoping Malcolm would want to see her by then.

Gwynn stared up at the ceiling letting everything about Evie and the site roll through her mind. It was keeping her from sleep, but there was something nagging at her she couldn't quite put her finger on.

"I can do without sleep, love, but you can no'. What is keeping you awake?" Logan asked as he rolled toward her.

Gwynn turned her head to him. "It's Evie and Malcolm."

"I think Larena and Ramsey will get everything straightened out in the morn."

"No, it's not that. It's the site. I told you I thought there was another hacker, and I believe it was Jason."

Logan rose up on one elbow and reached over her to turn on the light. "Tell me."

Gwynn scooted up on the pillows. "We all know Wallace wants revenge, right?"

"Aye."

"We also know he likes to make us think he's doing one thing while he's actually doing something else."

"Aye."

"So." She paused and shrugged. "What if we've done it again?"

Logan frowned. "You lost me, love. What do you mean?"

"I mean, what if we underestimated him again?"

Logan's hazel eyes narrowed. "You mean he's doing exactly what it looks like he's doing?"

"Yes. We kept looking for hidden meanings, but I don't think there is one. I don't think he has a clue as to what the necklace does. I think he wanted it because he suspects it does some magic."

"But he doesna know what," Logan said with a nod.

"We won't know if he did until we talk to Malcolm."

"If Wallace knew the necklace could bind our gods forever, he wouldna care about turning Evie *drough* right now. He'd have her release the spell and get us out of the way."

"Exactly!" Gwynn shouted and crossed her legs beneath her. "So if he doesn't know about the spell, then he does want Evie and Malcolm for the prophecy as Aisley suspected."

Logan leaned back against the headboard. "And therein lies the problem. We can no' allow that child to be born."

Gwynn slid down until she lay her head on his chest. "If it was us in Malcolm and Evie's shoes, what would you do?"

"Protect you and pray to find a way that our child wouldna be born holding all the evil of the world."

Gwynn's heart pounded in her chest so loudly she expected him to hear it. "What would you think about becoming a father?"

There was a beat of silence before he shifted so that he leaned over her. "Gwynn? What are you saying?"

"Answer my question."

His brown hair fell forward into his face, the shadows keeping his eyes hidden. "I would like nothing more than to have my child fill your womb."

"But just not now," she finished, trying to hide her disappointment.

Logan shoved aside the covers and placed a hand on her flat stomach. He looked back at her. "Gwynn?"

A lone tear slipped from her eye. "I didn't skip the spell on purpose, Logan, you have to believe me."

"Gwynn," he said in a soft, too quiet voice. "What are you telling me?"

She covered his hand with hers. "I'm going to have your child."

He tenderly wiped away her tear. For long moments he stared at her with an unreadable expression. Just when Gwynn was about to beg him to say something, he leapt from the bed and scooped her up in his arms as he spun about the room.

"Logan," she said with a giggle. "You're going to make me sick. Stop, please."

Instantly, he stopped and rained kisses upon her face. "I've never been so happy. I could shout it to the world."

"Don't," she said before he could. "I'm not ready to share with everyone else yet."

"How long have you known?"

She shrugged. "A week. I was trying to find the right moment to tell you."

"You thought I'd be angry?" he asked with a frown.

"Yes. I know you didn't want me pregnant while we battled *droughs*."

He held her close. "Nay, my love, we've put our lives on hold long enough. Larena and Fallon taught me that."

"I'm glad you believe that, but don't start thinking you can keep me out of any battles."

"Gwynn," he began.

She leaned back and put a finger over his lips. "I won't purposefully put myself in danger, but we're going to need all the Druids we can get to fight. You know this."

"All right," he said and started back to the bed.

She let out a shriek when he tossed her on the mattress and quickly followed. He held himself up by his hands, a wicked grin on his lips as he leaned down and flicked his tongue over her nipple through her silk nightgown.

Her eyes rolled back in her head. "Logan," she whispered.

There was a ripping sound. She looked down to find he had ripped her nightgown in half, but she didn't care, not when he kissed her and his knowing hands touched her.

Jason Wallace held the necklace he'd taken from Evangeline—Evie, as Malcolm called her—Walker in his hand. The pendant dangled from his fingers, the ornate Celtic cross beautiful in the design, but nothing more than that.

What could the necklace do? There had to be magic in it or why else would Evie have put it on her site? For hours he used spell after spell trying to get the pendant to reveal its purpose.

But it had remained silent.

If it was ancient, he would feel that magic. It was powerful and residual, and even a Druid could detect it. So if it wasn't ancient, and none of his spells worked, maybe it was just a trinket. A trinket used artfully to gain his interest.

His quest to get it made him appear a fool. And that was something he couldn't allow to pass without retribution. The more he thought on it, the more he was undecided about all of it.

"Nay. Ms. Walker didna want to be parted from it," he said to himself.

Then again, some people were sentimental about things handed down from family. He should've asked Brian about it when the lad was there.

Whatever the spell was, Jason knew he would get to the bottom of it sooner or later. There was no rush. His chessboard was almost complete. Once all the pieces had been moved into place and he captured the king—Malcolm—the game was over.

There were just a few more moves Jason needed to push Malcolm, Evie, and the Warriors and Druids into. It would be so simple, so easy they wouldn't realize anything until it was too late. By then Malcolm would be dead.

And Evie would do whatever he wanted.

He tossed the necklace on the coffee table and stretched out his legs, crossing one ankle over the other. So far his plan was working magnificently. Evangeline was *drough* and carrying the babe of prophecy. Malcolm, who was obviously smitten with the Druid, would do anything to keep both mother and bairn safe.

Yet, he wouldn't endanger Brian's life either. It was too perfect.

And with Malcolm and the *drough* together, it would ultimately split those at MacLeod Castle. Their once-solid bond broken by one person—Evie.

"Oh, I wish I could be a fly on the wall at the castle now," Jason said with a chuckle.

The Warriors would try to kill Evie, Malcolm would battle them for her safety, and Malcolm would leave them forever.

The only kink was those damn dragons. Otherwise Malcolm and Evangeline would be on their own. The dragons were an issue, but one that didn't pose that big of a problem for him.

Jason sat forward and held his hand, palm down, over the glass coffee table as magic formed in his palm. "Where do the dragons come from?"

A 3-D version of the Earth filled the space between his hand and the table.

"Here?" How was it he'd never heard of them before now? "Where do they live?"

The image changed from the planet to a range of mountains. The mountains could be anywhere, and nothing he saw showed him any indication of where they hid.

"Show me on a map."

Again the image shifted to a map of Scotland, with a red dot pinpointing the dragons' location.

"And how many are there?"

Image after image of dragon appeared, each a different color until he lost count.

"Enough."

The dragons were going to be an issue unless he could turn them against Malcolm and Evie. He'd demanded Evie kill them, but he knew she wouldn't even attempt it. That would fall to him. In a manner.

He needed the couple on their own. As long as Evie and Malcolm had friends, hope, and—most especially—love, the child wouldn't be the one from the prophecy.

It was a small thing no one needed to know, especially not the expectant parents.

CHAPTER
FORTY-SEVEN

In his chair near the hearth, Malcolm looked to the bed where Evie lay curled. He wanted to climb in beside her, to pull her against him, and make love to her until neither could move. But the strain of the day had battered her endlessly until she had barely been able to keep her eyes open.

He'd managed to get food into both her and Brian. Only after Evie had fallen asleep and he'd moved her to the bed did he then work on convincing Brian they were safe.

That had taken another hour, and in the end, the lad had been asleep on his feet when Malcolm walked him next door. Brian had fallen face-first on the bed, his feet hanging off the side. With a grunt, he had grabbed the pillow and turned his head, already lightly snoring.

Malcolm removed his shoes and hastened back to Evie. As Evie slept, Malcolm thought about all Wallace had said over and over in his head.

Wallace was a devious bastard. One could only believe half of what he said while trying to decipher hidden meanings. Deirdre had been scheming, but nowhere near the magnitude of Jason.

Deirdre liked to see the fear in the faces of her enemies.

Jason Wallace liked to go in for the kill at the last minute. And Declan, he had spent too long with money and power and thought that could give him all he wanted.

All three were wrong.

And Jason would join Deirdre and Declan in death soon.

Hours passed and still Malcolm was no closer to discovering how to kill Wallace than he had been months before. He couldn't go off on his own now. He had Evie, Brian, and his unborn child to think about.

He had gone from being a loner to having a family in a matter of days, and it still shocked him. No matter his efforts, he had done a miserable job protecting Larena. What made him think he could do better with those who counted on him now?

Malcolm closed his eyes and dropped his chin to his chest. As much as he'd like to take Wallace out on his own, that wasn't going to happen, not after what Wallace did to him the last time.

Malcolm's body still ached from his time with Death. There wasn't much that could give him pause, but Death certainly did. It adored pain, relished agony, and savored screams.

Soft hands touched his shoulders. Malcolm's head jerked up to find Evie kneeling in front of him. She smiled sadly and smoothed away the lock of hair that was always falling in his eyes.

"You should be resting," he said.

"So should you. I thought you would've joined me."

Desire shot through him like lightning, his cock immediately hard and his blood on fire. "If I did get in that bed with you, it wouldna be sleep you were getting, lass."

She gave him a smoldering look. "You say that as if I'd mind."

"I think my desires have gotten you in enough trouble."

The teasing light left her clear blue eyes instantly. "Don't you dare, Malcolm Munro. You can't think to shoulder the blame for this on your own."

"I do. If I could've kept my distance from you, you wouldna be carrying my child."

"And had I not put up the site Jason would never have contacted me. Had I not been looking for other Druids I wouldn't have stupidly trusted him and become *drough*. You can't take responsibility for those actions because they lie squarely on me."

He clenched his jaw as she traced the scars on his face, her touch reverent and tender, her eyes heavy-lidded.

"I thought I'd lost you. Seeing you lying on that bed with your wounds not healing was torture. You were so still." She sniffed and swallowed. "I tried to help you."

Malcolm took one of her hands in his and brought it to his lips where he kissed her knuckles. "I know. I saw you. I kept calling for you, but you couldna hear me. Death was playing with you."

"Death," she repeated with a shiver. "How did you come out of it?"

"I told you. You." When her eyes widened, he grinned. "Oh, aye. It was you. Seeing you, feeling your magic gave me the hope I needed."

"Con and Phelan helping to heal you didn't hurt either."

"They helped a little. You're the one who saved me." He should've told her that last night, but there had been too much other stuff going on.

She laid her head on his leg and sighed. "And you saved me. I saw what Jason did to you when you fought him. He's powerful. So powerful. I think the ancients are wrong. I don't think he can be killed. I mean, my God, he used Death!"

"Everything can be killed. You need to remember that. We just have to find what will do the job with Wallace," he said as he smoothed his hands over her head, letting the cool strands of curls glide through his fingers.

"With you, I think I can face anything."

"We will get through this."

The door suddenly opened as Brian stood there with one eye closed and his dark hair in disarray as he signed that he was starving.

"You're always starving," Evie said with a smile as she got to her feet.

Malcolm wanted more time alone with Evie. There was so much he wanted to say, and he wasn't sure how to do it. His smiles were coming easier, if a little tight.

She did that to him. He found himself grinning at the smallest thing because she had come into his life. How dull and dour his world had been before her. He couldn't fathom how he had survived it, not knowing her . . . loving her.

He watched her run fingers through her hair as she pushed Brian out of the room telling him to wash up and brush his hair before they went downstairs.

"Rhys went to the inn and got your bag," Malcolm said as he stood. "If you need anything, the women here said they could help."

"Give me five minutes, and I'll be ready to go down."

Malcolm got to his feet and strode from the room. He paced the hallway feeling trapped and cornered by Wallace and the predicament they were in. Malcolm couldn't help but feel as if Jason was playing them like the games he saw others play on computers or their mobiles.

"A good run might help."

Malcolm paused and turned to find Rhys leaning against the wall. "The only thing that will help is killing Wallace."

"We'll get to that soon enough. How is Evie?"

"Tired and frightened. She hides it well, but I can see it." He walked to Rhys and propped himself against the wall opposite the Dragon King.

"Has she had any effects from her time with Death?"

Malcolm stilled, his eyes narrowed on the dragon. "What? I saw her, but it was just her magic."

"Nay. She was there, Malcolm. When she tried to leave, Death burned her. Phelan healed her."

Malcolm ran a hand down his face, more frustrated than ever. "I promised to protect her yet she keeps getting hurt."

"She went in to save you. She had no thought of herself. You'd do the same for her, would you no'?"

"Without hesitation."

Rhys slowly smiled. "Just as I thought. Come. I've found clothes for you. I think you could do with a shower. And a shave."

Malcolm rubbed his beard as he followed Rhys. The beard was meant to hide his scars, but they didn't seem to bother Evie. Maybe it was time she saw him for who he truly was.

"Are you telling me I smell, Dragon?"

Rhys grunted. "Just take the damn shower, Warrior."

Malcolm walked into the room Rhys showed him to and found several pairs of jeans and four shirts laid out on the bed.

"The bathroom is there," Rhys said. "Doona keep your woman waiting."

The door closed on his words. Malcolm looked around the bedroom noting the masculine air. There were pictures of yellow dragons on every wall with the exception of a sword that hung near the bed as if waiting for someone to take it.

Malcolm knew he was in Rhys's room. With one last look at the impressive sword, he made his way into the bathroom and the sink where an array of shaving equipment awaited him.

"Sodding dragons," he mumbled as he lathered the brush.

* * *

Evie glanced at the clock to see she had taken thirty minutes instead of five. She shook the blow dryer, wishing it didn't take her hair so long to dry.

With her curls still slightly damp, she put on clean clothes. One look in the mirror, however, had her wincing. Dark shadows appeared beneath her eyes, making her look as tired as she felt.

She grabbed her bag of makeup and quickly dabbed some concealer on to help hide most of the circles. Then she added a touch of blush and some eyeliner.

"At least I don't look like death warmed over," she mumbled.

She walked out of the room and came to a halt when she saw Brian and Malcolm across the hall signing. Brian finished with a shrug of his shoulders, but it was Malcolm who captured her attention.

He had shaved his thick beard revealing the strong jaw and chin she had known were beneath. His scars were more prominent as they cut over his right cheek to his neck.

His head slowly turned to her while his azure eyes watched her intently. Evie felt all the air rush from her lungs as she was pinned by those mesmerizing eyes.

The Malcolm she'd first met—silent, withdrawn, and hiding his scars—had been handsome. But the man before her now—clean-shaven, confident, approachable—was heart-stoppingly magnificent.

She closed the distance between them and kissed him. After the briefest of seconds, his arms closed around her as he deepened the kiss.

Evie could have stayed kissing Malcolm all day if it hadn't been for Brian clearing his throat multiple times. She ended the kiss and looked up at Malcolm, wondering how it was that such a man fancied her.

"I like this new look. A lot. You wore that beard to

hide your scars, but you were really hiding the amazing man you are."

He put his forehead to hers. "You have no idea how much I need you, Evie. You've changed me."

His hand found hers and their fingers entwined. She tried to walk away, but then she saw the desire in Malcolm's eyes and they were kissing again, the heat, the fire of their need too potent to deny.

Brian grunted and stomped off. It was Rhys's laughing that broke them apart the second time, their chests heaving and a promise of pleasure silently exchanged.

"Your brother says you need to get a room," Rhys stated with a wide smile.

Malcolm chuckled. The sound was rough, and Malcolm grew uncomfortable after, but Evie knew it was another step to him becoming the man he'd once been. He was a marvel, and one she knew she would never tire of being around.

He was fire and ice, fierce and tender. He was Warrior and lover.

And for now, he was hers.

"You should laugh more often," she whispered.

Malcolm cleared his throat. "Food, then?"

Rhys's laughter filled the corridor.

Evie grinned when Malcolm held her hand as they walked down the stairs to the kitchen.

CHAPTER
FORTY-EIGHT

The next morning Larena wasn't surprised to find Guy waiting in the drive outside Dreagan Manor. As soon as Fallon jumped her and Ramsey to Dreagan, he teleported back to the castle.

"He's welcome to stay," Guy said of Fallon.

Ramsey shrugged. "He knows. It's no' a good time right now."

Guy nodded. "Malcolm, Evie, and Brian have been up for a bit. They're in the kitchen having breakfast. The room will afford you all some privacy."

"How is he?" Larena asked as she put her hand on Guy's arm to stop him. "Really. How is Malcolm really?"

"Why no' come see for yourself," Guy said with a kind smile.

Larena glanced at Ramsey before she trailed Guy into the large house. Before they reached the kitchen, she could hear the sound of conversation and a female's laugh.

Once at the kitchen Guy stopped Larena before she could go inside. "Watch. Listen," he urged.

Larena turned the corner and saw Malcolm, Evie, and

Brian sitting at the round table, relaxed as sunlight filtered through the many windows. The round table was littered with food and pitchers of juice.

Evie's long curls were down and falling over her back as she laughed at her brother. Brian stuffed food into his mouth as he signed with one hand, then had to cover his mouth with his hand as he laughed.

Malcolm leaned back in his chair, one hand resting on his thigh as he held a mug of coffee in the other. His gaze never left Evie's face as he goaded Brian into eating more. It was a cozy, comfortable scene the three of them made.

Larena looked closer at Malcolm and blinked hastily as she saw a glimpse of the man he had been before fate had set him on his path. He was more relaxed and at ease than she could remember seeing him.

"He shaved," Larena whispered in awe.

Ramsey moved behind her and made a sound of approval. "He's smiling too."

He was. It was almost too much for Larena to take in. "It's been so long since I've seen him smile."

"He chuckled this morning. Well, it wasn't really a chuckle, but it was close," Guy whispered. "Evie certainly approved."

Larena's eyes clouded with tears. "He looks at her as if she's his entire world."

"Because she is," Ramsey said. "He lived in darkness. Evie is his light."

Guy nodded. "Evie is a trusting soul. Too trusting at times, but only because she's no' been touched by evil before a few days ago. As a result, she was able to look past the wall Malcolm erected and find the man beneath."

"Where there is love evil can no' flourish," Ramsey said. "*Drough* or no', I doona believe Evie is evil or that she became *drough* with evil in mind."

"That was as we thought," Guy said. "The pair have a difficult road ahead of them. They need all the friends they can get."

Larena glanced at the Dragon King. "Fallon only wanted Malcolm home with the rest of us. He thought by having us all confront him that it would convince Malcolm to come."

"Con knew Fallon had a reason for it."

Ramsey leaned down and whispered, "Go to him, Larena. Your cousin needs you."

For several more minutes, she watched the three. Evie laughed at some story Brian signed while Malcolm smiled widely. It was a balm to her soul to see a glimpse of the man who had so valiantly stayed by her side when he was mortal.

Malcolm had been a charmer, a rogue who could turn the eye of any woman. Losing the ability to use his arm changed his world overnight, and he had never been the same since.

He had gone to a dark, nefarious place, a place of pain and solitude where no one was able to reach him. Yet, somehow, Evie found him.

Whether or not her cousin knew it, he was in love with Evie Walker. It showed in his eyes as he watched her, in his smile as she laughed, and in the way his entire attention was focused on her.

Larena walked into the kitchen. She'd taken only two steps when Malcolm's head turned to her. His coffee cup was halfway to his mouth when he spotted her. Slowly, he lowered it as Evie's laughter died and Brian grew still.

She couldn't stop the tears from flowing as she hurried to him. Malcolm stood and held out his arms. Larena rushed to him and flung her arms around him.

"You smiled," she said through her tears. She leaned back and cupped his face. "And finally shaved."

"It was time."

"It certainly was." Larena sniffed and looked at Evie. "Thank you for bringing him back. He was lost, and you found him."

Evie smiled wryly. "He was the one who found me."

Larena stepped away from Malcolm and held out her hand to Evie. "I'm Larena MacLeod, Malcolm's cousin. It's good to meet you."

"Likewise," Evie said as she took her hand. "This is my brother, Brian."

Larena signed "Hello," and a surprised Brian asked if she was really a Warrior.

"They wanted to know more about those from the castle," Malcolm explained. "Everyone is enamored with the idea of a female Warrior."

Larena laughed as she looked back at Brian. "I am a Warrior. What do you want to know?"

She wasn't surprised when he asked her to shift into Warrior form. Larena didn't hesitate. As soon as her iridescent skin glowed, both Evie and Brian gasped.

"It's so beautiful," Evie said in awe.

Brian's mouth was agape, his hands still.

"And that's a first," Evie said with a laugh. "Brian has nothing to say."

Brian gave her a shove. While brother and sister jested, Larena and Malcolm shared a look.

"I'm sorry for everything," Malcolm said.

Larena tamped down her goddess and took his hand. "There is nothing to apologize for. You were looking out for me."

"I did horrible things, Larena."

"We all do horrible things. Look at you now, though."

Evie wiped her hands on her napkin and motioned to the chair opposite her. "Please sit. I'm sure you and Malcolm have a lot to catch up on."

"Actually, I'm here to see the both of you."

"Oh." Evie glanced at Malcolm before she turned to Brian.

Brian stuffed a piece of toast in his mouth as he signed, "I know, I know. I'm going."

"Come with me, Brian," Guy called from the doorway. "I know where more food is."

Malcolm turned and spotted Ramsey next to Guy. With a wave, Malcolm motioned Ramsey to join them. If they were going to do this, they might as well do it just once.

There was a moment of awkward silence as Evie tried to figure out what to do. Malcolm reached over and took her hand. Their gazes met, and he saw her shoulders relax when he gave her hand a squeeze.

"I gather the two of you came for a reason," Malcolm said.

Larena crossed her legs. "I came to see you, but also to let you know why Fallon did what he did last eve."

"So tell me," Malcolm insisted.

"He wanted you to come home. Since you rarely answered your phone, he thought by having all of us there it would convince you."

"He was wrong."

"And he knows it," Larena said. She glanced at the table. "You're part of our family. You have to know that, Malcolm."

He rubbed his clean-shaven jaw and considered her words. "No one was willing to listen to us last night. Phelan told you Evie was *drough*, and you all made up your minds."

"No' all," Ramsey said. "Tara and I came to bring both of you back to the castle and to offer our support."

"You hurt him," Evie said into the silence. "Phelan and Charon saw what he went through just hours before. He confronted Wallace on his own and was torn to shreds. He faced Death, and then he tackled Wallace again to save Brian and me. We returned to find all of you."

Ramsey frowned. "Death?"

"That's what is in Wallace's blood now," Malcolm said. "Death had me trapped. If it hadna been for Evie, I'd still be there."

Larena looked at Evie. "Then I owe you a great debt."

"No. I did it for Malcolm," she said.

Malcolm wanted to pull her into his lap and kiss her. She wasn't cowed by the Warriors, and she had stood up for him. He couldn't remember the last time anyone had done that.

"We're glad you did," Ramsey said. "I suspect you risked your own life while doing it, Evie."

"She did," Malcolm interjected when she shook her head. "Phelan saved her. Did he no' mention how Death nearly burned her alive while she was trying to rescue me?"

"Phelan was doing what he thought best," Larena said.

Ramsey sat back in the chair and stretched out his legs. "Phelan is a lot like Fallon. He wanted you at the castle."

"But no' Evie?" Malcolm clenched his jaw in anger. "After what he went through with Aisley?"

"I think it's because of what he went through with Aisley." Ramsey's silver gaze slid to Evie. "Phelan recognized the strong feelings between the two of you. He knows firsthand what Wallace can do. Had Aisley no' been a Phoenix, she'd be dead."

Malcolm looked at the floor, unable to say anything. He was hurt by what had transpired with everyone the night before, but Ramsey made sense.

A chair scraped on the floor as Evie rose and came to

stand behind Malcolm. She placed her hands on his shoulders and said, "Malcolm needs his family. If it means that I remain behind, then so be it."

"Nay." Malcolm was up and had Evie in his arms before she could blink. "That's no' an option."

"Malcolm, please," she pleaded.

He shook his head and wrapped one of her curls around his finger. "Nay, lass. Doona bring it up again. I'll no' leave you alone. Every time I do, you get into trouble," he teased.

She laughed and then nodded. "All right, but you need to make up with your family. You've only got the one."

"It's us who need to apologize to him," Larena said. "Not the other way around. But I appreciate what you just tried to do."

Malcolm sat and pulled Evie onto his lap. He liked having her close so he could feel her curves and touch her as much as he wanted. She was a reminder of who he wanted to be—and who he wanted to be with.

"Is it true?" Ramsey asked. "Has Wallace put the prophecy in motion?"

Malcolm looked at his friend and gave a single nod. "I was his plan all along. I doona know how long he had the plan in place, but we fell into step exactly as he wanted us."

"So you're carrying a child?" Larena asked Evie.

Evie shrugged. "Jason said I was, but I don't know for sure."

Ramsey rose and walked to them. He squatted next to the chair and looked at Malcolm and then Evie, his hand hovering over Evie's stomach. "May I?"

"Ramsey is part Druid, part Warrior," Malcolm explained to her.

Evie's clear blue eyes widened. "Oh. And yes, you may."

Malcolm didn't move as Ramsey placed his hand on

Evie's stomach and closed his eyes. Several seconds ticked by before Ramsey opened his eyes and stood.

"She does carry a child in her womb," he announced as he resumed his seat.

Malcolm held Evie tighter. "Evie isna evil. The child can no' be born evil just because the prophecy says so."

"There is much left out of prophesies," Ramsey admitted. "The problem is, we rarely discover what was missing until it's too late."

"What do I do then?" Evie said. "Jason said if I tried to abort the baby he would kill Brian. I can't bring a child of pure evil into the world for Jason to raise."

Larena shook her head of golden hair. "No, that can't happen. Wallace first tried to bring about the prophecy with Phelan and Aisley. I wonder if they might know more."

"We need to ask then," Evie said.

Ramsey was silent for several moments before he looked at Evie. "Your site was hacked, aye?"

"Twice," Evie admitted.

"Once by our Gwynn. We think the second was by Wallace."

Evie shifted on Malcolm's lap. "It was. He wanted my necklace in exchange for my brother."

"Did he mention the necklace when you saw him last?"

Malcolm frowned and looked at Evie. "He didna to me. Did he to you?"

"No," she said in surprise. "I was so worried about Brian and then learning about the prophecy that I completely forgot about it."

Larena leaned a forearm on the table. "There's a chance he may not have actually wanted it."

"But you do?" Evie guessed. "Why?"

Malcolm thought back to what it could be, and when the answer came, he was shocked he hadn't realized it sooner. "They think it's from a cargo of magical items which left Edinburgh years ago in one of three shipments."

"I've searched Edinburgh Castle as well as the Tower of London, but the necklace isn't there," Larena said.

Ramsey shrugged. "At one time we wanted the necklace for us. Now, we want to make sure it doesna fall into the wrong hands of someone like Jason Wallace."

"What do you think my necklace does?" Evie asked.

Malcolm met her worried gaze. "Binds the gods inside us."

CHAPTER
FORTY-NINE

Evie stood atop the hill gazing at the majestic mountains around her without seeing any of it. Malcolm's words still rang in her head.

The necklace her family had guarded for generations contained the spell to bind the gods inside the Warriors. It seemed absurd, and yet . . . right.

And she had lost it to Wallace. If Jason knew what the necklace contained, he could use it against Malcolm and the others, leaving just the Dragon Kings to fight for mankind.

Evie couldn't imagine Malcolm as anything but a Warrior. His god was part of the man he was, the Highlander who had made such sweet love to her.

She swallowed and silently berated herself for being so trusting. She was to blame for the entire mess. To make matters worse, knowing those at MacLeod Castle wanted the spell so they could bind their gods made her feel even lower.

The only good thing to come out of the entire debacle was Malcolm. He was like the great oaks she'd always admired—strong, steady, and constant.

"This is one of my favorite views," Elena said as she walked up.

Evie jerked, surprised to hear a voice. She glanced at Elena to find her staring at the same view. "It's beautiful."

"But you're not really seeing it today, not that I blame you." Elena cut her a quick look. "Hal and Rhys took Brian and put him to work herding the sheep. The poor boy looked like he needed to get his mind off things."

"That'll be good for Brian. He won't tell me what Jason did to him. After seeing what Jason was capable of with Malcolm, I'm almost too afraid to find out."

"I'm sure Brian will tell you in time. Each of you is dealing with things in your own way."

Evie sighed loudly. "God, Elena, I can't figure a way out of any of this."

"You need to focus on the here and now. And remember, you're not alone."

"A month ago all I worried about was work, meeting a guy, and what Brian and I would do over the Christmas holidays. It seems a lifetime ago."

Elena shoved her hands into the back pockets of her jeans and cocked her head at the mountains. "When I first came to Dreagan, I almost died while caving in the mountains. My boss did lose her life, and it was Guy and the others who found me. We'd been trespassing, but it was obvious Sloan had come here to find something. Con thought I was part of it."

"Were you?" Evie asked as she looked at Elena.

"No, and only Guy believed me. I was so scared. My ordered life went into utter chaos. The only calm in the storm was Guy," she said with a soft smile before she faced Evie. "I put my faith in him, and I discovered who he really was. And then I set out to help all the Dragon Kings."

"How?"

Elena grimaced. "Much to Guy's anger, it involved

eturning to London and the company I worked for, Pure-Gems, to determine who was behind looking into Dreagan. You watch all the movies about spies and you think it looks easy, but it isn't."

"Did you find out who it was?"

"In a manner. It was the CEO, but someone else was behind him. It would've taken us even longer to learn that f it hadn't been for Jane. She and Banan met and fell in ove in London."

Evie let the gust of wind slide over her. "I'm carrying a child of a prophecy, Elena. A child who is supposed to ouse all the evil of the world. How can I let it live?"

"If you think Malcolm is going to allow Wallace to ake your baby, then you don't know him," she said with a wink.

"You're right." Evie couldn't believe she hadn't thought of that. She was so mired in everything else she had forgotten who Malcolm was at his core.

Elena bumped against her with her shoulder. "He's worried about you. He's been standing at the bottom of the hill watching you for the past hour."

Surprised, Evie turned and looked over her shoulder to ind Malcolm just where Elena said he was.

"Go to him," Elena urged. "Brian will be occupied for a while, and I'll make sure no one bothers either of you or at least two hours."

Evie nodded before she turned and started toward Malcolm. The closer she got to him, the more she saw his face was set in hard lines, almost as if he were preparing himself for something.

She stopped a few paces from him. "I didn't know about he necklace, Malcolm. I swear."

"I doona care about that."

"If Jason discovers what the spell is—"

"Then he will," Malcolm interrupted her.

She shook her head in amazement. "Does nothing faze you?"

"Everything when it comes to you, apparently."

Her heart skipped a beat as his words sank in. "Because I carry your child?"

"Because you are you."

She was entangled, caught, trapped in his azure gaze. An emotion, deep and profound, was there for her to see, to accept if she was but willing.

Evie didn't have to think twice. She closed the distance between them and flung her arms around Malcolm's neck. He held her tightly, his mouth descending upon hers in a scorching kiss.

His arms were like bands of steel holding her captive against him as he plundered her mouth, demanding she yield completely.

She offered everything she had—body, heart, and soul. With one touch he had ensnared her, enticed her. Enthralled her. He was everything she wanted, everything she needed.

The kiss deepened, his chest rumbling with a moan. Evie's body burned for him, craved to feel him inside her, filling her.

"I have to have you," he murmured as he kissed down her neck.

Evie's head dropped back. The cool wind raced over her heated skin. "Yes. I'm not complete unless you're inside me."

She barely took notice when he lifted her in his arms and began walking. How he could think, much less stand upright when his mouth was wreaking havoc against her skin boggled her mind.

The next thing she knew, she was on her back with Malcolm's delicious weight atop her. She groaned when she felt his hard arousal.

Her sweater was pulled over her head just before his lips claimed hers again. She sank her fingers into the silky locks of his thick, blond hair.

So much had happened between them, and yet they hadn't shared much in the way of words. Suddenly, she had to tell him how she felt, had to make him realize just what he meant to her.

Evie broke the kiss and pushed against his chest until he lifted his head and his gaze pierced her. Her breathing was ragged, her heart pounding as she looked into his eyes and saw the same need she knew was reflected in hers. The world melted away then.

With the feel of his heart beating against her palm she realized that somewhere along the way she had fallen hopelessly, madly in love with Malcolm.

The words tangled in her throat as her emotions welled high. She wanted him to know, needed to tell him.

Their gazes still locked together, Malcolm shifted until she sat upon his lap, her legs wrapped around his waist. When had their clothes been removed? And then she no longer cared as he lifted her over his rod.

Evie sucked in a breath when she first lowered herself onto his staff. He was thick and impossibly hard. Skin to skin beneath the sun and sky their bodies—and hearts—joined. The rhythm was slow, sensual as she moved her hips, causing her nipples to graze his chest.

His azure eyes darkened, a moan falling from his lips as he kept one hand on her hip and the other wrapped around her. They moved as one, taking the other higher with each thrust, each touch.

Evie was sinking into Malcolm, into all that he was. She could feel his heartbeat, hear his breath . . . savor his very essence.

He drew her closer until their lips nearly met as the desire knotted tighter and tighter inside her. Her skin sizzled, her blood burned through her veins. All for Malcolm.

As she welcomed the love for him, some shackle she hadn't known was around her heart fell away. She became . . . more. She was everywhere and yet nowhere. She could reach past the stars and into chaos. She was as small as an atom, as fierce as the sun.

She was a Druid.

And she had given her heart and soul to a Warrior.

"Evie," Malcolm whispered reverently.

Her body shattered, the climax sweeping her away on a current of bliss that took her higher, deeper than she thought possible.

As she rode the waves of ecstasy, Malcolm's fingers dug into her as he orgasmed.

Their breaths mingled, their hearts beating together as the pleasure coalesced into something bright and intangible. No longer were they two people—but one.

Whatever had just happened, it changed everything. But for once, Evie knew only good could come of it. Because she had Malcolm.

She cupped his face as the last tremors from her climax faded. "Whatever comes next, I can face it with you beside me."

"I wouldna be anywhere else." His thumb brushed her bottom lip. "I didna dare hope that I would ever find you. I'm no' going to let you go without a fight."

"I didn't know about the spell in my necklace."

He gave a shake of his head. "As I said, I doona care. The others may want to be mortal once more, but there has to be someone to fight evil."

"And that will be you?"

"Aye. If the Druids at MacLeod Castle can live four centuries, then so can you."

"If that's what you want."

"It's one of several things I want, but it's a start."

The teasing light in his blue eyes made her smile. "Together then."

"Together."

They weren't words of love, but for a man who hadn't experienced emotion in a long time, they were just as good.

Phelan stood at the windows of Con's office and watched Malcolm and Evie walk back to the manor hand in hand. "So you're pissed."

Con gave a snort. "Do I agree with what you did? Nay. And you know it. I'm no' the one you need to apologize to."

"I was trying to help him."

"Aye. And so were Charon and Laura when they told everyone you were with Aisley. I distinctly remember you being a tad on the angry side then."

Phelan rubbed his forehead and faced Constantine. "I admit I forgot all about that when I discovered what Evie was."

"What is Evie but a Druid who was backed into a corner and did what she thought best to save lives? Both Aisley and Isla have proven that just because they performed the ceremony to become *drough* doesna make them evil."

"Okay. So I fucked up. I knew Aisley wasna evil when I met her."

Con lifted a blond brow. "Malcolm uses the same argument, except Evie wasna *drough* when he met her. He's known her before and after the ceremony. I also sense no evil in her."

"Yet." Phelan leaned against the wall and shook his head. "Malcolm has been through so much. What if Evie is working with Wallace? What if she was meant to get close to Malcolm and turn him against us?"

Con's forehead furrowed. "Malcolm has been on the

edge of darkness for a while. We've known he could fall either way. You have a valid point when it comes to Wallace, but I agree with Malcolm that Evie is trustworthy."

"You're going to chance the entire world on that?"

"Aye. And I'd do the same for you if you were in Malcolm's shoes. I trust my instincts, Phelan."

Phelan blew out a breath. "I was on the outside looking in for so long. I think that's why I understood Malcolm before. He's been given the short end of the stick on most things. I doona want to see him lose it all now."

"Then we make sure he doesna," Con said, his black eyes full of determination and resolve.

One side of Phelan's mouth lifted in a grin. "Agreed."

CHAPTER
FIFTY

Despite the circumstances, Malcolm wanted to smile about everything. Nothing was sorted yet, but they had months before the baby came to find a way out of the mess with Wallace. And he wouldn't stop searching until he discovered how to kill the bastard.

He wanted more time alone with Evie, but the women of Dreagan, along with Larena, had pulled her into a room as soon as they returned to the mansion. Malcolm stared at the closed door for several minutes before he went in search of Brian.

Malcolm opened the front door to find Rhys walking toward the house.

"Just who I was looking for," Rhys said. "I need to patrol around the east side of our property. Fancy helping me?"

"Aye." Malcolm was never one who liked to sit around anyway.

"Good. I'll race you there."

Malcolm raised a brow. "I'm no' foolish enough to race a dragon."

"I'm no' going to shift into dragon form," Rhys said, affronted. Then he smiled. "But I still can beat you."

Never one to back down from a challenge, Malcolm nodded. "Where does this race end?"

"At the cabin on the east range. Do you need a map, Warrior?" Rhys teased.

"I'll find it, and still beat you, Dragon."

"What are you waiting on?" Rhys said with a laugh as he took off running.

Malcolm was quick to follow, feeling freer than he could ever remember. Evie had steadied him while giving light to his bleak world. By doing so, she released him from his prison.

There was evil to kill and Wallace's machinations to work out, but none of that mattered at the moment. He had his woman, a babe in her womb, and his friends. Nothing was going to hold him back from having it all. Not now.

Not ever.

Jason parked his hunter green Jaguar XF two miles from the border of Dreagan land and climbed out. When he discovered the dragons had been hiding on none other than Dreagan land, it all clicked into place.

The teleportation spell still hadn't worked, much to his fury. There hadn't been a spell he couldn't work with ease since he returned from the dead. Why the teleportation spell was different he wasn't sure.

He looked around the forest before he glanced at the sky. Any moment he expected to see a dragon. The dragons would sense him near, he was sure. It hadn't taken him long to work out that he'd been on Dreagan land when he had died during the battle with Charon and Laura.

At least the selmyr wouldn't return. Aisley had somehow managed to trap them again. The dragons, however, were still a concern. They'd remained hidden for so long that there wasn't much known about them.

No matter how many questions he had asked, Jason received few answers. He wasn't concerned though. His magic was strong enough to kill whatever he needed to.

"First, there's the little matter of Malcolm," he said with a smirk.

How easily Evie and Malcolm believed he would allow them to live together until the babe was born. He wanted them to let their guard down before he struck again. Jason's intent had been to wait a week, but he found he enjoyed toying with Malcolm too much to put it off.

With a simple spell, Jason discovered Malcolm and Evie were apart. The timing was perfect. He closed his eyes and thought of Malcolm, the link between them snapping into place.

His smile grew as he imagined Malcolm's furious expression. But the Warrior would come.

Malcolm instantly halted, grabbing his head as pain exploded. Then Jason's voice filled his mind. Malcolm roared, he and Daal both struggling against the intrusion.

"There's no use fighting," Jason's voice said. *"We have a link, Malcolm. My blood in you. There is nowhere you can run, no place you can hide that I willna find you."*

"What do you want?" Malcolm demanded as he fell to his knees from the agony of Jason in his head.

"You."

"Never!"

"How foolish of you to leave Evie. Even with the dragons."

Malcolm squeezed his eyes closed. He drew in a deep breath and flattened his hands on the earth before he lifted his head and searched for Wallace. "Come on out, you son of a bitch."

"Ah, my mother was a bitch, but I'd prefer if you didna

call her such. And I willna be the one coming to you. You will come to me. I have what's most precious to you after all—Evie."

Too many times Jason had fooled them. Malcolm wouldn't fall into that trap again. He yanked out his mobile and tried to call Evie. Only to find there was no reception.

Malcolm jumped to his feet and ran to the highest point on the mountain, scrambling over rocks, jumping from one boulder to the other, ignoring the pounding of his head. But his phone still wouldn't connect.

"I'm waiting, Malcolm. The longer I wait, the more I hurt her."

"You wouldna dare to harm the bairn."

Jason's laugh was loud as it bounced around Malcolm's head. *"There are other ways I can torture your woman. How long will you let her suffer before you come and claim her?"*

Malcolm knew it was a trap, but how could he not go to Evie? He glanced around hoping to catch sight of Rhys or even another dragon flying, but there was no one.

For the first time, Malcolm hated the solitude he'd always sought. He couldn't stand there a moment longer if there was even a shred of doubt that Evie could be in Jason's grasp.

"Turn southwest, Malcolm. I'll be waiting."

Malcolm wanted Wallace out of his head, and as soon as he found the bastard, he would make sure Wallace was never able to command him like that again.

The farther southwest he walked, the farther he moved from the manor—the one place where there were people who could help. Malcolm paused several times, debating on returning to Dreagan and getting the dragons in the hopes they reached Evie in time. But in the end, Malcolm couldn't stand the thought of Evie harmed by Wallace in any way.

A quarter of an hour later, Malcolm topped a hill and stopped. Wallace was somewhere in the forest below. Malcolm tried to feel Evie's magic, but he was too sickened by the stench of *drough*.

Malcolm walked into the forest, picking his way through the trees. He had gone a hundred yards when movement to his right caused him to pause. There, leaning against a tree was Jason Wallace.

"Where is Evie?" Malcolm demanded.

Wallace shrugged. "Back at Dreagan Manor I suppose."

"So you doona have her?" Malcolm was sick to his stomach, but that was soon replaced with blinding fury.

"Nay, I do no'."

Malcolm wanted nothing more than to rip him apart, but he wasn't fool enough to attack by himself again. He turned on his heel and began to walk back the way he'd come when Jason's magic slammed him face-first against a tree.

"Where do you think you're going?"

"You said Evie and I could be together."

Jason laughed as he walked to him. "And you believed me? How many times have I kept my word? You should know better."

Malcolm struggled against the magic holding him, to no avail. "What do you want?"

"Your child. And doona even try and tell me you were going to hand over the bairn. I'm no' daft enough to believe that."

Malcolm seethed, Daal plotted. But none of it did any good while they were trapped. Wallace then walked around the tree where Malcolm could see his face. "Evie willna leave the protection of Dreagan."

"You mean the dragons?" Wallace smiled slyly. "Oh, but she will. She cares a great deal for you. She'll do whatever I want."

"And what do you want?"

"To keep you two apart."

Malcolm ground his teeth together, desperately trying in vain to keep his temper under control. "Why?"

"You mean none of those at MacLeod Castle have worked it out? This is too good to believe," Jason said and rubbed his hands together. "Give me a second to enjoy this."

"Wallace," Malcolm growled.

The smile died and Jason glared at him. "No one gives me orders, least of all you. I think you liked your time with Death. He's been waiting for your return, but this time there willna be anyone to bring you back."

Malcolm ignored the bark of the pine biting into his cheek. He realized too late that Wallace was going to put Evie in a position to make a decision of whether to save him or not.

"She'll protect our child," Malcolm said. Evie was strong, she knew right from wrong. She would know the goodness of their child mattered more than his life.

Wallace leaned back against a tree and laughed. "Perhaps. But by keeping the two of you apart, I'm ensuring that hate and anger will fester inside her. That will then transfer to the child."

Malcolm closed his eyes and silently screamed his rage. Would Evie think he abandoned her, or would she know Wallace had him? Either way, he wouldn't be with her.

He wouldn't see her belly grow with their child, wouldn't hold her in his arms, wouldn't laugh with her. He wouldn't see their child born and hold the bairn.

Evie returned his feelings, but she gave him hope as well. Hope for a new life and a family—both of which he'd never thought to want. For a few precious days, they had been his.

But after all his sins, he should have known he could never have that kind of happiness.

"Doona worry, Malcolm. I'll let you see your child for a moment before I take it to raise as my own."

"Why no' just kill me?"

"Because I may need you. If something happens to this bairn, you and Evie need to be around to give me another."

It was the last straw. No longer did Malcolm contain his rage or hold back Daal. With one vicious roar, Malcolm released his god as lightning forked from his hands to split the trees around him.

But Wallace's magic was too strong for him to get away. He could do nothing but bellow his frustration as Jason cut him, then gave him two drops of his blood.

Agony exploded throughout Malcolm's body.

And then he saw Death.

CHAPTER FIFTY-ONE

"It'll be fine," Jane said for the third time, but as Evie stared out the window listening to the cry of the rocks and stone, she knew that wasn't true.

A door slamming was followed closely by boot heels striking the wood floors and growing closer. Evie faced the door, hoping to see Malcolm's form fill the doorway.

Instead it was Rhys.

"Where is that sodding Warrior?" Rhys asked with a cocky, lopsided grin. "I knew he wouldna pay his debt."

Evie's stomach dropped to her feet like lead. "He isn't here."

Rhys's smile slipped. "When he didna arrive, I thought he returned to you."

She shook her head and grabbed the back of a settee to remain standing. Jane and Cassie both began to ask questions of Rhys at once while Elena rushed from the room, and Larena wrapped an arm around Evie.

"Malcolm is strong," Larena said.

Evie swallowed hard. "You didn't see him lying on that bed. Something has happened to him, I know it. I feel it here," she said and put her hand over her heart.

"He probably just needed a bit of time to think," Guy said as he came into the room. "Malcolm has been by himself for a long time, Evie."

Larena gave her arm a squeeze. "Guy has a point. Malcolm often went off by himself. We'll go find him for you."

Evie looked to the doorway to find Ramsey and Banan standing behind Guy and Rhys. The men turned as one and strode out of sight while Larena quickly followed.

They put on a good show, but Evie wasn't buying any of it. She walked around the settee and into the foyer on wooden legs, deafened by the stones surrounding her from the mountains and beneath her feet.

"The shouting has gotten worse," she said. When the group talking amongst themselves didn't hear her, Evie repeated it louder.

Ramsey's head jerked around to her, his silver eyes pinning her. "What did you say, lass?"

"I think the real reason Malcolm didn't tell anyone about me was because of where he found me."

Guy shook his head slowly. "Shite. It all makes sense now."

Larena looked from Guy to Evie. "What are you talking about?"

"Malcolm followed me because of my power," Evie said even as the stones shouted louder. "I hear the stones. I wrecked and had no money. The mountain kept calling, and I needed somewhere to go."

"Cairn Toul," Ramsey murmured.

Evie nodded and reached behind her for the wall. The room was spinning, but she kept her gaze locked on Guy to remain standing. "He told me of Deirdre, of the evil that had taken place there. But I couldn't leave. Until Brian was taken. Now, the mountains all around me are shouting so loud it's deafening."

"What are they saying?" Guy asked as he took a step toward her.

"Just one word over and over."

Ramsey was suddenly beside her, one hand on her arm with the other wrapped around her. "What is that word, Evie?"

The room tilted and she with it. It was only Ramsey's aid that kept her on her feet. "Death. They keep saying death."

Evie heard the distant drums of the ancients. She tried to focus on them, but the rocks were too loud. She welcomed the darkness as it descended upon her.

Ramsey lifted Evie in his arms as she lost consciousness. He looked up to see Rhys's and Guy's worried looks. "You said Wallace had Death in his blood now. Is that what the stones are telling Evie? That Death is coming?"

"Perhaps," Guy said.

Rhys shook his head. "Or it could be that Death has Malcolm."

"That would mean Wallace is here," Banan said.

Ramsey glanced down at Evie. "And took Malcolm."

"But he let them go," Larena said, her voice rising in irritation. "Why would he let Malcolm, Evie, and Brian go if he would return for one of them?"

"Brian," Banan said and sprinted from the house.

Ramsey turned and started for the stairs. "Evie's had a shock. I doona know what it will do to her or the bairn she carries."

Elena was already on the stairs and motioned him after her. "Bring Evie. We'll look after her."

Once Evie was resting in her room with Elena and Cassie, Ramsey hurried back to the main floor where Larena was pacing the foyer.

"She kept saying she had a bad feeling," Larena said. "I dismissed her words, thinking she just missed Malcolm."

"You couldna know."

Larena halted and glared at him with her smoky blue eyes. "Malcolm didn't trust us, and because of it, we didn't know what Evie's magic could do."

"We know now. What we doona know is if Wallace was here and got to Malcolm somehow."

"Why take Malcolm?"

"So he can make Evie do whatever it is he wants."

Larena rubbed her temple. "This has got to stop. Jason Wallace has got to be stopped."

"Agreed. First, we need to find Malcolm," Ramsey said as the front door opened and Con walked in, followed by Hal and Banan. "We should call Broc."

"It may come to that," Con interjected. "We're patrolling right now."

"Wallace could easily evade your Kings on foot," Larena said.

Con's black eyes fastened on her with cool intensity. "They are no' on foot. And no' even his magic could shield him from us."

"Is there no magic that can hide someone from you?"

There was the slightest hesitation before Con said, "There is, but nothing a Druid can do."

"Then Malcolm could be fine and just needing some time alone," Larena said, the hope in her voice too great to ignore.

"We can no' know for sure just yet."

Ramsey was in complete agreement with Larena when she pulled out her phone and called Broc.

Malcolm had dealt with the debilitating pain hours before, but this time it dragged him down with a force that left him reeling.

It was excruciating, agonizing.

Horrific.

The darkness was consuming, the burning horrendous, and the muscle being ripped apart was unbearable.

Through it all he kept Evie's face in his mind. As his bones were broken one by one, he thought of her clear blue eyes.

As his limbs were ripped from their sockets he thought of her dark curls.

As the skin was flayed from his body he thought of her smile and how it could light up a room.

All the while, Death's sinister laugh sounded around him. That laugh was cold, callous. It was ruthless, merciless . . . unforgiving.

And it was never going to let him go.

Malcolm held on to the hope that Evie was safe. She was with the Dragon Kings. Neither the Kings nor the Warriors would allow anything to happen to Evie. Between all of them, they would come up with a way for his child to be born without evil.

He had faith in Evie, in the feelings she stirred in him. She would know he hadn't left her of his own accord. Wallace was wrong to think separating them would bring about Evie's hatred.

She already held hatred for Wallace, but it would be the goodness, the purity in her soul that would save their child. Malcolm should have realized that sooner. They had fretted for nothing, but there was no way to tell her now.

He threw back his head and bellowed in agony, as a white-hot poker was jammed into his spine. Death enjoyed pain and torment, he reveled in misery and suffering.

Daal's roar sounded alongside his in his mind, and Malcolm welcomed the god within him. If he could keep in contact with Daal, then there might be a chance to withstand some of what Death had in store for him.

It felt as if he had been brutalized for weeks, but it was

probably only hours. He had months ahead of him, months of the same cruel treatment.

If only he could use the currents of lightning that begged to be released. But Death managed to immobilize his power, just as Death was hindering Daal.

Malcolm had gotten free of Death once. He would do it again. He might have had help the first time, but he had something to live for, something he would pluck the stars from the sky for—Evie.

Evie opened her eyes, her heart just as heavy as before. The stones still chanted death, but they weren't as frantic as earlier.

"Evie," Cassie said as she rose from her vigil near the bed.

Evie sat up and pushed the blanket off before she swung her legs over the bed and stood. There was a new element in the voices of the rocks—sorrow—and it made her soul cry out.

Elena reached the door and put her hand upon the knob. "Evie, what is it?"

"Let me pass."

Elena hesitated a moment before she opened the door. Cassie and Elena fell in step behind Evie as she walked from the bedroom. She didn't care who followed her. All she wanted were answers, and the ones who could give them to her were gathered below.

Evie wasn't certain how she knew that, only that she did. She walked down the first flight of stairs and was descending the second when she heard Guy's voice. She couldn't make out what he was saying though.

By the time she reached the last set of stairs, she discerned another voice she didn't quite recognize. The door to the morning room opened and Evie saw the group gathered within.

She met Con's gaze as he stood in the doorway. There were no words spoken. Instead, he held out his hand to her. Evie descended the last few stairs and walked to him.

His face was set in grim lines, his brow furrowed with concern. "I was hoping you had woken."

She looked past him into the room and saw Fallon standing with Larena. There was a man with blond hair who stood near them, anxiety coming off him in waves. He looked vaguely familiar, and she realized he was a Warrior.

"Fallon jumped Broc here in the hopes of finding Malcolm," Con explained.

"A dragon needed help?" She hadn't meant it to sound so callous, but she was afraid to give in to the emotions filling her lest they take her soul.

Con smiled wryly. "Nay, but there was no stopping Larena. And before you ask, Brian is safe. He's with Kiril and Hal in the caves. He'll remain there until this is over. No Druid magic can penetrate the caves of a Dragon King."

Evie nodded stiffly. At least Brian was safe.

Broc's head suddenly lifted and in his dark brown gaze was sadness and grief. Evie wanted to cover her ears and sing loudly to drown out whatever was coming next, but she wouldn't. For Malcolm—for their child—she would be strong.

Con gently guided her into the room as Broc pushed away from the wall and strode to her. A muscle ticked in his jaw when he stopped before her.

Guy cleared his throat and led her to a chair. "You might need to sit."

She wasn't sure how her legs were holding her up now, but if she sat, she might give in to her need to cry. By remaining upright, it helped her keep her strength in place. Though she had a feeling that was about to be tested.

"We found Malcolm's mobile phone," Con said into the silence.

Evie looked at Broc. She recalled Malcolm telling her he could find anyone, anywhere. Now she knew why he had been brought to Dreagan. "Where is Malcolm?"

"Wallace has him."

CHAPTER FIFTY-TWO

Evie felt the room tilt around her, but she refused to faint again. She had to stay strong.

"There were signs of a fight," Con told her.

She turned her gaze to him. "Like what?"

Con clasped his hands behind his back. "Trees split in half and burning."

"Malcolm," she said. "It was his lightning."

"Our thoughts as well. There was also blood found. It's Malcolm's."

Anger began to simmer, and though she wanted to lash out at someone, she kept it directed at the individual responsible—Wallace. "I thought no one could get onto Dreagan land without the dragons knowing it."

The pity in Con's eyes made her stomach roll. "Wallace never touched Dreagan land."

"Then how did he get to Malcolm?" she demanded to the room at large. "We were safe here. Isn't that what we were told?"

Larena hurried to her and took her hand. "There is only one reason Malcolm would've left. He thought you were n danger. Jason must have done something to convince Malcolm of that. Otherwise, Malcolm would be standing next to you now."

Evie placed her hand on her stomach as nausea set in. How could she do this without Malcolm? How could she face what was to come without his reassurance and strong arms?

She sank onto the chair as something was pressed into her hand.

"Drink," Elena said.

Evie didn't even look at the glass as she raised it to her lips. As the liquid slid down her throat, it pooled like golden warmth in her belly, snapping her out of gloom, but not chasing it away altogether.

"Your color is returning," Larena said with a smile. "That makes me feel better."

Evie drew in a shaky breath. "Why did Jason come back for Malcolm?"

"It was probably his plan all along," Fallon said. He gave a shake of his dark head. "Malcolm suspected as much, but we were all lulled by the fact he released you."

"I trusted what Jason said. I should've known better." Evie fisted her hand and slammed it on the arm of the chair as tears threatened and anger grew. "That bastard has taken *everything* from me."

The magic that welled inside her was dark and nefarious. It promised wickedness and sin, retribution and triumph. As if it knew exactly what she wanted, an image of Jason Wallace writhing in pain flashed in her head.

"Evie!" Larena shouted.

Evie blinked. She looked down at her hand and felt the black magic pool there, sinister and lethal. She could go to Jason and inflict damage upon him. She could make him hurt as she hurt.

"Let it go," Ramsey said as he knelt before her. "Le the anger go, Evie, or it will consume you. This is wha Wallace wants. He wants your fury. Doona give it to him.

Evie thought of Malcolm. He'd warned her decision would have to be made. Here was one. Did she give in t the black magic and get him back? Or did she turn awa from it and hope the others could find him?

"What would Malcolm tell you to do?" Guy asked.

Evie bit back a sob as she looked at the Dragon Kin who stood next to her. "Follow my heart."

"And that is?" Larena prodded.

"To not give in to the evil inside me. But if I did, could get him back."

Con walked to the couch across from her and sat. "D you really think that?"

"It's what I feel."

"The evil will take you," Ramsey said. "You'll becom Wallace's. There willna be a chance for Malcolm."

Trust. She had always been a trusting person, but re cently she had been burned by it—twice. She wasn't sur who to trust anymore, not even herself.

"Malcolm said that just because I was *drough* didn mean I was evil. That came with decisions a person made He said I would always make the right ones because wasn't evil."

Ramsey's silver eyes were kind as he stared at her "Malcolm knows you well. Has he ever lied to you?"

"Never."

Evie drew in a deep breath, and as she released it, sh let go of her anger. The surge of black magic dissipate like smoke.

Malcolm was right. She had to trust herself and follov her heart. The black magic felt wrong. Just that small bi of holding it in her hand had made her soul wither.

"Do we go to Wallace's to get Malcolm?" she asked.

Fallon leaned a hip against the back of the couch Con was on. "That's the rub of it. He didna take Malcolm to his house."

"Then were is Malcolm?"

"I can no' find him. For days I've had a difficult time locating Malcolm. There were instances I couldna find him at all." Broc ran a hand down his face. "I thought for sure it was Wallace, but Guy says Malcolm was with you."

Evie frowned. "That's right. The only time Malcolm was near Jason was at Urquhart and then at the mansion."

"I doona believe it was Wallace hiding him," Con said as he stared at Evie.

She lifted her brows the longer Con stared. "What are you saying?"

"I'm say, lass, that your magic is stronger than you realize," Con stated. "I think you were the one shielding Malcolm from view."

"All I did was pray that Wallace didn't find us."

Fallon shrugged one shoulder. "With a Druid, sometimes that's all it takes."

"That explains earlier," Broc stated. "It doesna explain now."

"I thought you said he was with Wallace." Evie was trying not to get anxious but it was proving difficult.

"He was. Whatever Wallace did to Malcolm left an . . . imprint, for lack of a better word, in time. I saw that imprint."

"And what was Jason doing to Malcolm?" Evie asked.

Everyone looked away but Guy, yet he couldn't quite manage the words. It was Rhys standing quietly in the corner until then who drained his glass of whisky and said, "He gave Malcolm two drops of his blood."

"*Drough* blood," Evie murmured. Suddenly she understood why the stones had been shouting death. They weren't proclaiming someone's demise, but of Death itself. "Malcolm is in Death's control again."

"I shouldna have taken him out there," Rhys said. "He looked like he could use a little time to ease his mind. He wanted to run, so we were to race to the cabin. I'd no' have left him, if I'd known."

Evie rose and walked to the Dragon King. "We all know that. Ease your mind, Rhys. We'll get Malcolm back. I'm sure of it."

"Do you have a plan?" Larena asked.

Evie faced the rest of the room. "Jason will expect me to contact him now."

"If you do, you'll let him know we've figured everything out," Con said.

Fallon shifted as Larena sat on the couch. "Aye, but if she doesna, we may no' discover why he has Malcolm."

"I have no choice." One wrong move could land Evie in Jason's grasp once more. "I'm going to give Jason a call. I'm sure it's what he's expecting."

Every Dragon King in the room visibly winced at the same time. Con's gaze jerked to her, his nostrils flaring as he removed the silver dragon-head cuff links and rolled up the sleeves to his dark purple dress shirt.

Rhys walked around her and jogged out of the room, Guy fast on his heels.

"What's happened?" Elena asked Con as she stood and stared after Guy.

Con's eyes remained locked on Evie. "You doona need to contact Wallace."

"Why?" she asked as fear snaked down her spine.

"Tristan found Malcolm."

Larena stood and called up her goddess, her skin going iridescent. "What are we waiting on? Let's go to him."

It was Fallon who walked around the couch and took

is wife's hand. "We'll return with the others in quick rder."

"What?" Larena gawked at Fallon with wide eyes full f shock and anger.

Con nodded. "Elena, Cassie, and Jane will be here. hey can tell you where we'll be."

Evie met Fallon's eyes before he grabbed Larena's arm nd jumped her out of the manor.

"Come," Con ordered Evie as he stalked from the room.

Evie hurried after him, her heart pounding a sickening eat. She was afraid to ask what kind of condition Mal-olm was in, afraid that Wallace had killed him. And if e did, there was no amount of magic, dragons, Warriors, r Druids who would stand in her way of killing Jason.

She followed Con outside expecting to get into a vehicle. nstead she came to a halt when she spotted a massive ragon with metallic red scales watching her as he stood eside the manor. The red was shaded lighter on the under-ide of his neck and massive wings that ran from his shoul-ers to his tail.

"It's Guy," Elena said as she walked up beside Evie. He'll fly you to Malcolm."

"Guy," Evie repeated. She looked at the large head of ne dragon to see a mane of spines sprouting from the ack of his head.

He held out a front limb with four closely mounted igits and claws of black. Evie looked into Guy's dragon yes and saw patience and kindness, but also a willing-ess to take out their enemy. The Dragon Kings had been ere for Malcolm as well as her. They'd sheltered them, d them, and protected them. The least she could do was ust them now.

Evie walked to Guy and waited as he carefully wrapped is dragon hand around her. She rested her arms atop his

humongous hand. Elena gave them a wave, and with
jump that made Evie's stomach plunge to her feet, Gu
took to the air.

The wind whished around her while Guy's red wing
beat loud and steady. Evie gripped the hand holding he
amazed to find his scales warm instead of cold as she
expected.

A roar near them had her head turning to the side t
see a gold dragon as well as a blue and a yellow dragon
They flew on either side of Guy, their great wings stirrin
the air with as much force as a tornado.

The ground was a blur beneath her. Each beat of Guy
wings ate up the miles and brought her closer to Ma
colm. They passed over valleys full of sheep, mountai
peaks still capped with snow, and thick forests.

But she saw none of it. She kept her gaze on the dis
tance, searching for Malcolm. Evie caught a glimpse of a
amber dragon just before Guy tucked his wings and dove

She clutched one massive digit and closed her eyes c
a squeal of fright as the ground rose up quickly. At th
last minute, Guy's wings opened once more and he glide
low over the ground before he landed softly. He gently s
her down.

Evie stumbled out of his grasp and held her stomach a
a bout of nausea set in. She bent over at the waist an
closed her eyes to try and keep from vomiting.

"I'm sorry," Guy said from behind her. "I tend to fo
get how fast the descent is."

She frowned. Could dragons talk? She looked behin
her to find Guy in human form buttoning a pair of jean
She glimpsed a dragon head coming over his right shou
der to breathe fire across his chest. "It's all right," sł
managed.

Evie straightened to see Con walk out of a clump c
trees with only a pair of jeans on as well. He turned to sa

omething to whoever was still in the trees, and that's
when Evie saw the tattoo on his back.

It was done in black and red ink with the dragon lying
down and his wings spread wide, covering Con's entire
back. The dragon's tail wrapped from his left side around
his front to end once more on his back on the right side.

Rhys strode out of the trees and her gaze was riveted
on the tattoo on his chest she had glimpsed the night
before. It was done in the same black and red ink with the
head of the dragon on the right side of his chest and the
dragon leaning to the side with its wings tucked. The tail of
the dragon wound over his left shoulder and down to his
elbow.

She turned back to Guy. With a knowing grin, he turned
around so she could see the rest of his dragon. Its wings
spread from shoulder to shoulder with its tail wrapping
around to his front.

"All Dragon Kings have a tat," he said as he turned
back to her.

"Do you choose what design?"

"Nay," Con answered. "It's chosen for us. Just like what
dragons we rule."

She nodded numbly as her mind took it all in. "Just a
few weeks ago I thought I was the only Druid left. Then,
Malcolm found me, and I learned of Warriors and Dragon
Kings. It's surreal."

"I know," Guy said as he came to stand beside her. The
smile was gone. His mouth was set in a hard line now.

Rhys pointed to the sky. "Tristan has been keeping
watch since he found Malcolm. There's been no movement,
but the stench of Wallace is gagging. The bastard is around
somewhere. Keep vigilant."

"But Jason can't hurt me while I'm on Dreagan land,
right?" Evie asked.

Con gave a nod. "Just remember that, Evie. He somehow

convinced Malcolm to cross the boundary. He'll try the same with you."

"Let him," Guy said in a low, dangerous voice. "His magic can no' hurt us."

"Show me Malcolm," she demanded of the Kings.

Rhys took her left side and Guy her right as they walked her into the forest and down the mountain. It seemed wrong that everything was so green and vibrant when her heart was breaking so violently and her world was tearing apart.

"Does he know you love him?" Guy asked.

Evie shook her head. "Not yet."

"Doona be afraid to tell him," Rhys urged. "He feels the same. Anyone can see that by the way he looks at you."

She opened her mouth to reply when Rhys's hand shot out to halt her.

Guy pointed through the trees below. "There. Just a hundred feet from our border."

It took her a moment to see the crumbling stone cottage because it melted into the forest so well.

And chained to the outside stone wall was Malcolm.

CHAPTER
FIFTY-THREE

Jason Wallace smiled as he watched the amber dragon make another pass over the cottage. He spotted the others flying toward him. Any minute now they would surround him.

The boundary around Dreagan was one of magic, but not any magic he knew. Could it come from the dragons themselves? It was the only explanation. Not that he was worried. No one's magic was stronger than his.

After all, Death was a part of him. And he used it to his advantage.

Along with the dragons, the Warriors and Druids would arrive soon as well. In one fell swoop he would wipe them all from the earth. Malcolm and Evie would remain in his control, and everything Deirdre—then Declan—had aspired to would be his.

The plan was so simple and flawless he couldn't believe he hadn't thought of it sooner. The anticipation of it all kept the grin upon his lips.

The only thing missing was Mindy. How she would have loved to be standing beside him to witness the destruction of the Warriors. Jason was particularly interested in bringing the most pain to Phelan since he had been the one to kill Mindy.

Then there was Aisley who dared to betray him and fall in love with Phelan. The couple would know the horrors Malcolm was even now enduring.

"How fitting," Jason murmured with a chuckle.

Jason moved from his position in the shadows. He walked beneath the caved-in roof and around the crumbling wall to where Malcolm was chained.

"Evie will come for you. She'll take one look at you and come racing to your side. I willna have to force her to return to my home. She'll make that decision willingly just to be by your side. But while she's with me, I'll slowly and surely erode every ounce of good that remains inside her."

His smile grew as he turned and spotted Evie and two men walking toward him. Just as they reached the Dreagan border, one of the men stopped her.

The concern on Evie's face for her precious Malcolm made Jason want to pat himself on the back. Everyone was so predictable. The Warriors thought they were smart, but he had outwitted them this time. And how wonderful it felt.

He glanced at Malcolm's body and chuckled. Malcolm's chin rested on his chest, his long blond hair hiding his face from Evie. Not that it mattered. Malcolm was gone, locked in a never-ending battle with Death. No one could reach him this time.

Jason had made sure of it.

He took a deep, fortifying breath, and stepped onto the battlefield. The next few moves would be his last play, ending in checkmate. He almost hated to end it so soon, but then again, it was time the world knew a true leader.

"I knew it wouldna take you long to find me," Jason said, his voice raised to reach Evie. "Was it the dragons or Broc?"

Evie's eyes landed on him. For long moments she simply stared as one of the men said something to her. Then she lifted her chin and glared at Jason. "Does it really matter? You wanted me here, so I'm here. But I want to know why."

"Ah," Jason said as he put a finger alongside his mouth while he bit back his laughter. He knew Evie was steaming to have Malcolm so close, yet so far away. For the moment, she remained on Dreagan land. That wouldn't last long. "You mean you want to know why I didna keep you, Brian, and Malcolm while I had you."

"Yes."

"There are parts to the prophecy no one knew about until I found them. Setting this plan in motion has taken considerable patience on my part. You made it so easy. I thought I'd have to find a Druid, but you fell right into my lap when I ran across your site."

She shrugged. "If you hadn't forced me, I would never have become *drough*."

"How could you no'? You who communicate with the stones and found a home in Cairn Toul? You're following in Deirdre's footsteps. I just gave you a little nudge. I've no' doubt you'd have gotten there on your own."

"I'm not evil."

Jason laughed and let his gaze roam over the two men flanking her. With the dragon tats there was no doubt they were dragons. But would they remain on their land? He sure hoped they didn't.

"I choose to remain good, despite the black magic," Evie stated in a clear voice.

"Ah, but everyone has their breaking point. You have two. Brian and Malcolm."

Evie looked smug as she said, "You'll never get to Brian. As for Malcolm, he's strong. He's endured Death's torture before. He will again."

"Such confidence," Jason said as he rubbed his hands together. He would find out how they had learned about Death. Until then, he would continue to taunt her. "I may no' be able to get to Brian, but then I doona need to. I have the one thing you would sacrifice everything for—Malcolm." When only silence met his remark, he grinned. "What? No witty retort?"

"Don't you want to know how Malcolm survived Death the first time?"

Jason ground his teeth together. Of course he wanted to know, but after he had Evie in his hold. Damn them for bringing it up. He had to stay in control.

Evie saw the slip in Jason's smirk. She had thought bringing up Malcolm's shaking off Death's grip would find its mark. "Arrogant prick," she murmured.

"Good job," Rhys whispered from beside her.

So far, both of the Dragon Kings had let her do the talking. It took everything she had not to give in to the black magic calling to her, urging her to lash out at Wallace and get her reckoning.

It was only Malcolm and the love she had for him that reminded her of who she really was and prevented her from giving in.

"Don't you want to know how Malcolm walked away from Death?" Evie asked Jason. "You went to such trouble to hurt him at Urquhart."

Jason's lips peeled back in a scowl. "How?"

One simple word, but it boosted Evie's faith that she could get Malcolm back to Dreagan. However, it was in everyone's best interest if Jason didn't know everything. At least not yet.

"Phelan."

Jason's face contorted with fury when she said the name. "And where is Phelan now?"

"He'll be here soon enough."

"Just as I expected. You're too cowardly to face me on our own."

"Malcolm told me how you once had a number of Druids and Warriors at your beck and call. They left you to die all alone. Tell me, how did that feel?"

"I doona need anyone now."

"Somehow I don't believe that. You're just like Deirdre and Declan who had to be surrounded by those who feared them. It makes you feel more powerful."

He threw back his head and cackled. "And you'll be trembling in fear soon enough, Evie. No' even your dragons will be able to help you. No one will save you from what I have planned."

"Release Malcolm now."

"Let me think on that a moment," he said and glanced at the sky as if he were thinking. "That would be no."

Guy leaned close to her and whispered, "The Warriors and Druids are here."

"You'll die here today, Jason."

He threw out his arms and bellowed, "Nothing can kill me!"

Evie looked at the Dragon Kings. "I need to get down to Malcolm."

"It's what Wallace wants," Rhys cautioned.

Guy smiled. "It's time his arse dies."

The amber dragon let out a loud roar overhead as Druids and Warriors fanned out around Evie. Guy and Rhys turned and ran out of the trees before jumping into the air and shifting into dragons.

Evie kept her gaze on Malcolm. He needed her, and she wasn't going to let him down.

"We'll keep Wallace occupied," Ramsey said. "Do what you need for Malcolm."

Fallon came up beside her. "I can jump you to Malcolm."

"Then what are you waiting for?" she asked.

"Because it's suicide," Larena stated. "There's no way you're going down there without me."

Fallon waited until Larena released her goddess, turning iridescent before she used her power to shift invisible. "Larena will be beside you, Evie, but doona allow Wallace to get ahold of you. We'll free Malcolm no matter what."

Evie nodded. Fallon took her arm, and the next instant she found herself standing beside Malcolm. It was Jason's laughter that sent a chill of foreboding racing along her skin.

Malcolm had stopped trying to hold in his bellows of rage and pain long ago. Death was exacting in his torture, and if Malcolm hadn't been chained, he knew he'd have been brought to his knees.

His roars stopped when Death ripped out his throat. Malcolm struggled for breath as his throat began to regenerate. Whatever Death did to him, his body healed allowing Death to do it again and again.

Daal retreated deep in his mind, but at least this time his god hadn't totally deserted him. The fact the primeval god was frightened of Death when he was afraid of nothing put things into perspective for Malcolm.

It also gave him a clue to just who had trapped the gods in Hell so long ago. No wonder the gods wanted out so desperately. Malcolm understood their feelings all too well.

Smoke billowed around him as fire raged. It licked at his skin, the flames eagerly reaching for him. The fire was as alive as Death, and it wanted a piece of Malcolm.

He called up an image of Evie and squeezed his eyes shut to hold onto it as the fire reached his leg. The pain was terrible, the smell of burning flesh severe.

"Malcolm?"

"Evie!" he bellowed.

Had her voice only been in his mind, or was Evie with him? If she was, that meant Wallace had her.

Malcolm shook his head fiercely. That couldn't happen. Didn't she know the life of their child was more important than him? He was destined for Hell anyway after all the things he had done. Wallace just put him there earlier.

Evie. His wonderful, precious, headstrong Evie. It was unimaginable that he would never hold her again, never feel her warmth, never twine her curls around his fingers, never hear her laughter . . . never tell her how she had touched his soul.

Never tell her he loved her.

Something splashed on his face before rolling down his cheek.

Whatever Death had in store for him was nothing compared to the terrible, aching loss in his chest. There was a gaping hole where his heart had once been. Evie had brought him back from the brink, had shown him kindness, and he had gladly followed the shining light inside her.

Without Evie there was only darkness. Numbness took him, clutched him in her arms. And he welcomed her.

As the tear fell from his jaw, Malcolm looked at the flames that had risen to his hips. The blaze was green at the tips and hungry to devour him.

He felt nothing—because he was nothing.

Not without Evie.

CHAPTER
FIFTY-FOUR

Evie shot a bolt of magic at the chains holding Malcolm, but they didn't release him.

"As if I'd make it that easy," Jason said as he smiled maliciously.

She shot him a withering look. "You will be beaten this day."

"Oh, I think no'. I've come back from the dead once. There is nothing that could kill me now."

Evie wanted to slap him. She wanted to hit him, kick him, anything to knock that smug expression off his face. Never in her life had she hated someone as she did Jason Wallace, and that hate fed her black magic.

It gave her a moment's pause, because it was growing so quickly, taking over. And there was no turning back from it.

"You're afraid of your magic," Jason said, his eyes alight with a gleam of excitement. "The loathing you feel will grow, and the black magic inside you will infect your child. You, Evangeline Walker, will be the reason your child is born evil."

Evie shook her head even as she knew he spoke the

truth. Malcolm had forewarned her it would be decisions she made that tipped the scale one way or another.

Try as she might, she couldn't push aside the hate. The more Jason talked, the more her animosity grew.

"Easy," Larena whispered in her ear from behind. "He's goading you, Evie. Fight back. Do it for Malcolm."

Malcolm. Evie put her hand on his scarred shoulder. He was the reason she had the strength to face Jason. Malcolm was why she could look at herself in the mirror. He was the sun, the moon, and the stars.

Her life, her breath.

He was simply her universe.

She lifted a brow and gave Jason a bored look. "My child will be born good. I'll make sure of it."

"We'll see about that," Jason said as he flung a hand out.

Black smoke poured from his palm to scatter over the land in long, sinister, ribbonlike fashion. Dozens of human shapes took form, cloaked in solid black that hid their faces.

She knew the figure, because she would never forget her time with it.

"Death."

Jason's laughter echoed around the forest as the Warriors engaged the figures. Evie saw a red Warrior shoot fire from his hands while a white-colored Warrior formed spears of ice and hurled them at the figures.

The three MacLeod brothers stood shoulder to shoulder, the black skin of their god showing as they battled five figures of Death.

It wasn't just the Warriors who were attacked. The figures honed in on the Druids who stood in a group. They combined their magic, making the land hum with it. That magic held off Death, but it didn't kill the figures.

Jason sat back watching it all with such glee that it made

Evie's stomach sour. She faced Malcolm and ran her hands over him.

"I'm here, Malcolm," she said. "Hear my voice. Focus on me."

She tugged on the chains, but they didn't budge. Then she felt another pair of hands beside her. Evie was thankful Larena was with her because she had been near panic.

"Use your magic the same time I pull," Larena's disembodied voice said.

Evie felt her magic well inside her, but it wasn't black magic. It was her *mie* magic, and she welcomed it, embraced it. "One. Two. Three," she said as she poured her magic into the chains.

There was a soft shift, and then the chains broke, releasing Malcolm. He fell on Evie, and it was only with Larena's help that she could support his dead weight.

Evie glanced at the battle to see that none of the figures of Death had been killed. About that time the dragons dove from the sky to maneuver between the trees with skill and grace to join in the fray.

Jason clapped and jumped up and down as he shouted for the figures of Death to kill.

"He's gone daft," Larena whispered.

Evie couldn't agree more. She situated herself so that Malcolm's head rested in her lap. "Go help the others. We'll be fine."

"I shouldn't leave you."

"I'm not battling Death as your husband is. Go, Larena."

There was a pause before an invisible hand rested on Evie's shoulder. "I'll keep an eye on you."

And then she was gone. Evie drew in a deep breath and brushed the lock of blond hair from Malcolm's forehead. She ran her hand over his cheeks, feeling the bristle of his whiskers and the raised skin of his scars.

"What a mess I got us into," she said, hoping her voice carried to him over the roars of dragons, bellows of Warriors, and shouts of Druids. "I need you, Malcolm."

He looked so peaceful lying there, but she knew first-hand what it was like where Death had taken him. It was dark, malicious, and foul.

There was one way she could reach Malcolm, and that was by giving him her magic as before. But that would leave her isolated for Jason to do whatever he wanted.

However, it was a chance she had to take.

Evie felt for her magic again. This time both the black magic and *mie* magic welled within her. The black magic was more powerful, but there were risks involved. The *mie* magic was pure, but it would take her longer to reach Malcolm where Death held him.

She called for both, letting them blend and fuse, the two magics swirling about each other, twisting faster and faster as they expanded inside her.

And with a gasp, they exploded, filling every pore, every fiber of her being.

Evie lifted her hand and felt it buzz with magic. She traced a fingernail along Malcolm's jaw and saw the smoky tendrils of magic that vanished as soon as they appeared.

There was no denying the sheer force of magic at her fingertips. And for a moment, she considered turning it on Jason Wallace. Then she looked down at Malcolm. He had suffered enough.

She closed her eyes and called to the ancients. It took her awhile to hear the drums over the battle, but once she did, she let out a sigh of relief.

The chanting grew closer until the only things she could hear were the ancients' multiple voices and the drums. She gave herself a few seconds to bask in the glow of the ancients.

"I need help," she told them. "How do I free Malcolm from Death?"

"No release. There is no release."

She refused to believe that. "Then how do I kill Jason? You said there was a way."

"You already have it."

"My black magic? If I give in to it, I become evil."

"You already have it," they repeated.

Evie clutched at Malcolm's shoulders. "Please. I don't know what to do. I can't have my child born evil, but I can't let Malcolm go either."

"You must choose, but choose wisely."

"What? Are you saying I can have either my child or Malcolm, but not both?"

The chanting grew louder for a moment before tapering off again. *"You have all you need, Evangeline Walker. Trust yourself."*

And just like that, they were gone. No matter how much she tried to find the ancients again, they had left her.

Evie opened her eyes to see Jason watching her, but, thankfully, his gaze was jerked away when the gold dragon swooped down and one of its wings slammed into the cottage, knocking down the stone walls.

She used that time to gather the mixture of *mie* and *drough* magic to her once more, and then she pushed it inside Malcolm.

The feel of Evie's magic was like a kiss against his blistered skin. His burns began to heal instantly while his body grew stronger. But he noticed none of it as he exulted in Evie's magic.

Her magic was ecstasy, the pleasure of it as close to Heaven as he would ever get. Malcolm closed his eyes and let the strings of her magic enfold him in a cocoon of bliss.

With her magic came a bright light. He turned his face

away it was so blinding, but he knew it was her. If he could get free of the chains he could go to Evie.

It was dangerous for her, so very dangerous. At that moment, Death took notice of her. Malcolm tried to turn his head to find her, tried to shout her name, but Death refused even that.

Malcolm struggled furiously against his bonds, the rusted iron manacles ripping open his wrists. Blood poured from his wounds. Death hissed in enjoyment.

Evie was too trusting, too innocent to know how to deal with Death. She'd had a brush with it, but Malcolm knew Death all too well.

"Trust me," Evie's voice whispered around him like a breeze.

He stilled, and for the first time felt the full magnitude of her power. Her magic slammed into him, enveloping him in the pure, absolute phenomenon of all that was Evie.

Her magic was fierce, and her uncorrupted soul kept the area blazing with luminous light.

Malcolm was held immobile from the force of it all, and then with a loud clink, the chains holding his wrists fell away. His gaze turned to Death, and the figure cocked its material-covered head to the side as if waiting for him to attack.

"I'm waiting, Malcolm," Evie beseeched.

"You'll come for me again one day," he told Death. "You might be able to hold me then."

Death took a step toward him, but Malcolm had already turned his thoughts to Evie as he followed her voice. The next thing he knew he was staring up into her beautiful blue eyes with her curls hanging over one shoulder.

He took her hand and brought it to his lips. "You brought me out again."

"I can't believe it worked," she said in awe, her eyes filling with tears.

Malcolm then heard the sounds of battle. He sat up and saw all the figures of Death dotting the forest. The Warriors and dragons cut them down, but nothing killed Death.

"I need to help them," he said and started to stand when she put a hand on his arm.

She glanced past him. "I don't think we'll be leaving quite so easily."

"Ah, Malcolm," Wallace said from behind him. "It seems I underestimated Evie. My first mistake. I need to rectify that immediately."

Malcolm stood and helped Evie to her feet before he faced Wallace. "Your time has ended."

"As you can see, Death can no' be killed," he said as he swept his hand across the land to the battle. "The same goes for me."

"Everything can be killed."

"You're right, of course." Wallace's blue eyes narrowed on him, anger flashing in his depths. His normally perfectly coiffed hair was in disarray from his jumping around in excitement. "I thought I should keep you alive to give Evie the push she needed, but I see what really needs to happen is your death."

Malcolm got off a shot of lightning that hit Wallace once. Like before, Jason quickly had him immobile so Malcolm couldn't use his power again.

"That hurt," Wallace said as he looked at the scorch marks on his shirt. "Just for that, I'm going to make your death extra painful."

Evie wasn't going to lose Malcolm again, not after working so hard to get him back. There was no holding back her fury, no stopping the hate. It mixed with the love filling her until she didn't know which would win.

Her magic erupted within her as if someone had flipped a switch. The more she thought of how much she love-

Malcolm, the stronger her magic grew until it felt as if her skin was too tight and she might explode from it all.

And there . . . in the magic she felt something. It was small, tiny, but so powerful that it left her gasping for breath. The child growing within her, the child made from love and hope had added its magic to Evie's.

Evie looked at Malcolm to find his gaze on her. His azure depths were filled with worry and faith. She gave him a reassuring smile as she let her mind connect with her child.

"Trust me," she asked of him again.

And in his gaze, she saw his acceptance—and his trust.

Evie held her palms facing each other as a white ball of crystal tendrils swirled. The more she poured her magic into the ball, the larger it grew.

"You're wasting your magic," Jason said with a laugh.

Evie smiled. "Have you never heard the saying that love can conquer all?"

Jason's grin slipped, and just as she hoped, Malcolm used that opportunity to shift his hands toward Jason. Jason's attention was on her, giving Malcolm the chance he needed to be able to use his power.

"You're scared now," Evie said. "So scared that you haven't even realized you no longer have a hold on Malcolm or on your army."

Out of the corner of her eye, Evie saw the Druids and Warriors begin to gather around them once the figures of Death had vanished.

Wallace glanced around frantically.

Evie barely contained her joy. She wanted to laugh, but she would hold it in until the battle was over. "Death couldn't hold Malcolm because its strength was split in fighting your battle."

"Death is too strong for that," Wallace stated angrily, spittle flying from his lips.

Evie felt a tickle in her stomach from her child. Because of the babe, she was going to leave this battle with both Malcolm and the bairn.

"Even Death can be defeated," Malcolm said.

"Nay!" Wallace shouted.

Evie let the ball of magic grow larger. "Your overconfidence will lose you this game. You took your eye off the prize, Jason. You forgot how strong love and hope are. Because of that, Death walked away from you. It left you here, alone. To face us."

Malcolm moved beside her. "Ready?"

"Oh, yes."

She released the ball of magic the same instant Malcolm threw several lightning bolts at Jason. Wallace raised his hands to block the attack, but he couldn't stop it.

He fell to one knee, a shocked expression on his face. "How?"

"Love," Malcolm said. "Evil can no' withstand the power of love."

Evie threw several more blasts of magic at him as more lightning shot from Malcolm's hand until Jason was on the ground, his body writhing while he fought to drag in a breath.

The Warriors and Druids closed in around him and, as one, gave him one last blast of magic and power. Wallace yielded a final shout before his body disintegrated into particles so tiny they were taken by the wind.

Evie watched the last of Jason Wallace float away as rejoicing sounded around her. Suddenly, Malcolm stood before her, his hand on her stomach.

"Our daughter is going to have strong magic."

Malcolm's smile was slow as it spread. "Daughter?"

"Daughter."

"She gets it from her mother."

"She was the catalyst," Evie said as his hand slid around

the back of her neck. "She added her magic to mine. She is life made through love."

"Love. No' a word I ever thought to utter again, but you, Evie Walker, are impossible no' to love."

She looked into his azure eyes and melted. "I love you, too, Malcolm Munro."

His lips claimed hers in a searing, scorching kiss that set her body aflame with desire. Pats on their backs from the others broke the kiss, but Malcolm didn't release her.

"I doona want to live another minute without you. You saved me, Evie."

"And you saved me."

His brow furrowed, causing her to laugh.

"I learned something else today. You stopped the last drop of my blood from completing the *drough* ceremony. I can use the black magic, but I'm no' *drough*."

"How do you know?"

"The ancients told our daughter, and she told me."

Malcolm hugged her to him, burying his head in her neck. When Evie pulled back it was to see a tear roll down his cheek.

"I doona deserve you," he said.

"Too bad. You're stuck with me."

"Thank God. Now you must make an honest man of me and become my wife."

She giggled as he lifted her in his arms and carried her out of the crowd. "I thought you'd never ask."

EPILOGUE

One week later...

The great hall of MacLeod Castle was overflowing with Warriors, Druids, Dragon Kings, and mortals. Laughter and joy reached every corner of the castle.

Malcolm watched as Evie was passed from Arran, Phelan, and Lucan during the dance. She hadn't stopped smiling since they had walked away from the stone cottage, and that smile had only grown that afternoon when they had become man and wife.

"What now?" Con asked.

Malcolm shrugged. "I'm no' sure. Lucan and Camdyn found Evie's necklace at Wallace's. We have the spell to bind our gods."

"Are you?"

"I doona believe anyone is. There will be more evil to come. It's no' fair for you Dragon Kings to get all the glory."

Con gave a bark of laughter and slapped Malcolm on the back. "Wise choice. You know you and Evie, as well as Brian and the bairn, are always welcome at Dreagan."

"Thank you for that," Malcolm said. "I'll go wherever Evie wants."

"Here she willna age."

Malcolm nodded. "True, but we'll figure all of that out."

The music stopped and Logan jumped onto the table, knocking over wineglasses in the process. "I have another toast," Logan shouted.

Galen groaned and the rest of the castle burst into laughter.

Logan narrowed his gaze on Galen, but it was spoiled by his smile. He then turned to look at Malcolm and Evie. "To Malcolm, who we all never thought would find a woman who could put up with him—"

Loud cheers followed, and Malcolm winked at Evie.

"And to Evie," Logan continued, "who can easily hold her own against the brute!"

Malcolm laughed, still amazed at how easily it came to him now. It was almost as if the past few years hadn't taken place. He raised his glass in salute to Evie as she blew him a kiss.

When the bagpipes began again, it was Fallon who took Evie spinning around the room.

"I have something for you and Evie," Con said. "Consider it a wedding gift from all of us at Dreagan."

Malcolm accepted the gold band where a triskelion was etched into the top with dragon heads at all three points. "It's beautiful. Evie will treasure it."

"As long as she wears it, she'll be immortal."

Malcolm's gaze jerked to the King of Kings. "I didna realize you could do this."

"You both earned it. Any Druid here who wishes to live outside of MacLeod Castle will be offered the same token."

"You have that kind of magic?"

Con just smiled before he raised his glass in salute and walked away. Malcolm managed to pull Evie out of Fallon's arms as they danced by and shared what Con had given them.

"I don't know what to say," she said in shock.

For the second time that day, Malcolm slid a ring onto her finger. "We have forever."

"How I love the sound of that."

"Where do you want to live?"

She smoothed the lock of hair out of his eye. "Anywhere as long as I'm with you."

"We'll need to think of the bairn."

Evie glanced down at her still-flat stomach and the way the white silk hugged her frame. "I'll be waddling soon, so I guess we'll need to think about a home."

Malcolm found Brian near the hearth holding baby Emma in his arms as Camdyn and Saffron's daughter cooed up at him. "Brian will need to return to his school."

"Actually, Charon offered us a piece of land on the edge of Ferness as a wedding present. He said it was secluded."

Malcolm shook his head in dismay. "I doona know what to say to everything they are doing for us."

"You say thank you, and you take your wife out of here. I'm ready to have you all to myself, Mr. Munro."

Malcolm didn't need to be told twice. He took Evie's hand and made a dash for the door. Once outside, they took the first vehicle they found, the red Jaguar F-type, and drove out of the bailey, the shouts of their friends filling the air.

Con glanced at Kiril and said, "She took your car again. You can always ride back with me."

Kiril rolled his eyes. "No' the way you drive."

Lucan spewed his ale as he laughed. After he wiped his mouth, he grinned at Con. "We'll have peace for a while."

"Until another evil steps up," Fallon said, but he was still looking fondly at the Jaguar as it sped away.

"And we'll always be around to put evil in its place," Quinn said.

Con looked at the three MacLeod brothers and nodded. "We make a good team."

"Of course," Lucan said with a wink to his brothers. "It's why you were so hesitant to befriend us all those years."

Con barked with laughter. "What will become of everyone now? Each Warrior is married."

"Aiden and Britt are leaving first thing in the morning," the youngest MacLeod brother said. "I hate to have my son leave, but it's been a long time coming. He plans to propose to Britt on their travels, so we'll have another wedding in the next few months."

Lucan clinked his goblet with Quinn's. "Good for Aiden. We all like Britt. It's a good match."

"Logan and Gwynn willna be the only pair expecting," Fallon said, barely able to hold back his goofy smile. "Larena told me this morning she's pregnant."

Con looked at Lucan and Quinn expectedly.

Lucan shook his head. "No' yet. It will happen, because know it's what Cara wants."

"I'm waiting for Marcail to give me that look," Quinn said after he took a drink of ale. "I suspect it'll be any day now."

"And the others?" Con asked.

As one, all four turned on the steps of MacLeod Castle nd looked through the door into the great room. The agpipes were playing, the drink flowed freely, and smiles vere aplenty.

"It's odd, is it no'?" Lucan asked. "I think back just

four centuries earlier when I didna know how I would make it through another day alone."

Quinn leaned a hand against the doorway. "Then you brought Cara inside."

"And our lives were changed forever," Fallon said. "We went from three lost brothers, to a castle full of family."

"Doona forget about battling evil along the way," Con added.

Lucan raised his goblet. "Too true. Back then I wouldna have believed that all of us would find happiness or vanquish our demons. But we did."

"We triumphed," Quinn said. "Our parents would be proud."

"Aye," Lucan said as he clamped Fallon on the shoulder.

Fallon raised his goblet. "To the MacLeods."

"MacLeods," Quinn, Lucan, and Con repeated before they all took a long drink.

Fallon caught Con's eye. "The future is uncertain now."

"No' when you have allies. The Warriors can always count on the Dragon Kings."

"And the Kings can always count on us," Lucan said.

Con finished his drink and handed Quinn his empty glass. "Duty calls, but you'll be hearing from us soon."

He walked down the steps of the castle knowing he'd made the right choice in letting the Warriors know about the Dragon Kings, because evil wasn't gone. It was closing in on Dreagan, and Con suspected they would need every friend they had to keep the Dragon Kings a secret from the world.

In the months following, Lucan and Cara remained at the castle, though they took frequent trips, the first of which was to Egypt to see the pyramids. They decided to spend quality time enjoying each other before they started their family.

Fallon and Larena readied the castle for their impending child, though Fallon often jumped them to Paris or Rome for a night out. Both wanted a castle full of children. There were no lasting effects from the *drough* blood in Larena thanks to Britt's serum. Leaving the couple plenty of time to argue—and make up—about the name of their first child.

Quinn and Marcail decided to remain on MacLeod land and build their own home. Just as Quinn predicted, Marcail had given him that look. Three months later they learned she was carrying their second child.

Hayden and Isla embarked on an excursion to Australia and New Zealand for two months. They also remained on MacLeod land, choosing to build near the cliffs for a spectacular view. Just weeks after their home was finished, Isla surprised Hayden with the news that he was going to be a father. In Campbell fashion, it was a great excuse to throw a party and celebrate.

Galen and Reaghan also traveled, but remained closer to home and toured England, Scotland, Wales, and Ireland. Undecided on where they wanted to live, they remained at the castle while considering options on MacLeod land and in Ferness.

Broc and Sonya chose a spot on MacLeod land and built their home, only to leave and travel through much of Europe including the Netherlands, Hungary, and Belgium. After a brief sickness, which Sonya thought was brought on by food, they were surprised to discover she was pregnant. Broc cut their trip short and quickly returned home to the safety—and the shield—of MacLeod land.

It took some convincing, but Gwynn talked Logan into

a trip to Texas. Logan refused to get on a plane, so Fallon jumped them to her hometown of Houston. For almost three months they toured the US before Logan had Fallon jump them back to Scotland. The remaining months were used in building their home in a secluded part of the forest on MacLeod land where Logan knew his family would be safe, and the love of his life would always be by his side.

Ian and Dani took up residence in Ferness, in an old cottage they decided to renovate. Ian discovered he had a special talent for woodworking, and Dani loved decorating. They often shared meals with Charon and Laura as well Malcolm and Evie. Not a day went by that Ian didn't feel the loss of his twin. It was with Dani's love that he looked to the future, not the past.

Camdyn and Saffron remained at the house they built on MacLeod land. In between their duties as parents to Emma, Saffron was exposing Camdyn to the role of businessman. The family often went to meetings for the numerous companies she owned. Camdyn had a head for business, and it wasn't long until he was running the companies alongside Saffron while waiting for the birth of their second child.

Ramsey and Tara kept a room at MacLeod Castle while they traveled all over the globe for weeks at a time only to return for a month before traveling to a new destination. Because of the volatile magic running through Tara, it was decided it would be better if they didn't chance subjecting a female child to what she had endured. They adopted a menagerie of pets instead. They too built on MacLeod land. Ramsey had found a family with his brethren, and he wished to remain close.

Arran and Ronnie resumed Ronnie's archeological study, preferring to remain in the United Kingdom doing their digging. They discovered many ancient places som considered sacred to Druids. Arran worked beside Ronnie, making them an unbeatable team in the archeological field.

Charon and Laura continued on as before in Ferness, except Laura was now his business partner. Laura also accepted a ring from the Dragon Kings allowing her to become immortal as long as she wore it. Together, she and Charon grew his vast empire of holdings and businesses while looking after the people of Ferness.

Aiden and Britt did leave the castle right after Malcolm and Evie's wedding. They traveled first to Spain before heading to Italy. On a gondola ride in Venice he proposed, and Britt happily accepted. While in Rome, they decided to get married, and Fallon teleported everyone to watch the wedding at the beautiful Santa Susanna church. After a large celebration, Aiden and Britt continued on their journey to Switzerland and France before returning to Scotland so she could finish her studies.

Phelan and Aisley decided to spend some time getting to know the Fae side of Phelan's family, which took them to Ireland and there they remained for several months. Upon their return, they took up residence in Phelan's cottage near the loch where Phelan tended his flowers and Aisley learned to cook.

After long deliberation, Malcolm and Evie settled on the piece of land gifted to them by Charon and built a modest house atop a hill with views of the mountains and loch. As Evie predicted, she did waddle, but Malcolm was always at her side, finding ways to make her laugh or sharing moments where they both felt their daughter kick.

At exactly 4:16 a.m. on July 19th, Mallory Munro made her entrance into the world to the wondrous delight of both Malcolm and Evie.